The Ordeal of Stanley Stanhope

by *Richard Bousquet*

The Ordeal of
Stanley Stanhope

W · W · NORTON & COMPANY · INC ·

NEW YORK

Copyright © 1972 by Richard Bousquet

FIRST EDITION

Library of Congress Cataloging in Publication Data

Bousquet, Richard.
  The ordeal of Stanley Stanhope.

  I. Title.
PZ4.B775Or [PS3552.O835]   813'.5'4   72-39236
ISBN 0-393-08670-4

Published simultaneously in Canada
by George J. McLeod Limited, Toronto

DESIGNED BY ROBERT FREESE

PRINTED IN THE UNITED STATES OF AMERICA

1 2 3 4 5 6 7 8 9 0

TO SOPHIA
ever loving, ever loved.

The Ordeal of Stanley Stanhope

ONE

*T*HERE ARE FEW places in this world more un-
comfortable than a dry-cleaning plant on a hot
July afternoon with the air-conditioner broken
down. In the workroom of the Stanhope Cleaners
it was intolable. That was Harry's exact word, in
fact: "Stan, it's intolable in here."

With Irma it was another thing. When Stanley
walked into the workroom she gave him her usual
good-natured greeting, now somewhat dampened:
"Hiya Mister Stanhope. . . ." She worked steadily
on at her steam-press—ssss-phtttt—and when she
raised her arms, widening dark rings of perspira-

tion could be seen under her armpits. Her dirty-blond hair stuck wetly to the sides of her face spoke of the conditions in the workroom far more eloquently than Harry Putchek's barely bridled snarl, "Whaddya running here, a goddamn sweatshop?"

So Stanley closed down for the day, to everyone's relief but his own. With a vague uneasiness, he eyed the stacks of garments yet to be cleaned. At midweek they were behind in their work. It was because of the summer people vacationing nearby at White Cove. They were down now in force, so the plant was full. On every available table and bench clothes were stacked in mute limp piles, tagged and waiting to be cleaned. Harry was snapping off the banks of fluorescent lights two at a time. In the sudden dimness the garments looked incredibly forlorn—abandoned not only by their owners but by the people entrusted with their rejuvenation. As the dry-cleaning machines wound down and halted, the silence in the workroom was all but palpable.

Was it the twinge of responsibility Stanley felt? For didn't people entrust to him their very own second skins, as it were? He did not take the responsibility lightly. THE STANHOPE CLEANERS stood for something in Krumpit: Responsibility; Integrity; Honesty; Professionalism . . . .

"See you tomorrow, Mister Stanhope"—and Irma hurried on by as if glad to be away and quick to do so lest he change his mind.

He mumbled something vaguely affirmative and regretted it immediately: no employee of his should think he begrudged her an afternoon off on an intolerably hot day. So he called after her, as amiably as he could on the spur of his second thoughts, "Yes Irma see you tomorrow, keep cool!" He shouted it to Irma Kasendorf's soft round retreating bottom which was accented with an enormous *Y* of perspiration, turning the light blue of her denim dress into a dark and secret and—yes—seductive Question. He was still looking after her, still seeing the enormous dark *Y*, when Harry came by on his way out, his anger turned off as quickly as the lights had been.

"You gonna lock up, fella?"

"Yes. All right. . . ."

"Right." He stepped into the little office for his lunch pail, then popped out again. "We'll do it all over again tamarra, Stan."

"Goodnight, Harry." There was nothing to do but lock up and go home—to forget about the garments and the responsibility for a day; to forget about Irma Kasendorf's soft round sweat-laced bottom.

It seemed not so warm outside. Still, the thermometer in front of Holgrove's Hardware Store read 96, admittedly hot for Krumpit, Connecticut. But under the high old elms of the town, it was a not unpleasant afternoon, with the long urgent siren-whine of cicadas stirring the air. The elms themselves seemed timeless, as they always had for as long as Stanley could remember. The elms stood fast in Krumpit long before the advent of such a thing as air conditioning.

On many a warm summer's day, through both high school and college, Stanley himself had sweated away at the Stanhope Cleaners without benefit of air conditioning. He recalled the strangely *sensuous* sensation of sweat running down his own ribs and—yes—between his own buttocks. He smiled, feeling an absurd affinity toward Irma Kasendorf. Had he, too, those many warm days past, left the Stanhope Cleaners with a great sweaty Y on his backside and paraded down the street, a question unanswered?

Air conditioning spoke to Stanley of a race grown soft. Yet *Harry* could not conceivably be described with such a word. Barrel-chested, with legs like sturdy piers and arms like the able-bodied seaman he once had been, with hands like blunt instruments and fingers that could grip like pliers, Harry Putchek was anything but soft. Yet it was *he* who demanded air conditioning and, in its failure, the closing down of the plant. Irma, on the other hand, she who certainly *looked* soft, had only smiled and greeted him and worked on.

Was it merely a matter of conspicuous consumption, that blight of an affluent and acquisitive society? Then so much the worse, thought Stanley. For didn't that mean that people— Americans— had forfeited their birthright? Not for a mess of pottage (which might have sustained them, at least) but for the toys of an affluent society: the color television sets and the electric can-openers; the second cars and the vacation homes; the boats and the camping trailers; the stereo sets and the third cars; the frozen chickens in the microwave ovens; the air conditioners. . . . To become acquisitive and affluent, to consume conspicuously . . . could such possibly be the "blessings of liberty" which the Founding Fathers wanted to secure for their "more perfect Union"? Did the "pursuit of happiness" come down to *that?* Or was the ultimate softness not to be able to deny oneself those things which are not truly needed. . . .

The great elms he walked beneath had been often threatened by the dreaded Dutch elm disease that had wreaked such havoc throughout New England. The town's elms had been saved by luck and by immense effort. It seemed to Stanley that America, too, was threatened by a dread disease that might yet wreak far greater havoc. It was something insidious, like a syphilis of the spirit. And it seemed that the United States Government itself had become the keeper of the brothel of Conspicuous Consumption. For did not the Government allow and even encourage the production of things that were not really needed? Did not the Government depend on such programmed superfluities for a significant portion of the Gross National Product, that false god of modern economic policy? Did not the same Government grant licenses to those electronic hucksters so that the people might be in turns cajoled and shamed into purchasing the myriad unneeded items they might never lust after or acquire if left to their own simple desires?

The people were not blameless, Stanley realized. Somewhere along the way the people had ceased to be the People. It seemed as if the Government of, by, and for the People had perished from the earth in a Lincolnian nightmare. It had perished, Stanley decided, not catastrophically but imperceptibly, by degrees, so that now "the Government" and "the People" seemed not only different but antithetical. The Government was something grudgingly to pay taxes to and hope to be left alone by, while the People sat air-conditioned before their color TV's quietly lusting after the new cars boats appliances trips abroad—

"Hot one today, Stanley."

He looked up to see Old Beardsley pass by in paint-spattered overalls and general untidiness. "Yes, it is." And he caught the unmistakable whiff of booze on the old man's breath—or on his unkempt brush of a mustache. He'd known Old Beardsley all his life. At an earlier age he had, in fact, admired the man fiercely. In those days *Mister* Beardsley was an amiable enough sort who could fix the town hall clock or a bicycle sprocket. But over the years a bitterness had replaced the amiability, and the admired figure of Stanley's childhood had degenerated into the town character and a dirty old man. Beardsley had known Stanley's father, though —known him well, in fact—and nowadays the old man would often buttonhole Stanley and talk at him with a heavily boozy breath. Sometimes, like today, the old man only greeted him in passing. And sometimes Old Beardsley would ignore Stanley completely—ignore even Stanley's greeting—and pass sullenly on, a ship in his own peculiar night. It was the booze, Stanley had decided.

As he walked on Stanley could feel the midday heat, but it was not an unpleasant experience in the practically contiguous shade of the elms. Old Beardsley had moved out of his mind as quickly as he'd passed out of his sight, and Stanley's thoughts about contemporary America resurfaced before he'd gone another half-block.

But he could find no anchor for his judgments. He'd somehow grown distrustful of history. Was history, in the final analysis, anything more than propaganda after the fact? (He recalled something he'd read somewhere, about how different the history of World War II would have been had it been written by Joseph Goebbels rather than Winston Churchill.) It was well to be wary of history.

If he could not trust historians, Stanley had come to trust newsmen even less. He'd grown steadily aware of the way they continually opted for the sensational, reported misinformation as indiscriminately as verifiable truth, and seemed to blow everything out of proportion, from the weather reports on upwards. More and more Stanley had felt a sense of betrayal. Unfairly, he trusted none of them; but he felt it was his only defense.

Nor was all the blame to be laid on the news media. Stanley felt himself, and not the news media, to be master of the vessel of his own opinions. But it was also true that he'd always simply gone his own way, always steered calmly onward amid a seething sea of troubles, as America struggled not to drown. Had he ever, even once, tried to help? Had he ever even summoned help, raised his voice that *others*, at least, might hear and come to America's aid? He had not. He could not sit in judgment, Stanley decided, for he would have to judge himself as well. Besides, who was he to judge anyone? Who was he?

He was Stanley S. Stanhope. He had just celebrated his fortieth birthday not a week ago, on the Fourth of July. Forty years old. That had made Stanley a Depression baby —not that he'd ever known hardship. In those days his father didn't have the dry-cleaning business; he had a far more dependable job for desperate times: he'd been a mortuary assistant during those years. ("Even in hard times," his father used to say, "people have to die. More so, maybe.") So the family was never without a steady income, and Jock Stanhope was even able to put aside the money to open his dry-cleaning plant by 1942. It was something of a mystery why his father had left the undertaking business (which he said he enjoyed) to go into dry-cleaning, though Stanley once imagined a certain perverse relationship between the two enterprises: preserving clothes instead of cadavers. Stanley had meant to ask his father about it sometime but never got the chance, his father having died peacefully in his sleep one cool September night in 1958, his dreams perhaps full of the fishing expedition he'd planned for the following morning. So Stanley never found out. But of what importance was it, anyway? The important things were that Jock Stanhope had done well in his business and in his marriage and had raised his son Stanley in good middle-class comfort even in a difficult period in the life of the Nation. Stanley had known love and security and grew up accordingly, like a young tree well-nurtured. He could not have asked for more tenderlovingcare, from either parent. His memories of his mother, from his earliest to her latest years, were those of devotion and concern, unstintingly but discerningly provided. Stanley had never wanted for anything he truly needed; he had never gone cold or hungry. The Depression was only a word to him, one he understood only very much later and then only intellectually. His father and mother had taken care of his immediate world, and Franklin Delano Roosevelt had looked after the rest, like the right hand of God.

Stanley Stanhope had been brought up to believe that FDR was, if not God, then surely his prophet; and he had accepted the dogma completely, well into his college years, when finally he was able to see the man as mortal—and fallible—after all. But it was only years later that the deceased President had fallen off the highest perch of Stanley's estimation.

It had come about quite by accident. The occasion was a TV special, a report on the American economy. Stanley recalled it vividly (remembered, even, that he'd had to override his young daughter's demand that she be allowed to watch something on another channel, which denial resulted in her storming off complaining about how maltreated she was in not being allowed to have her own television set). The point of the program had been that the American economy, by then thoroughly Keynesianized (like Sanforized or Sanitized?), precluded anything like the Great Depression of his father's day. But time and time again during the televised report, tangential references to the "defense industry" or to "military spending" or to "the defense budget" had cropped up, and the point was inadvertently made (for Stanley, at least) that the economy of the United States actually *depended* on defense spending. Didn't those omniscient television commentators *see* that? Or didn't they want to. Or did they purposely turn away from it. A few years later they would not only recognize that fact but jump all over it, as was their way, swatting it with the switch of their latest catch-phrase, "the military-industrial complex." Stanley had seen the truth about the American economy before those omniscient commentators had, and he was secretly, childishly proud of the fact.

At the time, however, he was stunned. The program had ended and television had returned to its ordained purpose of selling him mouthwash. He had flicked off the set, his mind racing to the horrifying conclusion conjured up by his sudden realization of his Country's economic dependence on defense spending. *When had it started?* And Stanley had been shocked to discover, upon careful examination, that such dependence—which could in truth be called nothing other than a war economy—coincided in its beginnings with the final recovery from the Great Depression and was apparently the cause of that recovery. Perhaps the Second World War had been unavoidable and certainly President Roosevelt was not to blame for it, given the malevolence of the Axis powers. Yet didn't FDR *continue* to play the game and set the economic standard followed to this day?

WAR ECONOMY. For *thirty years*, whatever the reason, his Country had known no other. Poor FDR was perhaps less to blame than any of his successors, not one of whom had been either able or willing to alter the war economy's spiraling course. These seemed unavoidable conclusions, like admitting exposure to poison ivy when the itching starts and the rashes appear. Whatever the cause and whoever was to blame, the Nation was obviously in torment.

Stanley pushed open the wooden gate to his front yard and was arrested by the scent of the honeysuckle vines that hung abundantly from the front porch pillars. As he inhaled deeply a cicada cried out plaintively close by. He no longer thought about his business, about the uncleaned clothes, about the air-conditioner or Irma's sweatily seductive ass. On his own front walk, amid the scent of honeysuckle and the waning cry of a cicada, Stanley Stanhope thought about the United States war economy, about the billions it consumed and about how that money might have been spent seeking solutions to the race problems, the crime rate, the decay of the cities, the pollution of the environment—*if only* it had been properly channeled.

And then it struck him, like a slap in the face: Would there have *been* all that money *without* the war economy? Were not the billions in fact *spawned* by the very defense dependency he was lamenting? He went slowly up his front steps and into his house.

Emily was, not surprisingly, surprised to see him. He explained about the air conditioner, in as few words as possible. It was warm, not hot, in the house. The high ceilings undoubtedly helped. There was no air conditioning, nor would there ever be: "Conspicuous Consumption. . . ."

"What, dear?"

"Oh. . . . Nothing. Something I've been thinking about."

"Have you eaten?" She brushed a fallen wisp of dampish hair from her face—raven hair, full and thick. There was an arc of moisture over her upper lip: tiny cystalline beads like diamonds.

"I had a tuna sandwich at the drug store." And that was true, though he hadn't finished it: the mayonnaise was turning, or tasted like it was. He sat at his kitchen table, across from his wife.

"The thermometer on the back porch says ninety-four."

"One at Holgrove's reads ninety-six."

"Well, they're usually right. I believe it, anyway."

"They usually are. So do I."

"I bought some watermelon this morning—thank God I got my shopping done early. Want some?"

"Later, maybe. Where're the kids?"

"Billy's at the beach—swimming today, not working. It's his day off. Cissie's over to her friend Betty's house. They were supposed to go swimming, too—over at Riker Park."

"Good day for it."

"I think I'm going to go swim in the bathtub." But she didn't move—looked as if she couldn't. That wisp of errant hair fell again, this time over one eye. It was several seconds before she brushed it away, a superhuman task, it seemed. It was a lovely sight to watch, thought Stanley.

"Billy wants a motorcycle. . . ." Something seemed to click in Stanley's head, then flash, bearing lighted blighted words: CONSPICUOUS CONSUMPTION. He ran his hand across his mouth, felt the perspiration over his own lip. "Says he really needs one. . . ."

"That sounds familiar. These damn kids of ours equate *want* with *need*, Em. We ought to say no on principle."

"Whatever you say, Stanley."

"He's entering college in less than two months and his summer job won't pay for a third of *that*. Where does he suppose money comes from, anyway?"

"He wants the motorcycle for college. To get around more cheaply."

"You get around *cheapest* on shoe leather—that's how *I* got around in college. I want him in the dorm hitting the books, not roaring around the countryside."

"Well, I never liked those machines, myself. Aren't they dangerous, Stanley?"

"Walking across the street's dangerous today. Cissie's got to go to college eventually, too. Does he think about that?"

"Billy says he wants to pay for the motorcycle himself. . . ."

"Mighty damn nice of him."

"Well I only thought I'd mention it."

"You mean he put you up to it."

"Oh, Stanley: if you wouldn't always just bark at him . . ."

"If he'd only be *reasonable* sometime!" Emily only sighed. "Has he got any money?"

"He has fifty dollars."

"What's the motorcycle cost?"

"The one he wants sells for seven hundred and fifty."

"He's got a long way to go—beyond next summer, I'd say."

"He talked of financing it."

"Nobody'd give him the dough."

"He had you in mind." Stanley only snorted. It was actually, despite its sonorous quiver, a noncommittal sound, more safety-valve than protest. Emily was used to it and had long ago ceased to try to break him of the habit. "I'm going to soak in a cool tub for an hour." She finally hauled herself up out of her chair and left the kitchen, brushing Stanley's shoulder as she passed.

"The world's going to hell in a handbasket and the kid wants a motorcycle. . . ." (UNFAIR!—the lights flashed.) Perhaps it was unfair. But it was not enough to *want*, in Stanley's book; there was also the little matter of *doing*. He who wants, let him do. The boy had a job. . . .

But not at the Stanhope Cleaners. There was, Billy said, more money to be made at the Casino in the summer. *As if the point of working at the plant were simply remunerative!* Stanley'd almost given up hope that his only son would go into the business eventually. Billy apparently didn't think much of dry-cleaning as a life's work. (Did he secretly say of it, as he openly said of so many things, "That's *dumb*"*?*) But the plant was a money-maker: money—that same where-withal without which Billy would never have a motorcycle. Their home (inherited from his parents, it's true) was mort-gage-free, they ate well, they were well and seasonably dressed (and dry-cleaned regularly, of course)—and all be-cause of the family business, which also supported Harry Putchek and his wife and four children, and Irma Kasendorf as well. Billy could do worse than go into dry-cleaning. Maybe he'd feel differently about it after he got out of college (if he graduated), the army (if he was called), his adoles-cence (if ever he would). If not, to hell with it. Maybe Cissie would be interested in inheriting the business.

He got up and went to the refrigerator with nothing more in mind than a lingering sense of annoyance at the ingratitude of some children toward their parents. He swung the fridge door wide open.

A watermelon. It lay there dominating the topmost shelf of the refrigerator. Pale green, cool to see as well as to touch, ponderous in both appearance and actuality, a confirmation of its own reality. It was the first watermelon they'd had that summer. Stanley cut himself a generous piece—the entire umbilical end, in fact—stuck a fork into its juiceful flesh, and headed out the back porch, whose screen door didn't seat properly though Stanley'd fiddled and fooled with it on two occasions after painting it in a splurge of outdoorsy activity that spring. He opted for his gazebo and crossed his back yard to get to it.

The gazebo was as old as Stanley himself and was built, he knew, by his own father. It was a cool and private retreat of dark green latticework raised above a stone base. The gazebo was Stanley's own thinking-place (weather permitting) and he'd been able to prohibit his children's roughhousing in its sacred confines—his one indisputably successful exercise of parental authority. He sat, watermelon in hand, on one of the three greenpainted benches which alternated with the three entrances. He began to eat; absently at first, his mind trying to pick up the loose ends of thoughts which had so enervated him earlier. Then it hit him: the watermelon . . . !

Ice-cold, a direct antithesis to the July heat, yet burning like the fire of a prophet's word in his mouth. Sweet—not cloyingly so but like a fine sherbet: refreshing, titillating, making him hungry for more. It was incredible. It was delicious—no, the word wasn't adequate, wasn't inclusive or connotative enough to fully describe—. It was beyond description. Ineffable. He ate ravenously, barely taking the time to spit the seeds out onto the stone floor of the gazebo. Seeds . . . .

That, alas, was the snake in the garden. Or more precisely, the several snakes. That delicious melon—that exquisite ineffably *perfect* thing—was full of seeds. He spat them out machinegunlike as he thrust forkful after forkful of the sweet cold fruit into his mouth. His teeth hurt from the cold of it. He nearly choked on the seeds before he could spit them out. Watermelon juice trickled out of the corners of his mouth and fell to stain his shirt and trousers. Yet he could not stop: Stanley Stanhope was a man obsessed . . . or *possessed*. He felt—absurdly, he knew, but nonetheless truly— that he could *die* for that melon: die for the chance to consume it, as certain insects were given the chance to mate gloriously only to pay for the pleasure with their lives. He didn't care. There were all too few perfect things in this world, in nature, even in the minds of men at their noblest or most creative. But here, in a Krumpit, Connecticut, gazebo some forty years old, *here was* perfection! If only it had fewer seeds . . . .

Stanley found himself scraping at the rind with his fork. (Is this me? Can this be me involved in this unbelievable passion, this grotesque—?) He didn't answer his own question because he got up and ran out of the gazebo, up the back porch steps (savagely slamming the badly-seating screen door), ran to the refrigerator, and—yes—took, no, yes, kidnapped—carried away at any rate, as in some trans-Appenninean lust-raid (Is this me? Can this be me?) the unprotesting flushed-pink melon and hauled his prize, screen door banging, back to the darkgreenshade, his own safe gazebo—sweating now, profusely, face arms back (buttocks?) ribs legs, his perspiration mixing wantonly with the sticky dark stains of spilled watermelon juice.

He ate until he could eat no more, until his mad-lust was satiated. His jaw ached from the furious spitting-out of seeds. His stomach, numbed with coldness, throbbed protuberantly. Yet he'd eaten less than half of that gigantic melon. He sank to his knees on the stone floor, bringing the watermelon with him. Less than half . . . but *what* a melon. Ineffable. No words could be found. Could he find a *reason?* Why—*why* had this particular watermelon, so full of seeds, tasted so . . . ? Was he mad? Had he . . . ? Sweet Jesus no, let it not be that—not madness. He knelt there a long time motionless, convincing himself that he had *not* gone mad, going over in his mind his business accounts, the state of his finances, his monthly budget, his bills outstanding. The facts and figures presented themselves in quick order, with Stanley fully in command. He was not mad, he decided, very much relieved.

Was it, then—the melon?

Oh Christ, had he been victimized? Had some murderously antisocial yippie—? Had some demented drop-out filled that lovely Godgrown melon with some diabolic hallucinogen the way his father used to spike a melon with rum? There was only one way to be sure, and that was to taste it again. He had to find out—or wonder about it for the rest of his life, perhaps. With his fork he dug out a large chunk, ate it, spat out the seeds, felt its coolness in his gullet, and waited. Ten full minutes by his watch. There was no reaction at all—other than the throb of protest from his distended stomach. Reluctantly, he concluded that the melon was perfectly safe. Had the *heat* affected him?

A cicada sang in an elm somewhere, and that was what reminded him of the heat. He'd walked home from the plant in 96 degree temperature, after all. But the cicada also reminded him of the great old elms, beneath which he'd been sheltered most of the way home. It simply hadn't been that hot under the elms—as it wasn't in the darkgreenshade of his gazebo. As he knelt looking at the scattered seeds around him, Stanley simply had to admit to himself that he could find no reason for his . . . for his strange experience.

So many seeds! It was unbelievable. He began to brush them into a pile with his fingertips, gathering them rather absently over the stone floor spotted pink with stickily drying watermelon juice. Then, for no discernible reason, he began to count them. How utterly peaceful it was, to be seated on one's heels in one's gazebo counting watermelon seeds on a summer's day. Gone were his worries about America-the-troubled, about the stacks of clothes to be cleaned, about Billy's hotly desired motorcycle. The gazebo might have been a shrine and he an Eastern monk, serene in contemplation of the seeds of eternity: he was fully at peace, for the world consisted of watermelon seeds on a stone floor, and responsibility, nothing more than counting those seeds, numbering them as the Creator might have numbered the stars. . . .

Suddenly he'd run out of available seeds—no, there were a half-dozen more. Then it occurred to him that to do the job right (Can this be me?) he would have to get the rest of the seeds out of the remainder of the melon. But—no: that was wasteful—and absurd. Beside him, a pile of 306 seeds lay moist and sticky. A fly buzzed by and he brushed it away. Stanley took his handkerchief out of his pocket—not to wipe his hands with, as he intended—but (as it turned out) to spread flat on the stone floor. Then, to his own amazement, he calmly transferred the pile of seeds, all 306 of them, to the center of his hanky. His gaze fell on the half-eaten melon that remained. It was still cool to the touch, calm, and as collected as a partially eaten watermelon could possibly be. Stanley too was calm, and, more importantly, his thoughts were collected:

(It is bad enough for a man of forty, a respected businessman in his community, to be sitting on the floor of his gazebo counting watermelon seeds, after a spate of gluttony. But it is far worse still to contemplate destroying the rest of a perfectly delicious melon just to satisfy an infantile urge to know how many seeds are in it. If I really *have* to know, I can just as well ask the family to save the seeds and count them as the rest of the melon gets eaten. Or make a game of it with the kids: hey! let's see how many seeds are in the— "Oh, Dad, that's *dumb*." In any case, I am fully in control of the situation; that is, I don't *have* to take that melon apart and count the seeds in it; that is, I am not *compelled*. And because I am not so compelled I am free to choose whether or not to do so. Therefore, if I freely decide to take that melon apart and count the rest of the seeds in it—admittedly a pointless pastime—then it would be, nonetheless, an act of a free and unencumbered will, and *not* an act prompted by madness. *I* at least would understand it. But how would I explain such a thing to, say, Emily . . . ?)

He asked himself that question even as he ripped the melon apart, even as he squished the still cold fruitflesh between his fingers seeking seeds, even as he added them to the sticky pile in his handkerchief, numbering them. In his mind the lettered lights flashed: CONSPICUOUS DESTRUCTION. But he went on about his task, gouging out handful after handful of soft melonflesh and counting its seeds. Still, he was glad that he felt silly about it; for if he didn't, wouldn't it have been cause for worry?

"Heh-heh-heh-heh-heh . . . !"

Stanley heard the low laugh soft as summer air and looked up to see Old Beardsley standing there watching Stanley Stanhope count the last three seeds (numbers 997, 998 and 999) into his handkerchief. Stanley, unfortunately, also saw himself as he must have appeared to Old Beardsley: like some minor priest in his gazebo-temple, he had just finished slaughtering the sacrificial melon, the grisly remains of which were all about him, its life-juice dark and sticky on the stones, on his clothes, on his hands and arms, for all he knew on his face as well. He could feel himself blushing hotly, watermelon pink.

"Don't mind me, boy. Go right ahead . . . !" And oh those mocking old eyes.

"Oh for Chrissakes!" It was like being caught naked. "What do you want!"

"Heh-heh-heh-heh-heh! Whatcha *got,* Stan . . . ?"

"Will you kindly state your goddamn *business?*" If the old man would only turn off that mocking gaze . . . .

"Glad to. Running into you a while ago reminded me: Em'ly says you got a screen door needs fixing. I've checked the front one—nothing wrong with *it.* Just came around to check the back door when I saw you here, Stanley-boy. Sitting on the floor, I mean. Thought something might've happened to you." He popped a stubby pipe into his mouth, the stem being immediately lost under the scraggle of his mustache. "*Did* anything?"

(Jesus how those eyes can mock!) Stanley glared at the old man, but Old Beardsley hid himself in tobacco smoke. "No! And it's the *rear* door that's broken!"

"Okay, Stanley. Nothing to get excited about. I'm sure it can be fixed, heh-heh-heh-heh-heh. . . ."

"Get out of my gazebo!"—but there was only a drift of pungent blue-grayness twining itself through the dark green latticework. That and Old Beardsley's laugh retreating.

Stanley stumbled to his feet and surveyed the scene about him. His legs were numb from having been knelt and sat on; his trousers, which had begun to dry in a sitting position, now clung perversely to his legs, as if the devastated melon were having its revenge. A glance out his gazebo revealed Old Beardsley busy with the screen door to the back porch. Stanley gathered his wits.

The first thing to do, he decided, was to get rid of the melon—the evidence. He would bury it—return it to the earth whence it had sprung. He got a shovel out of his garage, to Old Beardsley's vast amusement: the old man had the screen door off and was looking down its edge as if *aiming* it at Stanley, heh-heh-heh-heh-heh. Stanley ignored him. (Ignore the senile old bastard.) Back of his garage Stanley dug a sizable hole. It took three trips, but he scooped up the corpus meloncholus by the shovelful and interred it. While he was behind the garage he urinated, though not on the grave. His water steamed out of him, bringing immense relief from the pressure that had mounted within him since Old Beardsley had appeared on the scene. Moreover, his urination gave him the idea of using the garden hose on the stone gazebo floor, and he went to fetch it. But before he took the hose to the stones, he carefully tied the watermelon seeds into his handkerchief, which he stuffed into his pants pocket.

He washed the stone floor down three times with the hose nozzle set for maximum pressure. In the heat the stones took only minutes to dry—had done so, in fact, by the time he'd put the hose away.

Stanley sat on a green gazebo bench and contemplated the residual pale pinkness on the gray stones. At first his thoughts were about how he, as a dry-cleaner, might conceivably remove watermelon stains from a stone floor. His mind mixed proportions of tannin stain remover, neutral lubricant, perchlorethylene, soap, and steam under pressure. But as the afternoon sun found its way into the gazebo, Stanley came to admire the pale pink cast on the gray of the stones. His hosing-down had diluted the stain and spread it practically evenly over the stones—though there was, of course, one particular spot (the sacrificial stone?) where the stain glowed rosier.

It was then that he looked up and saw Old Beardsley approaching with the erect, bouncy steps of a man half his age. Stanley apologized at once to the old man, who came and sat with him in the gazebo. Old Beardsley quietly lighted his pipe, and the nutty smoke from it drifted across to Stanley like a peace offering.

The handyman thumped one of the gazebo's uprights. "Still standing strong, I see. I built it, y'know."

"*You* built it!"

"'Course. D'you suppose Sanny Claus brought it one Christmas?"

"No, I thought—. My *father* built this gazebo. He told me so himself." There was sudden, choking laughter from Old Beardsley, whose own face flushed watermelon-pink.

"Is that what he told you?" And then there were cascades of laughter, mocking falls and splashes. "Jock Stanhope couldn't drive a nail straight if his life depended on it—much less actually *build* anything!"

"But he *told* me—"

"Painted it himself, though. Amateurishly, but he did paint it himself, he did that much." The mocking eyes appraised the sloppy paint job of forty years ago—saw it clearly beneath all the subsequent coats of paint. "Maybe that's what he meant."

"He *said* he *built* it."

"Waal . . . ol' Jock always did get carried away with a story. *I* built it. I can show you where every nail is and how the thing was put together, if you like. I put the floor in, too. The stones are resting on sand from White Cove beach. So's the frost won't throw 'em up, y'know. Heh-heh-heh-heh-heh . . . ! Your pa was a congenital liar—did you know that, Stanley?"

There was no point getting into an argument with the old man, so Stanley tried his own mockery, a feigned-innocent "No!"

"Neither did your ma. Never, I truly believe."

"They seemed happy enough." Why was he wasting his time with Old Beardsley?

"Guess they were. Jock wasn't a *bad* man, mind. All in all. . . ."

(This is ridiculous.) "You knew my father well, didn't you."

"You bet. We used to whore around New York City together in the Roaring Twenties, so-called. 'Course we were both young colts then. . . ."

"Did you say *whore around?*" (Who did you say was the congenital liar?)

"Just an expression, boy. Don't take it literally." He retreated into a smokescreen and didn't say anything for a while. It seemed a spell was being evoked out of remembrances of things past; it was the last thing Stanley wanted to put up with, so he summoned back reality.

"What was wrong with the screen door?"

"What? Oh, one of the hinges'd worked loose. Whoever took it off to paint it didn't know balls about how to hang a door. Those older screen doors are pretty hefty, unlike the crap they're turning out these days. Screen door wasn't rehung properly so the hinge worked loose. Simple matter, easily fixed—if you know what you're doing. You won't have any trouble with it now. (Puff-puff.) Did *you* paint it?"

"Yes."

"Thought so. You paint like Jock used to. With the wrong end of the brush, looks like. Lord knows what he ever did to those stiffs when he was in the meat-packing trade. Heh-heh-heh-heh-heh!"

"You know, you don't *sound* like a friend of my dad's." Stanley was getting angry at Old Beardsley, though he tried to suppress it.

"But I was. Maybe his best friend—after Mary Louise, your ma I mean. Now there was a princess. Too bad you never had a sister, boy. If you had, and if she'd favored your ma, she'd be a remarkable creature, you bet."

(Be nice to the old man.) "I didn't enjoy being an only child."

"What makes you think y'are—heh-heh-heh-heh-heh!"

(Dirty old man—dirty senile old bastard mouldering in the rotten dregs of your own fetid memories! How dare you cast dung at the shades of those you aren't fit even to look upon . . . !)

But suddenly Old Beardsley grew very, very serious, and his voice became soft as smoke. "Mary Louise—your mother —was an exquisitely beautiful woman. As you undoubtedly recall. . . ."

"Yes of course. Thank you."

"No thanks to you. (Puff-puff.) And *what* she was, was as beautiful *as* she was. (Puff-puff.) I tell you frankly, boy, I never saw the likes of her before or since. She was a . . . (Puff-puff) . . . a singular occurrence, like a comet that shows up once and never again. Better'n your old man deserved, if you ask me."

(I didn't.) "My mother seemed content with her choice. And it's my understanding that she had a wide choice."

"You bet she did. You can't imagine how wide, boy. Anybody with any sense and half an eye was after her—and lots with none of either."

"But she *picked my father*. That's historical fact." (Whether you approved or not, old toad.)

"*Might* have been happier with someone else, though—with any number of 'em—now that's a possibility, you got to admit." (Puff-puff.)

(Oh no you don't:) "Hypothesis. Speculation. Unverifiable. A pointless argument. As much could be said of anyone."

"Right: a universal truth, hence applicable. Heh-heh-heh-heh-heh."

"Not at all." (Go to hell.) "In human affairs I've always felt that somehow the Fates decide such things. Kismet. Or Providence. Or what-you-will."

Heh-heh-heh-heh-heh. Poppycock. Surprised at you, Stanley. Even your pa'd know better'n to say something like that. Even ol' Jock. Even Jock the Joke. . . ."

"Were you very much in love with my mother?" Anything, anything to unbalance the old bastard, to upset his mocking self-assurance.

"Ho-ho!" (Puff-puff. Puff-puff-puff-puff-puff.)

"Well, were you?" (Squirm, you bastard.)

"Trouble with you, Stanley, is that you got a peculiar kind of mind—come to think of it, Jock had it, too: the kind of mind that just has *got* to have answers to things and if it can't *get* answers, fabricates 'em. I mean *cree-a-shun!* Right out of thin air. If the cow's supposed to jump over the moon and there's no cow, you'd supply one—from the infinite resources of your eager imagination. Your pa was the same, 'cept Jock, he'd even supply the fuckin' *moon!*"

"I don't believe you've answered my question." His pipe was out. Was he defenseless?

"Number one, it's none of your business. Number two, you ought to be ashamed of yourself, dragging your ma's name down by associating her with the likes of me, even indirectly. . . ."

(Cheap trick, Beardsley: cheap, cheap trick and I see through you.)

"Number three, it's the future you ought to be concerned with, Stanley, not the past. The future's where the action is, boy. Concern yourself with that—and the ever-lovin' present, of course, 'cause that's the future incarnate, so to speak. Pay attention to that, if you've got any piss and ginger in you."

Stanley inhaled slowly and leaned back on his bench and against one of the gazebo's uprights. The old man was busy relighting his pipe and seemed engrossed in the task. Was it Stanley's imagination that the old man now seemed vulnerable? Suddenly he felt sorry for Old Beardsley: not a pity, but a genuine compassion for the old derelict. He did not want to argue with him, did not want to fence with him anymore. "Funny that you should say those things about the future, Mister Beardsley. This afternoon I've been very nearly obsessed by thoughts about the future." (Not to mention an obsession with watermelon.)

"Have you. . . ." There was no more mocking in his eyes, but rather—was it?—yes: *age*. Stanley watched him for a minute, but the mocking combativeness didn't return. The old man sort of slumped on his bench and puffed away on his stub of a pipe with a measured cadence.

"I've been thinking terrible thoughts today. About the Country. . . ." And suddenly he wanted to talk about it—needed to, perhaps. Even to Old Beardsley, the very last person in town he ever expected to confide anything to. Was it the old man's presently discernible age? You could say anything to the very old; nothing surprised them. Hadn't they seen it all before? He looked up at Old Beardsley, who was gazing at him ethereally through a wreath of tobacco smoke and saying nothing, not even with his eyes. Stanley felt encouraged: "It sounds . . . pretentious, perhaps, but I've been concerned about the Country—America, I mean. I look around me, Mister Beardsley, and all I see and hear about are race-riots, bombings of buildings and killings of innocent people, and policemen, and freedoms, burnings of cities and exploitation of ghettos—polarizations of interests. . . . And the people—the *People*, Mister Beardsley—don't even seem to give a damn. They lock their doors and windows against it all and settle down before their television sets." Stanley found himself getting wound up tightly and checked the tendency while he still could. "All I mean to say is that the whole state of affairs in America today strikes me as neither a desirable nor a healthy condition. And if I could—if somehow, *any*how I could—I'd like to *do* something about it. Help right the Ship of State, which seems to be foundering. If that doesn't sound too, too pretentious. . . ."

Stanley experienced a tremendous relief in just expressing what had finally, succinctly been articulated within him. Later that day he might have found the same relief by relating his fears to his wife; he had never expected to be put at ease by Old Beardsley's patient attentiveness. When he looked up at the old man again he was confronted by a pair of rock-steady eyes watching him for what seemed an eternity.

Finally Old Beardsley sighed audibly. "What we need today are patriots, a rare breed in any era. We've always needed 'em, and we've been lucky to have 'em at crucial times, from the very beginning. Maybe our luck's run out. All we got today are crops of overprivileged juveniles who never had to work for anything and don't know what it means to be without anything; a pack of self-hating failures who want to do away with all of society so that their own personal failings won't be noticed among the ruins; and—as always—flocks and flocks of unthinking sheep who are easily herded into any sort of pen imaginable, including slaughterhouses. And oh yes: then there are the goddamn flagwavers. Now that's nice for parades, but that's not what we *need*. We need patriots, Stanley. No country can survive without 'em—not as a nation, anyway. And we need patriots now more'n we ever did, maybe: 'cause now there's more to lose. . . ."

"What's a patriot, anyway?"

"Somebody who puts his country's good over the good of his own blood and guts. Over his own rhetoric, too. Somebody who sees the nation not as so much abstract humanity waiting to be molded or exploited, but as *people*, Stanley— individual persons to be joined together in the common effort of nationhood. That's what 'we the people' means in the American context. It means 'we the patriots'—or *should* mean that, if the kind of democracy this country's supposed to be all about is gonna work. Patriots . . ." He knocked out his pipe against one of the gazebo uprights. "You can't hardly get 'em anymore." Then he arose, slapped Stanley paternally on the shoulder, then plodded out of the gazebo, showing his age.

Stanley watched as the old man went over to the back porch steps, picked up his toolbox, and disappeared in the same uncharacteristic shuffle down the driveway, leaving Stanley to swallow his hollow accusations of senility.

TWO

*S*TANLEY washed up in the kitchen—stripped right down to his underwear, found *that* to be melon-soaked, and peeled bolicky. His clothes he stuffed into a paper bag, which he hid in the closet under the stairs.

Barefooted, bolicky bare-assed, Stanley Stanhope trod up the stairs carrying his seeds in a hanky, trying hard not to think about his father and Old Beardsley whoring around New York City together in the Roaring Twenties, so-called. He felt like a dangerous criminal—a rapist—stealthily entering a home on a sleepy July afternoon while the lady of the house, the fair and raven-haired Emily Camille Stanhope, lay unsuspecting vulnerable naked in a cool tub. Suddenly, to Stanley's dismay, his man arose. (Oh for Chrissakes.) His erection sustained itself, despite his unease, and nothing he could do could get it down again. On tippy-toe he made his way to the edge of the bathroom door. He put on his best casual smile, then popped his head in, so that only his face would show.

"Hiya Mister Stanhope—I'm keeping cool, like you said to . . . !" It was Irma Kasendorf, naked in his tub, smiling her toothy absurd smile. He yanked his head back. When he looked again there was only the raven-haired Emily relaxing in the tub, her eyes closed above placid water. The shock had knocked his man down, at least. He scurried to his bedroom and dressed quickly. For his secret hoard of seeds he found a fresh handkerchief, which he thrust into a pocket of his clean slacks.

"What would you like for supper, Stanley?" She looked like a million: the cool tub had worked wonders. (No, she's always looked like a million.)

"Oh . . . anything at all. . . ."

"It's so warm. How about a chicken salad? I've got some chicken left over from yesterday; I think there's enough for a salad."

"Sounds great."

"And we can have watermelon for dessert!"

He felt a stabbing pain in his bowels. "Oh. About the watermelon . . ." Why did he do it—why did he *lie?* He never lied to Emily—never—not even with the "white" variety. Yet there he was telling her it had been a bad melon and he'd had to dispose of it. He actually said that. *Lied.*

"I wish you'd saved it, Stanley. I'd have taken it right back and gotten another. It cost a dollar-nineteen!"

"Oh it's—uh—too much bother." (Oh what a tangled web we weave . . . .)

"I'm sure Felix would make it good. Where's the melon, in the garbage?" She started out toward the back door.

"No!" (Easy.) "No, Em, I . . . I broke it up, back of the garage. For—for fertilizer. I thought I'd—I'd plant the seeds, since the melon was overripe. Maybe we'll have a . . . late summer crop. . . ." (. . . when first we practise to deceive.)

"Do you think it's possible?" She was looking at him quizzically prettily trustingly.

"Well I—dunno. Might be worth a try. . . ." (But not the lie: Christ!)

"Canned peaches okay then? For dessert? They're already chilled."

"Sure, only—" He felt a terrible cramping now, a violent wrenching of his bowels. "What watermelon I did have—I think it's made me sick, Em!" He excused himself hurriedly and ran upstairs. Then: wretched diarrhea, minutes worth, the wages of sin.

In his agony a question of immense importance pressed: Why were there only 999 seeds? Why not a perfect thousand? Had he miscounted? He got the handkerchief out of his pocket and began to recount the seeds onto the sinktop beside him. He allowed nothing to distract him, not even the mating-call of a desperate cicada in its own private travail somewhere in his back yard. Emily called up once, "Are you all right?" but he only answered with a snort that either satisfied her or drove her away, as Stanley counted on.

What he found both pleased and puzzled him: there were exactly 999 seeds. He'd missed none in gathering them—not even the immature white ones. Might 999 then be *the* most perfect number?

The melon had been the very best Stanley Stanhope had ever eaten. *And* the one with the most seeds. Was there a correlative there? *Was any given watermelon more delicious in direct ratio to the number of seeds it contained*, the more seeds the more delicious? It struck Stanley as the discovery of an eternal truth. Hadn't he already experienced both watermelon and seeds to a degree beyond the grasp of most mortals? Lovingly, reverently even, he piled the seeds back into his handkerchief, which he stowed carefully back into his pocket. It is not given to every man to carry an eternal truth in his pocket.

The kids were home, the house was full of noise: Cissie playing records and Billy singing in the shower. Later Stanley would have to face the business about the motorcycle. He wasn't up to it. Here he had hold of an eternal truth far and above the common maunderings of mankind, and his son wanted to pester him and wheedle at him all in the unholy name of Conspicuous Consumption. Stanley wanted none of it. He had—a sticky pocket. Body heat or perspiration had moistened the seeds and he could feel the dampstickiness against his thigh. He looked down and saw a dark spot on his trouser leg. He went into his den and put the handkerchief with its precious freight safely into the top drawer of his desk.

In the driveway outside his den stood his aging Studebaker —a car, he reflected, no longer manufactured in America: a victim of the economic illness that was affecting the Country. He stared at it, lamenting its fate. Then suddenly—ESCAPE! —the thought flashed in colored lights. He could avoid wrestling with the ogre of Conspicuous Consumption for tonight, at least.

He kissed the raven-haired beauty in his kitchen and informed her that he didn't think he should eat so soon after his intestinal ordeal and that he was going down to the plant and then maybe over to Harry Putchek's house. On his way out he retrieved his melon-stained clothes from the closet under the stairs.

It was still hot in the workroom of the Stanhope Cleaners. Hopefully, he turned on the air-conditioner. It made a rising whirring noise, then died in a low moan that sounded

like CON-SUMp-tion. . . . But it was quiet at the plant.
Stanley would be able to think. To think out what was wrong
about his Country. Once President Nixon had appeared on
television, shaking his jowls in the serious way he had of doing that (as if shaking a finger) and intoning, in his very
intonable voice, that all Americans should pay more attention to "what is *right* about America." Stanley had heard him
out but was more than a little confused by the request. For
does paying attention to what is right about America mean
ignoring what is wrong? The President did not make that
perfectly clear. Stanley would think about that, as well.

Later that evening he would drive over to Harry Putchek's
and ask him to tend to the business for a week. That would
give Stanley time to think the Country out unencumbered.
It was, after all, a fearsome task. Was it a feasible one? He
reminded himself of the young Englishmen from Oxbridge
who came over periodically, spent a few weeks touring the
States, then went home to write their snidely critical little
volumes All About America. America was not so easily in-
gested. Yet Stanley would try: *must* try. He had an enormous
advantage over the young Englishmen, after all: he'd spent
forty years in America. Surely that gave him a solid base to
build his thoughts on? A week devoted solely to his Country;
it seemed the very least he could do. He definitely needed a
week off.

Right now he needed his trousers off. He took his water-
melon-stained clothes from the paper bag. His underwear,
shirt, and socks were dispensable, he decided. The trousers
were expensive and could be saved. He brought both pairs
over to the spotting board, where with water, tannin stain
remover, bone and brush, spotting fluid, live steam, and
compressed air, he worked the stains out. Then he put the
pants into one of the dry-cleaning machines. The perchlorethylene would finish the job nicely—that and the soap and
the sizing. He switched on the topper and legger presses, then
went to sit in his office, and think.

Stanley thought about the Watermelon Correlative, which was beginning to seem the very key to the universe! For might not the Watermelon Correlative change the world? Might not the seeds of perfection be implanted in mankind to bring about the *state* of perfection? It was an engrossing thought, new and shining and seemingly not only workable, but omnipotent; and Stanley was lost in its implications as if amid the stars.

He became aware, first, of the hissing of steam-pressure, and then of the fact that the dry-cleaning machine had stopped. He went to retrieve his trousers.

He held both pairs of pants up to the fluorescent lights. The watermelon stains had disappeared completely. Yet he knew not joy, but rather a sinking of the heart: for if the watermelon stains could be done away with so easily by the simple science of dry-cleaning, how difficult would it be for the darker sciences which plague the world to obliterate the Watermelon Correlative—before its application could bring about the New Eden? It was a terrible thought and he would not allow himself to think about it. Instead he concentrated on pressing his pants.

He stood in his skivvies before Irma's machines, working away, quietly reassured by the familiar sound of the steam. His own father had taught him how to press when Stanley was still a boy. How much Stanley would have given to be able to teach his own son how to press! To have him work there alongside him, with Harry and Irma . . .

It was then that the awareness gradually crept over him: the realization that it was indeed Irma Kasendorf's machine that he, standing there in his skivvies, was busily working at. Irma: she of the soft round—(Ssss-*phtttt!*). Stanley's mind became filled with the enormous sweaty Y which had imprinted itself on Irma's denim dress above her softroundass. Stanley found himself working Irma's machine for all he was worth: SSSS-PHTTTT! SSSS-PHTTTT! SSSS-PHTTTT! A crawling sensual feeling raised first the hair on his bare legs

and then, stealthily, steadily, his man. (Oh sweet Jesus!)—
somebody was tapping on the shop door, tapping loudly on
the glass with a coin or a key, demanding entry. It could not
be Harry: he had his own key. Then who? Not—oh Jesus!
—not Irma Kasendorf! His man retreated like a cur. The
tapping was now imperative. Stanley struggled into the pair
of trousers he'd already pressed, then hurried out front.

It was his son, Bill, tapping on the glass door with the ornament hung on the end of his love beads. Stanley let him in.

(You too could have a key, my son!) "What's wrong,
Bill?"

"Nothing wrong. I wanted to borrow the car, that's all. I
got a date. . . ."

(*I* had dates at your age—without a car.) "Oh. Well, I
was planning to stop over to Harry Putchek's." (What's
the matter, can't girls *walk* anymore?)

"Well I could drive you over."

"How'd I get back? It's too far to walk. . . ."

"Couldn't Harry take you back?"

"I wouldn't ask him to do that. He may have plans. . . .
He may not even be home, he's not expecting me. . . ."
(Youth inconveniences the world—for its *own* convenience.)

"I really need the car, Dad. Deborah lives all the way over
in Osterville. . . ."

"Can you stay a minute?" Did his son *have* to look at his
watch as if to calculate whether or not he actually had the
time to spare for his dear old dad? Was this Deborah that
exciting? Did his young man stand at the sight or thought of
her? (UNFAIR!—the lights flashed.)

"Sure." The metal ornament—the peace symbol in shining
chromium—hung on its own silverlike chain, not on the love
beads. The love beads were nothing but beads. Like fatted
watermelon seeds.

(I'd like to give you the business, son.) "Come out back.
I've got a pair of pants on the press. . . ."

Bill sat on the edge of one of the work tables, the ankle of one leg crossed over the knee of the other, an athletic youth who was already bigger and taller than his father. Miss Deborah (or whomever) would be a lucky girl.

Ssss-phtttt.

"Mom said she mentioned to you about the motorcycle. . . ."

(*Mentioned the motorcycle to you*—or is that equally bad grammar?) "Yes, she did."

"What do you think?" Stanley looked at him. Bill wasn't looking at his father but down at his sock, which he pulled at.

"I think you don't need any distractions your first year of college, especially." (Ssss-phtttt.)

"But it wouldn't be a distraction, it'd be a time-saver. And if I got it now, the novelty'd be worn off by the time I went away to school. And I wouldn't have to keep borrowing the car, until then. . . ."

(Ssssss-shhhh . . .) "There. That's done—didn't take long, did it?" Stanley switched off the steam. "This Deborah, she'd ride on the back of a motorcycle?"

Now his son looked at him—as if at a creature from another age: *brontosaurus stanhopus*, pea-brained, extinct. "Sure, Dad."

(In *my* day girls who—) Stanley found himself staring at his son and hoped the stare had not assumed the properties of a glare. "I never asked you, Bill, but I wonder if you wouldn't mind telling me why you wear your hair that way . . . ?"

"What way?" He seemed genuinely surprised. Of course it seemed the normal, acceptable thing: his peers approved; never mind his dear old dad. "*Long*, you mean?"

"Yes. And those necklaces. Why? I'm just curious, Bill, not critical, mind you."

Bill shrugged. His hair, freshly shampooed, shimmered and glistened under the bright lights. "All the guys wear it this way." His face fell into a puzzled expression. (". . . unthinking sheep who are easily herded into any sort of pen imaginable . . ."). Did he see something in his father's face? "It's not *real* long, Dad, just—average. . . ." He didn't mention the reason for the beads and the peace pendant; Stanley decided not to pursue the matter.

"Mind if I ask just one more question, son?"

Bill glanced at his watch. "Sure. I mean, no—go 'head."

"Well, I just wondered. . . . That is, have you given any thought as to whether you'd like to take over the business some day, Bill? After you get out of college I mean. . . ."

Billy seemed embarrassed. He shifted his legs, then his entire body. "GeeIdunno—I really couldn't say right now. It seems like . . . so far away. . . ."

"Well of course you don't have to decide now this minute . . ." (If you promise to go into the business you can have the motorcycle.)

"I just can't see that far ahead, Dad."

(If you swear you'll take over the business some day, I'll *buy* you the motorcycle, outright!) "Yes . . . of course. I understand, Bill. . . ."

"To tell you the truth, Dad, I just don't know *what* I want to do. With my life, I mean."

(I'll give you the motorcycle and the business and the house and the gazebo!) "But you *will* think about it, won't you, Bill? About going into business with me? Eventually?"

"Sure, Dad."

Stanley surrendered the keys to the Studebaker and watched his son roar away from the Stanhope Cleaners on his way to Osterville, Deborah, and Godknewwhat. He felt a slow turning-over of his stomach.

After supper Stanley asked his wife whether she wouldn't mind his shutting himself up in his den for the evening, as he had some problems to figure out. (And *that* was true.) Emily said she didn't mind, that she had a novel she'd been wanting to read. She even managed to get Cissie to turn down the television set. Once in his den he closed the door and opened the windows. The curtains billowed pregnantly, promising deliverance of a cool night.

Stanley Stanhope sat at his desk and stared at the wall before him. He felt . . . what was it he felt? Impotent? Was that the word for his feeling of not being able to find solutions to anything?

He had not gone to Harry Putchek's house after all: had not asked him to tend to the business for a week; had not arranged to take the week off in order to think. He might phone or ask Harry tomorrow . . . except he knew he would not. Some things had to be done on the spur of the idea or they were not done at all. Things like taking a week off to think about America. He'd had this opportunity and missed it— sacrificed it to the vagaries of his son's love life. (Do children ever really realize the extent of their parents' sacrifices on their behalf?)

Impotent. Was that the word? His eyes drifted to a framed photograph on the wall: his parents' wedding picture. How seriously they looked out at him! What on earth had they seen as that shutter was being clicked openshut so many years ago? Stanley went over to the photograph.

His father had not been impotent. He'd worked through the entire Depression, even when other men stood in breadlines and went on the dole. Later he founded a business and developed it and made it prosper so that he was able to hand it on to his son, a legacy of great value and continuing support. He'd whored around New York (whatever that meant and married the most beautiful girl in town and fathered a son and bought a fine house and built (or had built—painted, at any rate) an incomparable gazebo. And he died peacefully in his sleep on the last day of September, 1958, in the forty-ninth year of his life, unwracked by age or illness. *That* was not an impotent life, however brief the candle.

Stanley looked closely at his father's eyes and saw a fearless gaze leveled like a rifle: manly, self-assured, ready to take on the Depression. His parents had married, he knew, in November of 1929. The month after the Great Crash! Now that took courage, not to mention love. Perhaps that explained the solemnity of the wedding portrait.

Lovingly, he studied his mother's features. What a beauty she'd been! *Her* eyes were unafraid also, but they were receptive, like quiet pools. ("Mary Louise—your mother—was an exquisitely beautiful woman. And *what* she was, was as beautiful *as* she was. . . .") Stanley would have bet anything that Old Beardsley had indeed been in love with her. It would have been understandable. But it was his father who had won her—with that level unafraid gaze so fitting for the times, perhaps—and after that Old Beardsley could only putter around fixing other people's broken articles and taking credit for building other men's gazebos. His mother had chosen well. Whatever she'd seen from her vantage point in 1929 had been the true road, and she'd stayed on it until the winter of 1966, when she died of pneumonia, on Cissie's seventh birthday. Stanley turned away from the portrait: from the tender past to the harsh present.

The present was a sense of impotence. Yet somehow that hot July afternoon, somewhere under the ancient elms of Krumpit, Connecticut, Stanley Stilmore Stanhope, only-begotten son of Jacob and Mary Louise Stanhope, had picked up the conscience of America and carried it now as a burden. Not a physical one—not a weight which threatened to crush him—but a burden similar to the cicada's: the shrill brute knowledge that there was only a limited time in which to act or it would be too late—*too late!*—and something would die out in the Land.

"What we need today are patriots," Old Beardsley had said. But where were they, where were they now, now that America had need of them?

Stanley tried to visualize a Patriot—attempted to conjure one up: George Washington in the bitter cold and snow of Valley Forge; John Paul Jones on a pitching deck in a reel-ing ocean; Patrick Henry before a revolutionary convention pleading for Liberty or death; Nathan Hale, that fellow Connecticut Yankee who taught school over in New London, paying that last full measure at the end of a British rope and regretting that he had but one life to give for his Country. Patriots. They had put the good of their Country over their own blood and guts, their own rhetoric.

Yet they escaped Stanley: he could not conjure them up satisfactorily. They were larger than life: they had not only entered history but myth as well. Such familiarization bred, not contempt (myths are above contempt) but obscuration. No one knew, anymore, the true extent and nature of their sacrifices. Historians, damn their hides, had condemned the Patriots to fame and thence to remoteness. George Washington sat securely in the primal position of the American Pantheon, but he was no longer first in the hearts of his countrymen. It was a comedown, Stanley felt. A fall to rival Adam's.

But oh to have actually *known* a Patriot! To have grown up with him, perhaps, to have lived in the same town, to have shared a sense of—

Stanley shot out of his chair—rose on the wave of his own excitement as he remembered that he *did indeed* know a Patriot! Or at least lived in the same town with him, shared the same land, streets, air: shared some of the same old elms, perhaps. In a moment he was at his book shelves searching, searching for the volume he had so clearly in mind. All to no avail: he couldn't find it. Finally he remembered: his daughter had borrowed it to press leaves in, since he'd overruled use of the unabridged dictionary.

He ran out of his den—"Cissie!"—and up the stairs, slowed down only by the phonographic blare emanating from his daughter's room. "CAN YOU TURN THAT THING OFF A MINUTE . . . ?" He was certain she hadn't heard him but his gestures must have sufficed. The sudden silence nearly knocked him over.

"What is it, Daddy?" Only a few months earlier she had finally convinced her mother to free her forever from the ignominy of pigtails, and as a result she looked disconcertingly grown up. Emily had remarked on it some time ago but he really hadn't noticed the change until now: had never fully accepted the reality of little girls growing up; not his own, at least. "Okay, I'll keep it down. . . ." She wore her annoyance prettily. She'd be a knockout like her mother in a few more years. She would disconcert a lot of males in the years ahead.

"No, it's not that." The room was tidy, shipshape, after years of looking like flotsam and jetsam. Emily had finally gotten the message across in that regard, and Cissie now took an interest in her surroundings, as well as in herself. (Cissie-girl, what would you think of a career in dry-cleaning?) "I was looking for a book. The one you're pressing leaves in, remember?"

For several seconds she didn't, then she hoppedskippedandjumped, still the little girl, over to her desk. The volume was under the goldfish bowl. "Sigmund's helping to press them."

(How the sweet Christ does an eleven-year-old girl come up with the name "Sigmund" for a pet fish?)

She moved the bowl off the book and brought the heavy volume over to her bed, her littlegirlishness dissolving, suddenly, in gravity. Carefully she opened the book to several pages toward the center and removed three doubled-over sheets of wax paper. Stanley stood by as if at a ceremony, as Cissie lifted out three single leaves of the previous autumn. But they were not as they had been. She twitched her nose as she looked down at them. "They've faded."

"They'll do that. I think you have to pour melted wax over them, honey. Paraffin. Try that, next time."

Cissie made a softly whistling noise in her nostrils—an inchoate version of Stanley's own reverberant snort? "I thought the wax on the wax paper would keep them nice and fresh."

Stanley thought it a triumph still: she'd used her head, at least, even if the outcome wasn't what she'd expected. "Want the book back?"

"No. . . ." She crumpled the faded leaves into a ball in her hand, then tossed it into her wastebasket. "I've outgrown those things now." She strolled over to her phonograph, lifted the arm, and poised it over the record as she searched for a desired groove. Stanley left hurriedly before it made contact. A bongo beat pursued him downstairs and he shut the door of his den against it.

THREE

*T*HE BOOK was A HISTORY OF KRUMPIT, CONNECTICUT, AND ENVIRONS, 1645–1945, and was compiled by the members of the Krumpit Historical Society. The book had belonged to Stanley's father.

It had been published on the Tercentenary anniversary of the town, in celebration of that memorable occasion. Production of the volume had required the labor of ten long years, from 1935 to 1945—or approximately the decade a significant portion of Western civilization was undergoing the convulsions which nearly destroyed it. Despite that distraction, the members of the Society had kept their collective nose firmly to the task at hand; the Second World War would have to be left to Historical Society members of another, later decade.

An exhaustive tome, the Tercentenary volume consisted mostly of listings of land transfers, vital statistics, catalogues of catastrophes natural and otherwise—records of a million or so bits of historical, commercial, and industrial information. But it did contain an appendix in encyclopedic form, and it was to this that Stanley eagerly turned. Toward the end of the K's he found:

> KRUMPIT *(variously Krumpet or Crompette)*. A family name found in the records of Rhode Island and Conanicut Island as early as 1640. The family is believed to have originated in Wessex, England. (Point of origin contested. —F.B.N.). Best known members of the family were Aaron Krumpit (q.v.) and his great-great grandson, the American Revolutionary War hero Anthony Krumpit (q.v.).

> KRUMPIT, town of. Town founded by Aaron Krumpit (q.v.) and the band of settlers led by him, in the S.W. corner of the county in 1645 on high ground (elev. 155 ft.) 7 miles due north of Long Island Sound. The original name of the area was Oganeequonchee (the Wilmot Indian name meaning "high-place-where-the-wild-onions-grow-under-ever-changing-skies").

> KRUMPIT, AARON. *(Sobriquet: "The Terrible")*. Leader of a band of settlers who left the Colony of Providence Plantations nine months after its formation in 1644. Krumpit found himself the leader of a hardy band of pioneers recruited from the docks of Providence. The group arrived in what was then popularly known as Ball's Rise on January 3, 1645. Land, including that then occupied by Hosiah Ball (q.v.) and his family of 27, was

purchased by Aaron Krumpit from the sachem Quikqil (q.v.) for 25 English coats. (Number of coats contested.—C.F.O.). Aaron made further land purchases from Quikqil's son, the sachem Dimqil (q.v.) in 1655 and again in 1660 for an undetermined number of barrels of rum, thereby adding significant acreage to the town. The origin of his sobriquet "The Terrible" is not known.

KRUMPIT, ANTHONY. (*Sobriquet: Wild Anthony"*). Hero of the American Revolutionary War, first under Major General Israel Putnam (q.v.) then later on his own. He was the great-great grandson of Aaron (The Terrible) Krumpit (q.v.). He was born in Krumpit-town (q.v.) on August 9, 1753. Two of his exploits are especially remembered: his courageous journey from Princeton, N.J., to Philadelphia, Pa., with a warning for General Washington announcing the approach of the British; and the stunning upset he brought about single-handedly on July 29, 1779, at Riker's Field (q.v.) against 1,200 British light cavalry under the command of General William Tryon. (A monument raised by the Krumpit Historical Society marks the spot today.) Anthony Krumpit's untimely death occurred on January 17, 1787, in Paris, where he was serving his country as special representative to the Court of France. His body was returned to Krumpit, Connecticut, and now rests in glory in Riker's Field Park, near the site of his unforgettable victory against the might of the British Empire.

For a more complete biography of Anthony Krumpit, see the monograph "Anthony Krumpit: American Revolutionist" by Horace Wiley Pool, K.H.S., available at the Krumpit Free Library or from the Society ($1.00).

Stanley's blood thrilled in his veins. Wild Anthony Krumpit was that rarest of things, an authentic Patriot. One against twelve hundred: unbelievable odds! But for the authentic Patriot—one who put the good of his Country over his own bloodgutsrhetoric—even those odds were favorable. It struck Stanley that it was the Watermelon Correlative all over again: *One's efficacy was in direct ratio to the seeds of courage within one.*

From his desk drawer he took the hankyful of watermelon seeds. It left a widening rosy spot on the wood at the bottom of the drawer. Thought Stanley: as the wood absorbed the juices, so would America absorb the rosy glow which the Watermelon Correlative could bring about in the Land. He vowed that, somehow, he would sow those seeds in the provenly fertile soil of American Democracy and make the Republic *flower*, that it might bear its fruit once more. Stanley Stanhope was caught up in a reverie that was broken only by his sudden awareness of the Studebaker's headlights shooting up the driveway. The clock on his desk read three-to-midnight. In another minute Billy was at his den door.

"I saw your light. . . ."

"Saw the light?"

"Coming up the drive."

"Oh, yes, of course. Come in."

"I just wanted to know if you've been giving it any thought. About the motorcycle, I mean."

(Have I been—!) "Oh; yes." He tapped his tooth with his fingernail and concluded that he ought not to commit himself so soon. "But I haven't quite decided, Bill." He saw the fleeting annoyance which shot across his son's face. "Did you have a good time in Osterville?"

"Yeah."

"With—ah . . . ?"

"Deborah. Yeah, it was okay."

"What'd you do?"

"Sat around and watched TV. They got a color television, the Perkinses have. Pretty nice."

(Conspicuous Consumption, son. Worse: another totally

unnecessary consumer item foisted on the easily seduced American public by the panderers of Madison Avenue and the communications industry, aided and abetted by the F.C.C., infecting the Nation and the People with mediocrity and materialism.) "I'll have to let you know about the motorcycle, Bill." His son's love beads glinted dully—but the shiny chromium peace pendant was missing. "You lost one of your necklaces. . . ." Billy felt at his chest and looked down, obviously surprised. Then a delicate shade of pink flooded his face.

"I guess it fell off—at Deborah's. . . ." He moved toward the door. "I'll phone her tomorrow and tell her to keep an eye out for it. Goodnight, Dad"—and he was gone.

"Goodnight."

He found Emily propped up in bed, reading. She lay in the shorty nightgown she wore in summer, her tanned long legs ending in crossed feet. "Hi, handsome."

"Hi." He undressed quietly, put on his pajama bottoms, used the bathroom down the hall. "Is the book any good?"

"Fair. Sounds like something I've read before, though I can't imagine what." He could just see the title: *The Kingdom That Never Came.* Around and around the room he walked, unable to get into bed, his mind an apprehensive mishmash of Wild Anthony Krumpit's charge against the redcoats being viewed on color television by 200,000,000 complacent Americans. It seemed to Stanley that he would never sleep that night. "Something wrong, dear?"

"I'd like to get drunk. Stinko. Potted enough to be planted."

She put her book down over her abdomen, like a little hut. "Well, it wouldn't take more than one drink, would it?" She said it teasingly, not unkindly.

And it was true: he could not drink. Not at all—not a drop. To his immense mortification throughout his college years, when not to be able to hold one's liquor made one, somehow, less a man—and inevitably the butt of jokes. He'd discovered the grievous flaw in his physiology at his first American Dry-cleaners' Convention in New York City in

1948. His father had taken him. He was just 18—Billy's age. Stanley's gotten looped—flying high—on *one half* a highball. His father'd thought it a great joke, as would his future classmates. Stanley had thought of it rather as a terminal illness. But finally he'd accepted it: he simply could not drink. He was never able to acquire a tolerance for the stuff. He never even kept any of it in the house.

"Do you suppose it affects Billy?"

"Do I suppose *what* affects Billy?"

"Why, alcohol. Do you suppose he's . . . like me in that regard?" (He must be like me in *some* regard.)

"I don't know. Why don't you ask him?" (She's always direct like that. She'll tell her fruit man yet about that watermelon.)

"Do you think Bill drinks, Em?"

"Probably. Don't most boys by his age?"

"Jesus, Em, you don't suppose he's into *drugs*, do you? Pot—or *worse?* Did you ever smell marijuana-smoke on his clothes, or anything?"

She laughed. "I don't think I'd recognize it if I did."

He got angry. "It's not a laughing matter, Em, this is a serious problem today. Kids use drugs like our generation used alcohol! I don't want Billy getting all screwed up inside . . . !"

She was very quiet, but firm. "Neither do I. But I trust him to do the right thing, Stanley. That's the way we brought him up."

"I wonder how many parents have said just that. . . ."

"I feel certain about it. We did a good job with Billy."

(What the hell could we do about it if we didn't—now.) "I guess you're right. He's never . . . let us down. . . ." (Yet.)

"Is that all that's worrying you?"

"He lost one of those necklaces he wears—the peace pendant. Over at the Perkins girl's house, over in Osterville. He didn't even know it was missing. Know what I think, Em? I think he lost it on the sofa or someplace—they were watching TV—wrestling with her, *making* it with her, maybe . . . !" Emily's laughter cut his anger down to saner proportions. "Do we *know* this Perkins girl!"

"Deborah? Why, Stanley, she was over here for *dinner* not a week ago—on the day before your birthday, in fact."

"Oh. That one." (Which one? Christ, they all lookedalike talkedalike dressedalike giggledalike, were all in turn gravely polite: "Very nice to meet you, Mister Stanhope.") Or was it that he frightened them somehow? "Pretty girl, right?" It was a safe guess.

"Beautiful. Lovely dark eyes. Remember?"

"Not quite." He snorted, startling Emily. "I hope that kid behaves himself, I don't want any problems."

"Oh, Stanley, what *has* got into you?"

He threw his hands in the air. How was it to be explained? About America, the need for Patriots. The necessity to do battle against seemingly overwhelming odds which in reality are *not* overwhelming—given the validity of the Watermelon Correlative as verified by Wild Anthony Krumpit at Riker's Field in 1779. And how to explain the need to raise one's children free of crass materialistic cravings and lustful longings so that the supply of Patriots might be ever and ever renewed? "I feel so goddamn *impotent*. . . ." He sat down on the bed beside her. The book slid off her belly. She glanced at the title, then tossed it onto her bedside table.

"Poor dear, hasn't the kingdom come, yet?"

"No, I—" (How *did* she know?)

"You're still king with me, good-looking."

"Em, I'm not in the mood for levity."

"Am I being levit?" She looked at him with the innocent rounded eyes she affected whenever she was determined to tease him.

"*Yes!*" He was surprised by the anger in his voice. Emily

only raised her brows a moment, then heaved an immense sigh that lifted her breasts and let them slowly down again. "What's the book about?"

"Really want to know?"

"Sure. I guess. . . ."

"Well. It's about this absolutely *gorgeous* man, this virile American dry-cleaner who suddenly turns forty, see, and it hits him so hard he feels like he's been socked by Muhammed Ali or somebody, and—" Stanley sank to her and kissed her hard on the mouth to end the levity and because she looked so soft in the light of the bedside lamp. "Don't you want to hear the rest?"

"I already know that story. Sheer fiction. . . ."

"Is it . . . ?" She kissed him back lingeringly. "What's the ending, then?"

"Happily ever after. . . ."

"That's not fiction. . . ." He sought her mouth again, then freedom from the garments that kept them even so slightly apart. Her raven hair was sweet as night and as mysterious, as always it had been, and Stanley explored it, and all the other mysteries.

They spoke no more. They needed no words. They lolled together dreamlike, hearing a private melody. Christ, how he loved her; how lovely she was and how he loved her. Words couldn't say it. It was like the watermelon in the gazebo: ineffable. The music played on, more and more a part of them until it seemed that they could no longer distinguish themselves from the music, until its rhythm became the dance perfected over nineteen years, so that each other's movements were in fact their own, so that without consciously doing so they could anticipate and provide and fulfill, as finally they did, in the awful joy that was the crescendo of their own devising.

They lay as one as long as they could. There was only the blood-beat of the music now, but even that was to be enjoyed. When finally they parted, Stanley felt himself suffused with the peace which had eluded him all day. Surely, now, he would sleep that night. For a long time they lay quietly, bathed by the little yellow light from the bedside lamp. Emily said nothing, only smiled. Her lips were still flushed by the ardor of their kisses.

"Em, I think I've been some kind of fool. . . ."

She rolled against him. "If you're telling me you're crazy about me, I'll accept that."

Then oh the sudden rebirth of desire in him, the renewed thirst for peace, for the awful ineffable joy. Stanley led and they danced as on their wedding night, that night when the sun shone golden and tremulous as they themselves—who might indeed have been the sun. (Oh EmilyEmilyEmily!) "Oh Emily . . . !" (Oh JesushowIloveyou!) "Jesus how I love you . . . !" Then in the golden sun the final drive into the Gazebo of Peace and Fulfillment, where it was always summer in the darkgreenshade. . . .

Afterwards, as she lay with the blanket pulled up to her ears despite the warm night, sleep began to overtake her; but the beginnings of a smile played across her lips, coming and going. Finally she could contain it no longer, and the remark came out in a murmur: "Impotent, hunh . . ." Then she drifted off to sleep, well loved, well laid, the ghost of a smile still flitting about her face. Stanley watched her, loved her, for what must have been an hour. . . .

When he pulled the Studebaker up to his shop the next morning, Stanley was flabbergasted to see Irma Kasendorf picketing the plant—walking back and forth in her blue denim dress and carrying a large printed sign: UNFAIR. He leaped out of his car.

"Irma! For Chrissakes the air-conditioner is going to be *fixed!*" She only smiled her toothy absurd smile at him.

"Hiya Mister Stanhope. . . ."

"Irma why are you *doing* this to me?" She smiled—almost giggled—her ample breasts bouncing under the blue denim.

The Ordeal of Stanley Stanhope

Stanley realized that she was braless. Had she gone and joined
Women's Lib, this once-docile and devoted employee of his
—and had the Stanhope Cleaners been singled out for some
sort of retaliatory action for—? For *what?* What did Wom-
en's Lib want? Good God, what did they *want?* "Irma?"

"It hasta be done, Mister Stanhope. *Some*body hasta do it."
She squinted at him, apparently embarrassed that it had to be
she, then she turned her back on him and picketed in the
opposite direction. His eyes fell, naturally enough, on the soft
fluid roundness of La Kasendorf's bottom. Already over her
buttocks a great sweaty *Y* was spreading. Where was Harry?
Was *he* behind all this, he with his talk of sweatshops and
intolerable conditions? Harry Putchek, who'd been with the
Stanhope Cleaners since Jock Stanhope's day? Was it a plan
to force Stanley out of the family business?

Irma had about-faced and was now picketing toward him
again. Stanley threw his invective at her: "Go home and
change—your dress is all sweaty in back!"

She only laughed—but pleasantly, respectfully even. The
large white teeth were right under his nose now. "That's not
sweat, Mister Stanhope, it's watermelon juice." She actually
winked at him. "You oughta know about *that!*" Then she
turned on her heels, displaying the great watermelon *Y* with
a consciously importunate wiggle. Back and forth she went,
protesting:

—Y cannot the Country pull itself together into One Nation Indivisible with Liberty and Justice for all?

—Y cannot We the People insure the domestic tranquillity
without which we will cease to survive as a more perfect
Union?

—Y cannot we promote the general welfare regardless of
the colors of our skins in this the Land wherein all men were
created equal and endowed with inalienable rights to Life
Liberty and the pursuit of Happiness?

—Y must our politicians behave like power-brokers rightleftcenter exploiters of the very People who should be the Government of by and for?

—Y has the American dollar replaced the American Eagle will it ever soar again?

—Y must alabaster cities no longer gleam and

—Y must the fruited plain the amber waves of grain be poisoned by insecticides and

—Y must the spacious skies be continually polluted and

—Y must the mountains rills rocks woods templed hills be turned into dumping grounds and

—Y must the coldstream waters be contaminated from sea to sludgeful sea and

—Y must the Law be laughed at and behave laughably and

—Y must youth be worshipped rather than instructed and

—Y have the schools become playpens and amusement centers and

—Y have no prophets descended from the purple mountain majesties to lead the Chosen People of the New World to their own their Promised Land?

—Y Y Y Y Y Y Y?

Overwhelmed, Stanley collapsed against the Studebaker. For a brief moment he thought he saw Harry Putchek just inside the shop, standing with arms folded and looking out at him—but then stepping back into the shadows. . . .

Stanley heard the running footsteps behind him and turned as Billy rushed up, his face flushed in anguish.

"I have to borrow the car, Dad!"

"Help me, son. . . ."

"I *have* to have the car—I haven't any motorcycle!"

"Son, my s—"

"*Dad!*" His face was ablaze now. "I *have* to have the car!"

"Where's your peace pendant?"

"Dad, I have to go to Osterville—I have a piece pending!"

Then his son was searching through his father's pockets, looking for the car keys. (Oh Christ, don't let him find the watermelon seeds . . . !) The keys were in the car, as Billy soon realized. In a moment he was off, the Studebaker's engine whining desperately, like a cicada. Stanley began to stumble reel wobble like a drunk (Can't drink; never could) toward the entrance to his shop. Irma stepped aside politely.

"You all right, Mister Stanhope?"

—Y?

. . . He was alone in the middle of an ocean of watermelon juice, and he was drowning: sinking sinking sinking into a pink and seedless sea. Then before him swam Sigmund, his golden scales burnished by the surrounding rosiness. One walleye caught sight of Stanley and the fish approached him with little sculling movements of his fins. Stanley cried out "Sig-mund!"—but it came out "Blub-glub," with his precious breath rising out of him in large silvery bubbles through the pinkness. Before Stanley's face Sigmund's mouth worked slowly—silently, Stanley thought, until he began to hear the soft pop, pop, pop of Sigmund's translucent lips. And then he heard his tiny voice:

". . . delusions of persecution and grandeur . . ."

(No!) "Glub!"

". . . repression suppression aggression regression depression obsession . . ." (pop, pop, pop).

(Sigmund, *help!*) "Glubblub, *glub!*"

". . . fixation frustration castration gratification masturbation sublimation hallucination . . ."

(Please!) "Glub . . . !"

(Pop, pop, pop) ". . . reversion perversion immersion, inhibition exhibition premonition . . ."

(For sweet Jesus' sake, Sigmund, lead me out of this—take me to Cissie's room . . . !)

(Pop, pop, pop) ". . . fantasy reality sexuality orality anality . . ."

It was no use, Sigmund was not there to help, only to observe. Now there was a crushing ache in Stanley's chest, a feeling of impending implosion. There was nothing to be done, though Sigmund stayed by to watch him not do it. Stanley closed his eyes (could Sigmund?) and simply allowed himself to drift. . . .

Out of breath, terribly out of breath, he was running across Riker's Field, looking for the monument, the one erected by the Krumpit Historical Society. (What have they done with the monument? *Y?*) Then out of the park, out of the woods, a man on horseback thundered toward him, the stallion's hoofs sending clods of Riker's Field flying. Stanley tried to escape, but he could run no more. As he stood gasping for his breath, the rider galloped directly at him, waving a saber over his head. Stanley feared being trampled but could not move. At the very last instant the rider reared his horse and Stanley thought those upraised hoofs would come smashing down into his skull.

"I'm not a redcoat! I'm not a redcoat . . . !"

The hoofs flashed by, very near his head, and then the horse sidestepped against him, forcing him back. Wild Anthony Krumpit looked down at him, pushed the saberpoint against Stanley's chest, and spat the words out contemptuously: "You be worse than that—worse than any redcoat."

"No!" But the saberpoint was only raised to Stanley's throat.

"Where be the Kingdom which was to come, the Kingdom wherein the *People* were to be King, the Kingdom of Justice and Equality and Freedom for everyone—where be the Promised Land I fought for: *where?*" The saberpoint cut into the tender flesh of Stanley's throat; he could feel the sudden warmflush of his own blood. "Thin. Thin the likes of watermelon juice. No wonder the Kingdom has not come, with citizens the likes of this." His great anger abated, and Wild Anthony put up his saber. "To think that the Dream has died, that there be no longer dreamers left to dream it. . . ." Sadly he looked away, across the green expanse of Riker's Field to—? Stanley saw tears in the hero's eyes and wanted to speak—if only to say that he understood!—but he did not dare. Wild Anthony sighed audibly, removed his tricorn, pushed a gnarled hand through his thick curly brown hair, and looked off again across the field. The horse shuddered in the awful silence. When finally the warrior spoke it was with a melancholy quietude. "My Country 'tis of thee, sweet Land: for thee I mourn. Hath no God his grace to shed on thee? To crown thy good with brotherhood, *ever* in our time? Who, *who* more than self his Country will love, and in liberating strife make Freedom ring . . . ?"

"I WILL! I swear it—on my honor and on my watermelon seeds!" Stanley was overcome by a sense of history. He felt as if his very words would be remembered recorded recited by schoolchildren generations hence, when the Kingdom had finally come—when he, Stanley Stilmore Stanhope, had delivered it. Wild Anthony looked down at him from his perch atop the frothing stallion. For a long while he said nothing but just looked into Stanley's eyes: into his *soul*. At last he withdrew his saber and lay the flat side of the blade on Stanley's left shoulder.

"Raise thy right hand."

And together they recited the Pledge of Allegiance: "O changing skies of Oganeequonchee, high place where the wild onions grow . . ."

Emily was sound asleep beside him, her face just outside of the small arc of light cast by the bedside lamp. Stanley got up, found his pajama bottoms, then quietly made his way downstairs to his den.

Moonlight flooded the room, transforming the fluttering white curtains into spectral bodies. They frightened him. The very real presence of Wild Anthony Krumpit was still very much with him. Unthinkingly he put his hand to his throat, half expecting to find the sticky trace of blood. (Oh, Emily, where has the peace you brought me gone?)

From his top drawer he took the watermelon seeds and studied them under moonlight. For all their values in helping him discover the Watermelon Correlative, the seeds had also wreaked a small havoc in his life: they had caused him to lie to his wife. True, it was an insignificant lie, as the lies of this world go, but it put him just that much further away from his beloved Emily. (Emily! Oh, peace!) It was too far. It occurred to him that he could make partial amends for the falsehood by *making reality fit the lie*—or at least part of it. He arose immediately and went out and buried all 999 watermelon seeds behind his garage, as he'd told his wife he'd done. Then he went to sit in his gazebo.

The moonlight shone in diamond-shaped beams through the latticework. It seemed to raise the very surface of the stones. The pinkish cast of watermelon juice was noticeable only on the Sacrificial Stone. Somewhere an owl called softly.

With his eye to the latticework, Stanley gazed at the moon and thought of the billions of dollars that had been shot up there. On earth, the cities of the Chosen People of the New World slowly strangled in crime, pollution, injustice, and the lack of opportunity. Within the vast Land of Milk and Honey, people and the children of people knew hunger and deprivation. To right such wrongs would cost money, it was said. But no money could be spared. It was being spent defoliating Indochina and deflowering the people there. It was being spent on weapon-systems and safeguards of increasing sophistication because the Russians, God damn them, were doing the same. Yet still and all, the politicians—the power-brokers—had so far found *thirty billion dollars* to put men on the moon, at first to fulfill a foolish pledge made by a dead President who should have had the plight of the People foremost in mind, and later out of the sheer momentum of past appropriations, while millions cheered—and injustice and deprivation continued unabated.

On the moon itself, earthshine illuminated the footprints of American astronauts. Because of an absence of atmosphere it was said that those footprints would remain forever on the moon, unless disturbed by other men. Was that enough to make the moon American? When, Stanley wondered, would *America* be made American? But alas! footprints here were not so permanent. Who now saw, for instance, the bold imprint of the Indian moccasin?

He did not want to think of dead Presidents or dead Indians; he tried not to think of the death of the American Spirit. . . .

The owl called again. Was that call, like the cicada's, also a mating cry? Stanley decided not: it had none of the desperate urgency about it that the cicada's did. Yet the owl's hoot had none of the qualities of the songs of daybirds, who apparently sang out of sheer gratitude for the sun's warming their fragile bones. The soft chainlike hoohoohoohoohoo of the owl was of an entirely different order. It was a call with which to raise a spirit. . . .

And Stanley, to his immediate horror, saw one now, coming toward him across the grass of his back yard, barely touching the ground: a tall spectral figure in fluttering white. He was not dreaming; he was wide awake. As the spectral figure floated toward him, Stanley locked the fingers of both his hands into the latticework and waited for whatever was to come. His only thought was, "Thank God I had time to plant the seeds. . . ."

"Stanley?"

(Emily! Oh peace!) She sat down beside him, pulling her long nylon negligee around her.

"Is anything wrong?" He still had his fingers clenched, monkeylike, into the latticework. "Darling?" He took his hands down and put them onto his lap. "Aren't you cold out here, without your pajama top?"

"No. Feverish, if anything." They sat for a few minutes in silence, the diamond-beamed moonlight streaking across their faces.

"Emily . . . peace!"

"What?"

"Oh, Jesus . . . !" Inexplicably he began to cry. Great

tears rolled down his cheeks and dropped onto the stone gazebo floor. There was no sobbing: rather his tear ducts had simply opened like floodgates and threatened never to close again.

"Stanley what *is* it. . . ?"

"I'm not sure that the Kingdom will *ever* come, Emily. . . !" She took his head in her hands and pulled him to her wordlessly. He clung to her, then the tears stopped as suddenly as they'd started. The moon shone, the owl—yes—the owl raised a spirit. "Emily . . ." Then he had his hands in her negligee, under her brief nightgown, into the always startling softness of her breasts. (Emily! Oh, peace!) He began pulling her to the stone gazebo floor.

Her resistance was real, but not much stronger than her fierce whisper: "Stanley—surely not *here* . . . ! Stanley, it's nearly dawn . . . !" He took her, on the Sacrificial Stone as chance would have it. She submitted to him, a dutiful wife. It was not an act of love, for he had nothing to bring to her. He found no peace.

FOUR

*S*TANLEY nicked his throat while shaving. He stanched the bleeding with a little piece of toilet tissue, which he absent-mindedly carried out into the bright morning like a tiny flag of his Pledge to Wild Anthony Krumpit.

He generally walked to work and left the car for Emily. Yet there he was, driving up to the Stanhope Cleaners in his Studebaker, as if in a dream. . . .

But no one was picketing. Instead, the air-conditioner repairmen were going in and out, from truck to shop. In the workroom, all the dry-cleaning machines were hard at work, as were Harry and Irma. When he saw Stanley, Harry came over to him.

"They gotta put a new compressor in—gonna cost ya a bundle."

Stanley simply couldn't care; there were far more urgent things to think about than a broken air-conditioner. He announced that he expected to be gone for most of the day and left immediately, over Harry's sputterings that there was "too goddamn much work ta do around here, goddammit . . . !"

At the entrance to the Krumpit Free Library, Stanley saw a familiar pair of paint-spattered baggy-trousered legs atop a stepladder.

"Morning, Stanley. Going in for a little culture these days? Heh-heh-heh-heh-heh." Old Beardsley had the automatic door-closer disassembled and was pumping a lubricating compound into it with a grease gun.

(Pump that stuff up your ass, will you?) "Yes. . . ." He hurried inside.

"Always inspiring to see a young fella improving his mind, heh-heh-heh!"

He asked Clara Pearson for the book by name: Horace Wiley Pool's *Anthony Krumpit: American Revolutionist.*

"Gosh, Stanley, we haven't had a request for *that* since Judge Pool used to come in to autograph the copies." She was gone only a few minutes. "I got you a virgin edition." She blew dust off it and smiled, younger than her years. "Actually they're *all* virgin editions."

Out by the front door Old Beardsley began bellowing the verses of a bawdy song:

> "Oh I had a burning,
> And she had a yearning . . ."

"Would you believe that man?" Clara was checking the book out for Stanley.

> "We got on together
> Like birds of a feather . . ."

"Ten minutes ago he asked me whether I wouldn't like to go behind the stacks with him to explore worldly knowledge. The joker."

> "We learned from each other
> Things not taught by mother . . ."

"What makes you think he was joking?" (He used to whore around New York City, you know. With my father.) She looked up, startled, then laughed.

> "And what we invented,
> We never repented . . ."

"You know, my husband absolutely refuses to believe what I tell him about Old Beardsley."

> "We traveled and tippled,
> Our sinfulness tripled . . ."

"I've known him all my life and sometimes *I* don't quite believe him."

> "And she called me honey
> Till I ran out of money . . ."

"Your little Cissie's been coming in a lot lately. She's a very bright girl, Stanley."

> "I learned only later,
> From Doctor McPhaytor . . ."

"Thank you. Just keep her away from Old Beardsley, won't you, Clara?" They laughed together, then he thanked her for the book and started out.

> "That along with her kisses
> She gave me the business. . . ."

Old Beardsley was standing beside his stepladder wiping his hands on a red flannel rag. "Whatcha got there, boy?" He was also standing in front of the door and Stanley had little choice but to let him see the book. "Oh my. Heh-heh-heh. Oh *my!* Heh-heh-heh-heh-heh!"

"Something amuses you, Mister Beardsley?"

The old man sighed a great sigh, rippling the weedpatch of his mustache and wafting his alcoholic breath into Stanley's face. It was odd, though, the way he held the book: tenderly somehow. . . . "I tried to warn you about this sort of thing, Stanley. About the past, about wasting time on it. Time's precious, son—take an old man's word for it. Look ahead, boy—look to the future!—not backwards."

"The past is prologue."

"Oh that's cute. And smug. And only partially true, by the way: lots and *lots* of the past *wasn't* prologue, y'know."

Stanley yanked the thin volume out of Old Beardsley's hands. "You know what's wrong with this Country today, Mister Beardsley? People don't know *enough* about the past—America's own past, especially. Maybe if they did we'd have some of those Patriots you said we need. Men like Anthony Krumpit."

"Heh-heh-heh-heh-heh. That so. How much do you think Wild Tony knew? About the past, I mean. History and stuff like that."

"Why—" But he could only stare at the old man.

"Heh-heh-heh. Exactly, boy. Zilch. Nothing to speak of. Oh, he might've heard of Julius Caesar, or somebody like that. . . ."

"It's entirely possible to have a sense of history without ever even setting foot into a schoolroom!" How had he gotten *into* this needless, foolish argument?

"Course it is. *Contemporary* history, though—and that's the present, Stanley, not the past. And that's what Wild Anthony knew. Bloody King George, taxation without representation, petitions for redress of grievances—that sort of thing. Right?" Stanley started out but Old Beardsley grabbed him by the arm. "The past is a kind of graveyard, Stanley. Be careful where you dig in it." Stanley pulled away and forged out into the summer morning. Behind him the old man was cranking up again:

"Oh I had a burning,
    And she had a yearning . . ."

Riker's Field was once at the west end of town, but it was now the only sizable open space amid a dozen square miles of residential sprawl. The field and the nearby woods comprised Riker's Field Park.

There was no one about but an elderly man chipping golf balls down the meadow. Stanley walked from his car to the monument to Wild Anthony Krumpit. The obelisk stood thirty feet tall, a granitic phallus set atop a star-shaped base. Carved into the shaft were the words GOD, COUNTRY, LIBERTY and HONOR. On the ten walls of the star-shaped base were inscribed the names and dates of every battle, skirmish, or confrontation of the American Revolution, with Riker's Field, 1779, engraved in its proper sequence and filled with gold leaf, now unfortunately peeling. At the base of the phallus, under GOD, was a large blackened brass plate:

ON THIS MOST HALLOWED SITE TOOK PLACE
THE BATTLE OF RIKER'S FIELD
July 29, 1779

In Which Wild Anthony Krumpit, of Krumpittown, Single-handedly Turned Back a British Tide of 1,200 Light Cavalry, Thus Preserving the Town and the Continental Honor. His Revered Remains Are Interred South of This Spot in Honored Glory.

Erected in 1904, in Grateful Memory and in the Fervent Hope That His Courage, Dedication and Love of Country Will Be Forever Remembered . . . By the Citizens of Krumpit and the

★ KRUMPIT HISTORICAL SOCIETY ★

Suddenly for Stanley, the monument improved considerably. For it was the memorial aspect that counted, not the nature of its realization. If there was one point on which Stanley could wholeheartedly agree with the K. H. S., it was that Anthony Krumpit's courage, dedication and love of Country should be forever remembered. Yea, and acted upon: for God, for Country, for Liberty—

"*Fore* . . . !"

Stanley heard a voice faint with age and distance. The voice of God? He was forced to his knees in the meadow, overwhelmed (there was no other word for it) by the feeling that had hit him like a bolt: that it would be must be *he*, Stanley Stilmore Stanhope of Krumpit-town, who would *somehow* transform the People into Patriots! Hadn't the understanding of that quite literally bowled him over?

The old man who'd been puttering around with a golf club had apparently become concerned about Stanley and had solicitously come over. But why was he apologizing? For breaking into Stanley's reverie?

"Don't mention it." The old man could not possibly know what Stanley had just experienced—and Stanley could not explain it. There it was, another ineffable experience.

"Are you hurt?" Stanley could only smile and shake his head. "You *sure?*" The old man was becoming annoying. "I'll gladly drive you home, or to a hospital, if you like. . . ." Stanley got to his feet, the old man attempting to help him.

"No no—really!" (But isn't it exactly *like* people to mistake inspiration for illness?) The old man was sorry a few more times, and to get away from him Stanley Stanhope bid the duffer good day and turned his back on the erection of the Krumpit Historical Society.

In the park proper, in an open space, in the center of a circular brick walk lined with silvery benches, there was a raised rectangle of red brick, with a half-dozen steps leading to its grassy top through beds of surrounding marigolds. Beneath this simple elegance lay the mortal remains of Anthony Krumpit. In the spring, Stanley recalled, flowering dogwood trees embraced the area in delicate pinks, whites, and rose-reds. The shrine was maintained by the Krumpit Garden Club.

Stanley made his way up the little brick walk and stairs. He could not have been more thrilled had he climbed the greatest pyramids of the Mayas or the Aztecs: the view, to Stanley, was of the length, breadth, and depth of American history. At his feet was an unprepossessing granite slab:

ANTHONY KRUMPIT
1753–1787
HERO OF THE AMERICAN REVOLUTION

The Garden Club people had not been by to trim the grass for a week or more, and it had grown just long enough to waver gently in the summer breeze that dallied there. Stanley sat himself down atop the shrine, ready and willing to experience the thoughts he felt would surely come to him there. Instead his eyes fell on the used condoms, empty beer cans, and cigarette butts that littered the shrinetop.

(Jesus!)—the rage exploded within him and he could feel the heat of color in his cheeks. *Was nothing sacred?* Rebellious youth was one thing, but must the youth of Krumpit rebel on the very grave of him who once saved Krumpit-town? Was there no sense of decency among them, or gratitude? No notion of fittingness? No sense of the sacred, no reverence? Stanley Stanhope began to weep: for youth, for Krumpit-town, for America. If young people were so truly alienated that they could take their pleasure on a hero's grave, then from where oh where would the Patriots come? If the inheritors placed no value on the inheritance, what oh what was to become of America?

On his hands and knees Stanley Stanhope crawled over every inch of the shrinetop picking up the used condoms and the cigarette butts and stuffing them into the empty beer cans, weeping, weeping, weeping so that his tears watered Wild Anthony's grave in what he hoped was expiation. Then he fled the place, pausing only long enough to dump into a green trash can the detritus of the ideals and revolutionary spirit of America. He was weeping still as he started the Studebaker and drove away from Riker's Field.

On Sycamore Street he saw Old Beardsley crossing over toward Holgrove's Hardware Store and slammed the brakes on hard. The old man turned at the screech and Stanley yelled at him out the window: "The past had decency—and ideals! The past had God, Country, Liberty, and Honor! The present has only self-interest and self-indulgence! Gratification! Desecration! Abomination! And what will the *future* have? You tell me that!" But he roared off without waiting for an answer.

He drove recklessly, hoping to escape from his thoughts. If he could get drunk—obliteratingly and devastatingly drunk —that would do the trick. He needed to be transported out of himself entirely, to forget utterly what he had seen, if only for a few hours. Down the street was Brown's Little Jug; he slammed to a stop before it, went in, and bought a fifth of rum.

Waiting for the long light at Main and Elm calmed him down. Or was it the town itself, going about its business steadily as usual? Krumpit-town showed no signs of anguish. Yet did the townfolk *know* what went on atop Anthony Krumpit's grave? Did Anthony Krumpit know? The members of the Garden Club surely knew. Yet said nothing! At least Stanley had never heard anything about it. He drove around slowly now, aimlessly, the bottle of rum lolling beside him on the front seat. If the caretakers of the shrine could take it, week after week, summer after summer, who was Stanley Stanhope that his outrage could only be extinguished in rum?

He realized that he had overreacted. For surely, as bad as it was, the desecration of Anthony Krumpit's grave was not representative of *all* American youth. Surely there were inheritors who valued the inheritance. He stopped his car, obsessed by one important question: *How many* inheritors were there? A familiar voice intruded.

"Hey-hey, Mister Stanhope! What's this I hear about a bad watermelon?" Stanley had stopped alongside Felix's Fruit Stand. Felix Buonoparte's hairy arms were leaning into the car window. "I couldn't believe it—everything I get is fresh!"

Stanley wondered if his embarrassment showed. "Gosh, I—I told my wife not to bother you about it. . . ."

"No no no, I'm glad she did. I wanna hear about anything that's not right."

(Wanna hear about Anthony Krumpit's grave? Wanna hear about America?) "I wish she hadn't, Felix. We've never gotten a bad buy from you in fifteen years. . . ."

"Lookit, I value good customers, Mister Stanhope. I sent my kid around with another melon for you."

Stanley got out of his car. His lie now extended to Felix, as well. "I just won't have it"—and he took out his wallet. But Felix wouldn't hear of his paying, and the only thing Stanley could do to right the wrong was to buy another watermelon.

"Whaddaya need two for?" But Stanley insisted and drove off with an easier conscience and a watermelon on the front seat beside the bottle of rum. Was it the proximity of the two that suggested to him how he might avoid getting drunk that afternoon?

The house was deserted. It was nearly noon and getting hot. The watermelon Felix Buonoparte sent over was sitting in the shade of the back porch. Stanley put it into the refrigerator, then started to work at once on his own melon.

He recalled exactly how his father used to prepare it. You had to cut a three-inch plug out, then pour the rum into the fruit, a little at a time so it could be absorbed. It was a slow process, but Stanley waited it out patiently. Finally the melon would absorb no more; it had taken nearly half a bottle into its secret pinkness. His father used to melt paraffin over the plug (the melon had to be sealed or the rum would evaporate) but there seemed to be no paraffin in the house. Perhaps there never would be, now that Cissie had outgrown the preservation of autumn leaves. He settled for Scotch tape.

He brought the melon down to his vegetable cellar. The fruit would have to ripen a while—overnight or preferably longer. He would spring it on the family Saturday evening— and he would find out for sure whether son Billy could drink or not. Perhaps it hadn't been such a bad idea to have bought the rum, after all.

There was still half a bottle of it left. A half-pint would have been more than enough for his original purpose. He went out behind his garage, and with the rest of the rum he watered the seeds he had planted there. And wondered idly if melons could be grown pre-spiked. . . .

Stanley went into his gazebo to wait out the midday heat. He had not forgotten his copy of *Anthony Krumpit: American Revolutionist*. On the flyleaf was the Judge's quavery autograph: Horace Wiley Pool. In the cool of the darkgreen-shade, Stanley began to read:

What is best known about the life of Anthony Krumpit is, of course, the famous episode at Riker's Field on the 29th of July, 1779. That single act of superhuman courage in the face of so vastly superior an enemy (in numbers only, one must hasten to point out!) has lived both in the history books and in the hearts and minds of countless Americans. Is there a lad yet today, as the Axis foes threaten the peace of the modern world, who does not appropriate Anthony Krumpit's courage and derring-do as his very own, as exemplar and inspiration? Let Tojo and Mr. Hitler beware, for American courage springs forth ever anew!

Anthony Aaron Krumpit was born in what was then, but which has since tragically died out altogether, Krumpit-town's First Family. He was the only surviving son of Jeremiah and Rebeccah Krumpit and the great-great grandson of the illustrious founder of Krumpit-town, Aaron

Krumpit (sometimes called "The Terrible"). We can only speculate upon much of his family history, yet there are milestones along the way in the form of bona fide historical records, and we shall herein attempt a reconstruction of the Krumpit family tree. For it is only in better understanding the root and trunk that we will attain greater understanding of the flower, Anthony.

I is believed that the first Krumpits, possibly the brothers Phineas and Philip Krumpit (or Krumpet) immigrated from the environs of Wessex [1] in England, possibly as early as 1630, bringing their families with them. The brothers landed at Plimouth Plantation and separated almost at once. Either Phineas or Philip (the records show merely "P. Krumpit") arrived first on the island of Conanicut in the present State of Rhode Island in 1640 and in the same year moved his family to the island of Rhode Island. The number and sexes of the children of this P. Krumpit are not known. It *is* known, however, that one of his sons, apparently already well into his majority at this time, was none other than Aaron Krumpit.

It was this same Aaron who, dissatisfied with his lot in what had become (in 1640) the Colony of Providence Plantations, pushed westward, as American pioneers were wont to do. There was some innuendo [2] which implied that young Aaron was all but hounded out of the Colony because of an unspecified affront to one Miss Henrietta Cobbit; but in any event Aaron Krumpit departed the Providence Plantations in December of 1644, and a few weeks later, in January of 1645, he had established a camp in what was then Oganeequonchee (Wilmot Indian for "high-place-

---

[1] My colleague Forbes Bartlett Nair maintains that what evidence exists, largely in the form of several references to Wessex in a single letter by one Isaac Barlow who claimed to have immigrated with "two brothers Krumpet (sic) and wives and children" is of questionable authenticity since the aforesaid Barlow, according to records in Plimouth Plantation, was reputedly illiterate.

[2] In a diary of one Joshua Brown Billingsley of Providence Plantations—described as "sheer slander" by my colleague Peter Todd Jameson.

where-the-wild-onions-grow-under-ever-changing-skies") in the land once known as Quinnitukqut (Mohican designation meaning "at-the-long-tidal-river")—or, our present State of Connecticut.

Aaron must have been an inspiring leader indeed to have led the little band into the wilderness wherein the Red Indian still held sway. When they faltered, did they have to meet Aaron's strong and fearless gaze? Was that the origin of his sobriquet, "The Terrible"? We do not know. We do know that the settlement was subsequently named Krumpit-town and by Aaron himself, so that he must indeed have exerted a dominating influence on the little colony.

They were not, however, the first white settlers in Oganeequonchee. Indeed, the area was popularly known among other settlements as Ball's Rise, after pioneer settler Hosiah Ball and his family of 27. Next to nothing is known of him, the only verifiable record being the tombstone of his wife, Fertility, in the Old Churchyard—the first white grave in Krumpit-town. Apparently, Hosiah Ball had contracted some sort of agreement with the crafty sachem Quikqil which enabled him to live there, perhaps in exchange for agricultural produce or other artifacts.

Yet the ambitious Aaron Krumpit purchased land (including that on which Hosiah and his family lived and farmed) from the sachem Quikqil. The price paid was 25 new English coats which some of the hardy band had foresightedly brought with them all the way from Providence Plantations.[3] Quikqil was reportedly impressed by the fact that the coats were still packed in their original cases and thus had never been worn. The crafty sachem refused, however, to sell the settlers more than a modicum of land, despite emigrations from other colonies, notably those of New Haven (founded 1638) and the infant settlement which was founded a year after Krumpit-town and which was later (in 1658) to become known as New London. In this

---

[3] My colleague Charles Foster Owens believes the number to have been no more than 18—or one coat for each of the known permanent settlers. The view is solely his own.

latter migration came the family of Rachel Fogg, later to become Aaron's wife. Still, Krumpit-town both grew and prospered, partly as a way-station to other points in New England and partly as a result of brisk trade with the settlements which had been founded by Adrian Block in what is presently New York State. But the sachem Quikgil still refused to sell more of his land.

The prospering settlement succeeded in purchasing acreage nearly congruent with the present town limits shortly after Quikqil's passing, however; in 1655 and again in 1660, Aaron Krumpit completed the desired land-purchases with Quikqil's son, the sachem Dimqil, for an unrecorded number of barrels of rum. After the final land-purchase in 1660, both whites and Indians carried on prolonged celebrations to mark the historic event. It should be noted that there had never been the slightest hostility between the Wilmot Indians and the white settlers of Krumpit-town.[4]

Little is known about the Krumpit dynasty until two generations later, due to the disastrous fire of 1761 which destroyed the town's records,[5] although fortunately no lives were lost. By Jeremiah Krumpit's time (1729–1791) the family name was still well-respected, if not held in the terrible awe once reserved for the patriarch Aaron, who died full of glory and rich in lands in 1703.

It was to Jeremiah Krumpit and his wife Rebeccah that a child was born on the 9th day of August, 1753. The child was christened, perhaps with the legendary Aaron firmly in mind, Anthony Aaron Krumpit. It could not have appeared so at the time, but that humble event was destined to rock the foundations of the British Empire in North America! Verily, it was to shake the Tree of Liberty until the Apples of Freedom fell for all Americans to gather!

It may be well to pause here a moment to consider the lamented passing of this important Colonial family. Strangely, none of Aaron's children are buried in the Old

---

[4] The Wilmot tribe is presently extinct.
[5] The holocaust of February 3, 1761, destroyed the town hall, the church, the school, and fully three-quarters of the town. Invaluable records were forever lost to future researchers.

Churchyard in Krumpit. Why this should be is an unexplained mystery of tantalizing proportions to the Krumpit Historical Society even to this day.[6] Perhaps they simply migrated westward. Or were they lost at sea in an accident in the Sound? We can only speculate, for the town records which might have provided us with an answer were consumed in flames in 1761. Aaron rests today in the Old Churchyard, as does his great-grandson Jeremiah and his wife. Yet no other Krumpits rest in peace there, although the town abounded with them! [7]

We might well ask what Krumpit-town was like in 1753 when young Anthony awoke to life and to the calling which awaited him scarcely two decades thence. It was not the impressive community of 25,000 souls that it is today. Moreover, the great fire eight years later all but destroyed the town. Young Anthony had few of the opportunities, educational or otherwise, of today's youth. After 1761, Krumpit-town had literally to rebuild itself. One might reasonably conjecture that Anthony's greatest "education" was participating in that Phoenix-like act of a town's regeneration—a task scarcely completed in time for the Great War.[8]

It was the Great War which furthered the young man's education. One might call the prolonged prelude to that conflict his "elementary grades" and the War itself his "university." [9] Anthony's tutor in the cause of Liberty was, ironically, the British Parliament which seemed to go out of its

---

[6] There is no further mention in American history of any Krumpit other than Jeremiah's son, Anthony.

[7] My esteemed colleague, the late Charles Wilson Woodruff, devoted a lifetime to searching for signs of the Krumpit family's reemergence in other pioneer communities from western Connecticut to Ohio. His son, John Wilson Woodruff, is presently continuing the search as far as California, and something may yet come of such dedicated diligence.

[8] Might this participation in his town's rebirth have further steeled the hero's resolve when, 18 years later, the Redcoat Horde threatened his beloved town?

[9] One must not conclude that Anthony was illiterate, however. Later testimony by persons who knew him explicitly state that he could read and write with facility. Certainly the fact of his future diplomatic service supports the case for his literacy?

way to alienate the Colonies. A proclamation in 1763 forbade Colonial settlement beyond the Allegheny mountains, effectively ending westward expansion of the Colonies. The Currency Act of 1764 made it illegal for Colonial Assemblies to print their own paper money. As Colonial tempers rose, Parliament pursued its mad collision course: in 1764 the Sugar Act; in 1765 the infamous Stamp Act and the Quartering Act; in 1767 the Townshend Act—all direct and indirect forms of taxation of the Colonies that reached even unto Krumpit-town. In Massachusetts in particular was the citizenry outraged. It seemed but a matter of time before violence must surely erupt. It did so on the 5th of March, 1770, in the Boston Massacre. One would have thought that King George III would have had enough of such heavy-handedness. But in 1773 the British Parliament passed the infamous Tea Act. The Colonists rebelled: on the night of December 16th, 1773, a courageous group of Bostonians brewed a great batch of British tea in Boston harbor. Surely *now* the British Parliament would react more tolerably towards the Colonies.

It was to prove not to be the case. The very next year Parliament passed the Coercive (the Colonists called them "Intolerable") Acts, effectively closing the port of Boston and considerably lessening Colonial control in Massachusetts. Then, like drunken sailors, Parliament squandered what was left of its coinage of good will by passing a new Quartering Act, to support British troops in the Colonies, and the Quebec Act, which extended that Province's boundaries into Pennsylvania and Virginia. It did little good to petition for redress of grievances. In September of that year, 1774, the First Continental Congress convened at Philadelphia. Young Anthony Krumpit had turned 21 the previous month.

Mad King George and his equally mad Parliament persisted. Tensions increased, and on April 19th, 1775, first at Lexington and then at Concord, where the embattled farmers stood, there was fired "the shot heard round the world." Patriots from all over New England rushed to arms. First among these was young Anthony Krumpit.

The Continental Congress had just named the experienced

Israel Putnam a major-general in its newly-minted American Revolutionary Army. It was to Putnam and his company that young Anthony joined himself. By June 17th he had known the baptism of fire, at Bunker Hill. Americans, some 2,200 strong, had struck back, bloodying the British Lion's nose, in the person of General William Howe. No longer the earnest, carefree youth, our Anthony! This was War: a man's job. George Washington himself arrived a fortnight later to assume command of the Continental Army, at Cambridge, Massachusetts.

In the far north the War continued. On May 10th and 11th, the brilliant Benedict Arnold teamed with the crafty mountaineer Ethan Allen to capture Fort Ticonderoga and Crown Point in New York State to give the Continentals control of Lake Champlain. Arnold went on to Quebec in a daring attempt ot take Canada but was decisively routed and wounded in the bad bargain. The British were free to invade from Canada once again.

Yet the Patriots pressed on. Washington forced Howe to evacuate Boston on the 17th of March, and on the 4th of July, 1776, the Declaration of Independence was proclaimed to all the world. A die Caesar never dreamt of had been cast!

Then the Lion began to claw. General Howe's explicit orders were to reduce New England and capture New York City. Helping to secure New York at Brooklyn Heights under General Washington's overall command was Major-General Israel Putnam's troops—Anthony Krumpit among them. Howe attacked on the 27th of August with an infamous three-pronged offensive that outflanked and crushed the Continentals, causing them nearly 2,000 casualties with another thousand captured. In the dead of night Washington led the remainder of his forces across the East River. Howe sent Lord Cornwallis in pursuit of Washington while he himself occupied New York City. Cornwallis pushed the beaten Americans across New Jersey and finally into Pennsylvania. On orders from Howe, Cornwallis stopped at New Brunswick and began preparations for winter quartering.

Rather than go into winter quarters himself, Washington stealthily recrossed the Delaware River with 2,400 men on Christmas night of 1776 and surprised the Hessian garrison at Trenton, New Jersey, then seized Princeton eight days later. (Anthony Krumpit did not see action in either of these brilliant engagements, for Israel Putnam's troops had been securing the city of Philadelphia.) Once Princeton was in American hands, however, Putnam was assigned to protect the place. It was a routine duty, but it gave Anthony his first crack at overt heroism.

In the far north in August of 1777, the Patriots were holding out or routing the British at Oriskany, Bennington, and on Lake Champlain. But south of New York things did not look promising for the Continental cause. On the 25th of August, two weeks after Anthony Krumpit's 24th birthday, Howe landed his troops at the head of Chesapeake Bay. Advance word of the British troop movement came first to General Putnam at Princeton. He immediately called for a volunteer to ride at breakneck speed through country thick with Loyalists in order to bring the intelligence to General Washington. It was Anthony Krumpit who volunteered for the hazardous duty. As a result, when the British forces entered southern Pennsylvania, they found Washington awaiting them across Brandywine Creek, 25 miles southwest of the city of Philadelphia.

But again the Patriots—and Anthony—tasted bitter defeat at the hands of superior British forces. Overwhelmed by sheer numbers, the Americans were routed. Howe was then free to occupy Philadelphia.

Still Washington refused to accept defeat. In a bit more than a week he had assembled 11,000 eager Patriots—Anthony among them—and deployed the heroes against the 9,000 British defenders at Germantown, 7 miles north of Philadelphia and the front line of Howe's defenses. As bad luck would have it, the redcoats were accidentally alerted to the presence of the Patriots before an attack could be launched. The well-entrenched redcoats were not to be dislodged and the Continentals were forced to retreat.

Washington went at once into the long hard winter quartering that was Valley Forge.

All was not black for the Patriot cause, however. On October 7th, 1777, just three days after the debacle at Germantown, the second battle of Saratoga [10] was fought in New York State. There General Horatio Gates so decisively defeated the redcoats that General John Burgoyne was forced to surrender to him ten days later. The defeat dashed British hopes of reducing New England and served to bring France into open alliance with the young United States.[11]

It was Anthony Krumpit's difficult honor to share with George Washington and the other Patriots the incredible hardship that was Valley Forge in the winter of 1777–78.

It is difficult for us today to grasp the full horror of that hardship. Ravaged by hunger, disease, the pervasive cold, and the lack of suitable clothing, nearly 3,000 Patriots perished during the six-month-long encampment. Countless others suffered with seemingly perpetual illness. As all great hardships come to an end, so did that great testing of men and morale that was Valley Forge. In May, word of the French alliance reached camp—and so did Benedict Arnold. By June 18th Washington was ready to renew the American quest for freedom. Anthony Krumpit also had stood the test. Was that severe and critical winter at Valley Forge the essential preparation for the stunning display at Riker's Field a year later? It would certainly seem that it was.

Sir Henry Clinton was appointed commander-in-chief of British forces after Howe's resignation in 1778. Clinton was not interested in the occupation of Philadelphia, which he evacuated that June, moving his headquarters to New York. Washington filled the vacuum with Major-General Arnold, and Philadelphia was once again in American hands. There

---

[10] Actually fought at Freeman's Farm, near Bemis Heights.
[11] France had surreptitiously equipped American troops as early as the spring of 1777, however.

was an indecisive battle at Monmouth, New Jersey, on the 28th of June as General Washington attempted to prevent Clinton's return to New York City.

By late June of 1779, Anthony was once again in his home state and once again under Israel Putnam's command. The Major-General had begun to suffer from the paralysis that would force him into early retirement, but there was still fighting to be done and brave Patriots needed to do it.

As summer wore on, the British governor William Tryon invaded Connecticut from Westchester County, New York. The marauding governor led 1,200 light cavalry, advancing relentlessly across Connecticut, his men looting freely, seemingly unstoppable. At Greenwich, Putnam himself barely escaped with his life by galloping down a precipice. Still Tryon advanced, destroying the towns of Norwalk, Fairfield, and Danbury. Then he veered due eastward.

On July 29th, 1779, Governor Tryon led his 1,200 light cavalry against Krumpit-town. He attacked from its western meadows and out of the late afternoon sun. Major-General Israel Putnam, badly stricken with his paralysis, lay ill in town. An all but leaderless force of 800 Continentals waited at the high ground of Riker's Field.

As Tryon's cavalry galloped up the slope, the Continentals fled in disarray into the woods. It looked to be a total rout; Krumpit-town seemed sure to go the way of Norwalk, Fairfield, and Danbury. Then, from the town, thundering straight down the meadow and directly at the advancing Redcoat Horde, a lone rider roared, swinging his sabre over his head as if it were Excalibur itself, cursing his enemies and threatening their annihilation. The Redcoat Horde broke rank, backtracked, horses sidestepping and jerking at bridles, rearing and neighing in confusion, as indeed Tryon's vandals must have been confused—and, no doubt, terrified by the raw display of unbounded courage. But still Anthony charged on, splitting and scattering the ranks. Now it was the redcoats' turn to flee in disarray: they retreated at full gallop, as the setting sun shone through the dust of British expectations. The 800 Continentals cheered, took up their courage and their arms and followed on foot. Krumpit-town was saved. Tryon's light cavalry galloped back to Westchester County, never to return.[12] For his valor, Wild Anthony (as he was thenceforth known) received the commendations of General Washington himself in a personal letter to the hero.[13]

In the South, the War played itself out: the Siege of Savannah (October 9th, 1779) and the Siege of Charleston (April 1st to May 12th, 1780); the battles of Camden, S. C. (August 16th, 1780), King's Mountain, S. C. (October 7th, 1780), Cowpens in S. C. (January 17th, 1781), and Guilford Courthouse in N. C. (March 15th, 1781)—all of which eventually led to the Siege of Yorktown, Va. (September 28th to October 19th, 1781) and the surrender of Charles, Lord Cornwallis to General Washington on the 19th of October, ending the War and securing the Independence so forthrightly proclaimed five years earlier.

As George Washington's service to his country did not end with the War, neither did Anthony Krumpit's. He was appointed by the Congress, at the special request of General Washington himself, special representative to the Court of France, in which capacity he served with distinction, as an aid to Benjamin Franklin, until his untimely death on January 17th, 1787. The hero's mortal remains were brought back to the United States by a grateful government. He lies today near Riker's Field, enshrined close by the spot of his greatest triumph, first in the hearts of his townsmen.

Heroism is not easily defined. What *is* an heroic act but the performance of something which needs to be done, regardless of personal risk and ignoring the chances of success or failure? Yet heroism is surely more than the

---

[12] The ignominy of this defeat was so complete that the record of it has never to this day been entered into the annals of English history, despite constant appeals by the K.H.S. to the British government.

[13] The letter, long unknown, turned up in 1846 among the papers of one Josiah Fulsome, of Krumpit. It is now in the archives of the Krumpit Historical Society, through the efforts of Henry Woolridge Best, K. H. S., deceased.

accomplishment of any particular heroic act. It is also a state of mind—an habitual way of viewing the world and the ways of men. And it is surely a kind of rage at what is not right, that it be made right. It is not a spur-of-the-moment rising to an occasion; but rather it is a process of long maturation and fermentation of the spirit of the patriot.

Such growth and development is readily discernible in Anthony Krumpit, American Revolutionist, from the day that patriotic urge compelled him to leave his home for the Continental cause, to the glorious day four years later when he returned to save both home *and* cause. One gets intoxicated by the fermentation of such a spirit! The Hero of Riker's Field lives on wherever and in whomever a like spirit is found—truly kindred, truly eternal, always the best and only hope of all Mankind.

In his gazebo, Stanley Stanhope inhaled the summer air in a desperate draught. He felt as though he might burst with a pride and an urgency—spill himself out watermelon-pink over the gray gazebo stones. There were things that needed to be done!—regardless of personal risk and ignoring the chances of success or failure.

As he rose he could feel his blood thrilling in his veins, tingling in his limbs, pounding in his head. With Judge Pool's slim volume in hand, Stanley Stanhope marched down his driveway in heroic strides. Down the street he walked, under the high old elms, to—. He could not imagine where. He trusted his legs to bear him safely to wherever it was that Destiny was calling him, the best and only hope of all Mankind. . . .

It called him downtown: down Elm and Sycamore, past Morgan's Department Store and Holgrove's Hardware and Prescott's Pharmacy until he found himself before the Stanhope Cleaners, where he stopped, curiously surprised at the destination Fate had chosen for him. He looked up at the sign over the entrance of his shop:

THE STANHOPE CLEANERS

Suddenly it had a meaning for Stanley that it never had before. It seemed—yes!—as though it were announcing to America that *here* was the place to have its values cleansed, that the resident dry-cleaner possessed the skill and knowledge to render those values wearable again, like new, clean and pleasing—again.

The shop door opened with a tinkle of its little bell and Harry Putchek stepped outside. "Whaddya doing?"

"Wh-what? Oh. Looking at the sign. . . ."

Harry stepped out to the curb and looked up at the sign a moment. "Ya better come inside. The air-conditioner's been fixed. It's cool in there now."

"Yes. . . ." Harry stood aside for Stanley to enter first. "Thank you." Stanley was all but herded into the small office behind the front counter.

"Whyncha sit down." As Stanley sat at the desk Harry went over to the tabletop refrigerator in which they kept lunches and soft drinks. "We're in pretty good shape, believe it or not. Me and the kid got caught up on alla that-there pressing. I gotta hand it ta her: she's a regular little beaver when the pressure's on. . . ." He popped open a bottle of Coke and brought it to Stanley. "Here, ya look like ya could use this." Stanley accepted it gratefully, its icecoldness startling him. Harry stood looking at him with one arm propped atop the file cabinet.

"Maybe . . . Irma'd like a Coke."

"Naw. She ducked over ta Prescott's. She's got hot pants for the kid bahind the lunch counter there. I'm saprised ya didn't bump inta her, coming down the street." The shopbell tinkled and Harry went out to tend to business. Stanley could hear his voice over the partition: "How are ya taday, Missus Salzman . . ."

As Stanley finished his Coke he laughed quietly to himself about Harry's solicitousness. (Am I acting so strangely? Is it so very strange a thing to feel motivated to do something on behalf of one's Country?) Odd the way Harry took it for illness, like the old gentleman at Riker's Field that morning. Had the Patriotic Flush become so rare a thing in the Land that no one even *recognized* it any longer? Not even Harry Putchek, who'd once served in the—

"Have 'em for ya by this time tamarra for sure, Missus Salzman." In the tinkle of a bell Harry reappeared in the office. "Been slow all day out front. Nobody wants ta come out in this-here heat. Good thing: it let us catch up on alla work. . . ."

"Harry—tell me something, will you? How was it at sea, during the war?"

"The Merchant Morons, ya mean?" His huge shoulders heaved with a laugh that was part sigh. "It was a job. Hard work sometimes. And lotsa boredom. And lotsa worry about Jerry U-boats. We was usually carrying munitions, ya know. With stuff like that-there aboard, they wouldn'ta even needed a direct hit." He raised his eyes and hands to the heavens. "Va-*voom!* Goodbye Charlie. Ya know?"

"Yes—but why did you do it?"

Why does the sun shine. "How the hell do I know. I was only a dumb kid at the time."

"You didn't have to *keep* doing it; you could have quit."

"Aw—! If I quit I woulda got drafted, and somebody'd be shooting at me anyways. I was making good dough, ya know—more'n any goddam footslogger was making."

"You did it for the money?"

"Naw, I wouldn't say that. I said I was *making* good money —that ain't the same thing."

"Then . . . why *did* you do it, if you don't mind my asking?"

"Naw I don't mind. But it's like I told ya, Stanley: what the hell did *I* know in them days. . . ."

Stanley put the empty Coke bottle down on his desk. "Listen, Harry: it's important to me, personally. Won't you *try* to remember what made you ship out over dangerous waters?"

"Important! Why the hell should it be important? It was twenny-five, thirty years ago."

"Time has nothing at all to do with it. Look—" he held up Judge Pool's book—"I've been reading about Anthony Krumpit. That was nearly two hundred years ago, but time hasn't dimmed *his* accomplishment."

"Whatsat gotta do with me? Ya wanna 'nother Coke?"

"No. I want—I'd *like* an answer to my question: why did Harry Putchek serve in the Merchant Marines during those hazardous times?"

"And I told ya: I *don't* goddamn *know*. Whaddya want me ta do, tell ya goddamn fairy-tales for Chrissakes?"

"Harry, there must be a *reason*. There's a reason for everything. Anthony Krumpit had a reason for charging down Riker's Field!"

"Yeah? What was it?"

"Why—" (What *was* it? Was it something easily put into words, or was it . . . ineffable?) "We were talking about Harry Putchek, not Anthony Krumpit." Harry was standing before him with his mouth slightly ajar. "All I'd like you to do is to remember the reason you had for serving in the capacity you did."

Harry shrugged. "I was a seaman. I been a seaman since bafore the war. I was only a kid when I went ta sea the first time. I'd still be there maybe, if I hadn't met up with Ginny and wanted ta get married with her. What the hell's so mysterious about that? I had my papers and the government needed able-bodied seamen and I signed on. I'da got drafted otherwise. Lotsa guys did the same. That's simple anough, ain't it?"

"But surely it occurred to you that what you were doing was likely to be far more dangerous than—than—than *footslogging* or whatever it was you called it?" Something—the icecold Coke, perhaps?—had given him a headache: right at the back of his head, near the crown. . . .

"Oh yeah. We usedta talk about it."

"You mightn't have ever even gotten shipped overseas, in the Army—surely you thought of *that*." Stanley passed his hand over the back of his head; it seemed as if there were a slight lump there. . . .

"Aw— We usedta think the Army was chickenshit. That's all."

"You could've joined the Navy—that would've been right up your alley, Harry." Of course there could be no lump there; he hadn't bumped his head on anything.

"The *Navy!*" The big shoulders shook with laughter. "You think *that* wasn't chickenshit? Dontcha get the picture, Stanley? We had a pretty good life all in all. We was civilians and we didn't hafta play soldier-boy and we made good dough doing what we been doing right along anyways. So why not the Merchant Morons?"

"But what about the submarines? You knew the Germans would be trying to get you. . . ."

Harry shrugged. "They'da been after any other ship I'da been on—and I wouldn'ta been getting hazardous-duty pay maybe, or not so much."

Still, the lump *seemed* real enough. . . . "Harry, somehow I can't believe you risked your life just for money."

"So who said I did it just for money? What am I, some kinda whore? I already told ya: I was making good dough but that ain't the same as saying I was *doing* it for the dough."

"And my question remains, Why did you do it, then?"

He shrugged again. "It was my job. My line a work. What can I tell ya?" The shopbell tinkled and Harry went out. "Hi, kid. Didja have a nice coffee break? Freddie make eyes at ya?"

"Oh Mister Putchek . . . !"

"I think ya can cut out early if ya wanta, ain't nothing doing around here now. Hey Stanley, okay by you if the kid cuts out now? Stan?"

"Oh—yes. Whatever you say. . . ." There did not seem to be any aspirin in his desk. His headache seemed to be spreading. Odd the way that lump seemed real. . . .

"Maybe y'oughta cut out yourself, Stanley. Go home and take a little nap, maybe."

"I have a headache, that's all."

"Goodniiiight!"

"See ya, kid." The shopbell made Stanley wince this time, so shrill seemed its sound. "You been feeling okay lately, Stan?"

Was there any use in even *trying* to explain it all to Harry? Better to answer indirectly. "I've . . . been concerned, that's all."

"Yeah? Not about the business, I hope."

"No—no. It's about . . . about my son, for one thing."

"Billy seems like a normal kid. I wouldn't worry too much if I was you."

"I—I've been wondering if he drinks. And if he smokes pot—or uses drugs. Do you think your Larry uses the stuff, Harry?"

"Pot, maybe. The stuff grows wild out in Veetnam. I hear lotsa guys use it over there. But, I dunno. . . ."

Stanley felt the rosy rise of embarrassment within him. "Forgive me, Harry—I'd completely forgotten your boy'd joined the Marines and was shipped over. . . ."

"Kid didn't wanna go ta college. What could I do—force him ta? I was dumb at his age myself. The other kids are all hot about school though—'specially Sandy, she's the one with smarts. What's a chick need brains for, anyways?"

"Don't you . . ." (Should I *say* such a thing?) ". . . don't you worry about whether Larry smokes marijuana over there? I mean isn't it a dangerous thing to do, near an enemy especially?" (Why *did* I mention it . . . !)

The huge shoulders shrugged very slowly. "Sure I worry. Alla time I worry, like when I was on the munitions ships, 'cept it ain't me I'm worrying about. I wish it was. But I didn't bring the kid up wet bahind the ears. I think he's got the good sense not ta use the stuff on patrols, for instance—*if* he uses it. And the good sense ta stay away from the hard stuff—heroin and that-there. I worry a lot more about the bullets and the claymores than about any pot he might run inta."

"When is his hitch over? In Vietnam, I mean."

"Seven months and sixteen days." Harry looked at his watch. "Fifteen and a third days. . . ."

"It's a nasty war. . . ."

Harry shrugged. "It's his job. . . ."

Stanley got up and felt the back of his head again. "Maybe I will go home. . . ."

"Grab yourself a little nap bafore supper. Best thing ina world. Do it myself, whenever the kids let me."

"Maybe I will. I . . . I didn't sleep too well last night." He looked around the cubbyhole of an office then around the spacious workroom filled with garments neatly cleaned, sized, pressed, hung on hangers and sheathed in plastic bags. He had an overriding feeling that he was leaving something behind, but for the life of him he could not imagine what it might be. Finally he gave up trying. "Goodnight, Harry."

"We'll do it all over again tamarra, Stanley."

FIVE

*S*TANLEY stopped at Prescott's, picked out a tin of aspirin, and sat down at the lunch counter. It was Freddie Winslow who brought him a glass of water.

"What'll it be, Mister Stanhope?"

"Just the water. I've got to take some aspirin, that's all."

"Oh." And Freddie turned away. Was this thin angular creature the same Freddie that the lush ripe Irma Kasendorf had, in Harry's phrase, hot pants for? Freddie now sat reading a magazine taken from the display rack: *Hotrod International*. International? American culture had triumphed again;

the missionary efforts of Coca-Cola had not been enough. Did the rest of the world know us by such things? We, the People of George Washington and Anthony Krumpit?

For a long time Stanley just stared at the youth. Odd, the contempt he felt for Freddie Winslow all of a sudden. Freddie, the very one who'd served him a tuna sandwich only yesterday. Stanley hadn't hated him then—not even when he'd suspected that the mayonnaise had turned. He had always considered Freddie an inoffensive fellow—not particularly interesting, to be sure, but not . . . not *contemptuous*. Was that *really* the way he felt about him? Did he *deserve* Stanley's hostility? Was Freddie Winslow one of the crass youths who regularly desecrated Anthony Krumpit's grave—Jesus! with his very own employee Irma softroundbottom Kasendorf who had—as everyone knew!—hot pants for this very same Freddie?

Somewhere in the store a telephone rang. In a minute Sy Schwartz popped out of the pharmacist's alcove. "Freddie— two coffees with cream and sugar. Want to run 'em over to Holgrove's right away? Hi, Stan! How's business?" But with a wave he was gone, a gray-headed fox run back into his lair.

"Hi. Fine. . . ." (No, not fine: not at all.) Could business, or anything else, be fine when America was not? when the Freddie Winslows of America took their pleasure (UN-FAIR!) on a Patriot's grave?

Stanley glared at Freddie, who went about the business of filling paper cups with coffee as if he were not some heinous criminal. When the boy had left, Stanley opened Judge Pool's book and read again the final paragraphs, the speculations on heroism.

It was a complex proposition, not just one of behavior in battle. The American Revolutionary War was not the war in Vietnam. But the two wars had a common reality: death was death, whether visited on young Anthony Krumpit at Bunker Hill or Brandywine Creek or Riker's Field, or on young Larry Putchek at Da Nang, Khe Sanh, or Con Thien. Whatever anyone felt about the Vietnamese War, Stanley decided that to have a son in the midst of it was itself a burden of heroic proportions—enough to make a hero out of a parent. . . .

He imagined having his own son Bill off in the fetid jungles of Vietnam—and he trembled with fear at the very thought. ("Sure I worry. Alla time I worry. . . .") Stanley marveled now at Harry. For if he, Stanley Stanhope, had had Billy off in Vietnam facing bullets and rockets and claymore mines and pongee stakes and Godknowswhat, would *Stanley* have been able to go about his business, manage somehow to function every day as Harry did?

The Vietnamese War—any war—seemed unspeakably obscene. Was there any other word for an event which might rob a man of his bloodflesh own? Was all heroism merely a fine madness?

Stanley closed Judge Pool's book with a noise that startled him. Freddie Winslow was back on his counterseat reading *Hotrod International*. Stanley left fifteen cents on the counter for the aspirin and hurried outside.

At Holgrove's Hardware he stopped to check the outside thermometer: 91. It felt warmer than the 96 of yesterd—His glance went through the window, where Barney Holgrove and Old Beardsley stood drinking coffee out of paper cups. Old Beardsley raised his cup as if in a toast, then bowed in profound mockery to Stanley, who walked quickly away, head athrob.

"You're home early!" The house was full of the aroma of a baking pie. Apple, he guessed.

"Yes. . . ." He kissed his wife.

"Stanley, aren't you well?"

"I . . . I've got a bad headache. I think I'll lie down. Would you call me for supper?"

He kicked his shoes off and lay down on his bed. Stanley felt immensely at ease in the old house—his father's house. It was a good house, a solid house, one that had absorbed his fears and listened to his dreams and echoed with his tears as well as his laughter, dependably and without betrayal. An only child he'd been, but the house had been like a brother to him—an older one—a refuge from the harsher realities outside and a confidant to those within. The house asked no questions. Only sheltered. As still it did. It sheltered succored *saved* him, put him at his ease. As now. Peace; and quiet; the chance to rest. Sweet Jesus, wasn't it the simplest things in life that meant the most? Peace, and quiet, and the chance to—

Bongo drums exploded in the hallway in strings of electronic firecrackers. Stanley shot upright, his fingers clutching the bedspread, his brain seized with an inexplicable terror. He thought he heard Emily's voice but could not be sure. The bongos ceased abruptly.

"WHAT?" Could an eleven-year-old scream so loudly?

"I said your father has a headache you're not to play that phonograph . . . !"

And with what disdain the small self-righteous piping: "Well, *I* didn't know . . . !" Stanley fell back onto his pillow, his reverie shattered.

What was the old homestead to his children but a place not large enough to play a phonograph loudly in or a base for trips to Osterville and to the beach. He could have wept at the realization. Not in his wildest imaginings could he conceive of either Billy or Cissie thinking about the house as a friend or a brother. But if they took the old homestead for granted, did it have any value at *all* for them? Or was it just so much board and brick, pleasant enough, necessary for a time even, but nevertheless something to abandon eventually. Yet what else was to be expected of a generation brought up on wastefulness of resources as a prod to Conspicuous Consumption? He couldn't rest anymore; he only closed his eyes and tried not to think. . . .

"Daddy, Mother says supper's ready now." Cissie stood in

the doorway, an apology on her face if not on her lips. Stanley sat on the edge of his bed.

"Okay, sweetie."

"She says will you dress up a bit, 'cause we have a guest for supper."

(Oh Christ no.) "Who is it, Cissie?"

"Billy's girlfriend Deborah."

"Oh. Will my tux do?" She bubbled at the implied put-down: already a woman wary of the femininity of other females. Christ how fast they grew, how quickly the winning ways of childhood ebbed away.

"Deborah's pretty informal. The way she's dressed, I mean." Then with an air of great sophistication: "And you know Billy. . . ." He nodded gravely; one had to accept the fact of one's kids growing up—however much one suspected the process. "Is your headache better, Daddy?"

"Oh . . . I guess. Ask your mother to inform Princess Deborah that I'll be down as soon as I've had my pedicure." But Cissie just looked at him unsmilingly, unwilling to stretch the joke. The look said, "Oh Dad, that's dumb." Then she pirouetted gracefully, turning her back on his heavy-handed attempt at humor. It was the (goddamn!) generation gap; it sneaked up on one, presenting itself as an established reality while the hapless parent still fantasied about childhood charm and innocence. (SweetJesus.)

Stanley washed up and changed into brown slacks and a yellow sports shirt and concluded that that was preparation enough for dining with the fair Damsel Deborah d'Osterville, she who awaited a prince on a shining motorcycle. . . .

"Nice to see you again, Mister Stanhope." They'd spent the day at the beach and looked it. The girl had on a brief colorful summery thing (30% Dacron, Stanley guessed) and her loose long hair was tied up with something that looked like yarn, thick and electric-pink. Her pert young breasts thrust out at him unselfconsciously, and her eyes were dark and round and startlingly pretty. Billy could pick 'em.

"Have fun?"

"Yeah, it was all right."

(Isn't anything ever more than "all right"?) "That's nice." They'd gone to the beach with a carload of others and had been dropped off at Billy's house. After supper, Billy would borrow the Studebaker (in want of a motorcycle) and they'd end the day in Osterville, probably watching color TV. (Probably—)

"The water's just *beautiful*, Mister Stanhope—you can't imagine!"

(Can't I?) "I used to go there myself, you know. Of course in those days there were still dinosaurs and things like that around."

"Oh Daddy . . ."

(Don't you *dare* say it, Cissie: don't you dare!) She didn't say it. They all sat down to steaks and salads, with Deborah being very social, Emily very friendly, Cissie very aloof, Billy very ravenous, and Stanley quietly agreeable to anything that was said. A domestic enough scene, yet somehow it seemed unreal to Stanley. He felt little hunger and scarcely tasted his food. He smiled at the tanned and summery Deborah whose lips moved constantly but whose words Stanley had difficulty understanding for some reason. Mentally he ordered Billy to get his elbows off the table and stop gnawing on the steak bone, but apparently the message got shunted to Cissie, who delivered it to Billy via a deft kick under the table and a quick sweet smile, as Deborah Perkins talked on and on. . . .

Was it possible to withdraw spiritually from one's physical presence? Stanley could feel himself leaving, leaving the table while his body remained and toyed with his salad and arched his brows and nodded with feigned interest at the scintillating remarks of the Princess d'Osterville which he, the real Stanley Stanhope, the interior man, could no longer even hear. It was as if he were being called away, summoned to attend to some vitally important task and could simply not be spared for idle supper-table conversation. *Was it America call-*

ing, as Anthony Krumpit himself had once been called from hearth and home? Was Stanley only now hearing the shot heard round the world—*really* hearing it that is, echoing explosively in his ears, the pungent scent of gunpowder filling his nostrils? Inadvertently he looked out the dining room window, and for a split second he thought he *saw* Anthony Krumpit there, beckoning urgently to him—but the vision was gone in another instant. . . .

"—motorcycle, Dad?"

"Beg pardon . . . ?"

"I wondered if you'd come to any decision about the motorcycle."

"Oh. . . . No, Bill, I honestly haven't. I just haven't had time to give the matter much thought. I'm sorry. . . ."

"Billy really *needs* a motorcycle, Mister Stanhope—he *really does!*"

(For what? For hauling your pert little ass to the beach and back and all around Osterville and Krumpit and environs?) "It's amazing, though, how few things we really actually *need* in life, when you get right down to it." Deborah seemed stunned—not by the words, but by the surprising coldness of his tone. For once she was speechless. Stanley mustered a smile that apparently put the girl off even more. Billy sat with his mouth partly open, a piece of lettuce leaf clearly visible within it. Cissie only just repressed a giggle. It was Emily who returned them all to casual normality.

"Well. We have fresh apple pie and ice cold watermelon for dessert. Who'd like what?"

Everyone opted for the pie except Stanley, who decided he'd had enough. Then, inexplicably, he found himself saying aloud what he thought he'd been only thinking: "Suppose I make the motorcycle contingent on what you'd done for your Country, Bill."

"What?"

(UNFAIR!) "Or even on what you *know* about your Country. When, for instance, was the Battle of Riker's Field?"

"Well I . . ."

"Surely you should know *that*, at least."

"I guess I forgot. . . ."

"What was the Stamp Act?"

"Stanley, is this really necessary?"

"*What*, Bill, was the *Stamp Act?*"

"The Stamp Act . . . lessee; it . . ." He was thoroughly perplexed, perhaps not altogether by the question.

It was Cissie who piped up: "The Stamp Act: a form of direct taxation imposed on the American Colonies by an act of the British Parliament in 1765. It required the Colonists to purchase stamps in order to buy newspapers and other everyday commodities as well as for certain legal documents, like marriage licenses."

"Even your kid sister knew! Aren't you ashamed?"

"She just had it in school this year!"

"And I had it—thirty years ago!"

"Stanley dear, can't we forget the history lesson for now?"

"But that's just *it!* We *have* forgotten our history! We, the People, have forgotten—that's why we're in the mess we're in!"

Then from Cissie: "The Battle of Riker's Field: July twenty-ninth, 1779. Wild Anthony Krumpit single-handedly repulsed an attacking force of one thousand two hundred light cavalry under the command of the British governor William Tryon."

"Exactly right. Thank God there's *one* American in the family. Cissie: when was the declaration of Independence proclaimed?"

"July fourth, 1776. It was actually signed the day before, though."

"See that? Cissie: on what date did the Boston Massacre occur?"

"March the fifth, 1770. A group of angry Colonials massed in front of the Custom House in Boston to protest—"

"When and what was the Boston Tea Party?"

"On the night of December sixteenth, 1773, some citizens

of Boston dressed up like Mohawk Indians and boarded British ships and—"

"When and where did the Continental Congress meet?"

"The *First* Continental Congress met from September fifth to October twenty-sixth of 1774 in Philadelphia. It demanded the repeal of the objectionable acts passed by the British Parliament since 1763. The *Second* Continental Congress met from May tenth to December twelfth, 1775—"

"When was Washington at Valley Forge?"

"Stanley—"

"Valley Forge: the winter of 1777 and 1778. General George Washington and—"

"When did the American Revolutionary War end?"

"At the Siege of Yorktown, Virginia, September twenty-eighth to October nineteenth, 1781, with the surrender of General Cornwallis to General Washington."

"There! There! See? *Someone* knows our history! *Someone* hasn't forgotten!"

"Does that mean I can have my own television set, Daddy!"

He was standing at the table—he did not remember having risen. Cissie's face was abeam, Billy's mouth was open, Deborah's eyes were saucer-round. With a bottomless feeling to his stomach he turned to his wife. "*Emily* . . . !" She folded her arms, spatula in hand; her look said, "You started it." (Jesus. Jesus Jesus*Jesus!*)

Without so much as excusing himself he fled the dining room, a shrill young voice pursuing him: "*Can* I, Daddy? *Can I* . . . ?"

His head hurt anew—more than before. What could he do about America—about its materialism and the Conspicuous Consumption which had already enslaved his own offspring, they who thought only of motorcycles and television sets and lolling in the sun on beaches and probably screwing by the light of the NBC peacock in Living Color, or on the grave of Anthony Krumpit! (UNFAIR!) Sweet Anthony Krumpit, what *could* he, what *must* he do?

After a while there was a soft knock at his door and Emily

looked in. "Billy wanted to use the car to take Deborah home. I told him it was all right. You weren't planning to use it, were you?" There was a yelp of tires and of slipping clutch as the Studebaker shot by his den windows, with a screech of brakes at the end of the driveway.

"If I was, it'd be too late now, wouldn't it." (CHRISTAL-MIGHTY.)

"Well . . . the girl does have to get home. . . ."

"He's gonna *ruin* that car! Did you hear him? That car's not new anymore, it's got to be handled judiciously!"

"Maybe he ought to have a motorcycle. He could ruin that, instead."

Stanley was on his feet, stalking around his den. "Oh no. No! Christalmighty no, Em! That kid is *not* getting a motor-cycle—I've decided. I've made up my mind, Emily: Bill is *not to have a motorcycle!*"

"Whatever you say, Stanley." She leaned against the door-jamb, and gradually Stanley ceased his pacing. "Come sit out on the front porch with me? The honeysuckle's in blos-som. . . ."

It was peaceful on the porch. It was still early evening and the world was full of pleasantly reliable realities: the creak of the glider which had made that sound since his father's day; the drapes of honeysuckle vines and the seductive scent of their blossoms; the last of the day's sunlight filtering down through the elms and falling onto the brown porch floor he'd painted only a month before. So it was all the more discon-certing when the bright yellow car with the broad red stripes stopped in front of the house. Its driver raced the engine a few times and it growled mightily, a caged beast. Its muffler had a startling, throaty sound.

"What in the world, Stanley . . . ?"

"Some goddamn friend of Billy's. . . ." He rose, and Emily with him. The car's horn blared twice. A woman in the right front seat waved pleasantly.

"Stanley, isn't that Ginny Putchek?"

It was. And Harry was driving. Stanley led his wife down

the front walk, opened the wooden gate, and together they approached the car unbelievingly. It was raised in the rear and lowered in the front—chopped, channeled and sectioned. A chromium air-filter stuck up through the hood, and there were chromium nuts holding the wheels in place. Stanley thought he saw a Chevy somewhere beneath it all. Emily was bug-eyed.

"For heaven's sake . . . ! Hi!"

"Hi! We were just passing by and saw you sitting out there."

"Whaddya think a this baby, Stan!"

"Where in the world did you . . . ?"

"It's the kid's car. Larry's. He asked us ta look after it for him till he gets back."

"He just couldn't bear to part with it."

"He done most of the work on it hisself. Practically rebuilt it. Ya know how it is, Stan: ya can't just sell a part a yourself."

"It's . . . really something."

"Yeah. We gotta drive it a little each week. Larry didn't wanna put it up on blocks. Kinda nice ta have a second car, though—even if this-here one gets a lotta stares."

"It looks . . . very fast. . . ."

"Had it upta a hunnert on the turnpike once. But I chickened out after that."

"I don't like for Harry to drive so fast. . . ."

"Listen, won't you come in?"

"Naw, thanks. . . ."

"Yes, please do!"

"We were just out riding, just passing by."

"But listen, we have some ice-cold watermelon! You don't have to rush off anywhere, do you?"

"Well . . ."

"Well . . ."

"Fine, then!" Stanley opened the door for Ginny, and Harry stilled the engine. They all walked together to the porch.

"Is that *honeysuckle* I smell?"

"Yes—isn't it lovely?" There were wicker chairs besides the glider, and a low wicker table. Stanley left the Putcheks chatting with Emily while he headed for the kitchen. At the foot of the stairs he paused to call up to Cissie, to inquire whether she wanted any watermelon. The phonograph was silent.

"No thanks. I'm reading."

He stuck napkins and forks into the pockets of his sport shirt. *What* was the kid reading—that was the question. Next time he was near the library he'd stop and ask Clara Pearson what sort of books Cissie checked out. The melon was a hefty one. He could not help but think of the other melons in his life: the sacrificial one in yesterday's gazebo; the secret watermelon in the vegetable cellar. And of course, the great Watermelon Correlative. . . .

". . . We kinda like driving that-there car of Larry's."

"It's like we're near him somehow. Does that sound silly?"

"No, not at all!"

They ate the watermelon under honeysuckle and talked together easily: about their children; about the endless war in Vietnam and Larry's presence in that ravished land and about the Putcheks' concern for their son; about the Middle-East powder-keg and the trouble-making Russians; about the persistent inflation and the steadily rising cost of living; about work and home-life and plans for next year—a common dialogue being repeated countless times that very evening all over Krumpit, the United States, the world. Yet how rare somehow, how soul-refreshing was that commonplace conversation, how like the cool sweet taste of watermelon in their mouths.

It was dark when the Putcheks decided that they had to leave. They all walked to the car, which sat in the street as if ready to spring, its paint-job glowing under a street lamp.

"Tell me, Harry . . . how'd your boy get the money to pay for this . . . this chariot?"

"Well he usedta work after school for years, ya know—

over at the West Side Garage. Becoming a first-class mechanic, they tell me. Most a this-here car is really salvage, if ya can believe it. That and the kid's own talent and hard work."

"Larry was always smart with his hands—even when he was little."

"This-here car's his pride and joy." Harry stroked the fender with a gentle, loving hand and seemed to be smiling to himself. Ginny began thanking her hosts for the watermelon and the hospitality.

"Please"—Stanley found himself saying, nearly begging —"please stop by again . . . !" The car roared into life and the Putcheks drove off with Ginny's "Thankyouuu!" hanging in the backwash.

Emily put her arm through Stanley's and pressed in closely. "God I hope their boy comes home safe . . . !"

"I was thinking just this afternoon, Em: what if Billy had to go? To war I mean—to Vietnam. And it struck me—it never had before, I don't know why—that all war, *any* war, is totally and inexcusably obscene. . . ." The honeysuckle was overpowering, and dire thoughts or no, Stanley paused to inhale deeply.

"Even the Revolutionary War?"

They sat on the porch steps. Crickets had begun their incessant, cast-of-thousands concert. It was the light of street lamps which now filtered through the elms. Stanley ran his hand down his face. The American Revolution obscene? (No!)

"No."

"It was war. Where do you draw the line?" It was not a question for a summer night under honeysuckle.

"At intention? At necessity? I don't know. . . ." Emily put her head onto his shoulder. "Was that a pretty bad scene at table?"

"Unh-hunh."

"Sorry about that. I don't know what got into me. . . ."

For a long while they sat in silence, until finally Stanley broke it. "The Revolution couldn't be helped. There was no other way—absolutely no other way, Em. The Colonists didn't want war—they tried everything they could to stay within the Empire. All they wanted was the redress of grievances, a say in their own governing. It was all very clear-cut. Liberty or death."

"I don't like slogans. They're untrustworthy."

"Not this one. Not to be free—that is, to be enslaved, told what to do—*is* a death: a death of the spirit."

"But the Colonists weren't really *enslaved*, Stanley! In fact, they had it pretty good, from what I remember of American history. Apart from the 'no representation' business, I mean. In fact, they probably had it better than any *other* British colony—better than Canada, even. Didn't they?"

"Interesting point. You may be right. Maybe the People just got fed up. With British rule, I mean."

"But weren't nearly half the people Tories? Didn't something like fifty thousand Loyalists fight for King and Mother Country?"

"More than twice that number fought for the Patriot cause."

"Still, it was anything but unanimous."

"Is any war? Anyway, that explains why the Colonists tried so hard to reconcile themselves to the Crown. When they found they couldn't, they had no other choice but to declare themselves to be free and independent—and be ready to fight to back that up. The danger always lies in our not having true representation. We the People, I mean, in relationship to the pols. That's what really annoyed the Colonists. . . ."

"You know, when you think of it, Stanley, taxation *with* representation seems to be getting every bit as bad as taxation without."

"It's become a complex world. That costs money to live in. And make work."

"But don't we in fact have a 'Stamp Act' of our own these days, what with all the sales taxes, license fees, and the rest?

Didn't the Colonists fight to rid themselves of such things?"

"It all comes down to the same thing, Em: the Colonists lived in a far less complex era. They had no Social Security, or Welfare, no Medicare or Medicaid or a hundred other services which, unfortunately, cost money."

"So what's a *cause célèbre* in one era—what men fight and die to rid themselves of—becomes government policy in another."

"I'm afraid so. *C'est la vie*. And *la guerre*. But *toujours la patrie*."

"As long as it isn't *toujours la guerre*." She shuddered. "I keep thinking about that Putchek boy. And about Billy. You're right: war *is* obscene."

"Except the American Revolution. I could never call *that* obscene. If anything it was one of the nobler acts of man."

"Stanley . . . What if this were the 1770's instead of the 1970's. Would you want Billy to fight in that war, and maybe . . . die for his country . . . ?"

(Christ!) She had a way of putting things, of holding them up to the light to get a view of them at a different angle. It made him uneasy at times. As it did now. "The only answer is that some things are worth dying for, if it comes to that. Like one's own Country, but not necessarily another. I'm beginning to feel that Vietnam isn't worth dying for; but I'm convinced that the Patriot cause *was*. But I'm with the Colonists in their belief that everything possible ought to be tried first to *prevent* war."

"I can't help thinking that 'worth dying for' has the ring of rhetoric. . . ."

"Maybe it has. But that doesn't alter the underlying truth."

"Which is?"

(Damn!) "That man must live free." Her head fairly popped off his shoulder.

"Stanley Stanhope, that's every bit as rhetorical!" And he knew that it was.

"I phrased it badly. It's just that some people have to live

—you know—in a certain style, under certain philosophies."

"I *don't* know. That's very vague."

"You know: like being Red or dead."

"That smells suspiciously like a slogan to me." Not even the sweet odor of honeysuckle could mask the fact. Stanley sighed. What was the answer?

"Most people live and die by slogans. . . ."

"Maybe that isn't good enough any longer! Stanley, I want Billy to *live!* And Larry Putchek, too!"

"So do I. . . ."

"And Stanley, I hope this isn't treason but I'd rather have Billy *alive*—whatever his political coloration, if it came to that!" Her voice quavered. Stanley put his arm around her and pulled her close. The lump in his throat refused to be swallowed, and he would not let it up and out: he had neither her courage nor her honesty. It was a long time before he felt it safe to speak.

"Perhaps the only real solution is to outlaw wars altogether —all wars."

"Fat chance." How abysmally despairing her tone was. He could only hold her more tightly, for long silent moments. "Stanley, do you think there'll ever be another civil war in this country? I mean black against white, rich against poor, radicals against the rest of us—that sort of thing?"

"If there is—real civil war I mean, not just insurrection— it'll be the end of us. As a Nation. And as a People. But I think there are enough sound minds—black, white, radical, and otherwise—to bring about change by other means. They're aware of the alternative."

"If it should come—real civil war—Billy'll be right in the middle of it. Cissie, too. No one will escape. No one, Stanley!"

"I don't think it'll ever come to that. There's too much to lose. Nobody would win."

"What about people who don't feel they're winning the way things are? What have they got to lose?"

"Nothing, I guess. But I wonder if they'd ever number anything more than a small minority. That wouldn't be enough for a civil war—only for an insurrection. And that would be put down in hours. Days, at the most."

"Could the Civil War—our original one, I mean—have been avoided, do you think?"

"I don't know."

"Because if it couldn't, you've no right to believe that another could be avoided—call it revolution or insurrection or what you will."

(Jesus!) "So often wars are economic in origin. The Civil War was. Maybe if we can solve the economic problems, we could go a long way toward putting an end to war entirely."

"There was slavery too, remember. In the Civil War, I mean."

"But slavery was an economic issue before it became a moral one, Em. Historically, I mean."

"But people *were* enslaved, Stanley. A few minutes ago you were calling that a 'death of the spirit.' Was that worth fighting for, to abolish slavery?"

"Perhaps there was a way to abolish it without fighting. It was done in other countries. In the South, slavery was an enormous economic factor."

"Tell that to the people huddled in the slave cabins. Or in the ghettos today."

"Lincoln himself—the Great Emancipator, hon—said that if he could preserve the Union without freeing a single slave, he would do so."

"That wouldn't have settled the moral issue; it would have ignored it completely. Shame on Mister Lincoln."

"I think he had another moral issue in mind: the lives of thousands."

"What about the lives of the thousands of slaves?"

"I guess he figured it was better to be a live slave than a dead freeman."

"Would he also have preferred being Red than dead?"

(Damn.) "His actions speak otherwise. He fought a civil war to preserve the Union."

"Because he had to?"

"Yes."

"Because slavery had become an economic rather than merely a moral issue?"

"Because the South, pursuing a different economic system, an agricultural one based on slavery, tried to secede from the Union, thereby threatening it."

"And slavery wasn't a moral issue?"

"Only later. It became one. As fodder for popular consumption. And as a spur for war recruitment."

"Stanley, are you telling me that slavery only became a moral issue *after* it became an economic one?"

"Em—it was always a moral issue, of course. But it was only when secession threatened the economy of the Union that something had to be done about it."

"So brother killed brother, as it were."

"Yes. A rotten solution."

"Not so much to free the slaves, but to save the Union."

"To save the Union *and* free the slaves."

"As a kind of afterthought?"

"As two wrongs righted by the same effort. You have to remember that the reason the South wanted to secede was because of moral agitation against slavery, which was the keystone of the South's economy. But the South could not be permitted to preserve its economic system by secession because that would have raised havoc with the rest of the Country's economy. Aside from Constitutional questions, of course."

"And Lincoln had to preserve the Union, at all costs. . . ."

"Or be impeached."

". . . But not necessarily to free the slaves."

"Correct. As witness the fact that blacks are still not really free. The slave cabin has been replaced by the ghetto, the slave-owner by a more impersonal system of economic exploitation, the plantation by an illusion of mobility and freedom. But their work has remained pretty much the same: mostly menial. The few cracks in the dike only serve to demonstrate the presence of the ocean—a great sea of bigotry and indifference."

"And all those *thousands*, Stanley—how many died in the Civil War, six hundred thousand?—all those people died for *economics?*" She shuddered violently at the thought; the realization of an absurdity had chilled her blood. "Was it worth all those *lives*, Stanley? Would it have been worth Billy's life, had we lived at that time?"

"I . . . rather think not. . . ."

"Better that Negroes remained enslaved and the Union split and six hundred thousand men remained alive, North and South?"

"I . . . don't know. . . ."

"Better enslaved than dead?"

(Christ!) "It was never a question of that, Em."

"Is it now?"

"What?"

"Better Red than dead? Better law than justice? Better order than liberty? Better repression than revolution? Better privilege for the few than opportunity for the many?"

"Oh Christ, no!"

"Then what's to be done, Stanley? What's to be done?"

(What indeed.) "I don't know. . . ."

"I'm cold."

They put what was left of the melon away and washed the dishes. When they went to bed they held each other very closely and listened to the throbbing of the blood in their veins. They heard Billy drive up, slam the car door, come up to bed. They listened to the myriad crickets and fought for sleep.

(Oh sweet Anthony, what's to be done?)

SIX

*S*TANLEY STANHOPE was walking the perimeter of Riker's Field Park with none other than Anthony Krumpit himself. The gravelly path was illuminated by moonlight, and Wild Anthony's boots made a scraping sound as his heels dug in. They walked slowly and in silence, Anthony's tricorn cradled under one arm, his saber swinging creakily at his belt. The woods beside them were deep in darkness.

"I have but the most abject fear for the Nation, good Stanley. . . ." What weariness in the hero's voice! "Where, where have all the Patriots gone?"

"Grown fat of soul and indolent of spirit, Anthony. Lulled into indifference by the mixed blessing of affluence, by the sop of crass materialism, by the curse of Conspicuous Consumption. . . ."

"I know nothing of such things—know not how to fight them. Tyranny I knew, and injustice; but of the materialism and affluence of which you speak, of the Con . . . Conspic . . . ?"

"Conspicuous Consumption."

"Of such things I know nothing. In my time I feared no man, Stanley—not bloody King George nor any of his minions. Ours was not an easy task. We were pursued and hounded, beaten in battle and oft in spirit; we had little food and less money and we froze in the wintertime for want of fit and proper clothing. But our enemy wore red—was easily identifiable and susceptible to musket shot and saber thrust. But how, friend, does one take a saber to Conspicuous Consumption? No, Stanley: yours is the greater battle. . . ."

"*Mine!*"

Anthony stopped and put a strong hand on Stanley's shoulder. Even in the moonlight Stanley could see the sparks of urgency in the Patriot's eyes. "Hear me, lad. 'Twas we who founded the Nation. With our blood and our vital energy. When the Nation was endangered, 'twas other Patriots who secured it. There is a different kind of war upon us now. The Nation is not primarily threatened from without but from within this time—by forces and philosophies alien to this Chosen People yet—sadly!—*embraced* by all too many of them. 'Tis you who must be the present-day Patriot, Stanley: 'tis you who must be the best and only hope. . . ."

"I'm not worthy! Not *capable* . . . !"

"Who among us is worthy? I dare say that there were times when General Washington himself felt neither worthy nor capable. If you could have witnessed the hardship and the pitiful dwindling away of spirit at Valley Forge!"

"Tell me—tell me, Anthony!—what is to be done? What's to be *done?*"

They resumed their walking, Anthony deep in thought, his eyes fixed on the moonstruck gravelpath. When finally he spoke, his words were measured. "You see, 'tis not in the least a classic war. The object is not to conquer an enemy, nor even to convert him. For there is no enemy—no *person* to be considered as such, that is. *Let no American be thine enemy, Stanley, I abjure you!* We are One Nation Indivisible and cannot exist otherwise. Rather consider thy enemies to be lassitude and indifference and infidelity to the ideals and declarations, to the Constitution my generation left to guide this Nation in its historic evolution into the true Land of the People." He stopped and gazed at Stanley anew. "You must lead a revolution, Stanley Stanhope. Not the glib and facile thing bandied about by the soft-brained misfits with uncalloused hands with which the present generation abounds, but a true and complete Revolution: one redounding to the *basic values* of 1776. Your time is not my own, lad—nor will solutions to your problems be the same. Make not that mistake. Yet unless both our eras be anchored to the same Foundation, America cannot continue to survive *as America*. It is up to you. It is still my Country but it is, after all, your time."

(Sweet Jesus!) "How—*how*, Anthony? Who am *I* to lead the Revolution?"

"It is interior disposition that counts. When I charged the twelve hundred in Riker's Field, *that* was my real armament. Do you suppose one saber would have sufficed? Interior disposition, Stanley. It is the secret weapon of the ages—of any age."

"But—*what exactly* is to be done?"

"To begin with, free the Nation from the grasp of the politicians."

"Do you mean, 'Power to the People'?"

The hero only laughed—a very sad laugh indeed. "Your

good spouse was quite correct in warning you of the untrustworthiness of slogans, Stanley. Whenever you hear a slogan you can be sure of one of two things: either a lack of intelligence or an attempt at deception on the part of the sloganeer. For the simple truth, lad, is that no great cause or idea or movement can be encapsulated in a catch-phrase, and to try to do so is necessarily to leave out essentials. You must exercise great care that the persons who shout 'Power to the People' do not in fact mean power to *themselves*—over the People. For there are many in your era, Stanley, who would simply disenfranchise the present power-brokers —the politicians—and substitute themselves in their stead. Such is hardly Government of, by, and for the People."

"Is it the politicians then who have betrayed us—betrayed the Dream?"

"The betrayers have had the enthusiastic support of the betrayed. Consider the free hands allowed the politicians by popular indifference. The People have allowed the politicians to become power-brokers. As a result, the Nation, Stanley —the *Nation!*—has become a commodity. It is the power-brokers who profit, not the People. The People are the ones who are being sold, traded, devalued—their freedoms bartered away."

"It must be *stopped!*"

"Aye. And the first step is to make the politicians relinquish their role as power-brokers. It will not be easy; they will resist. Patriots will be called vile names, flags will wave and anthems will sound, dire warnings will abound, people will be encouraged to mistrust and suspect one another."

"But—what to do with the politicians?"

"Reform them, if you can—or retire them by the election of better men. Make the politicians become, not power-brokers, but true representatives of the People, as the Constitution ordains. Then and only then will America stand a chance to be truly liberated and solve its problems and . . ."

He kicked some gravel with the toe of his boot. "And survive. . . ."

"But *how*, Anthony? Where do I start?"

"Begin where you must always begin: with the People. They must be instructed, good Stanley, not to allow themselves to be led by those politicians who play on their fears, but by Patriots who speak of national aspirations. They must not cast their precious ballots as if to stone the bogies implanted in their minds by self-seeking politicians, but rather to build a support for the Citizen-Patriots who would maintain the Republic and raise it up to still greater glory. In a phrase, the People must dethrone the politicians. It is the People who should be King, in these United States."

"The task is—immense! How can *I* do it? How can I possibly get word to two hundred million Americans?"

"Attend." Anthony shoved his tricorn into Stanley's hands, then drew his saber. He grasped the haft in both his hands and with two resounding whacks cut a slash into a sturdy oak beside the path. "But two small blows, really, yet if I kept at it this mighty oak would fall."

"But if *I* tried to fell the great oak of indifference—the tree of lassitude, the growth of infidelity to the ideals of the Constitution—I myself would be cut down. That would be no great loss, I grant you, but the oak would still stand. The sound of my labors would bring the woodsmen running— those keepers of the dark forest of American apathy—and they would prevent my felling the oak. . . ."

"Consider then the tree from yet another perspective. Consider the bark as but the thin protective shell upon the oak of indifference. Were I to hack away a few inches' width completely round the tree"—(with short chops of his saber he demonstrated the process)—"would not the mighty oak of indifference wither away and die?"

"The woodsmen would find a way to maintain it, Anthony. They'd swathe the wound with the tar of corruption and the burlap of self-interest, and the sap of indifference would flow freely again. And then they'd hunt me down as a vandal. . . ."

Anthony returned his saber to its scabbard. "No; you will succeed. You will have your Long Islands and your Brandywines and your Germantowns, but you will also have your Saratogas and your Trentons and eventually your very own Yorktown. I promise it, lad. Come. . . ." He took his hat, placed it on his head at a jaunty angle, and led Stanley off the path and into the woods. Apparently Anthony saw clearly in the blackness and Stanley followed him with confidence. Finally they emerged onto the broad expanse of Riker's Field. Moonlight blessed the meadow, and even the Krumpit Memorial Monument stood bathed in a silvery sheen which somehow ennobled it. "Come, lad."

"I've seen the monument, Anthony. Only this morning."

"You've not seen what it is I want to show you." Obediently he followed the Patriot across the moonwashed meadow until they reached the monument. "There now. Look ye." The hero pointed to the large brass plaque:

ON THIS MOST HALLOWED SITE TOOK PLACE
THE BATTLE FOR THE REFORMATION
OF THE UNITED STATES OF AMERICA
July 4, 1976

in Which Wild Stanley Stanhope, of Krumpittown, Single-handedly Inspired the Regeneration of the American Dream and the Restoration of Justice and Liberty for All. His Revered Remains Are Interred South of This Spot in Honored Glory Beside the Revolutionary War Patriot, Anthony Krumpit, a Kindred Spirit.

Erected in 2004, in Grateful Memory and in the Fervent Hope That His Courage, Dedication and Love of Country Will Be Forever Remembered . . . By the Citizens of Krumpit and the

★ UNITED STATES OF AMERICA ★

"Aye, lad: you'll have your Riker's Field, as well." The hero had to steady Stanley as they walked away from the monument.

"How will I ever do it, Anthony? How will I ever manage?" It seemed utterly impossible, yet he *would do it*—it was writ large upon a public monument!

"I cannot tell you how. I can be of little further use to you, lad. I have my era as you have yours. But we are brothers of a sort, you and I, and you will succeed, as I have. That much I can tell you. . . ." Stanley felt a great incapaciousness about himself. He could barely swallow, never mind speak, so they walked in silence across Riker's Field and toward the little park. Stanley stopped short when he realized that they were heading straight for the Patriot's tomb. "I must leave you now, lad. Never to return."

"No—no! Anthony, I'll *need* your help, I can't do it alone . . . !"

The hero only smiled. "You can. And you will." He started up the little brick walk to the shrine and Stanley grabbed him by his Continental cuff.

"I'll need your advice . . . !"

"You've had all I can give, lad; I know not your era even half so well as you do."

"Your encouragement, then! Stay by me, Anthony! *With* me . . . !"

"Be your spiritual crutch? You'd never succeed, in that case. And you *must* succeed, Stanley. 'Tis *you* who must decide the matter. And the manner. You must look to your own counsel and your own conscience. I will indeed be with you, but from there"—and he nodded in the direction of his tomb. Already the hero seemed somehow less substantial to Stanley, although that illusion was dispelled as Anthony grasped his hand and squeezed it warmly. "Do not be afraid, lad. Remember it is interior disposition that counts." The Patriot started up the half-dozen brick stairs to the shrinetop.

"I'll come with you!"—and Stanley bounded up beside him—"As far as I can. . . ."

They reached the top. "The Nation, Stanley, is in your hands. . . ." It was then that they spied the couple writhing on the grassy roof of Anthony Krumpit's grave. They saw the pair clearly in the moonlight: a tall angular youth thrust full between lushwhitethighs widespread. "Attend!" Anthony liberated his saber and raised it in ireful menace. The angular young man, hotrodding into the homestretch, was unaware of anything else. It was the girl who first saw the flash of the Patriot's saber.

"Mister Stanhope—save me!"

Anthony gripped his saber with both hands—as he had when he'd slashed away at the great oak. His eyes were furious, his voice snarling. "Vandals . . . !" There was a scream from Irma Kasendorf, curdling the moonlight. A moment before the blade of wrath descended, Stanley grabbed Wild Anthony's wrists and struggled to prevent the act of certain retribution. "Aside, lad! Aside, I say!"

With all his strength Stanley resisted. "Anthony—please! The girl's an employee of mine! Slay the other one—he's the despoiler!—but spare the girl, Anthony! Anthony . . . !"

". . . Anthony . . . !"

"Stanley, what's *wrong?*"

"Wha . . . ?"

"You were dreaming?"

"Yes. . . ." (Was I?)

"Who in the world is Anthony?"

"Why . . . Wild Anthony. . . ."

"*Who?* Oh. . . . History lessons even in your sleep, darling?"

"I . . . That is . . ." (Ineffable!)

He went down to his den and snapped on the desk lamp. He was not at all certain that what he'd experienced was merely a dream. Absently, he opened his desk drawer. The rosy watermelonstain eyed him mercilessly. The Watermelon Correlative restated itself, barging about in his mind: "the perfection the perfection of watermelon of watermelon is in direct ratio direct ratio to the number of seeds seeds seeds therein therein." He also recalled its first great corollary: "one's efficacy is in direct ratio to the seeds of courage within one." And Stanley asked himself the inevitable, vitally important question: What seeds of courage had Stanley Stanhope?

"Stanley . . . ?" Emily entered in a powderblue nightgown that fell clear to her ankles. "Stanley, I'm worried about you. . . ." She sat on the edge of his desk, the gown falling away from one leg: a long graceful stretch from bare foot to naked thigh. "Stanley . . . ?"

"You remember what we were talking about out on the front steps, Em? About America, and what's happening to us?"

"Yes, of course. . . ."

"I want to *do* something about it, Em. Not just talk and berate my son for not knowing about such things. I want to *help*—no. It's more than that. How can I put it . . . ?" He looked at her as if he expected her to tell him.

"Just—go ahead and *say* it, Stanley. I'm not exactly unsympathetic where you're concerned, you know."

"Em: I think I've received a calling of some kind. I can't explain it better than that—I don't fully understand it myself! But in the last couple of days— Something's been building in me, Em, something bigger than me. Something as big as . . ." (should I say it?) ". . . America!" She put a hand to his forehead but he shook it off. "I'm *not sick*, Em." (Why, *why* does everyone mistake the Patriotic Flush for fever?) "Please believe me!"

"I believe you, Stanley. You feel you have to act—is that it? To do something, in some special way?"

(Oh priceless jewel!) "Yes—yes!"

"What, Stanley . . . ?"

He was up, pacing around his den and wringing his hands. "I *don't know*. The only thing I'm sure of is that I've got this calling, this need and capacity to serve the Country in a very special way—*to change the People into Patriots*, Em . . . !" He looked at his wife from across the room; she sat perfectly motionless on the edge of his desk, one long lovely leg stuck out of a cloud of blue, her raven hair down, her calm eyes watching him. "Em . . . ?"

"Do whatever you feel you have to do, Stanley. I'm with you."

"No matter what?"

"No matter what. As long as you don't auction off the children."

"Thank you, Em." She smiled, pulled her nightgown around her, and rose from the desktop. "Do you really mean it, about being with me, no matter what?"

"As long as you don't sell the kids—remember?"

"I'm serious, Em."

She came to him, stood face to face with him. "*I* am with *you*. Come hades or hurricane-flood." She wrapped her arms around him. "Period." They swayed in each other's arms, and Stanley nuzzled her neck as he held her tightly against him. Ineffable. . . .

They went upstairs arm in arm, careful not to step on any of the squeaky places. In less than a minute Stanley fell into a deep and thankfully dreamless sleep. A decision was made, if not known.

He awoke at dawn, his brain milling away at a rapid rate. Something was in production—he knew it, could feel its process of manufacture and passage through the factory of his mind. Finally it spewed out, whole and entire, a finished product, all its parts in place, irresistible in its appeal.

"Em—Em! Wake up!" (Eureka!) "Em, I've got it! I've *got* it!"

For Emily, sleep was irresistible. "What . . . time is it, for heavenssake . . . ?"

"Time for *action,* Em!"—and he leaped out of bed. Emily murmured something acquiescent and toppled back into sleep.

The first thing to do would be to put an ad in the paper. If he acted at once he could make that day's edition of the *Patriot-Call.* Stanley found a yellow legal pad and began drafting his advertisement. The Revolution had begun!

This time it was Stanley who roared out of his driveway in the Studebaker. He seldom skipped breakfast, but that morning there simply wasn't time for such frivolity. It was not quite eight o'clock when he pulled up in front of the *Patriot-Call* office.

It was Harvey Palmer he had to see, and Harvey wasn't there yet. "When does Mister Palmer get here?" The girl in the front office looked up from her morning cigarette and blinked herself fully awake.

"Mister Palmer? Oh, about nine, usually. He generally checks out a few accounts on his way in. Won't you . . . have a seat?"

Stanley could not have sat still and opted for the front sidewalk and despairing glances at his wristwatch. Did they have to wait around for Benjamin Franklin to go about *his* newspaper business before they could get down to signing the Declaration of Independence? Then it occurred to Stanley: would his humble advertisement someday reside in protective display at the Library of Congress *along with* the Declaration of Independence and the United States Constitution? Was that *possible?* He rechecked his spelling. . . .

"Morning, Stanley. Beautiful day, isn't it?" Harvey Palmer was walking briskly past him lugging a dozen manila folders bulging with tear-sheets.

"Harvey, I've been *waiting* for you!"

"Well, here I am. C'mon in." They entered the *Patriot-Call* offices and walked to the advertising department at the far end of the long front counter. "Got another special on, Stan?"

"No—this isn't a business ad."

"Would you like a cup of coffee?—Won't take but a minute, the girls usually have it made by now."

"Thanks, Harvey, but I simply haven't time, I want to get this into today's edition"—and he handed him the yellow sheet of paper. "I want a *full-page ad*, Harvey."

Harvey Palmer gave a low drawn-out whistle. "Stan . . ." He rubbed his forehead a moment, just over his eyes.

"Is something *wrong?*"

"Ah . . . no! Only . . ." He looked up at Stanley— strangely, Stanley thought. "Are you sure you want to print this?"

"Of course I do—that's why I'm here!" (Does *no one* understand? No one but Emily?)

"Stan . . . , a full-pager will run you eight hundred bucks. You sure you want to spend that much on— What I mean is, a smaller ad can be pretty effective, the way we set it up. Maybe a series of small ads, scattered throughout the paper. . . . Cost you a lot less. . . ."

"Harvey, I want a full-page ad. Cost isn't a factor." (The Nation is in jeopardy, man!) "Now will you kindly place that ad for me?"

"Okay, Stan. You want it printed as is, the way you got it laid out here?"

"Yes. Exactly."

"Right." He made a notation across the copy. "You want it billed to your business account?"

"No. I'll write you a check for it now." He did so, in a hurried scrawl. "For today's edition—right, Harvey?"

"It's short notice, but I'll get it in for you."

His next stop was the Krumpit National Bank, where he switched $800 from his savings to his checking account. Eight

hundred dollars—money that might have gone into the pro-
motion of Conspicuous Consumption!—was instead being
dedicated to the Nation. How much *more* money would be
needed, before the project was completed, before the Nation
would be secured in its reformation? He immediately switched
another thousand dollars into his checking account. From
across the bank lobby Wolfe Harrison waved to him. Would
he soon be seeing Wolfe—the Krumpit National's chief loan
officer? Stanley's project would take a great deal of money
before it got on its feet. Later he would be able to solicit
funds; but in the beginning it would have to be Stanley
Stanhope who shouldered the financial burden.

He checked the new balance in his savings passbook: accumulated savings of $15,756.34. There was another savings
account, but that was for Billy's and Cissie's education. That
was sacrosanct, untouchable. Or was it? For if the Nation
fell, what use— And there was the business account, of course.
If need be, if his Country needed it, even that would— But
there was really not so very much money, not for a project
of national dimensions. Not with full-page ads in the *Patriot-
Call* costing $800, for instance. (What did the New York
City papers charge—ten times that much?) Money! Sweet
Jesus, did the salvation of the United States of America depend ultimately on *filthy lucre?* Could that *be?* Surely Patriots could be raised up in the Land by means of the honor-
able coinage of Countrylove. Surely America was not—
bankrupt!

But money was an inescapable reality, and right there in
the marbled lobby of the Krumpit National Bank Stanley
Stanhope held his passbook to his heart and formally dedicated
his savings to the cause he'd undertaken. It was little enough.
He was not, after all, laying his very life on the line as
Anthony Krumpit had done and as Larry Putchek even at
that moment was doing and as Billy Stanhope might. The
project *had* to succeed. Cost indeed must be no factor. After

his savings were depleted, there were his house and his
business to draw on. . . .

He was like a surgeon objectively evaluating a delicate
operation on someone else's brain—but then it hit him, a
scalpel thrust into his own mind: *sell the house?* And the
gazebo with it . . . ?

Stanley found himself wandering around on the sidewalk
outside, nearly rudderless at the thought of actually *selling*
the homestead. He pulled himself together and straightened
his course. There was the Ship of State to consider, and that
was to be valued far and above the dinghy of his own security.
The loss of the house was little enough to pay for a secure
America. For how much security did Anthony Krumpit
know? A secure Patriot was a contradiction in terms.

The house would go before the dry-cleaning plant, but
if his Country's good demanded the sale of the Stanhope
Cleaners, why then that too would go. One could not stop
half way. Being a Patriot meant putting one's Country's good
over one's own blood guts rhetoric *and possessions*, as well.
Over one's home, one's gazebo, one's business, one's savings,
one's own and one's wife's security, even over one's children's
future. For would there *be* any future if the Country collapsed in anarchy and injustice? *That* was what he had to
keep in mind—and labor to prevent. The cost might be
enormous, but he would succeed: it was writ large upon the
Stanhope Memorial Monument. . . .

The plant was humming as Stanley arrived. "Where ya
been, for Chrissakes! We're snowed under here, the kid'n
me. You wanna make daliveries this morning or ya want me
ta?"

"Why don't you go, Harry? Sounds as if you'd like to get
out for a while." Harry only glared at him. "Hello, Irma."

"Hiya, Mister Stanhope!" (Ssss-phtttt.) She was wearing a
white Dacron dress with a short pleated skirt that revealed

a generous amount of rolling thigh as she worked. (Ssss-phtttt.) She was smiling her absurd toothy smile, even after she'd returned her full attention to her labor. There was plenty of that: piles of clothes fresh out of the dry-cleaning machines were patiently queued up on racks waiting to be pressed. Stanley turned on the steam press he always used.

Outside, Harry started up the delivery van. Its muffler needed replacing; Harry was supposed to have tended to it but hadn't gotten around to doing so. A moment later, the red, white, and blue Stanhope Cleaners van (which little old ladies constantly mistook for a mail truck) shot past the shop with a noisy blurt.

There were no summer doldrums, thanks to the White Cove crowd. They made for busy days, and Stanley was grateful for them. Across from Stanley, Irma Kasendorf worked busily away at the topper and legger. (Ssss-phtttt.) She glanced up to see him looking at her and gave him a quick kooky smile. (Ssss-phtttt.) It was comfortable with the air-conditioner on; it was not, Stanley decided, Conspicuous Consumption in this case. It was an investment in employee efficiency and morale. Irma, for instance, still looked fresh and perky; Irma would have no great Y upon her backside today.

"Why do you keep looking at me like that, Mister Stanhope?" (Ssss-phtttt.)

(Oh Christ—was I?) "Like what?"

"Funny like. . . ."

"Was I? Sorry. . . . I was just wondering, Irma . . ." (Were you in Riker's Field Park last night?) ". . . How long have you been with us now?" (Ssss-phtttt.)

"Six months I think, Mister Stanhope."

"Harry's . . ." (Ssss-phtttt) ". . . been telling me you've been doing very well indeed, Irma." (With Freddie?) "And I know Harry isn't easy to please." (On Anthony Krumpit's tomb?) "You're by far the best and most reliable assistant we've ever had, in fact. . . ." (Ssss-phtttt.)

"I do my work, Mister Stanhope. That's what I'm paid for."

"How—" (Ssss-phtttt) "—how old are you, Irma? If you don't mind my asking, that is."

"I don't mind. I'll be twenty-two on Hallowe'en, Mister Stanhope"—and she laughed, mouth open, her tongue a coiled pink shrimp.

"I see. . . ." (Ssss-phtttt). "You're not originally from Krumpit, are you, Irma." He knew that she wasn't.

"No, sir, I'm from—(SSSS-SHhhhh).

"From where?"

"From Osterville, Mister Stanhope." She finished the rack she'd been working on and pushed it aside for another. When she walked, Stanley noticed, the pleats in her skirt fairly danced.

(Ssss-phtttt!) "What made you decide to move to Krumpit?"

"Oh . . . I dunno. It's bigger. Osterville's awful small, Mister Stanhope. There's never anything to do there."

(What? No hero's grave to dally on?) "Nothing at all to do?"

"Except pick peaches. They grow lots of them there, you know. Osterville peaches?"

(Don't they ever!) "So you . . ." (Ssss-phtttt) ". . . moved to the 'big town,' hunh?"

"Yeah. I worked in a coupla drive-ins over on the West Side first, but business was kinda bad winters, and you can't live on tips around here. But I like Krumpit okay. It's nearer the beach, for one thing. . . ." (Ssss-phtttt.)

(And nearer Anthony Krumpit's tomb!) "I'm surprised you didn't go to a much bigger town, Irma. New Haven or Bridgeport—New York City even, lots of young people head right on down there." (You could whore around New York —Grant's Tomb, maybe. UNFAIR!)

"Oh . . . all those places confuse me, Mister Stanhope. They're . . ." (Ssss-phtttt) ". . . just too big. And unfriendly. I always get the feeling people are looking *right through me;* do you know what I mean?"

(I *know!*) "Yes, I know." (Ssss-phtttt!)

". . . But not really *seeing* me. It kinda gives me the creeps. I'm just a small-town girl, I guess. . . ." (Ssss-phtttt.)

"Well, we're very happy to have you here, Irma. As I said, Harry's been praising your work. You can look forward to a substantial raise starting with your next paycheck." (SSSS-PHTTTT.)

"Oh—! Thank you, Mister Stanhope . . . !" Her big teeth rippled into a smile that spread fully across her face. She had a *very* large mouth, Stanley realized: a generous, sensuous mouth. The smile stood affixed to her countenance as she went about her work—thinking, perhaps, of the things she might do or buy with the extra money.

Had he said a "substantial" raise? Yes he had. Well, she was a good worker. Stanley went into his tiny office, found the phone number and extension for the payroll department of the Krumpit National Bank, and when he got through he quietly instructed the clerk to raise Irma Kasendorf's wages by fifty cents an hour. There was a stray thought—a kind of gentle probing, really—around the darker corners of his mind, asking whether there was any other motivation in proffering the raise, but Stanley managed to suppress it, scarcely aware that he did so.

He spent the remainder of the morning pressing clothes with Irma, who smiled at her own private thoughts and totally ignored her employer. It was just as well, for Stanley found himself staring unabashedly at her. Once he nearly burned himself on his steam press because of inattention to his work. And once he had a wild unruly moment when Irma dropped a garment to the floor and bent down to get it, her short pleated skirt moving up, up, up as she went down, down, down. And still he stared, uncontrollably now. (They grow nice fruit in Osterville. . . .) He stared and stared at the ripe peach across from him. (God damn that Freddie Winslow . . . !)

"It's so nice having you home for lunch, Stanley!"

"I really shouldn't have come. We're overloaded with work, Em. Harry'll be furious with me."

"Well, you *are* the boss, Stanley."

"I—just had to get away, that's all. . . ."

"Would you like some watermelon for dessert?"

"All right. . . ."

They were eating the watermelon, savoring its cold translucency. "What was all that excitement about early this morning, by the way?"

"Oh—that was another reason I wanted to come home for lunch. Em, do you suppose you could whip up some little party sandwiches—enough for maybe a hundred people, for tonight?"

"A *hundred people* . . . *!*"

"On second thought maybe you'd better call a caterer." (More money spent. Well, it's unavoidable.)

"Stanley—for *tonight?*"

"Coffee, too—and maybe some cookies, or something. . . ."

"Stanley—what *is* this all *about?*"

"Em, you said last night you were with me, no matter what. You . . . still mean that, don't you?"

"Yes, Stanley, of course! It's just that I'm— It's just a little unnerving to be faced with the prospect of a hundred or so guests with just a few hours' notice. And I still don't know what this is all about."

"I placed an ad in the paper, Em. It cost me eight hundred dollars."

"*Eight hundred dol*—! When business is so good?"

"It wasn't a business ad, Em. I've . . . I've invited some people over for eight o'clock this evening."

"*People*, Stanley? *Who?*"

"Do you think a catering service can handle it? On such short notice, I mean?"

"I—I don't know. I think they demand a week's notice, or something. . . ." She got up immediately and went to the telephone in the front hall. Stanley picked away at the seeds in his watermelon. So many seeds. . . . So much courage. . . .

"Stanley, I called both caterers in town and neither of them can handle all those sandwiches in a few hours' notice. They're just too busy weekends. Chilson's has a wedding cake they can sell us—seems the wedding was called off— but I don't imagine you'd want *that*."

"Why not? They could take the bride and groom off the top. And I imagine they could provide us with an urn of coffee easily enough. Call 'em back, would you, Em? Tell 'em we'll take the cake."

"All right, Stanley—but we'll need cups and saucers and silverware and dishes, as well. I simply haven't enough for— for a hundred people. . . ."

"Get whatever you need, hon." He wiped his lips with his napkin, rose, and kissed his wife. "I've got to be getting back. Harry'll be furious."

She walked to the front gate with him. "Will you be free tomorrow? We promised to take Cissie to the beach. . . ."

"Tomorrow?" (Tomorrow the world may end; America, maybe.)

"It's your turn to have Saturday off, Stanley. We planned the trip three weeks ago, remember?" The plant had to be kept open Saturdays. But Harry and he took turns, democratically, and it was indeed Stanley's turn to be off. "Cissie'll be terribly disappointed if we don't go. She's invited three of her friends along. . . ."

"I'd completely forgotten about it. You may have to take them without me, Em. Depending on how the meeting tonight turns out. You don't mind, do you?"

She kissed him again, at the front gate. "I guess not. . . ."
He started off. "Say—you still haven't told me what this
meeting's all about . . . !"

But he was already well on his way down the street. "See
today's paper, hon . . . !"

The work load had increased, if anything, but seemed to
be progressing at a manageable rate, with Harry and Irma
making their presses fairly sing with a sibilant pace. Harry
glared at his employer but said nothing. The ripe peach only
smiled—very pleasantly indeed. Stanley worked along with
them in the air-conditioned workroom until nearly three
o'clock, when he announced that he had to leave. By then the
work seemed well under control.

He walked toward the *Patriot-Call* office but saw its truck
drop the first bundles of newspapers off at Prescott's Pharmacy, so he headed there instead. He tried to wait patiently
as Freddie Winslow snipped the wire off one of the bundles.

"That'll be a dime, Mister Stanhope."

Stanley went inside and sat down at the lunch counter.
"You may bring me an iced tea."

His ad, which occupied all of page five, on the obverse
side of the funnies, quite took his breath away:

Attend!

AMERICA IS IN JEOPARDY!

Race-riots erupt, student protests sweep the campuses, minorities struggle against injustice, hunger and insecurity . . . while millions of complacent Americans, mired in an affluence which has become materialistic, madly pursue the inglorious goal of *Conspicuous Consumption*.

THE IDEALS OF 1776 HAVE BEEN FORGOTTEN.

You are hereby
INVITED
to join with other AMERICANS in
RIGHTING these historic WRONGS.

ANNOUNCING:
**THE FORMATION, BY WE THE PEOPLE,
OF THE**

ANTHONY KRUMPIT GUILD

a nonpartisan assembly of concerned citizens joined in common effort and dedicated to the regeneration of the American Dream and the restoration of Justice and Liberty for all Americans.

THE NATION IS IN NEED OF PATRIOTS.

THE NATION IS IN NEED OF *YOU*.

☞ ATTEND: Charter Meeting,
8:00 P.M. this evening
at the home of
Stanley S. Stanhope
37 South Woodlawn Street
Krumpit-town, Connecticut.

ALL ARE WELCOME.

Stanley Stanhope walked up Elm Street with his head held high. Under the elms of Krumpit-town a Patriot walked once more, and soon there would be thousands. The Anthony Krumpit Guild would spread throughout the Land; for everywhere, surely, there were other Stanley Stanhopes who cared about the Country and were only awaiting the sign the word the *call*. The great work had begun: the *Second* American Revolution. The delivery of the Nation was at hand.

SEVEN

THE DINING ROOM was in readiness. Besides the wedding cake, the catering service had come up with half a hundred liverpaste and chicken sandwiches. The coffee urn was perking merrily, and at five minutes to eight the first Patriot was ringing Stanley's doorbell. . . .

"Mister *Stan*hope how do you *do* how do you *do* how do you *do* I think this is the finest *idea* anyone in this *town* if not in this entire *na*tion has had and I want you to know I am *with* you Mister Stanhope one *thou*sand percent—we'll lick this thing to*geth*er don't you worry we'll put Krumpit on the *map* and shake up a few *heads* around here this sort of organization is so *long* overdue and there is such a crying *need* of *exact*ly this sort of thing in this country today that I *know* it can't *pos*sibly fail and most assuredly will *not* if we all but put our *shoul*ders to the wheel . . . !

"I'm s-sorry, you do look familiar but I can't quite place—"

"Missus *Herk*imer Murgatroyd Mister Stanhope my husband the *late* Herkimer Murgatroyd was if you'll recall past *pres*ident and *foun*der of the *Anti*-Socialist League which has for so many *years* preserved our precious American freedoms from the *diabolic* incursions of creeping socialism through its un*flag*ging educational efforts although its work came to an un*for*tunately premature end with the un*time*ly passing-away of *Mis*ter Murgatroyd who for almost *forty* years Mister Stanhope fought the good *fight* to keep America the land of the *free* and the home of the *brave* under the *God*given capitalist system. . . ."

The telephone was ringing in the hallway. Stanley took Emily by the hand and brought her forward. "My—my *wife,* Missus Murgatroyd—*Mis*sus Stanhope . . . ! Ah— would you *excuse* me? The—the *tel*ephone. . . ."

"As I was *tel*ling your husband Missus Stanhope—"

It was Old Beardsley on the phone. "For Chrissakes, boy —what the fuck are you *doing?*"

"What's that supposed to mean?" (You can go—)

"I just saw your ad—I saw your goddamn ad! Stanley-boy: tell me it's all a joke . . . !"

"Mister Beardsley, this is as far from being a joke as you are from being an angel. I'm determined to see this thing through to the end—which will *be,* Mister Beardsley, in case your impoverished and syphilitic imagination cannot arrive at that end, nothing short of the complete and utter Reformation of the United States of America, So Help Me God." Then he slammed the receiver down, cutting off the stunned silence at the other end.

Stanley hurried to greet the thin serious man he saw

hesitating at the front doorway. "Hello—please come in, I'm Stanley Stanhope." The stranger was slow to take Stanley's hand, but when he did so his grip was like steel. His eyes were steely gray and so was his hair, which was kept in a brush cut. There was no nonsense in the line of his jaw.

"George J. Danton." Even his voice was steelgray.

"Please, please come in. . . ." Before they had reached the dining room Danton halted.

"Is that Missus Murgatroyd I hear?" Stanley admitted, a bit uneasily, that it was. Danton seemed visibly relieved. "Well, that's good news. You can't be too careful, you know."

"Careful?"

"This might have been a front organization. You never know."

"Front . . . organization . . . ?"

"For the Communist Conspiracy. They love to pose as patriots. Trap the unwary that way. People with all the good intentions in the world. They end up getting used. Duped. But if Missus Murgatroyd's with you, I know you're the real McCoy. She's been fighting Commies for forty years—her and her late husband."

"She says she's against socialists. . . ."

George J. Danton gave him an astonished look. "What's the difference?" The doorbell rang.

"Ah—since you already know Missus Murgatroyd, why don't you . . . go ahead in. The other lady is my wife." Mr. Danton took a pipe from his pocket, perched it in his right hand, then entered the dining room. Stanley hurried to the front door.

"Well, *hi* . . . ! Barry Bell's the name—ol' Liberty Bell, if you prefer . . . !" He was hamhanded and broad and smiling of face and he radiated good will like a used car salesman. "That's what they used to call me in the Navy . . . !"

"They used to call you what . . . ?"

His eyes fairly twinkled. "*Liberty* Bell—get it?" His smile was full of flashing white teeth. "Dontcha get it?"

"No, I'm afraid I don't, actually. I'm sorry. . . ."

Liberty Bell clanged with laughter. "Now you just think about it a while—I'll check you later on it!"

Stanley noticed an elderly gentleman coming up the front steps. "Would you mind seeing yourself in, Mister Bell, it's—"

"It's Barry—*or* Liberty . . . !"

"Uh—Barry. It's just to your left. . . ." But Barry Bell was already laughingly on his way.

The old gentleman stood before the screen door waiting patiently. He wore a pressed seersucker suit, and the hat he held was a yellowed boater. He bowed slightly and smiled winningly. "Do I have the Stanhope residence, sir?"

Stanley opened the screen door. The old man did not step aside, however, and Stanley nearly hit him with the door. He laughed apologetically, the old man laughed winningly, but it was several moments and two attempts later before the old man moved to one side so that the screen door could swing open and admit him.

"Yes, sir. I'm Stanley Stanhope." He held out his hand. The old gentleman dropped his boater to the floor. They both stood looking down at the hat. Then they both stooped to pick it up—unfortunately in unison, banging heads resoundingly. I'm—I'm terribly sorry! Are you all right . . . ?" Stanley's own head hurt. The hat still lay on the floor.

"Yes . . . thank you. . . ." The old man proffered his hand now to Stanley. "W. Farley Simpson. Amalgamated Fruit Company. Retired."

"Very happy you could come, Mister Simpson."

"Happy birthday to you, sir."

The old gentleman bowed and smiled winningly yet another time. Stanley found it difficult to look at him and dropped his gaze to the floor. "Oh—your hat, Mister Simpson . . . !" Stanley retrieved the boater and put it on the hall table by the telephone. "Won't—won't you come in?" The old man smiled and nodded pleasantly, and Stanley led him into the dining room.

". . . because the *one* thing the American system *needs* is the free and unim*ped*ed flow of capital as *Mis*ter Murgatroyd pointed out on so *ma*ny occasions. . . ." From a cloud of pipesmoke George J. Danton nodded in brisk agreement, looking infinitely wise. Emily looked infinitely lost. Barry Bell stood by the table wolfing down liverpaste and chicken sandwiches and coffee. "So *much* depends on the con*tin*ued exercise of free enterprise Mister Murgatroyd *al*ways said for what is the American *dol*lar but the *key*stone not only of our e*con*omy but of Western Civili*za*tion!"

Stanley felt strangely light-headed. "I would like you all to meet Mister W. Farley Simpson, lately of the Amalgamated Fruit Company." (This is *not* happening . . . !)

". . . But don't ask the *so*cialists about the importance of the American *dol*lar to the stability of world order Mister Herkimer Murgatroyd asked them often e*nough* without *ev*er getting anything in return but *gob*bledygook—'Martha' he told me time and time a*gain* 'what the *so*cialists want is nothing *less* than the des*truc*tion of the world by de*base*ment of the American *dol*lar.' . . ."

The doorbell rang. With a deep breath and a desperate glance at his wife, Stanley turned to answer it.

At the front door was a woman of uncertain age, by no means old but no longer young. She was free of both make-up and any sense of style. But a positive glow emanated from her face, virtually transforming her into someone oddly appealing.

"I'm so sorry to be late . . . !" The clear stream of her countenance was refreshing, and as he let her in Stanley felt an easing of the tension that had been building within him.

"Not at all—nothing's really begun. . . ." (*Would* anything?) "My name's Stanley Stanhope. . . ."

She shook his hand, vigorously. "Imogene Ulbricht." Then

the words gushed forth like a hidden fountain in a desert: "I *so* hope we can light one little candle here tonight!"

"Y-Yes. . . ."

". . . sad *sad* day indeed when the word *'dollar'* is classified by some as a *dirty* word. . . ."

Stanley made the introductions as quickly as possible. At the name "Ulbricht" George J. Danton lowered his pipe and narrowed his eyes to blatantly unsubtle slits. Mrs. Murgatroyd smiled sweetly and rather indulgently. Barry Bell mumbled a greeting through a mouthful of disenfranchised wedding cake and Mr. Simpson bowed and smiled winningly.

"I can't *tell* you all how exciting I find this re-awakening, this renascence . . . !" The gush of genuine emotion quivered her unlipsticked lips. "As Tolstoy might say, 'We must discover what needs to be done!' " George Danton's fist tightened around the bowl of his pipe. Martha Murgatroyd marched on.

"*Not* that the socialists haven't won *bat*tles mind you but battles are *not* thankfully the *war* as Herkimer Murgatroyd never *tired* of pointing out. Minimum *wage* Social Se*cur*ity *Medi*care dear people now it's national *health* schemes they're talking about will they *never* stop their dilution of American *life* . . . ?"

Stanley drew himself a cup of coffee and surveyed the scene: the nonstop mouth of Martha Murgatroyd; the nonstop hand *into* mouth of Barry Bell; the relentless scrutiny by George J. Danton of the beaming woman who bore an infamous East German name and who talked of Russian writers; the rapt attention of Imogene Ulbricht herself as she sat crosslegged on the dining room floor and actually *listened* to Mrs. Murgatroyd; the endless smiling and agreeable nodding of W. Farley Simpson. (*Christalmighty!*) It was not what the $800 ad had called for!

It was then that he noticed the young man seated in the living room and gazing thoughtfully at the assembly. Stanley made his way to the stranger, who couldn't have been older than twenty-eight or nine. He had sideburns that curved toward his lips, and when he looked up at Stanley and smiled, the sideburns smiled too.

"I'm Stanley Stanhope." The stranger rose immediately.

"Hope you don't mind my walking right in. The door was open, and . . ." He offered his hand. "I'm Jim Tarber. The paper sent me over."

"The paper?"

"The *Patriot-Call*. I work for them. I'm their political reporter."

(Jesus! Oh-oh sweet Jesus, of all the—!) "I—I—!"

"What exactly is the . . ."—an amused glance toward the dining room, then a grave one at Stanley—"point of all this?" The reporter wet his lips (licked his chops?) and gazed at Stanley while he awaited an answer.

"Point . . . ?" Jim Tarber—*James* Tarber! Stanley read his columns regularly—cutting sardonic pieces that took the state's political biggies to the woodshed with all the fury of a young man's impatience. He'd won several awards for his hatchet-work. (Journalists would have awarded citations for good coverage of the Crucifixion or the weekly production rate at Buchenwald.) Tarber had his reporter's pad out and was turning a page.

"Yes. Why are you forming this . . ."—he read from his own notes—". . . this 'Anthony Krumpit Guild'?"

(Christ!) "It—has not been formed yet . . . !" Tarber looked into the dining room.

"Is Missus Murgatroyd a member?"

Stanley decided to brazen it out. "No—of course not. She . . . she just—dropped by, that's all. That's *all*."

"The guy who looks like a storm trooper: I've seen him somewhere before. What's *his* name?"

"His? Why— I really don't know! I— I wasn't really expecting him, either. Or Missus Murgatroyd!" (JESUS!)

Jim Tarber smiled drily and closed his notepad, much to Stanley's relief. He laughed a brief interior laugh, then thumped Stanley on the arm a couple of times. "Mind if I talk to your guests?" And without waiting for any such permission he sauntered into the dining room. Stanley watched him head straight for Martha Murgatroyd—then Stanley retreated to the front hallway.

He found himself backing furtively down his own front hallway until he bumped the screen door. Then he slipped outside. He stepped gingerly down his front walk and through the front gate, then he fled up his driveway and across his backyard to the safety of his gazebo, where he huddled on a wooden bench and suffered the humiliation of his personal Long Island. What, sweet Anthony, would his Brandywine and Germantown be like?

"Stanley, who *were* those people? I've never seen *any* of them around town—ever . . . !"

"I've seen Missus Murgatroyd's picture in the paper. Years ago, it seems." He had a hollow, empty feeling about him.

"It was terrible of you to desert ship like you did, you rat." They were sitting at the dining room table nibbling at wedding cake.

"Em, I panicked. I'm sorry. I *had* to get away." He pushed his piece of cake aside. "I had such *hopes* for the Anthony Krumpit Guild, Em! You know: I actually saw it saving the Ship of State. And then suddenly the Guild itself was in the shallowest of waters. You know what it was like, hon? It was as if I were one of those little grunions that drive themselves so hard they land on the beach and flap as they may they can't return to their natural habitat and they die agasping in the hostile environment. Only I was one of the lucky little fishes: I managed to get back to the saving sea of sanity. . . ."

"Yes and left your wife on the hook."

"Sorry about that—I really am, Em." And he really was. "When that Tarber fellow started his prying . . ." He shuddered, "Just . . . what did happen, anyway?"

"I'm not sure I should tell you."

"Em, for Chrissakes!"

She got up and drew herself a cup of coffee from the nearly full urn. "Mister Tarber was quite polite—he can be very charming, actually, though I had the feeling he was using his charm as a kind of tool. A burglar tool. It was fascinating to watch him, Stanley—it really was! He hardly asks any questions—not directly, at least. He learns things by getting people to talk about themselves. Apparently people are more than willing to."

"A favorite pastime, I'm sure."

"Information just spilled out of them, Stanley. Even that Danton fellow, who before that hardly said a word!"

"How could he, with flannel-mouth Martha blabbering on. . . ."

"Mister Danton just went on and on and *on*, Stanley, about how air and water pollution, hippies, the Black Panthers, the New York *Times*, sex education in the schools, fluoridation of water, gun-control laws, the civil rights movement, and the troubles on the campuses were all parts of the Communist Conspiracy, and about how just about *every*body but J. Edgar Hoover was probably pinko—or worse."

"How did he handle Missus Murgatroyd?"

"He kept throwing her off guard. He knows a lot about her personal life—that she keeps parakeets and hates cats and plays bridge with Judge Carter's wife, for instance. So whenever she started to blab he steered her onto parakeets or something and eventually worked in a subtle query or two and got an honest answer—or at least an unprepared one. And when old Martha finally realized the conversation had turned political, he switched her onto cats or bridge or what he said to Judge Carter in the courthouse cafeteria this afternoon. Stanley, she was putty in his hands. I'm telling you, it was an education to watch Jim Tarber work."

"I didn't like him. Not at all."

"And you know what else, dear? Right in the middle of all this interviewing he kept *flirting* with me . . . !"

"How'd he manage that?" (The sonofabitch. . . .)

"Well he started *playing* to me—like to an audience, you know? He was sort of saying, 'Watch how I twist these yokels around my little finger, baby'—like that. I think he even winked at me, when he was turning away from that Imogene girl."

"He's a merciless reporter, you know. They give awards for that, and he's won them."

"What sort of story do you think he'll write about tonight, Stanley?"

What indeed. How *would* that mordant cynical sardonic political shiv report on a gathering of the sort he had witnessed around the defrocked wedding cake in Stanley Stanhope's dining room? (CHRIST!)

"He'll kill it. The Guild, I mean. He'll puncture it with the rapier thrusts of his oh-so-clever remarks. Oh he'll be very deft, hon: Missus Murgatroyd won't even realize she's been stabbed. She'll clip out his column and paste it in her scrapbook beside all the yellowing articles about *Mis*ter Herkimer Murgatroyd and the *Anti*-Socialist League. But anyone with half a brain will see the Anthony Krumpit Guild portrayed as just another oddball political society. A branch'll probably spring up next week in Southern California. . . ."

"What if you don't let it happen?"

"I have no power at all over what happens in Southern California."

"For goodness sakes, Stanley, I mean what if you just *ignore* Tarber and build the Guild up the way you think it ought to be done!"

"One doesn't so easily ignore Mister James Tarber. The wire services often pick up his stuff—and they'd pounce on this sort of thing, the vultures."

"What would Anthony Krumpit do?"

The question cut deeply into his despair, effectively sheering it away and leaving him unburdened. If Anthony faced the twelve hundred armed with no more than his own interior disposition and *that* sufficed to turn back the Redcoat Horde, why indeed should Stanley fear James Tarber—or twelve hundred James Tarbers, for that matter? Interior disposition is mightier than the pen.

"To hell with James Tarber! Stanley Stanhope rides again!" (And Anthony Krumpit too: for in whomever a like spirit is found—truly kindred, truly eternal, always the best and only hope of all Mankind—in him the Hero of Riker's Field lives on!) "What happened later—after Tarber left?"

"Well—things just sort of resumed as they were before he came. Stanley, I don't think *you* were even *missed* . . . !"

"But did they talk about the *Guild*, Em? Did they . . . Sweet Jesus!—they didn't *elect themselves officers* or anything like that, did they? Because that crew could kill it—by *being* the Guild!"

"They *did* talk of meeting again—at Missus Murgatroyd's place. But the talk—her talk—was all about the threats of creeping socialism and I really think, from the gleam in her eye, that what she's actually interested in, Stanley, is in resurrecting the Anti-Socialist League, not in forming the Anthony Krumpit Guild."

He looked up to find Emily gazing at him with round solemn eyes.

"What is it?"

"Oh . . ." She began collecting the soiled dishes. "I'm so sorry things didn't work out the way you planned. . . ."

"It was my fault. I planned badly. Naively. The public appeal was a big mistake. The many will join after a dedicated few—a *selected* few—make the Anthony Krumpit Guild a thriving reality."

"Elitism, Stanley?"

"Oh God no. I don't want the Guild to be an elitist organization, Em. I want it to be of, by, and for the *People*."

"Stanley, that's what the U. S. Government's supposed to be."

"Precisely. And when the Anthony Krumpit Guild grows

larger—becomes national, Em—the U. S. Government will again be of, by, and for the People: in self-defense. The Guild will have served its purpose. It can then disband."

"Will it?"

"What? Why—of course. Why wouldn't it, once its aims have been achieved?"

"I don't know, Stanley. I guess I just can't imagine a nation-wide organization powerful enough to influence the U. S. Government voluntarily disbanding. I mean, would the John Birch Society or the S.D.S. or the A.D.A. or the Ku Klux Klan disband, if any of *them* were able to call the plays?"

"Emily, I am *not* attempting to build that kind of an organization! For Chrissakes! The Anthony Krumpit Guild is to be utterly and completely nonpartisan!"

"But really, Stanley . . . can any group of politically oriented people banded together for some kind of action *be* nonpartisan? And if it succeeds, *could* it disband?"

It was Stanley's turn to gaze at his wife. He felt his mouth open, but no words came forth. The thought would haunt his sleep that night.

Stanley was up before seven. In the kitchen, Bill was spooning a bowl of Wheaties into a sullen-looking mouth.

"What time do you have to be at the beach?"

"By eight o'clock." He concentrated on his breakfast—noisily, in the uncommon quiet of early morning. Stanley prepared himself a cup of instant coffee.

"What do you do there so early?"

"We work around. (Slurp, slurp.) We clean up, mostly. Saturday mornings it's the beach. We gotta rake up, pick up seaweed (slurp, slurp), bottles, paper cups—stuff like that. A lotta people come down on weekends. (Slurp.) They like it nice and clean. . . ."

(And you'd rather *rake sand* than work in the plant you may someday inherit?) "You might see your mother and Cissie there today. Does the bus go down there this early?"

"No. (Slurp.) Jerry Swenson picks me up. We work together. (Slurp.) He's got his own car now. . . ."

(Has he . . .) "Bill, about the motorcycle . . ."

"I know. (Slurp.) Mom told me." He was spooning in the last of the Wheaties with closer attention than was necessary.

"I'm sorry, Bill. I just didn't think the situation warranted—"

"That's okay." He scraped his chair in rising. "I've got to get my gear together. Jerry'll be out there any minute. 'Scuse me." He wiped his lips on the back of his hand and then Stanley sat alone in the kitchen, sipping his instant coffee and watching the morning sun pour into Billy's empty bowl.

How does one communicate with one's children?

Once it had been easy—effortless, in fact. Once his children had been . . . children, not these strange humanoids who sometimes seemed not *possibly* the offspring of him and Emily. And once he had been their father: he had talked to them, and they to him, freely and spontaneously and without the strange wall of sophistication each had now raised—Cissie even more than Billy. There was no "Oh Dad that's dumb" then. Once there were bicycles to help fix, tears to dry, birthdays to delight in with them. Once there were family outings, trips to the beach and the zoo and the movies. Once there were badminton games in the back yard and basketball tosses through the hoop mounted above the garage doors. And once—with dedicated regularity—there were the marathon games of Monopoly which occupied nearly every Sunday afternoon for years. What *ever* had happened, that those games had been discontinued?

The front door slammed. Billy had left the house for the tawdry charm of a painted casino. One day he would be leaving the house for good. Cissie, too. And Stanley would no longer have his children who somehow had ceased to be his children but whom he loved that way regardless. He would have had them, loved them, seen them retreat into their inexplicable aloofness (retreat from his love?) and finally he would lose them. Would he ever, he wondered, get them back?

He went upstairs. Morning sunlight filled the hall, and quietude the house. He went into Billy's room, hoping to find a clue to the mystery, a lead on which to base a plan to seize the initiative again and renew communication.

His son's bedroom was a pleasant clutter. Prominently displayed on the dressertop was an eight-by-ten-inch photo of Bill with Deborah taken at the recent Senior Prom. Then Stanley saw the small oval frame with a picture of him and Emily in it, and he was absurdly and profoundly touched.

But mostly there was merely the midden of an eighteen-year-old's existence: old movie-ticket stubs; sports magazines; tie clasps long unused; hair brushes almost too well used; six different brands of after-shave lotion; three paperback books; thirty-seven scattered cents in change; a broken key ring; a single shoelace. If there were clues among them, Stanley could not detect any.

He put a hand on the top drawer of the dresser but removed it immediately; he would not pry. But he wondered: would he be justified in looking into his son's wastebasket? (Don't spies do that, in embassies around the world?) By the time he reached the wastebasket he'd decided against it.

There was a colored folder on the floor where it had apparently fallen out of an already overflowing basket, and Stanley stooped to replace it. But the illustrated cover snared his attention: an obviously enthralled young man sat on a speeding motorcycle surrounded by an enormous blue sky. Across the top, in large yellow letters like an incantation, was YAMAHA, and below the spinning silvery wheels the simple phrase "Feel Free." He put the folder into his pocket. Somehow it might give him an indication, a lead. . . .

Stanley found himself staring at his own image in his son's mirror. It was then that he noticed the chromium peace pendant hanging there. Gently he lifted the emblem off the mirror-post and held it in his hand.

What the sweet Christ did it *mean* to Billy? Kids were far too prone to mistake ideals for knowledge: to confuse the way things ought to be with the very different problem of how to get them that way. Did they imagine they were the first generation to feel the stirrings of idealism and the only one ever to consider itself generous and honest and incorruptible? Stanley felt an anger rising within him. What right—what goddamn *right*—had Billy Stanhope to flaunt a demand for peace when he had no real idea (had he?) what efforts went into merely holding the world together, never mind getting its inhabitants to live peaceably! Stanley stuffed the pendant into his pocket—confiscated it, until he could decide whether his son had any inalienable right to wear such a thing.

He went downstairs to his den, opened the top drawer of his desk, and tossed both the peace pendant and the Yamaha brochure inside. Then he heaved an immense sigh, which all but emptied him.

Stanley Stanhope sat in his den and stared at the watermelon stain in his desk drawer. Through his open door and windows he could hear his wife and daughter and three or four other little girls happily loading the Studebaker with picnic lunches and beach gear, running in and out of the house and letting the screen door slam. Stanley would not be joining them. Emily understood. Cissie, the trip secured regardless, didn't care. It was nine-thirty when he heard the gruff voice from his kitchen.

"Em'ly, where can I find your goddamn husband—he wasn't at work."

"Mister Beardsley, I've told you before about using that language in front of my children—and other people's children."

"Well goddammit woman tell me where Stanley is so's I can use it on *him*."

"Mister Beardsley, this is *my* home and I won't have you —" But she gave up what she knew to be a hopeless battle. "He's in his den."

The Ordeal of Stanley Stanhope

Old Beardsley filled the doorway. At first he said nothing but only rubbed his mustache with his hand. Stanley closed his desk drawer, hiding the watermelon stain. He looked at Old Beardsley, but what he thought about was closely related to the watermelon stain: Was there a sort of *reverse* correlation to the Watermelon Correlative? Was the number of Patriots in a patriotic organization in *inverse* ratio to the purity of its intent and the sublimity of its accomplishment? For after all: Anthony Krumpit had charged the Redcoat Horde *alone*. . . .

"Lookit, Stanley . . ." But the old man only snuffled. Stanley folded his arms, leaned back into his chair until it squeaked. "You're gonna get yourself in a peck of trouble if you pursue this thing. . . ." He was actually waving a scolding finger at Stanley, who merely continued to stare at the handyman. Old Beardsley wiped his face with a red bandanna. "I know goddamn well what a full-page ad in our local rag costs—and I also know you can't afford this mad-ass scheme of yours." Stanley didn't say a word. Finally Old Beardsley took a deep breath and let it out with an air of reluctant decision. "And I can't let you do it, boy. I *won't*."

"*Won't* you, Mister Beardsley." Just then Emily came down the hall and Old Beardsley stood aside to let her into the den. She wore the shorts she could still wear in glory, and Stanley saw Old Beardsley take notice of the fact. (Get your libertinic eyes off my wife, you old bastard!)

"We're leaving, Stanley"—and she bent to kiss him, to what delight of Old Beardsley Stanley could only indignantly guess. "I imagine we'll be back by six or six-thirty, unless the traffic gets heavy."

"Okay, hon." (Get out—get away from those violating old eyes . . . !)

"Good day, Mister Beardsley." She waltzed prettily out, with Old Beardsley looking brazenly after her.

"Just how do you think you can stop me, Mister Beardsley?" (And just you goddamn *try!*)

Old Beardsley came over and sat on the edge of Stanley's

desk, placing his coarse paint-spattered overalls where recently Emily's powder-blue nightgown had been. "Listen, boy. I've been around a lot of years and I've seen a lot of things. Will you buy that?"

It was too much. "I do *not*, Mister Beardsley, consider you an authority on anything but fixing broken screen doors and the like."

"Also, I've been more kinds of fools, more times, than you even know the names of."

"I'll buy *that*."

"But I learn from my own folly, Stanley." He tapped his skull with a strong blunt forefinger. "Y'see, that's the *one way* I've never been a fool. Maybe the only one. . . ."

"I await your words of wisdom, O Multiple Fool."

"And I'm telling you plain as piss that what you're trying to do will not only fail, Stanley, but will ball up your own life in the process. And Em'ly's. And your kids'. Think of *them*, Stan, if you don't give a fuck about yourself." The Studebaker appeared outside the den windows. Emily tooted the horn and a car full of little girls shouted and waved excitedly.

"Mister Beardsley: Not that it's any of your business—as surely you realize it is not—but Emily is in full agreement with what I'm doing and supports me completely in this."

"God deliver us from women in love. 'Cause that's when sense goes out the window."

"And you, Mister Beardsley, are going out the door. The back one, if you please; I don't want the neighbors thinking you're front-door company."

"Heh-heh-heh-heh-heh. I could tell you stories about some of the back-door tactics of some of the front-door people in this town, m'boy."

"I don't care to hear them. I would very much like to be left alone."

"Can't do that, Stanley. Not as long as you insist on ruining your life."

"What makes you think you have a goddamn right to interfere in my life? You look after your own affairs and I'll look after mine. Is that clear, Mister Beardsley?"

"Waal, for one thing, you're Jock Stanhope's boy, and I was his friend. Now you may not like that, Stan, but it happens to be the truth. Jock isn't around any more, and I—"

"I do *not* need a stepfather and if I did I think I could make a better choice than *you*." Old Beardsley took out his pipe. It was apparently already filled for he lighted it immediately, making cumulous piles of a heady nutty aroma. "Look, Mister Beardsley: I know you were my father's friend, but that does not make you my friend. I know you've known me from the cradle but—"

"I even *made* your cradle. But don't worry, Stan—I'm not about to get maudlin about it. The fact remains, though: I did have a long and unusual friendship with Jock. Plenty of good times and experiences. . . ."

"I know. You used to whore around New York City together in the Roaring Twenties. So-called. . . ."

"*You know*—you don't know a goddamn fuckin' thing, so don't get flip. I'm trying to help you. Can't you at least try to understand that?"

"And can't you understand that I neither *need* nor *want* any help from you? Haven't I made that—plain as piss?" Old Beardsley calmly smoked his pipe, thoroughly at ease on the edge of the desk.

"Stanley, I gotta get you to abandon this Anthony Krumpit Guild nonsense. It's that simple. Now I'd *like* to reason you out of it, but if I can't . . ." (Puff, puff, puff . . .)

"You'll *what?*" Stanley laughed aloud at the thought of what Old Beardsley imagined he could do, but the laughter soured in his mouth. He was being childish; there was a better way to behave—a better way to confront the old man. "*You* call it nonsense. But only the day before yesterday—right out in my gazebo—you were saying that this Country needs *Patriots*. Well, Anthony Krumpit was a Patriot: a man with an interior disposition so strong and so profound that he overcame stupendous odds, Mister Beardsley, and not only saved this town we call 'home' but helped to secure the American Revolution, as well. And I do not believe that he paused to consider whether it was *reasonable* to charge that Redcoat Horde . . . !"

Calmly, the old man pointed his pipestem at Stanley. "You've been reading Hory Pool's fairy tale."

"I've been reading American history! And observing contemporary events, Mister Beardsley, which convince me that once again Patriots are needed to overcome stupendous odds. To reform America—to make it truly American again!—before it's too late. Well, Anthony Krumpit's dead and gone, yet he still lives, wherever and in whomever a like spirit is found, Mister Beardsley: truly kindred, truly eternal, always the best and only hope of all Mankind . . . !"

The old man winced. "That sounds like unadulterated Pool—Light Horse Horace at his galloping worst." He paused to knock his pipe out into Stanley's metal wastebasket. "None of it is true, Stan. Not a word of it."

"And all the other historians are wrong too, I suppose."

"Yep." He blew air through his empty pipe.

"I thought you said you wanted to be reasonable, Mister Beardsley."

"I do." He stuck his pipe into a shirt pocket under his overalls. "They're wrong—they're all dead wrong—and I can prove it."

"How."

"The proof's at my place. C'mon. . . ." He rose and started out of the den.

"I can't waste the time—I've got thinking to do, plans to make. . . ." (Go home, old man: just . . . go home.)

"What's the matter? Afraid I might be right? That I might be able to prove that old Pool-fool wrong?"

"Certainly not. I just haven't the time. And Emily's got the car. . . ."

"And I've got mine. Right out front, Stanley-boy. Unless

you're really *afraid* of the truth, that is. The . . . documented, historical truth. . . ."

"Did you say *'documented'*?"

"Tha's right. Heh-heh-heh-heh-heh."

"Let's go." (Let's finish this nonsense once and for all.)

Old Beardsley stood aside. "Back door or front?"

"Where in the world do you live, anyway?" They were
well down the Osterville Road but still within the Krumpit
town limits.

"As far away from people as I could get."

"Why out this way?"

"It's convenient. I do work in Osterville too, y'know."

"I didn't."

"You wouldn't."

"What's that supposed to mean?"

"Doubt you'd understand. It's your goddamn burgher
mentality. Keeps you from ever knowing how the other half
lives—and what's worse, caring."

"My, aren't we self-pitying today. . . ." They bounced
along, Old Beardsley's battered twelve-year-old Plymouth
taking every irregularity in the pavement. They turned down
the road to the town dump and the ride became even worse.
Where the rear seat used to be, the handyman's tools, paint
buckets, and myriad other bits of paraphernalia of his several
related trades rattled and clunked against each other and the
car. Hitting a pothole meant being subjected to a cacophony
as well as a jolt. "You might invest in new shocks, one of
these days."

"I like the feel of the road."

"Directly?"

"Trouble with you townies is, you're soft. Among other
things." They shot past the town dump.

"How much *farther?*"

"Coupla minutes. Keep it in your knickers, Stanley."

His house was set back a hundred feet from the road. Old

Beardsley grabbed the emergency brake and stopped the car at the rural mailbox with its faded metallic red flag upraised. Stenciled on the once-white box in black letters was A. BEARDSLEY. The old man got out to retrieve what looked like junk-mail. The car's engine throbbed noisily as he scowled through advertisements.

"What's the 'A' for?"

"What's that?"

"I was wondering what your first name was. You know, I can't even remember. . . ."

"That's 'cause nobody uses it anymore. It's 'Mister Beardsley' to my face and 'Old Beardsley' behind my back." He released the brake, shifted with a grind, and drove slowly toward the house. "The 'A' stands for Anton. My mother was an actress—a long, long time ago when theatre was still an art form. She named me after Anton Chekhov, for whom she had unbounded admiration. I had a brother named Constantin, after Stanislavsky, and a sister named Sarah, after Bernhardt. Does that surprise you?"

"Yes. Perhaps it shouldn't, but for some reason it does."

"It's your goddamn burgher mentality. You've conveniently pigeon-holed me in the 'town-character-and-handyman' slot."

"If anyone's responsible for the 'town character' reputation, it's your own clownish self."

"At least part of it has been in self-defense. . . ." He pulled the emergency brake again, and the car skidded to a halt among the weeds of his front yard. The house was in need of painting (the handyman has no time for his own repairs). Stanley noticed that the windows in the aging wooden structure had been moved up to the roof-line and ended a dozen feet above ground-level. The front door wasn't locked. The entryway was a blind hall with a short flight of wooden stairs leading up. The walls were painted a light serviceable green, the color of a public restroom. "You've never been here, have you, boy."

"You know damn well I haven't."

"Well, try not to be too shocked, will you." He pushed open the door at the top of the stairs and went in, leaving Stanley to follow. Stanley stopped short. Except for the high windows that pierced the room, the walls were lined from floor to ceiling with bookshelves, and the shelves were loaded with books. Stanley could only stare. "What's the matter? Isn't a handyman supposed to be able to read?"

"Yes of c— Where in the world did you *get* all these books!" Stanley walked to the shelf nearest him and looked at the bound volumes. The books in that particular section were all in German. Here and there he saw a familiar name. Goethe. Heine. Krafft-Ebing. Marx. Nietzsche. "Those belonged to my father. They're first editions, every one of 'em. About half the volumes in this room were his. He was a librarian by training—the first librarian the Krumpit Free Library ever had, by the way. He organized it. Later he went into the rare book business, working mostly through the mails. The other half of the volumes you see were actually acquired by your humble and obedient servant. I've even read a few of 'em, if you can believe that."

"In German?"

"I get along. My old man taught me the value of reading in the language a book was written in. Don't get flabbergasted now, Stanley, but I also get by in French, Spanish, and Italian, which my mother spoke fluently. Most of these are in the mother tongue, naturally enough." He picked a book off the shelf next to him; he held the volume as if it were a living creature. "Ever read Macaulay?"

"No, I'm afraid I haven't."

"Y'oughta read this, Stan: you're about ripe for it these days. I'll lend it to you, if you're interested." But he put it back on the shelf.

"What's . . . what's under us, if I may ask?" They were, after all, some dozen feet above ground-level.

"Storage, mostly. Tools and things. Second-hand this and used that. Stuff people throw out. Some of it comes in handy sometimes. I made a killing on old Tiffany lampshades a few years ago when that damn-fool craze started. I had dozens of 'em in storage. Same with brass cuspidors. Now I'm waiting for chamber pots to make a comeback—got lots of them, too."

"And the rest of the house?"

"Just my digs. A kitchen, a bathroom, and a bedroom. I eat in the kitchen, on that counter there—see?" It was a bachelor kitchen, not very well equipped. "You want a drink?"

"You know I don't drink."

"You may need one, after a while."

"What do you mean by that?"

"Have a seat." There were two armchairs, one by a window and another near a secretary that was set against the far wall flush with the bookshelves. "Have you forgotten why we came?"

"I guess I had." Stanley still hadn't gotten over his surprise.

"Waal—sit down, boy." The old man seemed a bit nervous suddenly. Stanley sat in the chair beside the window. He watched Old Beardsley remove a key from behind an end volume on one of the shelves beside the secretary, unlock the bottom drawer of the desk, move some leather-bound volumes aside, and finally come up with a thick notebook bound in blue plastic. Then the old man stood holding the notebook and looking solemnly at Stanley. "I want you to know . . ."

"Yes?"

Anton Beardsley looked very uneasy now. He turned abruptly and went into his kitchen, returning in a moment with a glass and bottle of Early Times, which he put onto a little table beside the other armchair.

"Stanley . . . I don't like doing this to you, I want you to know that. . . ."

"You spoke of proof. Documented evidence, I believe you said."

"You'll need some background." He snuffled, rubbed his

nose, shook his brush of a mustache. "To begin with, did you know that my family, on my father's side, goes back to Colonial times, right here in Krumpit?"

"I didn't. But so does mine. What do you suggest we do, join the D.A.R.?"

"Fuck the D.A.R. What I want to tell you is that a certain ancestor of mine, one Jonathan Beardsley, was a contemporary of Anthony Krumpit. In fact, he was his cousin. And he was also his best friend. Y'see they were both about the same age, and they grew up together—sort of like Jock Stanhope and me, except *we* weren't related. Waal, anyway, Jonathan had a little accident and his right leg got badly mangled. The only reason this is important is that when the war broke out in the 1770's, Jonathan Beardsley couldn't take part in it. His cousin Tony did though—as everyone knows. Jonathan later became a schoolmaster, right here in Krumpit. He taught here the rest of his life. This book here is a diary. . . ."

"Jonathan kept a diary."

"No, Stan. Tony Krumpit did. . . ."

Stanley felt his eyes were quite literally about to pop out of his head as he fixed them on the blue plastic notebook. "What are you saying . . . !"

"Y'see, when Tony went off to war and Jonny had to stay behind, he promised his crippled buddy that he'd keep him informed of the whole adventure. So, he kept a diary. Carried it with him right through the war. When he got back, he gave it to Jonathan. Waal, it's self-explanatory. It won't exactly jibe with anything you ever read in Pool's book or any other—except for dates and places, maybe. . . ." The old man brought the notebook to Stanley and laid it in his lap; then he turned his back and walked slowly over to the other armchair and sat down. Anton Beardsley uncorked the bottle of Early Times and poured himself half a tumblerful. "You're on your own, Stan. . . ."

Stanley Stanhope's hands trembled as he opened the notebook. The original pages of the diary were mounted between thin transparent sheets of acetate. The handwriting was small and swift and covered both sides of each sheet—for paper was well utilized in those days.

The man named after Anton Chekhov, the man who got along in German, French, Spanish and Italian, who hoarded junk and rare books, who boasted a scholar's mind and a sailor's vocabulary, brooded into his glass of bourbon in the shadows by the secretary. Stanley felt a lump forming in his throat as he turned his attention to Anthony Krumpit's diary.

EIGHT

Charlestown, Massachusetts
June 16, 1775

*D*EAR JONATHAN,

By the bleeding Jesus I do wish ye be here, old friend. In me cups especially I be sore in need of ye, dear coz. For ye should see the veritable clods with whom your Tony-boy must share his mess and days. 'Tis truly enough to send a body home to mother—be it not for certain difficulties awaiting your humble and obedient servant there in Krumpit-town, of course. How be Miss Nancy Primrose? Has her time arrived?

And of course, coz, how be ye, I do wonder? The leg, I mean. Damme but I do regret that accursèd incident at Burridge's farm—how it ended, I mean. For if 'twere not for that tragedy—that insane leap we did make from Burridge's hayloft—ye would be with me now for sure and certain, lad. But ah! I do often think of old man Burridge's buxom twin daughters (as do ye, no doubt!) and needs must smile at the episode, even tho' 'twas the very sad occasion of the mangling of your leg. If only ye did not have to *run* so far with the bones sticking out the way they were! Still, I suppose 'twas a good deal better than a blast from old Burridge's blunderbuss. But thank the Lord, Jonny, that your devoted cousin Tony was there to bear ye up as a living crutch. (And thank the Lord for that old bastard's failing eyesight, while ye be praying.) But ah! those twins, those buxom willing lovelies in the sweet hay on a spring night! 'Tis enough to make this soldier's bones ache for home. For the Burridge twins, at the least.

'Tis this soldier's business that urges me to take pen in hand. For a promise be a promise (save when made to a wench, of course) and 'tis past the time when yours truly should be telling ye of me adventures in this Great War, as I have indeed given ye word that I would, good friend. I propose herein to make entry of me observations about the War. About the next sixty days of it, I mean, for I've no intention to reënlist when me present three-month term be expired. By then the entire Primrose fracas should have settled down.

But now wouldn't ye think, coz, that the lass would have had the *decency* to move out of town? I know she has an auntie in Hartford. Ah, how pitiless women can be, lad—even the sixteen-year-olds the like of Nancy Primrose. Spring flowers on the outside, vipers on the inside. But ah! such lovely blooms, dear Jonathan! Who can resist the picking of them?

I cannot begin to describe to ye how many silly feminine hearts a shred of Continental blue can set to flutter. The country be filled with females fairly *acheing* to soothe and comfort injured Patriots. A case in point: but last week I did have a rare time with a most energetic lady over in Lexington. Her late husband, alas, was slain in a skirmish there earlier this spring. The good lady did take me in to tend me slight head wound (as I did tell her 'twas; actually I'd fallen down drunk the night before) and 'twas easy picking from that moment on. Ah, Jonathan! what I might achieve with but a *slightly* mangled foot!

It has been—what?—something more than a month since last I saw ye? Army life, dear friend and cousin, be one unending bore. How I do regret the folly of me enlistment— even tho' I did have to hie meself from Krumpit-town upon the blossoming-forth of the Primrose affair. (Why *didn't* the ungrateful wench go off to Hartford!) As I did tell ye when I left, I had full intention of joining meself to the militia of good Connecticut men which Captain Benedict Arnold was said to be recruiting at New Haven. I did miss Captain Arnold entirely—if ever he *were* in New Haven. So I did start northward after him. Well, 'tis not an interesting tale and I will not dwell upon it. Suffice it to say that, hungry to the point of starvation and with not a farthing in me trews, 'twas Major-General Israel Putnam's company I caught up. I did sign up with the company—in time for supper. I be with them yet. None too happily, to be sure, but stuck for another two months at the least. The wages be only somewhat better than the slop they do feed us. We have yet to see the War or hear a shot fired in anger, thank the bleeding Jesus.

If it be me own opinion of the War ye may be wanting, I do *not* believe that we can win it. For who will lead us? Old Put? A joke in striped trousers. Who will fight? The Continentals? Farmers and bumpkins all, as undisciplined as the redcoats be not. And then there be the Tories, lad— thousands of them, Loyalist to the core. I do give our woebe-gotten attempt at Revolution a year at the most, before King Georgie's lobsterbacks put an end to it.

Presently, Boston be under siege. We be quartered here

on the peninsula across the River Charles. There be not much we can do, tho'. If anything will happen, 'twill be up to the bloody British. The "siege" be a joke, Jonathan. Here we be in Charlestown, and there be General Howe in Boston getting all the supplies he needs through Boston harbour. Here we be, sitting on a river-bank making faces to the lobsterbacks on the other side who in turn make faces to us. Worst of all, we have been kept from the town—and hence from the solaces therein—for a fortnight now. Thus has the soldier ever suffered, e'en when not thrown into the ravenous jaws of battle, lad. I be so bloody bored, Jonathan.

Captain Arnold is said to be on Lake Champlain. Would I were with him. Surely 'twould be cooler there, at the least. By the Jesus, I must have missed him in Connecticut by mere hours! And now I have Old Put—and this sad state of affairs. Such, I suppose, be fate. But will nothing break this bloody boredom?

Cambridge, Massachusetts
July 10, 1775

Dear Cousin Jonathan,

Did I say boredom? It did end—for a while, at the least —on the morrow of the last entry in these pages.

We be on the Charlestown peninsula, if ye recall, and the redback Howe does get it into his head to break the so-called siege by attacking us—*us*, who did no more than make faces to the man! So the bastard leads seasoned *soldiers*, Jonny, against our bumpkin *farmers*. We met on Breed's Hill and also on Bunker Hill to the northwest. 'Twas horrifying, cousin: there was no way for me to leave without getting meself a musket-ball for desertion, I did realise, so I did have to wait with the bloody bumpkins to be shot like hogs in a pen. There be this big buffoon beside me, coz, and the idiot keeps looking up to see the redcoats charge. 'Keep your bloody head down, poxbox!' I tell him; but will he listen? He will not. But the greatest absurdity of all be none other than

Colonel Prescott, who goes about shouting 'Don't shoot until ye see the whites of their eyes!' Says I to meself: 'Be ye bloody *serious?*' Prescott be rattling his sabre and yelling about the whites of British eyes and the God-damned farmers, coz, do *dig in*—all save the big buffoon, who keeps looking up and finally gets the first British volley smack in the mug. And still our side fires not a shot! Never one to let an opportunity pass, I pull the bloody pulp of the big buffoon's face to me breast—to me white shirt, as that would show the blood the better—and I shout: "A hero has fallen! Avenge him, avenge him!" Then the second British volley comes—and this time the bumpkins answer. Me second opportunity be at hand, Jonathan. Before the redcoats can reload and as the smoke-pall from our own volley does fill the air, I do drop the big buffoon and stagger rearwards clasping me hands to me bloodied chest and bleating like a lamb. All the bumpkin farmers be far too busy to tend to me, but they let me pass to the rear, thank the Jesus.

Well, the battle did end as ye might have expected: the British now have Charlestown. But at a fearful cost to them for charging up those hills that way: some thousand casualties, of which perhaps a third must have paid the Final Price for that ludicrous spit of land. I do think less of Howe for it, frankly. The bumpkin farmers did surprising well, I must admit. Old Put, of all people, is said to be a hero. For meself, I value the big buffoon's services the most. But what was accomplished on either side? Charlestown be not strategic, and the British have Boston yet. The siege be neither broken nor lifted. If this be war, Jonathan, then let me say it be the most insane of pastimes of which human folly be capable.

We have now a Commander-in-Chief, by act of the Congress. He be one George Washington, of Virginia. He did take command of the Continental Army here at Cambridge-town today week. I cannot yet tell much about him, save that he lives like bloody King George himself and does appear far too soft for the impossible task the Patriots have set themselves. He rides about the town in a fine carriage and keeps aloof from the troops (not that I blame him for that). He's not the sort, I do fear, to turn farmers into fighting-men. He never smiles; I do think he has bad teeth. Why on earth the Congress chose this Virginian when they might have picked Captain Benedict Arnold for the job, I shall never know. The choice well illustrates the ineptitude of the political imagination in this country.

Cambridge
November 7, 1775

Jonathan—:

By the bleeding Jesus all we have been doing since September has been to play soldier-boy. I say "play," coz, for that be bloody all 'tis. Marching in Cambridge Common, up the street, down the street, and not even firing a shot because powder be scarce and does cost too bloody much to be wasted. And *talk!* Jonny ye would not *believe* the palaver. Old Put in particular does get wound up with the most incredible patriotic blather. So we spend our days Yankee-Doodling. The locals love it—and there might be some profit in it among the wenches—save we are kept *in barracks* of nights!

Ye may be wondering at this point why I be still here, in this bloody army. 'Twas true that me first enlistment did expire in August, and it be further true that your humble servant and cousin did have no intention whatever to reënlist. Yet I could not leave, dear Jonathan. For in the twelve weeks past, in that enforced fraternisation with these lowly bumpkins and unpolished farmers, I did learn an important and most valuable truth. Namely, that however much they attempted and desired, they simply could not, almost to a man, play cards. Yet *loved* to, Jonathan—that be the rub. Now the Continental pay be a pitiful small thing, 'tis true, but a penny from here and another from there, by the Jesus cousin it *can* add up. All of July and August did provide truly bumper days as an early harvest was gathered by *this* eager "farmer." Therefore I did patriotically reënlist for yet another three-month term.

'Twas a glorious summer, coz! There were a handful of small skirmishes with the lobsterbacks (I did manage to avoid every one of them) but army life was scarcely affected. Mostly the British did merely stay in Boston and we on the perimeters—keeping the siege, ye know. Redcoat or Patriot, it did seem a goodly summer on both sides. If wars must be fought, cousin, I do heartily recommend that they be waged in precisely such a manner. For why do nasty things, one to another?

Thanks to the pasteboards and to the devotion to that pastime by me comrades-in-arms, I did live the sort of life to which I do fervently believe I could easily become accustomed. I ate no army slop and tarried amongst the troops only long enough to get meself bankrolled regularly. During the heady month of August, in particular, I be convinced that I did live better than General Washington himself. Certainly I did get laid more often.

For 'twas then that I did make discovery (actually, I was *invited* to discover) a certain establishment in Cambridge-town not far from Harvard College. I should say that said establishment (I be sworn to secrecy concerning its identity, Jonathan) does cater to only the better classes of gentlemen in the town (tho' upon occasion it does break the custom by admitting a Harvardian or two). And the accumulated pennies of me comrades-in-arms made *me* a member of the better class, cousin. By then I did have me own rooms in the town and habitually went abroad in the fine civilian clothes which I had tailored to me. (Indeed, would I have been "invited to discover" the establishment had I persisted in going abroad in coarse Continental garb, as common as any soldier?)

But of that establishment, what can I tell ye! Amongst the other delicacies available there were, if ye can but imagine it, Jonny, actual French wines! How they did get there—*do* get there—I have not the slightest notion. Perhaps by way of Canada, despite the War, or perchance the establishment simply possessed a well-stocked cellar before these asinineous hostilities did begin. I have tasted Champagne, dear Jonathan, and I can report 'tis like mother's milk to me. 'Tis said that even General Washington does get an occasional bottle sent him. (What else he may get I truly cannot say.)

But it all did end in September, Jonny. When me own reënlistment and that of hundreds of others was a fact accomplished, *then* were the screws of discipline tightened. Surely 'twas upon General Washington's orders. Why the fellow be under the mad delusion that he can make an *army* out of his farmers! But I tell ye, he will no more make soldiers out of bumpkins than coaches out of pumpkins. Alas, no more freedom of the town for Tony; no more tailored clothes nor private rooms in the town; no more gentle bubbly evenings amongst the delights of the better-class establishment of Cambridge-town. But 'tis not the *worst*, Jonathan. Ah, no! Since September it has also been soldier-boy, soldier-boy and Yankee Doodle Dandy until I do feel I might retch at the sound of reveille and the mere thought of yet another day of Mother Washington's nursery for little tin soldiers. There will be no further reënlistment, by the Jesus. If 'twere not for the pasteboards and the knowledge that by their use I be storing up treasure against calamitous days, I do sincerely believe I would take to the beckoning hills. But it does go to show, does it not, cousin, that there be always something for which to live. The cards and me comrades-in-arms do succour me.

Yesterday week I did get a brief reprieve from Yankee-Doodling when I was assigned to a detail sent out to Concord to escort a payroll wagon in-coming. At Lexington I bid the lads fare-well, planning to meet them upon their return from Concord. Methought: I would pay me very dear respects to the lovely widow of Lexington who had so kindly tended me "head wound" this previous June—she who finished by tending to ever so much greater a need. I had no difficulty locating her house. Indeed, 'twould have been difficult *not* to find it, with that long line of Continental blue queued up outside it. Alas, I had not the time to wait me turn to pay courtesy to her. But it does the Patriot's heart good to see the citizens of Lexington doing their part for the war-effort and the Continental cause—even tho' that cause be hopeless.

The days do kill the spirit by small degrees, Jonathan; already I be losing interest in things—even in the card-playing. For of what use be money won, coz, if it cannot be spent? I do wonder whether I might be able to bribe me way out of the barracks, some snowy evening. Ah, for a gentle hour once again at the better-class establishment in Cambridge-town . . . !

> Boston
> March 31, 1776

Good cousin!

Your letter be received this day—but three months in reaching me. I be overjoyed to have word of ye, friend Jonathan.

So pretty Nancy had herself a man-child, eh? Alas, dear Jonathan, ye did not say whether the lad favours me or nay. It be a good thing, I do suppose, that old Clement Stanhope did marry the girl and that the boy has a name, at the least, and a home. I do remember the fuller very well—did we not used to throw stones at him as he gathered firewood for his vats? Still, I do suppose old Clem be solid citizenry, if rather taciturn. He has a good house and garden, anyway. The lad will have a reasonably set up "father" in him. And old Clem of course will have a pretty piece to warm his winter nights and the lengthening winter of his days—tho' how much heat he will produce in turn be quite a matter for speculation. Ye did not mention the boy's name; perhaps he had none yet. I will write ye a letter this day (tho' when 'twill reach Krumpit-town be anyone's guess). I must be sure to ask ye—besides what name the lad bears—to give me *very dearest* respects to sprightly Nancy Primrose—that be, Stanhope. By the Jesus Jonathan, that seems an unholy union, sweet Nancy and Old Clem. . . .

Ah me, dear friend and coz, this spring-time finds me *yet* in the army, and what be worse, in 'till the merry month of May. I can give ye no reason for the reënlistment; indeed, I can give *meself* no proper accounting. It did seem the only secure thing. The army has that effect on one—the "incarceration effect"—produced by months of being told when to act and what to do. And what to *think*, coz! Ye come to feel ye cannot function at all without the army. I did feel meself *above* such mind-shackling. Yet there I was, Jonathan, in line with the bumpkins reënlisting again.

There was an invasion of Quebec December last, led (as ye must have heard) by Captain Arnold, now Brigadier-General. Apparently he did plan nothing less than the conquest of Canada!—which mystifies me, coz, for if this Great War be to secure independence for we ourselves, why should Arnold be off conquering another colony? Be that not imperialism? Ah well, however it be, I meself at long last be resigned and even grateful to having missed Arnold in Connecticut a year ago. Can ye *imagine* fighting in the bloody snows of Quebec in deep December, lad? Even General Washington has sense enough to go into winter quarters.

I have new respect for our General, I must candidly admit. He has . . . a certain craftiness, shall I say? I witnessed same but a fortnight past, in the manner by which he did force the lobsterbacks out of Boston. Now 'twas plain even to General Motherwash that he could not throw his bumpkin farmers against the lobsterback garrison in Boston with any chance whatsoever of courting success. So he got his cannon to Dorchester Heights, which o'erlook the city. The British very quickly decided they were in inauspicious position. General Howe did evacuate Boston on the 17th of this month, and General Washington marched in at his leisure. Nothing really risked and an entire city gained. Yet it cannot be called a great military victory, cousin, for indeed there was no battle.

With all the troops here assembled, I had high hopes of lucrative pasteboarding. But 'tis not to be, for the word be out already: we are to leave Boston and hasten to New York, there to defend that city from the expected British assault. Already, 'tis said, the lobsterbacks crawl over the sands of Long Island. But surely 'twill take Howe all summer to mount an offensive against New York city—and me enlistment does expire in May, dear Jonathan.

I shall not be sorry to leave Boston. Methinks not even the British were. The weather be atrocious here, Jonny, and the women worse. I be still under the command of Major-General Israel Putnam, who be now preparing us for the journey to New York with all the fervent speechifying of a Romeo for his first Juliet. He wears heroics like a uniform these days. Methinks Old Put sincerely loves the War. Generals be dangerous people, it looks to me.

Would that we be passing close to Krumpit-town, dear friend! But I do fear that we must take a more circuitous and westward route, for GW be not prepared to toot his bumpkins any more a fortnight hence than a fortnight past. But spring be in the air, lad—even in frigid Boston!—and I do feel the primal sap begin to flow anew and a glory rise within me that be entirely something other than what Old Put does feel. I do wonder how the wenches in New York city be, this sweet re-borning spring?

New York city
August 9, 1776

My dear coz,

'Tis me birthday to-day. Age of 23, by the Jesus. But 'tis not to be termed a happy day, alas, for not only has the army become *work*, dear Jonathan, but a trap as well. And 'tis Tony-boy who be caught fast.

Since *late June*, coz, we have been set to work barricading this city of New York. We be stationed at the very brunt-point of any attack the British will mount: smack at the western tip of Long Island, at Brooklyn Heights. There be no escape. From the first of this month General Washington has ordered that all troops remain at their posts without exception. Old Put struts about while your humble and obedient servant does shit his trews. 'Tis conservatively estimated that Billy Howe has 30,000 lobsterbacks gathered on Long Island. The worst part of this entire bleeding-Jesus business, Jonathan, be me own realisation that I did *freely put meself* in the midst of this forthcoming hellfire.

I know I did swear off further reënlistment in this most lost of causes. But to understand me folly, coz, ye must consider the situation as 'twas here in April and in May—especially in April, when spring was upon the city and all of New York was receiving us as *heroes*, Jonathan. And the whore-houses, Jonny! New York be a veritable place of pilgrimmage for the devoted adherents to that oldest of religions. None have I found, 'tis true, of the *calibre* and *gentility* of the Cambridge establishment (New Yorkers being by nature more crass) but in numbers alone, dear Jonathan, the houses astound one to the point of stupefaction. Why, 'tis a major industry here.

But I must needs explain to ye the reason for me *fifth* reënlistment. When I tell it ye, I do believe that ye will agree that 'twas an entirely reasonable decision that I did make. *Then.*

'Tis obvious that the mere abundance of houses of pleasure alone would not suffice to keep me in Continental blue. But look ye, coz, a bit more closely at the situation as 'twas at the beginning of April. Continentals were pouring in—more than 10,000, Jonny! Now coz, I did sit meself down and ponder: '*Surely* there be opportunity here for a bright lad of proven enterprise and ingenuity.' The pasteboards were not truly feasible for *optimum* success, for I might work but a minimum of the 10,000 and would profit but little more than I did in Boston. Nay, coz, among this horde the opportunity lay not in cards. It lay in *lays*, it did not take me long to realise. For consider, coz: was not the combination of 10,000 bumpkins in a city of whore-houses a natural opportunity all but crying out for the deft hand of an *entrepreneur?*

Me first task, of course, was to assume a position of absolute control over the projected commerce (I did nearly say "intercourse"). And Jonny, 'twas as easy done as falling into bed with someone the like of sweet Nancy Primrose. Attend. Immediately I did spread the rumour of rampant disease raging amongst the houses of pleasure—a fabrication which did circulate amongst the troops in less than 24 brief hours, Jonathan! Me own reputation was secure enough amongst Old Put's company that the lads came first to your humble servant, cousin, to seek me advice. I did solemnly promise to investigate. (What do ye suppose they thought I'd do—catch the clap for them?) Of course, all I did was sample the increasingly empty whore-houses for the remainder of the week. By the following week the madames of the city were wailing in woe, Jonny, so empty were the houses. I then sent word to the leading proprietresses that I had quick solution to their financial grievances, and a meeting was quickly arranged. Me proposition was direct in its simplicity: I would personally clear their respective establishments for Patriot patronage at the tariff of one shilling per Continental—otherwise they could go on entertaining empty houses.

Well, Jonathan, as ye can imagine, the wailing did *worsen*, but your humble servant did hold his stance and at last the good madames (sound business-women all) did capitulate, tho' not altogether good-humouredly. Those who did not, made do without Continental trade. For I did forthwith draw up a list of "safe" houses and had the sheet distributed amongst the troops with me compliments. I was a minor hero for it, I do not mind telling ye.

But large profits be not so easily raked in, lad. For ye must realise that the madames of New York be not the most trustworthy of personages and would have cheated poor Tony blind, had I but let them. So, I did set counters at the whore-house doors—street urchins firmly in me own employ. I did pay them well to keep them loyal. The lads did serve me faithfully, staying at their posts 'till dawn's early light, if need be. Many of the madames did attempt a bit of "inaccurate accounting," but me urchins caught them every time. And I, in order to encourage the accuracy of their count, did both check their tallies against that of *other* urchins and did reward them liberally each and every time an "error" was turned up—which for a while was daily, those black-hearted madames being the greedy grasping creatures that they be. But the profits *rolled in*, Jonathan, with little labour on me own part save receiving the tallies of me urchins and the payments from the madames. Can ye wonder, coz, why I did reënlist at the end of May?

But fate, Jonathan—fate and the slow determined grinding of the army millstone—did your Tony in. Towards the end of June word did reach General Washington that *there be disease in the whore-houses* of New York city! Me very own rumour, coz—ten weeks after I meself had launched it! Well, what could Mother Washington do? He could not face the British with an army racked with disease and panicked by worry. So, lad, all the troops were ordered to remain at stations *and the houses were declared off-limits!*

I could have wept, dear cousin—methinks I did. And to *think* of the *good* I did do: employing countless street urchins; considerably raising the morale of the troops; even, coz, teaching the madames of New York perhaps their first lesson in honest accounting. But 'tis all done and gone now. The houses will survive: were they not here before the Patriots arrived? The Patriots too will survive—long enough to be scattered by the British. Ah, but Jonny, 'tis the street urchins for whom I do feel heartfelt sorrow: *they* be cast out once more into the gutters with neither victuals nor income. I meself did clear £15,000.

Well, 'twas but a few days later that the Declaration of Independence was proclaimed, in feeble attempt, I do suppose, to stiffen the Patriot spine. Methinks personally that the bleeding Congress might have waited 'till we had won a bloody *battle*.

Old Put does arise at dawn to gaze eastward with a spyglass. I know not what course others may take, but as for me, 'twould be quick across the East River, had I half the chance. GW's reason has fled him, and I do not wish to be fodder for his illusions. He has become incapable of coming up with a viable alternative to the mass slaughter which will surely occur.

For consider but one obvious, rational alternative, coz: if he does truly believe that the whore-houses of New York be direly infected, would not the *logical* strategy then be to let the British *have* the bloody city so that *their* troops might be paralised with disease? *Then* might the Patriots attack and decimate the redbacks. But no, 'twill not be done that way—and I'll tell ye why, Jonathan. 'Tis because the generals and the politicians would not fain give credit to the whores of America for securing the Independence so grandly proclaimed. For how would *that* look in the history-books, lad? 'Tis those bleeding glory-mongers in the Congress and the general staff who want to hog the whole bloody show—no matter how much common soldier's blood be spilled out upon Brooklyn Heights! This, Jonathan, *when the whores could win it for us without firing a shot*—as Benedict Arnold took Fort Ticonderoga! If only the God-damned whores *were* infected . . .

Somewhere east of us the British Lion crouches, and one morning before the month be out, 'twill spring into view in Old Put's spy-glass. I cannot swear that I will see me 24th birthday, or ye these pages. I will wrap this volume in thick greased paper, friend, and inscribe upon the package your name and address. If perchance I do fall, it may yet reach ye.

Bless—I say *bless*, Jonny, the mangled leg that keeps ye from the fate which beckons to your humble and obedient Tony.

And if ye could, dear Jonathan—hear, hear what may prove me parting request, made to me dearest friend: sometime, should the occasion arise or should ye be able to bring it about, would ye lay the lovely Nancy for me? It be me dying wish, good chum; ye know I would do the same for ye.

Farewell, then—if this be the end of it all—good friend and cousin and companionous lecher . . . !

> Somewhere in Pennsylvania
> November 15? 1776

Dear friend,

By the bleeding Jesus, Jonathan, these be times to try men's souls. I had even to thaw the ink by the camp-fire in order to write. We travel through the black Pennsylvania forests like wolves in the night, with none other than Lord Cornwallis riding to the hounds.

How can I begin to describe the debacle of New York! Israel Putnam disgraced himself with his posturing incompetency, and Mother Washington did find himself thoroughly outfoxed and outmanoeuvred by General Howe, who flanked us on both sides and hit us up the middle as well, cutting through our lines like so much butter on that August day.

I comprehend not how we did escape New York—how in unholy hell Howe did *allow* us to escape. For the lobsterbacks *had* us, coz: backsides against the harbour and the river. Yet GW got us (what did remain of us) safely across the East River under cover of darkness. Some of us had to *swim*, lad. 'Tis a good thing I had wrapped me diary in the greased paper.

Howe did chase us across the River Hudson as well. Then Lord Cornwallis was sent against us, at a most unlobsterlike pace, forcing us clear across New Jersey, the Delaware River, and into these bloody Pennsylvania woods, wherein we still encamp, our asses and our brains frozen into inactivity. We cling together for warmth and out of fear, not out of any blathering patriotism.

The only gain has been silence from Old Put, who dares no longer speechify after his ludicrous failure at Brooklyn. And the loss? New York city and very likely the Continental cause, which I can in no way see being salvaged, Jonathan. Aye and one thing more was lost. Somewhere on the muddy bottom of the East River lay me wooden chest, containing £15,000.

Someone has the mess-fire begun now. Soon 'twill be breakfast-time. Melted snow, I fear. At best, damp flour-cakes. Shit—the ink has once more froz

Philadelphia
January 15, 1777

Good coz!

At last some good has come out of this War—for your humble Tony, I mean. I have Old Put's incompetency to thank for it: GW will not have him about when large scale operations be afoot, so we be stationed the winter at Philadelphia.

GW has not even had the decency to go into winter sequestration as of this late date and instead has been harassing the British (who at the least be gentlemen enough to observe such niceties) first at Trenton—on Christmas night, Jonathan! —and then later at Princeton, both of which the bumpkins actually captured.

Philadelphia be securely ours, coz, and our "duty" be mostly parading about rather informally on order to demonstrate the Patriot presence. 'Tis an easy life, and I have reënlisted, for a three-year term this time. 'Tis not so foolish as it may seem, for the rebellion will not last beyond next summer, and the reënlistment did get me in good standing with Old Put, who seems to weep at such things. Ah well, each to his own madness.

Let Mother Washington chase across frozen rivers after

Hessians to his mad heart's content, cousin: your Tony does prefer the warmth and conviviality of Madame Sally's. Would that we could sample its delights together this very evening! It be an institution the like of which I have found nowhere else, lad. Not even the establishment in Cambridge can match the breadth of *choice* which Sally can offer the war-weary and world-fatigued. True, there be no French wines at Madame Sally's. But there be French *women*, Jonny—and Dutch, and German, and Italian, and Greek, and *Oriental*, lad, and West Indian—I have not as yet concluded a complete inventory, but I be pursuing the task with utmost diligence, coz, and hope to render ye a full accounting before the winter be out.

Me evenings at Madame Sally's have forced me to re-activate the faithful pasteboards (pleasures there do not come cheaply) and as usual, the cards fail me not. Madame Sally, alas, permits no gaming in her salons, so I must deal the pasteboards strictly amongst the far less affluent troops. *But*, lad: we be getting paid these days in scrip, which even the local merchants will not oft-times accept—tho' we be protecting their bloody hides. Luckily, Madame Sally be most generous to negotiate in the bastard currency, yet she cannot easily dispose of it and hence must charge a "surtax" of sorts upon the already taxing costs of the pleasures of her establishment.

The evenings at Madame Sally's be necessarily limited then, dear cousin. Aye there be other women in the city—young girls, too, all of whom, everywhere, do respond with some degree of favour to the uniform. Yet for some reason I cannot fathom, Jonny, they do appeal to me less and less the more time goes by. Also, I be less inclined to undertake the endless lies and cajolery so often needed to bed the wenches. I be less inspired, really. More and more, good Jonathan, it be the high professionalism of Madame Sally's staff that I do seek. There be something to this I do not like in me, but I cannot understand it. It seems that I have lost something, somehow, somewhere, but I cannot imagine what, or how, or where. Yet read me well, coz: 'tis not the morbid sounds of repentance I be making. But 'tis the softer sound of wonderment, I do suppose, as at a dream one has—yet does confuse with reality in an unguarded moment. . . .

But I will spend this evening at Madame Sally's ('twas in the cards!) and all will be well in Philadelphia, if not in this sad entire world. Somewhere this night in the wilds of New Jersey, Mother Washington will gather his frozen chicks about him and feed them the sorry grain of his mad delusions. But that be *his* problem—and theirs. 'Twas not I who began this War. And coz, I be content to fight the remainder of it right here in Philadelphia—at Madame Sally's.

Penn's Woods
April 30, 1777

Dear friend and cousin,

'Tis in GW's own camp I do find meself, lad—more a prisoner of this bleeding War, methinks, than a soldier in it. 'Twill be May on the morrow, and the good weather will bring battles and death as surely as 'twill bring flowers and flies.

I did not spend the winter in Philadelphia, Jonathan. I did not know the pleasures of Madame Sally's place, as I had so longed to know them. GW did order Old Put to Princeton in January. There be a college in the town, filled with blue-nosed boys who cannot hold their ale, and once the Continentals did arrive the wary townsfolk did lock up their daughters (who were not endangered by the blue-nosed lads, apparently). Methinks the damned Princetonians would fain have had the bloody British in their midst than we poor miserable Continentals.

'Twas but yesterday week that I did get the chance to leave that pox-hole, and I be indebted once again to Old Put—tho' he thinks 'twas *I* who did serve *him* (and the bloody Patriot cause as well).

The occasion was an urgent message to be delivered to none other than Old Motherwash himself. 'Twas from one of our spies in New York city and did inform of a plan of General Howe to land an army in southern Pennsylvania this summer. He's to sail up the Chesapeake Bay after coming round from New York. The courier from New York came ill into Princeton. The message, of course, needed be relayed postehaste to General Washington. But with the return of warmer weather General Cornwallis' lobsterbacks were again acrawl about New Jersey. Getting through to Philadelphia was said to be a risky affair. (In fact 'twas not: I saw not a single redcoat or Loyalist in the passage, tho' I did leave in broadest daylight.) Old Put did call for a volunteer to replace the courier, and your humble Tony did step forward without hesitation—face screwed into selfless valour, lad, chin stuck out in fearless determination. It meant a chance to get to Philadelphia, Jonny; your Tony would gladly risk a few redcoat musketballs for the chance to loll again at Madame Sally's!

'Twas not to be. A Continental guard did stop me just outside the city. When I did mention an urgent message for General Washington, I was escorted to his headquarters—northeast of the city. I never did get to see the Great Mother himself but had to surrender the billet to an aide. Well, methought, 'twill be simple enough to head for Philadelphia before returning to Old Put at Princeton. But Jonathan, at times the gods be against us. For even as your humble cousin was riding through New Jersey and hastening on his very determined way to Philadelphia, to General Washington and to Madame Sally's (not necessarily in that order), an emissary from GW was already riding to Israel Putnam with another message: Old Put was to move out immediately and take charge of the defenses of the highlands above the River Hudson. I meself, Jonathan, was re-assigned then and there to the Headquarters Company!

Tomorrow 'twill be May. In the streets of Philadelphia young lasses will be blossoming like flowers. Last night I did dream of Nancy Primrose. How she must by now be tiring of her old man! Ah well. By end of summer Generals Howe and

Cornwallis will have put an end to GW's mad schemes and we can then return to the pursuit of our own happiness, rather than this revolutionary idiocy. We poor soldiers will go home again. And I to Krumpit-town, dear cousin. I fancy that the exquisite Nancy be all the better for a couple years' experience, and I shall look forward to returning, dear Jonathan, with the very fondest of expectations.

Valley Forge, Pennsylvania
Christmas Day, 1777

Good friend and coz.

By this time ye would have heard for sure and certain about this summer's turning of the War—this tragedy of errors, this comedy of incompetency. Ye would have heard by now of Brandywine and Germantown, no doubt, but ye could not know the worst, dear Jonathan, unless ye yourself had laid your unbelieving eyes upon that pair of parodies of warfare. Only then might ye comprehend what a bad joke of a Commander-in-Chief we have in Mad George Washington. By the bleeding Jesus, Jonathan: if we cannot have General Arnold let us have General Gates as our Commander-in-Chief! What Gates did to Burgoyne at Saratoga he might well do to Cornwallis and Howe in Pennsylvania. Or at the very least *lose gloriously*. But must we go down in ignominy led by Bad Joke Georgie?

Howe's lobsterbacks came at us up the Chesapeake Bay, as expected. Well our Commander-in-Chief did prepare himself for Billy Howe, 'tis true. But damme, coz, Mother Washington did allow Cornwallis to flank us to the right as Howe attacked head on. 'Twas a complete rout—and we did suffer a thousand casualties in the very bad bargain. And Billy Howe took Philadelphia.

Now wouldn't ye think, Jonny, that Old Motherwash would have had the sense to go off and lick his wounds and give his bloodied bumpkins a bit of rest? But no, lad: 'twas back to the fray without a by-your-leave.

In desperate folly Mad Georgie led us against Germantown. Oh he had it planned, Our Georgie did. He did deploy us in four columns against the lobsterbacks. There was, that day, one of those October fogs which do arise in these parts. I meself was glad of it, for it made it all the easier for me to slip to the rear of the column I was in. Methinks Mad Georgie was glad of it as well, for it did mean that his four columns might slip up close to the redcoats before being discovered. Well, Jonathan, the bumpkins did surprise the British, 'tis true. Of course not quite as much as they did surprise themselves when in the fog one column of bumpkins did begin to fire upon another—doing an excellent job of alerting the redcoats in the process. I will say this much for the bumpkins: they have a fit and proper commander.

Mad Motherwash did lead us to this place to-day week. 'Tis called Valley Forge, and we be quartered here for the winter now. If General Howe has any sense he will come after us and put an end to this revolutionary farce before New Year's Day.

Christmas last, Mad Motherwash did lead his bumpkin farmers against Trenton; but I can assure ye he will lead them nowhere to-night. 'Tis bitter cold in this God-forsaken fastness, and we have nothing *near* what a winter's sojourn here will demand by way of provisions. I would fain be with Old Put up in New York State. 'Twould be no warmer there, but at the least we did always get our bellies full in Israel Putnam's company. One way or t'other. . . .

Madame Sally's
Philadelphia
March 11, 1777

My dear Jon-Nathan:

'Tis fed up I be with the entire Revolution, and, quite simply, I have quit it. Give me the sweet sanity of Madame Sally's place, any day.

Valley Forge, dear friend, was as frigid as must be any of the great northern glaciers. Never have I known such *intensest* cold, Jonny, such bone-numbing and unspeakable frozenness. There were not enough food, blankets, *clothing*, shoes, even. And then death and disease did set in, as if GW's madness were not enough to bear. Had Bad Joke Georgie but a smattering of humanity he would have led those bumpkins down into Philadelphia in surrender. But every vestige of humanness has fled GW along with his reason, Jonny. In memory I see the madman yet: cape tight about his shoulders and pacing in the snow totally absorbed by the creak and crunch of his own bootsteps. *As men died about him*, Jonathan, as they never had in battle! Indeed, 'tis old Generalwash who has become the enemy.

I did me best to see things out. The pasteboards were returned to duty: for food (what little there was of it), for clothing, for *rags for me feet*, cousin! Yet, I might have stuck things out if 'twere not for that bleeding-Jesus of a Hun. I swear 'tis true—a veritable Hun!

This Hun—Baron von Steuben be his handle—did arrive at Valley Forge in the beginning of the last week in February. There we be, Jonathan, half dead and the other half dying, minds boggled by despair and asses frozen by the cold, and GW sets the God-damned Hun *drilling us in the snow*— marching us, coz, back and forth, in muskets and back-packs —as if we be in the bloody Prussian army! Need I tell ye, good friend and cousin, that your humble Tony did find such behavior the last bearable degree of insanity?

On the last day of the month, there did arrive a supply shipment from God knows where: food, clothing—medicinals, even. And oddly, a payroll! The delivery came via sled, pulled by a sturdy pair of mares. We had not seen a horse in months, Jonny—we had eaten the few we had, including the General's. Well, I did leave behind the food and the medicinals. God knows the bumpkins needed them. I took the better mare, tho' it meant riding bare-back. And what use for money had those farmers at Valley Forge? 'Twas not scrip, lad, but real gold and silver. There were no shops at

Valley Forge, and your humble servant would truly have need of such monies in Philadelphia. Look at it thusly, coz: if the payroll had been distributed to the bumpkins—and because they had no place to spend it—I would have won it all from them anyway. Did I not, then, by me decisive action, relieve them of the embarrassment of loss and meself of the needless time and effort 'twould have taken to accomplish the inevitable?

It be pleasant here at Madame Sally's. That good woman, who did remember me from better times, did graciously take me in. As a paying guest, of course. Philadelphia be yet in British hands, but Madame Sally's, Jonathan, be neutral ground. It be share and share alike at this establishment ('tis all the same to the whores, after all) and I have e'en become quite friendly with some of the gentlemen in red. Society in general, Jonathan, might learn a good deal in tolerance from the whore-houses of the world.

I was not at Madame Sally's a week when I did notice that me funds were dwindling away at an alarming rate. It did occur to me then, Jonathan, that the monies which had come with the supplies to Valley Forge might *not* have been payroll-funds, after all. For if 'twere meant for wages, why would not the usual Continental scrip have sufficed? And why would not the sum have been considerably more? The thought did then occur to me that *perhaps* the monies were meant for the purchase of other supplies. I would not have taken such from those miserable bastards. So, I did feel bad about the gold and silver confiscation I had made upon leaving their wretched company.

But it did just so happen, coz, that through one of me redback acquaintances here at Madame Sally's (one Captain Reginald Morehouse by name) I did learn of an active little sideline in which the Captain and a few other officers be engaged: the selective pilferage of British provisions and their subsequent sale throughout the city. I did see immediately a way out of me own financial bind!—as well as a way to help the suffering bastards of Valley Forge, of course.

As I did point out to Captain Morehouse, the Continental Army would pay far more for certain commodities than would the house-wives and back-door merchants of Philadelphia. Food and clothing and medicinals, I did suggest. And 'twas obvious to the bright Captain, of course, that an American would be necessary to serve as go-between—and that a modest remuneration for such service would be only reasonable. Thus the bargain was struck: Captain Morehouse to provide the supplies, your humble Tony to find the buyers.

'Twas from Madame Sally herself that I did acquire (for a sort of "consultant's fee," I do suppose 'twould be termed) a list of prospective Patriot financeers in Philadelphia. 'Twas to these noble gentlemen that I did present meself: as a man sent upon this "hazardous duty" for the Revolution's sake by a Patriot "cabal" the identity of which, I did inform them, I was not at liberty to reveal. And they did *believe* it, coz—for such be the insidious illness of patriotism that the mental faculties be o'ercome by blinding emotion. Well, 'twas for a good cause, don't ye know. (I will not reveal *which!*)

Ah, Jonathan, 'tis a beautiful operation! Reginald provides the booty, the financeers not only pay for it but do see to its distribution, and we all of us do profit. So smoothly does the operation run, in fact, that when I did suggest to Reggie that I be allowed a small five per-cent discount on me purchases from him, he did agree without demurral. This does make for a very tidy profit, coz, as I have been steadily raising me margin of profit from the financeers from 10 to 20 per-cent, pleading an increase in expenses. Me profit runs currently at £2,500 the week.

But I do fear that me good friend Reggie Morehouse be getting somewhat suspicious concerning exactly how large me own cut of the pie be. Methinks 'tis me life-style here at Madame Sally's which did alert his suspicions. Perhaps I should not have engaged the grand suite with the private garden and the weekly change of "maids." And yet why not? For does not the successful businessman deserve the rewards of his labours?

Well, I shall not bother me head about Captain Morehouse.
He will do naught to curb his own considerable income from
our joint operation. As for life-styles and such, if the mutton-
eater has not yet learned to enjoy life, 'tis but his own bloody
fault. On this point Madame Sally does agree with me wholeheartedly, tho' she does but seldom take sides. Now if I can
but get her to change me sheets a bit more often, I will have
near everything a man could desire in this world, dear Jonathan. The army, cousin, was never like this.

Madame Sally's
June 12, 1778

Ah, cousin,

Reggie Morehouse did bring bad news to-day: General
Howe has resigned his command and Sir Henry Clinton has
been appointed Commander-in-Chief of all the British forces
in North America. Clinton be of stiffer lip and harder nose
than Howe, according to Morehouse. Reggie says Sir Henry
did fight at Bunker Hill and at Long Island and in the South
—at Charleston, methinks 'twas. The new commander does
see no value in keeping Philadelphia British, the Captain tells
me. There be no strategic value to the city, he does feel, and
an uprising of Loyalists which General Howe did expect has
never materialised. Lord Cornwallis be Sir Henry's second in
command, and tho' 'tis said Cornwallis does oppose the evac-
uation of Philadelphia, Reggie Morehouse be convinced that
General Clinton will have his way. And when the British
leave, Jonathan, their supplies go with them—and me own
business ends abruptly.

I have already economised by moving out of the grand
suite and into humbler quarters here at Sally's place. And to
show the pettiness of men, dear coz, what did Reggie do but
immediately move into me vacated quarters—and he with but
a week or two to stay in Philadelphia. Sal and I had a good
laugh about it. Of course she did laugh the louder. She could
well afford it: that suite does rent for £50 the week (services

included). Had I but known that the scoundrel Reggie wanted the suite, I would fain have kept it. For me purse be not flat by any means, good cousin. I have got me another wooden chest—quite a larger one this time—and in it, friend, be some £30,000. I will return to Krumpit-town in a golden carriage, coz. And sweep that fragrant Nancy Primrose off the fulling-mill floor. Be *that* any place for such a blossom?

There be *more* disturbing news. Sal did take me aside to whisper it me. How she got the information I can but guess, tho' her methods be many and her contacts legion. Last month, she tells me, Brigadier-General Benedict Arnold did join General Washington at Valley Forge. Naught but raucous revolution can come of that, I do fear. Sally did also inform me that France be now in open alliance with these united States.

And when General Clinton pulls his redcoats out of Philadelphia, where go I? Methinks 'twould be best to find General Israel Putnam again, wherever he might be. I shall have to enquire of Sal.

Madame Sal's
July 4, 1778

Dear Jonathan,

Philadelphia be in American hands once more. I did awake late one morning last month to find the British gone and none other than General Benedict Arnold in charge of the city. He does rule it now as military commander, appointed by General Washington.

A few days after Arnold's arrival, I did find meself summoned by Madame Sally to the reception chambre at ten o'clock in the morning. When I did see the guard there—four stalwart Continentals, coz—I do confess that I did feel a sickening within me. I was duly informed that General Arnold did want word with me. Sal's face revealed naught but fear.

When I was ushered into General Arnold's office, there

stood three of the bigger financeers with whom I had so long done business. They did stand sternly by, grim in banker's black, and Jonny, I did fear the very worst: the firing-squad. Had me great heroic act of provisioning the Continental Army been *misunderstood?* Ah, dear cousin, the very opposite proved to be the case. The worthy gentlemen had commended me good actions to General Arnold.

There did follow one of those stupid little ceremonies of official thanks, then the financeers were shown out. General Arnold did shut the door to his office, walk to his desk, look out his window, then finally, coz, he did walk to a table across the room where he poured a whisky which he did *bring to me!* I did accept it, wordlessly, lad, as ye might imagine, then the General's laughter did fill the room. Still he laughed, even as he went to sit behind his desk. I did attempt a smile—not too successfully—and he did but laugh the more. He did laugh, in fact, until tears formed in his eyes. "Drink up," said he, "I've need of ye, lad!" And by that time, Jonathan, I did sore need a drink.

A most perceptive man, General Arnold. He had seen a certain "managerial ability" in your humble cousin, Jonathan, and did want to utilise it—to *both* our profits, said he. Well, coz, the details be both lengthy and involved. Suffice it to say that General Benedict Arnold does also favour the higher style of life, which, as any of us who do pursue such an end may testify, does consume an alarming amount of monies.

'Twas over a second drink that General Arnold broached his plan. As military commander of the city, Arnold had closed the shops on what he did announce to be a "temporary" basis. A "partnership" was then formed amongst certain notables and merchants of the city (Loyalists all, I do suspect) whereby goods bought and sold within Philadelphia be done so at the direct profit of this organisation—for which your Tony, coz, does humbly, faithfully, and most profitably assume certain managerial and procuratorial duties. Need I say more, dear friend, than that I have since moved back into the grand suite at Madame Sally's? The suite's private garden be of especial delight these summer evenings, when me wench-of-the-week and I do frolic in the pool there. General Arnold did inform me but this morning that the "temporary" closing of the shops would have to continue some considerable time longer, in order to "prevent the exploitation of the good citizens of Philadelphia by certain unscrupulous merchants" —that be, those not within our organisation.

Yesterday I made purchase of a larger chest—one with a stronger lock on it. I do fear that soon I may have to depart from these jolly premises, however. Both Sal and the girls have taken an inordinate interest in the trunk. Wealth be a great burden, Jonathan, and a constant worry. I would not advise that state for the faint of heart.

Philadelphia
October 17, 1778.

Dear coz,

Ah, Jonathan, the world be full of amateurs, I do fear. Fortunately, I had long since learned the art of circumspection.

Me meditations upon the rather obvious interests of Sally and the other wenches in me great locked trunk did but urge me to action as those interests did increase. Ah, the sweet petitionings I did receive, lad, to but open that chest and permit those lovely damsels but to gaze upon its contents. And ah! what promises were made of untold paradisical pleasures if but I and she (whichever she did happen to be swearing the oath at the time) but did flee away together to some golden corner of the world. And ah! ah! how delightful their individual attempts at persuasion! 'Twould have been enough to have turned a lesser man's head, cousin Jonathan.

So, I did make preparation for what I did feel certain would be the inevitable outcome. Daily as I did leave Madame Sally's for me labours on behalf of General Arnold and the Cause, I would take with me as much coinage as I might secretively carry—always remembering to lock the great chest before leaving me chambres. And upon me return each day, noon and evening, I did bring a pavingstone—equally concealed upon me person—and I would deposit said stone within the chest. For more than a month now, coz, there has not been ha'pence in that trunk. Rather, the monies in question do rest safely in yet another trunk beneath floor-boards in me office. At last count that trunk did contain, dear friend, £200,000.

'Twas but yesterday when the "great theft" did occur. I had returned to Madame Sally's for me usual rest after the noonday meal when I was greeted by a very distraught Sal who bore the terrible news that *armed robbers* had come to the house and did haul off me precious chest and all therein. Tearfully, tearing at her hair and at her bosom, cousin, she did vigorously relate the terrible tale of how the ruffians did burst into the place, threaten them all with instant death, and then did search the premises (with Sal herself taken as hostage lest the others cry out for aid) until me own quarters, and the chest, were found. The thieves then did lug the heavy chest away, groaning under the weight of it. (*That* much of the tale be true, I'd wager!)

Well, Jonny, I did make cries of great distress and the wenches did moan and weep, then I gathered me fine clothes and few possessions (which the "robbers" had thoughtfully left behind) and vacated that place. I be now reëstablished in quarters provided me by none other than me good friend Ben Arnold. The armed guard which marches outside the compound should prevent any further "day-light robberies." But methinks I would have given a full quarter of the booty under me floor-boards to have seen the look on Madame Sally's face when the lock on me old chest was forced and she did discover herself the possessor of some of the finest pavingstones in Philadelphia!

The shops in Philadelphia be open now, but 'tis we ourselves (the department of military governance, Brigadier-General Benedict Arnold commanding) who do provide the permission for goods to enter and leave the city. There be a stipulated tariff for our services, of course (tho' the cost be cleverly incorporated into the prices of the commodities as they pass through).

Your cousin Tony does get on with General Arnold in fine compatibility, Jonathan. He does listen to me in reference to matters other than those of me own responsibilities. Just this very morning, for example, the General was much taken with me plan to levy direct taxation upon the whore-houses of Philadelphia. I did further suggest—and he seemed agreeable to it—that Madame Sally's place be the first so taxed. Me reasoning, coz, was lucidly clear to the General: as the leading establishment of pleasure in the city, successful enforcement of the tax on Madame Sally's place would bring immediate compliance from the lesser houses. And I was able to offer the General me very considered opinion that Madame Sally had far too much to lose *not* to comply with such a tax.

There be but one factor giving me cause for worry, Jonathan, and that be the behavior of General Arnold himself. He has been keeping open company with certain prominent Loyalists of the city. I did casually remind him that the British *did* evacuate the city nearly four months ago and that Philadelphia *be*, after all, an American city again. Already he has aroused suspicions among certain of the Patriots here because of both his Loyalist connections and his superb style of living. General Arnold wants naught but the preëminent social standing in Philadelphia, cousin—and he will have it.

But what does truly worry me, Jonathan, be that the man seems not to know when and wherein to restrain himself. To wit: he has been paying court to Miss Margaret Shippen of this city. Now 'tis not so much danger, methinks, in the fact that Ben Arnold be 37 and Peggy Shippen 17 as in the fact that this same lass be the daughter of one of the more prominent Loyalists in Philadelphia! But, Mother Washington be far away chasing his mad delusions.

The military governour of Philadelphia, meanwhile, does

have his own plans—and means to fulfill them, coz. If he does continue in this fashion Philadelphia will have its first doge. But I have no intention of being caught in any doge's palace at the Revolution's end—no matter *how* it does end. Your Tony has not grown witless in the flush of his success. Fear not for me, friend Jonathan, for I shall keep a wary eye on things.

Krumpit-town
May 20, 1779

Dear friend and cousin,

But do imagine me consternation at finding ye not here in Krumpit-town! Aside from not having the pleasure of reunion, I must needs confess that I do find meself flabbergasted indeed by what they did tell me in the town: that ye have gone off to Harvard to train as *school-master!* Be *this* the same Jonathan Beardsley who with me did once burn down the local school-house—and half the bloody town along with it? By the bleeding Jesus, Jonathan, I could not have been more dumb-founded had they told me ye had taken to the cloth.

General Benedict Arnold did last month wed Miss Peggy Shippen, of Philadelphia-Loyalist stock. And I, coz, did plainly see upon the wall of that stupidity a handwriting I did consider most inauspicious. There was ugly talk in the city—and accusations of misuse of the public property and polity. So, I did make purchase of a sturdy carriage pulled by two strong steeds and serviced by a coachman and footman, and off we did start, as spring came again to Philadelphia. Ah, I did not like to leave that city, Jonathan, for I had good friends, good times, and good profits there. Once in Krumpit-town, I did dismiss me navvies, giving them the carriage and horses for their wages and suggesting that they hie themselves to Boston to find their fortune.

On the very day of me return, I did choose me best new uniform (one of the dozen I had tailor-made in Philadelphia) and did prim and preen like a bloody peacock for an *entire hour* before me mother's looking-glass. Also, I did drench meself with the French cologne I have affected since me happiest days at Madame Sally's. And then, Jonathan, I did start out to pay me best respects to lovely Nancy Primrose—or whatever she now be called.

There I be, lad, walking down the main street of Krumpit-town in me fine tailored uniform, me new boots ashine, me tricorn set at a rakish angle and a fine sabre of Toledo steel with its haft of inlaid ivory with gold filigree and its scabbard of German silver. (I had acquired the weapon at Madame Sally's, from a Hessian officer on the brink of penury.) Me head full of thoughts of Nancy Primrose, I did not see 'till I did near collide with him, General Israel Putnam, accompanied by his guard. He gave such a *look*, Old Put did! And a smell, I'd wager—for the scent of me was not the every-day odor of your average Continental recruit, if I may say so. But his only words were: "Seize him!"

'Twas in his own temporary quarters in Krumpit-town that he did face me down. He did move with painful difficulty, for a paralysis of some sort be laying siege to him. In his face I could see that he be thinking the very worst, coz, so I did set me tongue to work forthwith. "I be on me way to see ye, General!" says I. "Ye smell like a Philadelphia whore!" says he. I did stiffen me spine militarily and saluted the old bastard smartly (anything to reënforce the military image.) "Explain," he did say simply, "where ye have been these last two years."

Well, 'twas a fortunate thing I could begin with the truth—of how I was kept on at GW's Headquarters Company because Old Put had been already ordered north to New York State. And then, Jonathan, I did play upon the old soldier's sensibilities like a preacher upon a spinster's soul.

Eloquently did I speak of the battles at Brandywine Creek and Germantown, of gallant attacks and bloody sad losses—I nearly wept meself, as Old Put surely did. When I did then launch into me most spirited account of the brutal winter at Valley Forge (tho' I did not mention me premature departure), General Putnam arose, albeit painfully, and did embrace me, Jonny, his unashamed tears splotching the fine linen of me new uniform. "Forgive me, lad!" croaked he, "for I had doubted ye!" I did feel 'twas the fit and proper time for the coup de grace, Jonathan, so unbuckling me sabre I did make present of it to Old Put. "Taken by me from a Hessian I slew at Monmouth, sir, a year ago next month," says I, and, "I would be honoured if ye accepted same." He did accept it, as if within a dream, wond'ringly and misty-eyed.

Finally, he went to where his own sabre hung upon a peg, removed the weapon and brought it to me, the paralysis jerking his movements. "As a mere recruit ye've no right to wear a sabre, lad, but I want ye to have me own—to have it and keep it," quoth he, "as a sign of me personal admiration. 'Tis a sabre I have had since the French and Indian War. 'Twas carried by me in the English expedition against Cuba in '62 and in the skirmishes against Pontiac after that." He did raise up his dented tin sword as if 'twere the bloody weapon of King Frederick the Great and pushed it into me hands. "And of course at Bunker Hill, and Long Island, and the rest. I be an old soldier, now, lad, and I will not see the year out in uniform, for age and a paralysis grab at me bones." And the bloody old fool did hug at me again, then did croak: "I cannot think of another I would have possess this weapon which has fought so long and well for its country's honour."

Well, coz, 'twas too bloody much for Tony-boy, so I did smartly salute, spun round on me new boots and left the blithering old imbecile to his teary mumblings. 'Twas a close call, and it did cost me a fine Hessian sabre; but it might have ended before a firing-squad—had not wit once more won out.

By the bleeding Jesus, Jonathan, methinks I do deserve some kind of medal for just *surviving* the madness of these God-damned times. And what do I get? Put's old sword. The God-damned thing be not even pawnable. (I tried.)

Well, I've not yet seen fair Nancy Primrose. Methinks that

God-damned fuller Stanhope does keep the girl locked up. And it be well enough for him that he does. For Jonathan, I do swear to thee by me own dear testicles that I will again have that lass—and *keep* her this time, along with me own natural son. For will not £300,000 buy us happiness *somewhere* in this bloody, bleeding world?

Krumpit-town
July 28, 1779

Good cousin Jonathan,

The War has come to poor Tony, who would not go to the War. It did come on the crest of Old Put's senility— or whatever 'tis which drives him on and drags your humble and obedient cousin along with him. For we have been all about Connecticut, Jonny—usually being chased by the light cavalry of William Tryon, who be the British Governour in Westchester County, New York, but who has taken it into his head to invade this State of Connecticut, wreaking bloody and merciless havoc along the way, the bastard.

'Tis said that his command be comprised entirely of Loyalists, but the cavalry we have engaged thus far do ride like regulars and do outclass our bloody Continental bumpkins. The "engagement" at Greenwich-town was fiasco, cousin, with Old Put himself nearly being killed or captured. Were it not for his galloping *down the face* of a most precipitous embankment, Jonny, the old man would surely not be with us this day. ('Twas a bloody lucky thing Put's horse be not as paralytic as its rider.)

Governour Tryon has his way in the State, and the blackguard does his redcoat-worst. Danbury has been destroyed, and Fairfield, and Norwalk. I speak of *homes*, Jonny, the habitats of non-combatants. Does he not realise that such action does serve but to anger the people further and stiffen the Patriot spine? For the destruction of domiciles be an unpardonable act in any war. For where will people live—the innocent, I mean, who had no part in the proclamations and declarations of the politicians who did start the bloody business? Where be the politicians, to take the homeless in? And where be Mad George Washington, now that he be needed? And the victorious Horatio Gates? And the wily Benedict Arnold? *Where be the generals?* Connecticut be overrun by Black Billy Tryon's cavalry, and what have we to stop it with? Paralytic Old Put and useless Hubert Fulsome.

This same Captain Fulsome be assigned to lead us when Paralytic Putnam cannot mount his horse. If Hubert Fulsome had ever any talent at all, Jonathan, 'twas in choosing himself a wife. His Molly keeps a farm here in Krumpit-town. A buxom flaxen ample juiceful apple of a woman, Jonny (did ye know her at all?) *and she has smiled on me already upon three occasions* in the town. There be invitation there, lad—promise aplenty. But of course, the few times the company be in Krumpit-town, Hubert Fulsome be with his Molly (for which I do not blame the pox-box).

Rumour has it that Tryon be heading this way. I do not believe it, nor, methinks, does Old Put. In any case, General Putnam this day can think only of himself, for he lay quite painfully ill in the Reverend Mister Baily's house. But the rumour concerning Tryon has raised great fear in Krumpit-town, and Old Put has ordered us to stand at Riker's Field—and did place the useless Hubert Fulsome, the bumpkin captain, in full command there. Well, there be no chance of the redcoats coming to Krumpit-town, and it does strike me that there be far more pleasant pastimes in which to engage meself than to wait in Riker's Field all night and perhaps all day tomorrow. For example, there be ample Molly Fulsome alone at her farm—now that Captain Hubert be off to the War.

But I must frankly admit failure with the other wench, Jonathan. No, not wench. Cousin, she be lovelier than e'er I did imagine in me loneliest moments in Penn's woods or Valley Forge! She be a *woman* now, and what was but budding at sixteen has bloomed at twenty. I was unprepared for me first sight of her again—so much so, cousin, that I did lose the advantage of surprise. She had just come out of church and was surrounded by Sunday morning. I meself was on

me way to the livery-stable to hire a mount for a morning
canter. When she did see me, a delicate pinkness did rise unto
her cheeks, dear Jonathan. Ah, the incredible keen loveliness
of her, coz! I did stand there as if smitten—could find neither
tongue nor wit, could move neither limb nor will. 'Twas only
afterwards that I did recall the dim figure of the old man with
whom she did walk away. I did not see the child—me own
flesh and blood, Jonny—tho' perhaps he was indeed about. I
could but stand motionless—speechless—me poor heart ahum
with a madness, coz, as that vision walked away from me. Yet
still I stood there—as if me feet had grown roots to keep me
there till the Sunday next, when the vision might re-appear.
I would be standing there still, methinks, had I not seen the
Reverend Mister Baily coming toward me grinning like an
ass in heat at the imagined pleasure of finding me outside his
church. I found me legs and ran.

That was two months ago, Jonathan. I did see her thrice
more—the last time at close-quarters in the market. I had
scarcely gotten used to the bombardment of her beauty—do
not *yet* know how to defend meself against it. That day in
the market-place, I did call her name—"Nancy!"—hoarsely,
cousin, me voice cracking and hardly me own. She did look
at me with pitiless eyes. Not a bit of colour rose to her cheeks
this time. How cruel such lovely eyes can be, Jonathan—how
brutal their merciless dismissal—yes, 'twas that, *dismissal*, un-
mistakably. And not a *word*, coz—not so much as a mention
of me name upon those perfect, precious lips. I do see her
yet—see her in me dreams, Jonathan, as she was that day:
standing with a cabbage in her hand, her pitiless, pitiless eyes
piercing me breast like musket-balls but without granting me
the minimum mercy of death, and then turning, turning away
from me, cousin—and even her back smiting me. I have not
attempted closer meeting since that time—have not had the
heart nor belly for it. Methinks I would prefer the hardship
of Valley Forge, Hun and all, to the hard look of Nancy's
eyes.

I have not seen the child as of yet, tho' I have learned his name: Thomas Jefferson—after the Patriot. Over and over would I repeat the name, coz: "Thomas Jefferson Krumpit, Thomas Jefferson Krumpit"—until it did occur to me, with a sickening twinge of me innards I cannot describe, that 'tis "Thomas Jefferson *Stanhope*" by which the boy—me *own son*, cousin!—be already known, and will be known, unless I can put an end to it.

By the bleeding Jesus Jonathan, 'tis not right! 'Tis *not right* to rob a man of both his woman and his son! And I *will not have it*, Jonathan: I will *not*. I will take Old Put's bloody sabre to that scoundrel of a fuller, that robber of cradles and lecher after young girls—I will sever their hideous union with Old Put's sword if need be—a use for it after all, cousin. What a *vile* state of affairs that ignominious fuller has brought about! I do feel I would be righting an immense *evil*, Jonny, in ridding the world of him and liberating Nancy and Thomas Jefferson from that ogre's filthy grasp!

A great pain does suffuse me this evening. Krumpit-town does appear deserted, for the townfolk be huddled behind their bolted doors and shuttered windows, awaiting an attack that will never come. Me comrades-in-arms, the dear bumpkins, be already assembled at Riker's Field. And I be alone, Jonathan—alone as I have never been, not ever in me life. And incomplete somehow, as if a part of me be missing. I do not understand it, coz.

But I will not be alone to-night, friend. 'Tis a long ride out to the Fulsome farm—why 'tis nearly to Osterville, lad—but I will take Old Put's horse, if need be. For no man should know the loneliness that I do feel, cousin Jonathan. No man. Onward, then, to Mistress Molly's . . . !

Krumpit-town
September 21, 1779

Dear Jonathan.

Fate, cousin—Fate. Who can comprehend the mysteries of its workings?

Surely, word of your humble servant's "heroism" has reached even Cambridge-town by now. I did receive a letter of commendation from none other than Old Motherwash himself (tho' I have the letter no longer, as 'twas in the pocket of a pair of me tailored trews which had to be abandoned one fine afternoon at Mistress Molly Fulsome's, the Captain returning unexpectedly). Ah well, 'tis no great loss; I do miss the trousers more.

The one good thing about this hero-business be, however, the society of fine ladies (who be not so very much different from Molly Fulsome—tho' not so honest). But there be bloody few of them here in Krumpit-town, or even all of Connecticut. So 'tis off to Paris I will go, cousin—there to flaunt me new-minted hero-status amongst the legendary ladies of the French Court. Ah, Jonny, if ye would but accompany me, what a bleeding-Jesus time of it the pair of us might have in France!

But I must tell ye of me heroism. Since ye will be teaching it to young ones some day (unless ye have the bloody good sense to come away to Paris with me), I had better fill ye in with the details.

If ye do recall, cousin, I had intention of visiting juiceful Molly that evening when the troops took their stand in Riker's Field under the dubious command of Captain Hubert Fulsome. Well lad, I did present meself to Molly at me best: newest uniform, French cologne—and General Putnam's horse. I did even—bless me—wear Old Put's sabre, Jonathan.

But ah! that eager winsome Molly, coz! She'd taken to practising her craft o'er the many years her Hubert has been off to the War, and I can report to ye that the perfection of her movements be worthy of Philadelphia Sal's most gifted purveyor of pleasure. And with truer dedication, lad: for juiceful Molly does not demean the act by subjecting it to the crass commercialism of her Philadelphia sisters. No! 'tis for the love of love that she does labour, generous soul that she be. And labours well, Jonny—ye might keep that in mind,

should ye choose to return to Krumpit-town. Or—blimey!—
do ye *know* that already, loathsome whore-monger!

'Twas Molly, hard cider, and your humble Tony all that
night, cousin Jonathan, while Captain Hubert and the bumpkins took the night air in Riker's Field. And when the cock
crew the last time, we were scarcely aware of it. 'Twas afternoon when we did awake, ravenous for food and for each
other. (I do not quite recall the order of our satisfaction.)
Then 'twas more of the cider. Molly and I did drink it, coz,
seeing who could guzzle the longer before taking a breath
(would ye believe that ample Molly won?); we did *bathe* in
it, lad—we did bathe, *each other* in it. 'Twas fully as riotous
a time as ever I have spent with a wench.

Yet 'twas Molly herself who did call attention to the hour:
the sun was already low in the west. From the direction of
the town all had remained quiet, all the day long. We knew
it did mean that Black Billy Tryon and his galloping Tories
had not come to Krumpit-town. But if such were the case,
why then Captain Hubert would be returning soon to Fulsome farm. "The troops!" cried I in mock-heroics. "I must
away to the troops!" But 'twas a bit embarrassing for a
soldier of three years' experience to have to be helped up
upon a horse (even tho' I hardly ever rode one in the army).
Molly did come to me assistance. Twice. The first time the
wench did give me a leg up she sent me over t'other side.
(There be a thumping good arm on her, Jonny.) 'Twas a
bloody good thing I was as drunk as I was, cousin, for I might
have gotten hurt, elsewise. Then she did bring me the sabre
(Old Put's decrepit thing—how Moll did laugh about it!).
"Point me west—duty calls!" cried I, who knew not up from
down at this point, cousin, never mind the cardinal directions.
"Ride into the sun, bold warrior!" quoth she (or words to
that effect).

And so I did ride, Jonny—or so the General's agile horse
did run. At length I could see the grassy spread of Riker's
Field before me. I did feel absurdly light in the saddle, Jona-

than—as if I did but float above it and Old Put's horse ran on beneath me. And absurdly *happy*, coz—I do not to this day know why—so gloriously drunken happy methought the whole bleeding-Jesus world was mine to do with as I pleased.

When I laid eyes upon me comrades—upon those whom I did *believe to be* me comrades—me own outrageous happiness did explode in laughter, cousin. "Oh the bumpkins, the bloody Fulsome-led farmers"—methought. And: "What fun 'twould be to rattle their asses—their rigid-with-fear-of-the-British bumpkin asses!" By this time I was nearly upon them, coz. I swear to ye that I did see no redcoats. All I did perceive were faces and golden sunlight—aye, sunlight, lad, as if we be all swimming in a sea of it, Jonny! The bumpkins (as so methought them) did seem genuinely startled at me sudden arrival, and to startle them more I did turn me laughter into curses—every bloody curse I knew—and waved Old Put's pathetic sabre over me head as if I did mean wholesale harvest of bumpkins!

By this time I was in the midst of them, and they did understandably pull back. That me "comrades" were all on horseback did not surprise me: for was I not also mounted? (The jug does lend its own peculiar logic to one's actions, as ye well do know, Jonathan.) Well, the "bumpkins" broke rank. Inspired, I did begin to shout: "I've got the syph, I've got the syph, ye coarse and bloody bastards—who will share me syph?" The faces around me did scatter like minnows, cousin—frighted fishes fleeing into a golden sea. Methought: "No wonder ye be losing the bloody War, ye poxbox bumpkins!" And after them I did go, Jonathan, westward into the sun, waving Old Put's sabre and shouting at the top of me voice, "Who'll have some syph to-day, laddies? Who'll share me syph?" I did ride after them at full gallop, Jonny, but after the sun went down I could no longer point me way westward, and I did lose them.

Well, your Tony did wander aimlessly about a while and stopped at last to rest, for 'twas by then dark. 'Twas by a brook, methought, for I could hear the tinkling sound of water, so I did tumble off Put's horse—and into a puddle of its urine. But I had ridden hard, lad (on various mounts) and drunk e'en harder, and I do remember thinking, "Oh what the sweet hell," then I did sleep like an infant, Jonathan, in a peaceful sudden slumber that was to last 'till break of day.

When I did awake, Put's horse be cropping grass nearby. Me head did feel the seize of Mistress Molly's ample buttocks. It did take me some time and considerable effort to mount the bloody animal, which seemed unduly skittish, for 'twould never keep its stirrup where me foot was. Ah, the perversity of dumb beasts, Jonathan, when man be not at his masterful best. Yet finally I did manage, and the animal did regain its respectful behaviour. I was confused at the time, as ye can imagine, Jonny, but I had the vague conviction that I should be riding into the sun, so that was what I did.

But I did soon become aware of the pungent odors of horse-piss and spilled cider, so at the first stream I did come to, I did bathe meself, wash me malodorous clothes, and water Old Put's horse. Ah, 'twas peaceful there, coz. 'Twas a slow but goodly stream, with trees o'erhanging on one side and a sunny meadow on t'other. In the meadow I did spread me clothes to dry, then to a shady tree I tied Put's horse. Close by, also under trees, there was a mossy bank, and I did lay me naked self down on that soft bed and slept—for how long I do not know, tho' me clothes were dry when I awoke.

Back in Krumpit-town I could not at first discern the cheers from the continuous buzzing in me head. By the bleeding Jesus, Jonathan, I was *still drunk*. I did decide that the best course would be to assume a dignity which might, with luck, be mistaken for sobriety. But 'twas the people of the town who did seem intoxicated, cousin. I was all but pulled from Old Put's horse and lifted upon shoulders and paraded through the town! I was carried to Old Put himself, who had since regained his feet if not his wits, and methought: "Oh Christ, he'll have me veritable ass for stealing his horse." But imagine me surprise, Jonny, when the blithering old fool began to weep and kiss me in front of the troops there assembled!

'Twas yet *another day*, Jonathan, before I was to comprehend that the "bumpkins" I had ridden into and cursed and threatened with the syph were Black Billy Tryon's light cavalry—1,200 of the bloody bastards! *This*, I do swear to thee, good friend and cousin, be the *true story* of "Wild Anthony Krumpit, Hero of Riker's Field."

By the bleeding Jesus it did all but ruin me with the lasses here, Jonathan. For what girl will feel at her ease with a bloody *institution?* There be willing Mistress Molly, of course, but after that afternoon's quick departure without me trews and GW's letter of commendation, Captain Fulsome has been ever on his guard—keeping his eye upon your humble servant when not upon his buxom wife. Of course, there be nothing he can do to me, your Tony being the hero and all, and his spiteful glares do bother me not at all.

For a time, dear Jonathan, I did seek to play the rôle which Fate did thrust upon me. Methought to profit by it—not financially, for I have lucre aplenty laid aside, and not sexually, for except for the few high-placed ladies I be severely limited in such pleasure precisely because of me God-damned heroics. No, lad. I did play the rôle for an audience of but one.

For near a month I did give patriotic speeches in the town (quoting liberally from past remarks of blathering Old Put, much to the old man's teary approval). I did train the village boys to march with wooden muskets—not neglecting even the very youngest (yet young Thomas Jefferson was never sent to join them). By the Christ, Jonny, I did even go to church (but the lovely Nancy sat forever at a distance from me and left with her old man immediately after the service).

Late one night, at home, after long hours of private drinking, I took Old Put's sabre and tested its edge against a fireside stool—imagining same to be old Stanhope's neck. 'Twas then I knew I had to have it out—directly. Cruel Nancy—the mother of me son, coz!—had not e'en *spoken* to me since me return to Krumpit-town! Be *that* any way to treat the father of her child?

I had me chance a bit more than a month ago. I did observe old Stanhope begin to unload a cart of fire-wood at his fulling-mill. With immediate haste I did make me way to his cottage on the Elm road. I had but entered the gate when I did spy the lad—all four years of him, Jonathan—hoeing away in the kitchen garden as if there be great harvest to be gotten in. He has his mother's eyes, coz—clear and serene as the sky—tho' without her recent cruelty. But his features be mine, Jonathan, no mistaking them. The lad did cease his labours and looked up as I did kneel beside him.

But the boy said no more to me than his mother had. There was dirt upon his clothes, from the lad's ardent gardening, and I did begin to brush it gently from his shirt. I was ill prepared, cousin, for the *un*gentle yank that pulled me to me feet—and less so for the swinging slap that sent me senses spinning, so unexpected and so unexpectedly hard was the blow from such a prettily dainty hand. Nancy's eyes had veritable fire in them, coz—not hate, methinks, but anger and determination and that same, that terrible, that appalling look of dismissal, Jonny, all exploding together. 'Twas the look which God must have given Adam, or perhaps the demon Lucifer. "Belovèd"—I did petition weakly. But again the pretty arm did swing: once, twice, thrice—and the piercing soul-shot glare that slew me, Jonathan, with a death no man should suffer. She took the boy by the hand and led him away into the house. She had still not uttered a word. Me poor brain did reverberate, cousin, from the incredible fury and finality behind her slaps. Especially the immense *finality* of those blows. Ah! Jonathan! so stunned was I that I know not to this day how or when I came away from that place. . . .

I do sail for France in a week's time, aboard a naval ship, no less. We will have three days together, if ye be free, or can make the time. Would that we have three *years* together at the least, dear friend, and I do hope ye shall lend sympathetic ear to me offer to sponsor your studies abroad.

Dear friend and cousin: must we *all* go our separate ways, touched only by the memory of better times? Surely *ye* of all people will feel adventurous enough to sail an ocean in search of a better life, as e'en our forebears did? I go to the Old World, Jonathan, as they came to the New. Be me life so topsy-turvy that I cannot tell the difference? Come then, friend, and steady me—as I did once steady ye when madman Burridge did make attempt upon your life. Come, Jonathan, if only for a year . . . !

And if ye have remained behind despite me pleas and read these lines and by good chance do change your mind, why then, good friend, I will gladly send ye passage to join me in Paris. The Revolution be a farce, Jonathan; no good can come of it. The Congress will elect a President, should the Patriots somehow succeed, and 'twill be someone the like of Old Motherwash—mark me words. And if the Patriots do lose, as 'tis most likely that they will, why then there will be repression throughout the Colonies, and ye will live the life of the vanquished, Jonny. Come away with me then to France!

If ye remain in these young united States, dear friend, I do wish ye naught but happiness. And request in exchange a fond remembrance of me. Sweet bleeding Jesus, Jonathan, do not forget me. . . .

Your friend and cousin,
Anthony Krumpit.

NINE

I'M SORRY I had to do that to you, Stanley. I truly am. . . ." Anton Beardsley sat motionless in his armchair, his glass empty of Early Times.

Stanley Stanhope felt bankrupt, as if he'd just lost a Monopoly game with life. "Yes. . . ."

"But I had to disabuse you of this infatuation with Anthony Krumpit. If there'd been any other way . . ."

"Yes. . . ."

"You'll be forgetting about that 'Anthony Krumpit Guild' so-called, won't you now?"

"Yes. . . ."

Anton Beardsley nodded. "Good. 'Cause y'see, Stan, all you would've gotten to go along with you would've been crackpots. Like the characters who showed up last night—oh, I know all about it: Jimmy Tarber's a good friend of mine."

"Tarber is going to make me a laughingstock in Krumpit."

"He'd probably like to. He's a sonofabitch, Stan. He's used lots of heads as stepping stones."

"And now mine. . . ."

"I doubt it."

"I feel stepped-on already."

"Heh-heh-heh-heh-heh. What a leader of men. What a founder of organizations. You're so fuckin' naive it's pitiful. The *Patriot-Call* won't print anything nasty about you because you're a steady advertiser and they want to maintain good business relations. It'd be different if you upped and murdered somebody—they couldn't ignore *that*—but the little foolishness with the ad, why that'll be kept in the family, so to speak. Tarber was prob'bly sent over only to give you a little free publicity, had your little soirée turned out to be some kind of viable idea. As a sort of service to a steady advertiser—the way they run pictures of new houses in the real estate section. Newspapers are primarily money-making enterprises, Stanley, and it all boils down to a matter of mutual back-scratching. Hell, I thought you knew that, boy. Y'know, you remind me more'n more of old Jock, the better I get to know you. Heh-heh-heh-heh-heh."

(Go directly to hell. Do not pass God, do not collect two hundred pardons.) "Will you take me home, please?"

Anton Beardsley snuffled and rubbed his hand over his mouth. "Sorry, boy. It wasn't any time to tease you. Fact of the matter is, I've got more to show you. Six letters from Tony. Sent from Paris. All six to Jonathan. You might as well know the whole business, how it ended." And he was opening the bottom drawer of the secretary again, rummaging for the letters.

"I don't care to see them." Old Beardsley came up with a

much thinner notebook. Stanley could see the gleam of acetate sheets within it. "I don't *want* to see them."

"Don't *want* to? Aren't you interested? *Curious,* even?"

"No." (No! No-no-*no!*) "Please take me home." The
old man was visibly disappointed, but grotesquely so, Stanley thought: like an executioner who usually gets to give
the *coup de grace* but doesn't get the chance for once, because the victim is, quite obviously, dead. Anton Beardsley
returned both notebooks to the bottom drawer. Stanley
struggled to his feet.

The ride back to town seemed bumpier by far than the
ride out had been. They careened past the town dump, with
Old Beardsley leaning on the horn and swerving to avoid a
truck just exiting.

"Life goes on, Stanley. Believe me, boy, life goes on. It's
not the end of the world, just the end of folly. Of one particular folly. . . ."

(Jesus, keep your bloody peace.) "If you don't mind, I'd
rather none of your platitudes." And Anton Beardsley held
his peace. But he was right, if platitudinous, Stanley knew.
Life did go on. Wasn't that the hell of it, when things went
wrong? Life just—went on. And on and on and on, and a
man just had to ride the fool thing out. Was that how it had
been, for instance, with Wild Anthony Krumpit in Paris?
"How did he die?"

"What's that?"

"How did Anthony Krumpit die?"

"Why didn't you read the goddamn letters, then you'd
know."

"I—I couldn't, that's all. Can't you accept that? Can't you
just *tell* me what the letters are about?"

"Waal . . ." They were tearing down the road heading
into Krumpit-town along the approximate route that Wild
Anthony must have taken to Riker's Field that sundrunk
afternoon in 1779, fresh from the boozy boorish embraces of

juiceful Molly Fulsome, amateur whore. "Tony-boy had him a helluva time in Paris—found all the better brothels, for one thing. But it was court-life he craved for. Or courtesans, maybe. Ben Franklin was still over there—the war, y'know, was still going on. Then, after Yorktown, Franklin had to stay in Europe to negotiate the peace. And he was to hang around a coupla years more after that—doing public relations work for the new nation, was what it amounted to. He was enormously popular not only in France but in the rest of Europe. Our Tony-boy saw this—and saw the advantages in being assigned to Franklin's staff, in however insignificant a capacity. So, he exploited his new hero-status and got himself an appointment. Wild Tony was what we'd call a hustler today, Stan-boy: he saw what he wanted and went after it and usually got it. 'Cept for Nancy Primrose, heh-heh-heh-heh-heh. He didn't get *that* little bitch, did he."

"He . . . died so young. I can't help wondering just how. . . ."

"Heh-heh-heh-heh-heh. Waal, boy, to begin with our Tony had himself a case of syphilis—or so it sounds from the letters. Maybe he brought it to France—maybe he really did have a case of it at Riker's Field! Anyway it blossomed over there by spring of 1780—along with the chestnut blossoms, heh-heh-heh-heh-heh!" Stanley held his temper as the old man, as insensitive as the shocks in his wreck of a car, enjoyed his crass joke. "But it wasn't the syph that killed him. Drugs did him in, no doubt. Prob'bly an overdose. Our Tony-boy discovered laudanum in France. That's opium in cognac, Stanley, in case you don't know. Tony really took to it. The last of his letters in particular has a long account of his experiences with the crap. Too bad you didn't read 'em. . . ."

"Maybe you could tell me one more thing, Mister Beardsley. . . ."

"Maybe you'd like to read the letters for yourself sometime. Anytime." He leaned on his horn again as they shot through an intersection.

"What I wanted to know is, am I . . . my family, I mean . . . directly descendant from—from Anthony Krumpit? By way of Thomas Jefferson Stanhope, I mean . . . ?"

"Knew you'd ask that, Stanley. Knew you'd figure it just *had* to be. It's that romantic little burgher mentality of yours. There's nothing the bourgeois mind likes better than to find a little rascality or horse-thievery somewhere in its ancestry. Makes 'em feel there may be life in the line after all, heh-heh-heh-heh-heh. Sorry to disappoint you, but you don't spring from the energetic loins of Anthony Krumpit. Repeat: you do *not*. You *do* descend from Clement Stanhope, however, heh-heh-heh-heh-heh."

"And—and Nancy?"

"Strike two, Stan. Sorry 'bout that. You derive from Clem's *first* marriage. From his son—I forget his name. I checked it out a long, long time ago. But it's all in the town records, you can verify it for yourself." Old Beardsley erupted into a boozy laughter that quickly degenerated into a cough. "Why, you don't have the *balls* to be descended from Wild Anthony, boy. But that Nancy must have been a pretty piece to send our Tony off like that, don't you reckon?" The old man shook his head and sighed audibly. "A piece and a half, I bet. . . ."

They were in the town now, and Old Beardsley shifted into second gear, to slow the car down.

"What happened to Nancy? And to Thomas Jefferson . . . ?"

"Waal, Clem Stanhope up and died—the girl was prob'bly too much of a strain on him, heh-heh-heh! Nancy wasn't even twenty-five, I don't think. And the kid not more'n ten. The business went to Clem's son—your ancestor, Stanley—but Nancy prob'bly got something for the house, 'cause it was sold about the same time. Nancy left town with the kid. No telling where she went. But neither she nor the youngster ever got buried in the Old Churchyard. Waal, she prob'bly got married again—odds certainly favor it, if Tony's description of the filly was any fit testimony. But—who knows:

maybe she ended up in one of those New York whorehouses Tony wrote about, heh-heh-heh-heh-heh."

(Jesus!) "It seems *far more likely to me* that things went better for her!" (You calamitous old—)

"That's your bourgeois sentimentality acting up again, Stan. Makes you tend to close your eyes to the harsher realities of life."

"And you, Mister Beardsley, seem incapable of seeing anything *good* in life." (Damn your unseeing eyes and unloving heart.)

"Waal, you've read Tony's diary. Didja read of anything like Social Security or welfare payments or aid to dependent children?"

Suddenly Stanley felt an anger rising within him—one that swept away any petty arguments he might have with Old Beardsley. "Why was that diary kept secret for so long— *why?*" It seemed an incredible injustice, a betrayal both of Truth and the seekers after it.

"Don't be bitter about it, Stanley. It was done with the best of intentions, I'm sure. I guess all the keepers of the journal must've felt pretty much the way my own father did: that people and countries need heroes. As long as the example of Anthony Krumpit somehow served the country, then why, hell, there was no point disturbing the fairy tale."

"The People deserve the *Truth!*"

"Listen, Stanley: the truth is the last fuckin' thing most people want. Most people prefer their comfortable little falsities. Then there's people like the K.H.S. and the D.A.R. and the goddamn Descendants of the Mayflower—all those idiots with minds and hearts turned solidly to the past while the goddamn country goes to hell in the present. Got a theory about 'em, Stan; they cling to the past 'cause they're so fuckin' afraid of the future."

"Who isn't, these days."

"Anybody with enough intelligence to face today realizing it isn't just another yesterday."

"I don't believe that—I don't believe it's that simple."

"You will, when you've seen as many yesterdays as I have."

"One would think they'd all begin to look the same."

"Only to ignoramuses." It was useless to try to argue with the old man, so Stanley said nothing. "Y'know, I nearly made the Krumpit Papers public once—was right on the verge of doing so." Stanley wouldn't comment. "This was back in 1945—our Tercentenary year, if you recall. The Krumpit Hysterical Society was making all that fandango about 'glorious Krumpit-town' and it was just too much, Stanley, it was just too fuckin' much." They were turning into Stanley's street, under the arches of ancient elms. "I gave serious thought to bursting their hot-air balloon. I was going to call in the New York *Times* and give 'em the Krumpit Papers— just before the fuckin' celebrations began. Heh-heh-heh-heh-heh . . . !"

"But you didn't." (Out of cowardice?)

"No. I wanted to live in this town. This is my town— more'n any of those Hysterical Society bastards. Fact is, *my* family's been here longer'n any of theirs, though you don't find me making any waltz royale about it. Also, I wanted to keep working. Had to, really: all my money got spent on books." They were in front of Stanley's house and Old Beardsley yanked on the emergency brake, stopping the battered Plymouth. "Maybe when I can't work anymore I'll begin selling off the books. They're a pretty solid investment, y'know—'specially the first editions."

"And the diary? And the letters? The Krumpit Papers?"

"I'll keep the secret. Don't really know why—this goddamn town sure as hell doesn't deserve its little fairy tale of an illusion—but I will. Unless somebody else decides to ruin his life by forming some goddamn 'Anthony Krumpit Guild' or some such."

"I suppose I should be grateful to you, but instead I despise you, Mister Beardsley. I goddamn despise you."

"Waal that doesn't matter. But you're an accomplice now, Stanley. After the fact, so to speak. You're the only other person alive who knows the truth about Anthony Krumpit."

"That doesn't concern me. Not in the slightest." He opened the car door.

"I'm not going to live forever, Stan—eventually I too must pass on to my great reward, or whatever."

"I think you can count on the 'whatever.'"

"Be that as it may, I am not going to destroy the Krumpit Papers: they're historical evidence, boy—and priceless."

"What's that got to do with me?"

"I thought I'd bequeath 'em to you. As sole accomplice." Stanley froze, half out of the car, then slumped back into the front seat. "They'll be made public, Stan, if they're discovered among my things. You're the logical inheritor of the Papers— you, the sole accomplice."

"Stop calling me that! I've had nothing to do with that diary—nothing! Or any letters! And I don't want to! I *won't!*" He scrambled out of the car and slammed the door shut. "I absolutely and positively refuse to have anything whatsoever to do with *any* of the Krumpit Papers. Or with *you*, for that matter. Ever again." The Plymouth's engine throbbed, as did Stanley's head.

"Waal, I guess they go to Jim Tarber, then. I'm not going to just abandon 'em, Stanley. They've been in my family too long for that."

"What you do with them is entirely your own affair. Just don't bequeath them to me, Mister Beardsley, because if you do, I promise you here and now on my mother's honor that the Krumpit Papers will go straight into my incinerator."

Old Beardsley was rubbing his mouth with his hand. "Lookit, Stan . . . I don't *want* to give 'em to Tarber. What I mean is, I'd rather not. But they *have* to go to *somebody*— the Papers are too important to be left to chance. I'd . . . rather they go to you, than Tarber. . . ."

"Sorry. Your little plan worked very well, Mister Beardsley: you've completely 'disabused' me of any attachment I might have had to the memory and—and—and ideals of An-

thony Krumpit. Good day, Mister Beardsley. Many thanks
for . . . for the ride. . . ." He walked away, and after a
moment the old man rattled off.

On his front porch Stanley spotted the *Patriot-Call*. He sat
on the glider and began to search for the report on the charter
meeting of the Anthony Krumpit Guild.

Tarber's regular column was devoted to an exposé of criminal water pollution in the Bridgeport area, with pointed attacks on the State pollution control board. Finally Stanley
found what he was looking for, beside an ad for orthopedic
shoes. It was brief, merciful:

CITIZENS GATHER

Krumpit. A group of concerned
citizens met at the home of Stanley S. Stanhope for a discussion
on current political problems.
The group announced no further
plans to meet again.

He felt a sinking to his bowels, as if his intestines were about
to spill out in spontaneous agony—a sort of hara-kiri of the
spirit. What he had been, was a goddamn fool. Incredibly
naïve—Old Beardsley was right. Perhaps others would forget
in time—forget that full-page ad which flaunted his naïveté
before the world. But would *he* forget? *Could* he, ever? Or
would it be like a seed within him, growing to gargantuan
proportions until it could no longer be hidden or kept secret,
like the old joke about the young lady who'd swallowed the
watermelon seed. . . .

And Stanley Stanhope remembered his own watermelon
—not the Sacrificial One in the darkgreenshade of his gazebo
—but the melon in his vegetable cellar, the one transubstanti-
ated into a mystical sacrament that could relieve his anxiety
and subdue his memory: the Mystic Fruit of Forgetfulness.
He had only to partake of it. . . .

He stopped by his kitchen to get a knife. But before he descended into the depths of his cellar, Stanley stood in the front hallway like some Agamemnon home from the war, weapon in hand, and called out his wife's name. It seemed to echo in the emptiness: "Emily Em-Em-mi-mi-ly-ly . . . !" —and then there was only a terrifying stillness.

In the deepdarkcool of the cellar of his father's house, Stanley sat cross-legged with the Sacred Watermelon on the burlap bag before him. The melon had a virginal integrity about it. His hands trembled as he raised the knife so that his thumbs pressed against his forehead. (Is there no other way? No way but this?) He dragged the depths of his personal resources. All he dredged up was despair.

Suddenly the terror within him knew no bounds—was about to *break the bounds* that comprised Stanley Stilmore Stanhope: his flesh and sinews, heart and brain, blood and lungs liver kidneys pancreas bowels—"Em-i-lyyyy!"—he plunged the knife desperately deep into the melon. There was a very loud *cccrackkk!* and then the watermelon lay divided before him, its secret pinkness sending vapors of nepenthean promise to his madly flaring nostils. . . .

He sought his forgetfulness by eager mouthfuls: small cold explosions of sweetness and liquidity, with yet another wilder fluid going directly to his brain and quenching the febrile anguish there. (More, more, sweet Jesus more . . . !) Again, again, and yet again. . . . He was a sultan in rut amid his harem: there seemed no end to his pleasure. Or was he in the cave of Ali Baba? Then "Open, Sesame!"—sesame sesame sesame-seed seed seed seed, melonseed melonseed seed seed, watermelonseed: "Open, Watermelonseed!" Before him lay the treasure of the Forty Thieves—before him yes before him —before—fore—forty—forty thieves—forty years old, years like thieves: and the treasure lay before him. He had only to *grasp* it . . . !

As Anthony Krumpit himself had grasped at things. Today he would be called a hustler: he saw what he wanted and went after it and usually got it. Except he did not get that primrose Nancy (was that the name?—no, Nancy *Stanhope*, though no relation to Stanley). Wild Anthony didn't get *that* little bitch, did he, no he did not, he didn't, because she'd let him have it once, twice, thrice and stunned our Tony-boy so that he never did recover and went off to France to die of syphilis and dope, poor Anthony. . . .

Stanley could not prevent the swell of sorrow that rose within him, though he was not quite certain whether it was Anthony or he himself the sorrow was meant for. Strangely, the two seemed to coalesce: Stanley Krumpit, Anthony Stanhope . . . Anthony Stilmore Krumpit, Stanley Aaron Stanhope. Strange, strange the way a fusion seemed to be taking place. Stanley suddenly *understood* Wild Anthony. In a single intuitive stroke he *knew* the man—could see him clearly for the first time. Anthony was less the lecher now—less the traitor, less the cheat, less the card-sharp, less the whoremaster, less the adulterer, less the regimental pimp, less the exploiter of human misery, less the thief, less the conniver, less the war-profiteer, less the self-aggrandizer, less the selfish insensitive betrayer of the Revolution and of Mankind itself. Suddenly, there amid the deepdarkcool and melonpink and quenching-sweet deliverance, Anthony Stanley Aaron Stilmore Krumpit Stanhope had become, clearly, a tragic figure—more to be pitied than pilloried, more to be lamented than lambasted, more to be—yes!—*understood* than undone. Yes, understood, especially. For wasn't to understand all to forgive all? Stanley understood. He did not know exactly *how*—could not have put it into words (it was . . . ineffable)—but he understood Wild Anthony as well as he understood himself. . . .

He could think freely and clearly about Anthonley Krumhope now, for now he had been delivered of the blind prejudice with which Old Beardsley had momentarily blinkered him. For *whatever* that diary said—did not HISTORY proclaim Stanthony Stanpit a hero? Was there not a monument to him standing in perpetual erection in Riker's Field? Did not

the Krumpit Hysterical—Hysterectomical—Hys—whatever
—did not all those learned gentlemen bear testimony to the
heroism of Anthonley Krumhope—whatever his personal
traits? It was all mixed up, that was true, yet it was strangely
clear to Stanley, who pushed another piece of Mystic Fruit
into his still-eager mouth.

And as he began spitting out the seeds anew, a new corollary to the great Watermelon Correlative asserted itself: *The
perfection of Patriotism is in direct ratio to the seeds of lust
within one.* Why hadn't it occurred to him before! Would it
not explain the Patriot Anthony Krumpit? It was so simple
that mere words clouded the concept. Perhaps that was true of
all Great Truths: one knew them best in the wordless simplicity of one's soul. (Ah sweet Mystic Fruit, sweet new Awakening, I shall come forth reborn from the cave of my father,
from the deepdarkcool . . . !)

But care must be taken: his exhilaration must remain suspect, for bad mistakes could be made in the flush of great
excitement, ofttimes nullifying the gain of discovery. The new
correlative must be examined dispassionately. And tested, if
possible. *Tested?* No, that was not possible. For whom could
he lust after? And why? Y? Y . . . ?

But *no!* That was beyond the bounds of the decency he led
his life by. And he loved Emily. His Country had no right
to demand such a thing of him. The state had no right over
the physical integrity of the individual. What on earth did
they *want* of Stanthony Krumhope? ("Ask not what your
Country can do for you but what you can do for your Country.") But what of Emily? Any "test" necessitated virtual
unfaithfulness—in body if not in spirit—and he was not prepared for that. Infidelity simply did not fall within his defini-
tion of marriage.

Stanley gouged himself a large chunk of Mystic Fruit and
closed his mouth over it. Its coolness flooded his being with its
secret communion. Stanthony closed his eyes—then before
him leaped the vision of Irma Kasendorf, alone, writhing on

grass under moonlight, her lushwhitethighs widespread. She was crying out in alarm: "Save us, Mister Stanpit! Save the United States of America . . . !"—and she held her strong yet pleading arms directly out to him. . . .

Did duty clearly call? Was a personal sacrifice due, for love of Country? And must his fidelity to his wife be also part of that sacrifice? ("Ask not what your—") But if it meant the discovery of the key to Patriotism (surely the method would prove popular)—if it meant the salvation of the United States of America!—had he the right to *refuse* to test the theory?

For his Country's sake—for its very survival, perhaps—it had to be done. Perhaps Emily would never understand; he would keep it from her—spare her the agony he himself now suffered. . . .

How light Stanley's legs felt, how easily he floated up the cellar stairs. How absolutely effortless it was to walk, to think, to posit the most abstruse of problems and solve them immediately. "Em-m'ly?" But not to talk. There was no answer. Emily was at the beach, roasting happily in the sun, unaware of his ordeal. The kitchen clock read a quarter to six. He exercised his jaws and moved his tongue about, as if to limber it. It was time for action, that's what time it was. "The perfection of one's Patriotism is in direct ratio to the seeds of lust within one." Of course! How exceedingly stupid of him not to have seen that before now! He limbered up his tongue all the way to his den. He found his address book, then Irma Kasendorf's number. . . .

"*Hallo?*" It was a shrill harridan voice that answered. A landlady?

"Miss Irma Kas-en-dorf, please."

"Hang on." The clunk, clunk, clunk of a receiver bumping against a wall. Then the screaming shrill "KASENDORFFF!" Then long moments of silence, during which Stanley limbered his tongue and rehearsed in his mind, as encouragement for what *had to be done*, the great new correlative: "The perfection of Patriotism is in—" "KAS-EN-DORF!—GEN'LE-

MAN ON THE LINE!" There was an indistinct response
from a distance—perhaps from up a flight of stairs—and then
the harridan voice again. "HALLO? Hallo? This Freddie
Winslow?"

(JesusChristalmighty.) "No this is *not* Freddie would you
let me shpeak to Mish Kas-en-dorf, if you please." (Freddie
Winslow! Jesus!)

"She's takin' a bath right now. Can ya call back?"

"No! And it's impor'ant—it's vi-tally im-por-tant, you tell
her that!"

"Hang on"—clunk, clunk, clunk. "KASENDORF COME
ON DOWN HE SAYS IT AIN'T FREDDIE IT'S IM-
PORTANT." An indistinct query from a distant Irma, and
then from the harridan: "Who is this?"

"Thish is *Mister* Stanhope. I am her employ—"

"IT'S A MISTER STANDOPE." And again indistinctly,
from Irma, a long and seemingly urgent explanatory message
—which was relayed by the harridan simply as "Hang in
there, Mister Standope," clunk, clunk, clunk. Then long, long
silence. It was ridiculous: the salvation of the Nation being
delayed by Irma Kasendorf's bath. Such things seemed to
happen only to the Stanthony Krumhopes of this world. . . .

Her voice, when it came, was breathless and somewhat
timid. "Hullo Mister Stanhope . . . ?"

"I'm—sorry if I . . . disturbed you. . . ." (Your Nation
has need of you, girl!)

"Oh—that's all right. . . ."

"Irma . . ." (Miss Kasendorf?) "Hello, Irma . . . ?"

"Yes sir?"

"Irma . . . there's shumthing of ut-most important . . ."

"Are you okay, Mister Stanhope? You sound kinda
funny. . . ."

"Will you *lishen* to me?"

"Uh—yeah. Sorry, Mister Stanhope. . . ."

"Without ques—, without question?"

"Sure, Mister Stanhope. Go ahead, shoot."

(Bang! Bang-bang! Bang-bang-bang!) "Ir-ma, *lesson* carefully: *can* you . . . *will* you . . . come down to th' plant—right now?"

"*Now?*"

"Of coursh now—right now. It's—it's ver-ry impotent."

"You mean—right *away?*"

(Christ!) "Im-med'tely. If not sooner."

"I—I still have to get dressed."

"Nat'rally. Have—have you that den-im dress you shumtimes wear. To work?"

"Un . . . yeah. . . ."

" 'X'llent. Would you wear it? Tonigh'?"

"Mister Stanhope—have you been *drinking?*"

"Of *coursh* not. I have not—been drinking. *Will* you wear the den'm dress—and come as soon as you can. To th' plant."

"Awright. . . . If you want me to. . . ."

"I do. And Irma: would you *not wear anything under it?* Under the d'nim, I mean. Under the dress." (Is this me? Can this be happening?) There was an extended silence from Irma's end of the line, then a bubbly giggle, quickly suppressed. "Well?" (Can this be *me?*)

"Wha'd'you say . . . ?" And again the bubbly giggle, not suppressed at all this time.

"I shaid, when you come ov-er to th' plant will you pleazhe wear that blue den'm dress and noth-ing underneat'." (Can this be happening?)

An explosive giggle—but muffled by her own hand, it sounded like. "You *have* been drinking, Mister Stanhope!"

(By the bleeding . . .) "I as-sure you that I have *not.*" Uttered with all the dignity he could muster. But it evoked only more bubbly giggles, unsuppressed and unmuffled. Then, after a moment's silence:

"If that's what you want, Mister Stanhope!"—with still more bubbly.

"I shall be awaiting." He hung up. (Can this be me? Can this *really* be happening? Ask not what your Country, but what can you do. . . . Can this be me?)

How easily he walked—or floated—under the high old elms full of late afternoon sun. The strange feeling that he was somehow not walking on his feet at all, but on the stubs of his thighs. But yards and yards taller—higher, actually: up, up among the topmost branches of the elms. . . . Or was it that he was walking with his head back, looking up? He had best be careful, he decided. He might trip and fall. Off a curb, perhaps. Break his neck. Who, then, would save the Nation? Anton Beardsley? Freddie Winslow? He had best be careful, for he stood alone. Stanthony Krumhope. The best and only hope of all Mankind. . . .

It was warm in the plant. He flipped on the air-conditioner but it made so much noise in the silence and emptiness that it disturbed him and he shut it off. And he left the lights off: the business at hand had no need of the brilliant fluorescent tubes that challenged daylight itself. Would there be, some day, a brass plaque there on the wall, marking the historic occasion that was about to occur within the Stanhope Cleaners? The ushering in of the Second American Revol—

He heard the gentle tap-tap-tapping at the shop door. Irma Kasendorf had her hand to her brow and was peering through the glass. When she saw him she cupped her hand over her mouth. Beneath her blue denim dress her ample breasts shook like breadfruit on a vine in a gentle wind. Or the way Stanley *imagined* breadfruit would shake, never having actually seen any. In any case, there was something both fruitful and staff-of-lifeful about those generous appendages. He let her in.

"H'llo, Molly."

"*Molly!*"

He put a hand to his forehead, shook off the error, and locked the door. "I *am* sorry. *Ir*ma! Of coursh it's Irma. . . ."

"That's a funny way to greet a girl—after *asking* her here." There was the beginning of a pout on her full, naturally very pink lips. He took both her hands in his.

"Can you ever for-give me?" (Jesus!)

"Who's Molly." It was not a question, it was a demand.

"Molly . . . is dead. . . ." Was the quiver in his voice intentional? He made the most of it in any case, and dropped Irma's hands dramatically.

"Oh I'm so *sorry*, Mister Stanhope!" Her eyes were round, her eyebrows arched, her mouth open with the lower lip fleshly pensive and the tips of her big white teeth just showing. "Was she—?"

"No matter. You're here. Perhaps you'd better . . . come out back?" Slowly the full lips spread and bared most of her teeth. The dead Molly was forgotten. "You're . . . not afraid, are you, Irm—Irma?" The giggles bubbled out of Irma Kasendorf so irrepressibly that she had to cup both her hands over her generous mouth and large white teeth.

"You *have* been drinking, Mister Stanhope!" But she turned and walked slowly, very rhythmically, into the comfortably subdued workroom. Juiceful Irma . . . .

"I have *not!* I have been eat-ing wat-erm'lon . . . !" From within the workroom, an explosive giggle. (Is this happening? By the bleeding Jesus, can this be *me* . . . ?)

Stanley found her sitting on one of the large worktables, her feet dangling; her denim dress had ridden up her thighs. Behind her was a full rack of garments waiting to be pressed. In the diminishing light they appeared to Stanley as ghostly witnesses: the shades of Washington and Jefferson and Franklin and how many others, there to observe the rebirth of the Nation. Stanthony Krumhope felt his blood boil within him. To how many was it given to be aware of their own historic importance? Irma smiled her toothy smile and swung her well fleshed legs back and forth, forth and back under the table, causing the skirt of her denim dress to rise another millimeter or so each time. It was up to him now, Stanthony realized. To seize the moment. To grasp, to hustle. To test the newest correlation. "The perfection of Patriotism . . . !"

"What's that, Mister Stanhope?" Alas, he was not used to this sort of thing. Stanthony Krumhope must not falter, yet there were rules to the game. Weren't there? Of course there

were. There were rules to everything in life. To lust and seduction as well. Endless lies and long cajolery were needed to
bed wenches—as was well known. "Is there . . . something
the matter, Mister Stanhope?" Still the lush legs swung.
Above them goodly amounts of thigh had been revealed,
like waxing moons. But Irma's thighs did not appear the
moonstruck white of Stanley's visions. Perhaps it was the
darksome workroom. . . .

It was time to proceed with the seduction. By the rules, of
course. Lies and cajolery. "I—I was wondering, Irma, how—
how would you like to see the world . . . ?" (Oh Dad, that's
dumb.)

"The world!" Even the legs stopped a moment.

"W-Well—parts of it, anyway. You know: the Costa del
Sol, Juan-les-Pins. . . ."

"*Where?*"

"San Remo? Punta del Este?"

"I don't understand. . . ."

"P-Pampelonne? Saint Tropez?"

"Wh-*What?*"

(Jesus!) "The Côte d'Azur . . . !"

"Whose coat, Mister Stanhope?"

It was not working out. Not the lies *or* the cajolery. He
felt his opportunity fast slipping away from him. And what
would the Nation do, with the new correlative unproved!
("Ask not—!") Another, a desperate try: "Where would
you like to go, Irma—what place would you most like to visit,
if you could, if . . . if someone were to—to take you there.
On—on a trip. . . ."

"Oh. Oh! Well I've always been *dying* to see Oklahoma
City, Mister Stanhope!"

"Okla—" (Jesus!)

"—homa City. I heard it's just beautiful there. Out West,
and all." She wore her brightest, toothiest smile, dazzling even
in the subdued light.

"Uh—yes. Yes. . . ." (No. No, this is not happening to

me! What doth my Country ask that I—?) But he could not back out. Would not. Did George Washington back out at Valley Forge and leave the Continental Cause to shift for itself, leaderless? Stanthony Krumhope must also persevere. Press on. On! "Why . . . why don't you . . . make yourself comfortable, Irma . . . ?"

A giggle. Then another and another and then a gust of them, shaking the breadfruit. She slid down off the worktable, the full moons of her thighs disappearing beneath a scudding cloud of denim as she stood. She turned her very rounded backside to him very, very slowly and started the zipper a short way down the back of her dress. "Will you lend a girl a hand?" He fumbled at the slide fastener, fingers turned inexplicably to thumbs. Irma giggled. Stanley got the zipper jammed into the unraveling edges of the cheap dress.

What was that noise, that pounding? It was his heart. He pulled at the zipper, but it wouldn't budge. He put the fingers —thumbs—of his other hand beneath the zipper, feeling the silken texture of Irma's skin and eliciting a long chain of bubbly giggles. His hands were sweating now. It was ridiculous—ludicrous. The destiny of the Nation caught up in a jammed— He yanked at the zipper as hard as he could. It came off in his hand. The meshed closures, like a slow and sinuous symphony of movement, gradually slid open all the length of Irma Kasendorf's spine. Without turning, she pulled her shoulders inward, first one and then the other, and the denim dress slipped to just below her waist. She shifted her hips in a like but infinitely slower movement, then juiceful Irma stood naked before him. With an irrepressible giggle she stepped out of the little pile of blue denim heaped around her ankles. But before she could turn around and face him, Stanley Stanhope had retreated behind his clothes press. Only then did he dare look up. . . .

Her smile—if not the rest of her—was a maidenly, even coy affair. The breadfruit of her breasts hung heavily, exotic extravagances. But where were the lushwhitethighs of Stanley's visions? Mostly she was deeply tanned, bronzed almost, except for stark white breasts and pubes—which had obviously been protected from the ravishing sun by a bikini. The outlines of the brief swimsuit were distinctly discernible —and that was the trouble. That is, that's what unnerved Stanley. That is, the starkwhite of her breasts disturbed him. For the outline left by her bikini-top resembled nothing so much as a huge burglar's mask, with the whiteness of her untanned breasts as dazzling as her toothy persistent smile. But that was not the worst of it.

What so profoundly disturbed Stanley were Irma Kasendorf's nipples, situated as they were in the center of each side of the burglar's mask, like unblinking eyes staring relentlessly at him. Then to his horror, as he stared at them, he saw those nipples swell in erection like eyes growing larger and larger, the better to see him.

"Mister Stanhope . . . !" She was calling to him. Her mouth was open now, not in a smile but in a kind of bovine anguish. But Stanley felt himself withering under the relentless piercing glare of those burglar's eyes dazzling starkwhite out of the bronze lush night of Irma's tanned torso. He could not stand it—had to turn his face away—had to escape that merciless terrifying scrutiny. "Aren't you gonna—?" He closed his eyes and summoned the spirit of Wild Anthony Krumpit; but if there had been a recent union of his own and Tony's spirit, there had been a very sudden sundering of the two. What was left was simply Stanley S. Stanhope. A paper Patriot. He tried to look into Irma's eyes, hoping she might read his distress. But she had her own, it seemed: the strange distress of not knowing (for the first time, perhaps) what was wanted of her. And again Stanley's gaze was drawn to the starkwhite burglar's mask and the merciless nipple-eyes—which immediately frightened him off again. "Mister *Stanhope* why don't you—!" She took the breadfruit in both her hands. There was no giggling now, but rather a soft quick cry like a moan. "What do you *want?*"

He knew he had to do something. *Anything.* His eyes fell

on the rack of garments behind her—the shades of Washington, Jefferson, Franklin, and how many others—but empty now, deserted perhaps when the Patriot-ghosts finally realized they were not about to witness the spark of the New Revolution. "I want you to press those clothes. The ones on that rack behind you." He was relieved to hear how distinctly the words came out. But he had lost the peculiar lightness which had previously suffused him.

"Clothes . . . ?" Bewildered, she turned to look. For long puzzled moments she seemed to stare right through the garments. Did she see them? Stanley decided that he had to jolt her into action.

He all but barked the order: "Turn on your press. Start it up." Bewildered still, she did as he commanded. "Now: roll the rack of garments over." She looked over at him once then went to fetch the rack of clothes. The narrow slashes of starkwhite across her backside gave her something of the appearance of a convict set to work in the prison laundry. She smiled nervously as she pushed the laden rack to a spot beside her machine. When finally the steam was up, she set to work. (Ssss-phtttt.) She was in three-quarter profile to him now, and Stanley no longer had to look directly into those burglar's eyes. (Ssss-phtttt.) Soon Irma Kasendorf was working at a rhythmic pace, the breadfruit rising and falling, swaying and plunging, in a nearly predictable pattern. It was soothing, somehow, like the movement of soughing pine boughs against an evening sky. (Ssss-phtttt.)

"Why are you looking at me like that, Mister Stanhope?"

"Like what?"

(Ssss-phtttt.) "Funny like. . . ."

"Because you're very nice to look at, Miss Kasendorf. You have the ageless qualities of Mother Earth about you. Looking at you reassures me, somehow, that the world will go on, with men and women in it, and that life will continue to flourish on this planet. Because you yourself flourish, Irma. A flower—an orchid, perhaps. Something . . . something tropical and lush, at any rate—and a little overwhelming." (OhforChrissakes.) But it was *true:* she was exactly that, all of what he'd said.

Her full lips spread slowly into a wide and dazzling smile. The pace of her work increased—as did the steady rhythmic rise and fall, sway and plunge, of those singular breasts. (Ssss-phtttt. Ssss-phtttt.) And although Stanley continued to stare at her, continued to mesmerize himself with the rhythmic patterns of a movement older than philosophy or politics, Irma Kasendorf seemed completely unaware of his presence. (Ssss-phtttt. Ssss-phtttt Ssss-phtttt.) She began to hum as she worked. There was a sheen over her nakedness now, but she seemed neither to notice nor mind it as she kept up a torrid pace at her machine. (Ssss-phtttt. Ssss-phttt. Ssss-phtttt. Ssss-phtttt.) Already she was half-way through the rack, totally absorbed in what she was doing. Or was she? For every now and then she would smile to herself in purely unselfconscious delight. Yet worked on, not missing a stroke. Plunge, rise, fall, sway. (Ssss-phtttt! Ssss-phtttt!) She was almost like a machine, only much more animated and better designed.

Stanley discovered that he liked her. Personally. And he envied her: for she was, by nature, what he most in all the world wanted to be—uncomplicated. (Ssss-phtttt.) How had this whole ludicrous episode begun, anyway? (Christalmighty, *how?*)

Stanley Stanhope was first aware that the rhythmic pattern had been broken, then stilled. The entire rack of clothes was neatly pressed, stiffly aligned, and smartly hung. The juiceful hips rolled as Irma bent down to pick up her denim dress, which she then began to press. (Ssss-phtttt.) When she was finished she looked up at Stanley as if for further instructions. She seemed absolutely at ease in her nakedness. She shone as if she'd been oiled. Damp hair fell over her face and she looked at Stanley Stanhope through several dirty-blond wisps of it. And awaited his command. If Stanley had said "Stand on your head" he felt she would have done so. But facing him the way she was, the burglar's eyes were staring at him again. Stanley suggested that she get dressed.

The denim dress, of course, did not fit her very well with the zipper busted. Stanley gave her money for a new dress. He kept a raincoat in his office, and he offered her that to wear.

"I'll look ridiculous. It isn't raining and it's July."

"I'll drive you home, then."

There was only the van, of course. Like secret lovers, they waited until dark, then sneaked out, Irma being loaded into the back like a garment to be delivered. There was only one seat—the driver's—so Irma Kasendorf sat in the van proper, her legs dangling down into the driver's compartment. It was only minutes to where she lived, which was a good thing. The worn-out muffler made conversation practically impossible—which was also a good thing. When he pulled up in front of her rooming house, she arose from the ledge she sat on and screwed her face into a tough little tightness. Her voice was not only firm, but demanding:

"Mister Stanhope . . ."

(Oh Jesus, what now? Blackmail?) "Yes, Irma . . . ?"

"You're gonna have to pay me time-and-a-half for tonight. It's been a coupla hours, at *least*."

(By the bleeding Jesus . . .) "All right, Irma. And . . . thank you." (Thank *God*.)

"Goodnight." She got out and hurried into the rooming house, clutching the rear collar of her dress. Stanley pulled away as fast as the van could take him, setting up a terrible roar and rattle that attracted the attention of countless stoop-sitters that warm July evening. He didn't care. He drove his red, white, and blue delivery van through the streets of Krumpit-town not giving a solitary damn about the noise he made. He only wanted to get home.

TEN

*S*TANLEY was all but overcome by an extreme fatigue as he stopped the Stanhope Cleaners van outside his home. The house was ablaze with lights, including the one on the front porch. From somewhere on the second floor came the amplified thrum of base notes to base music. He heard the screen door bang and looked up to see his wife hurrying down the walk to him.

"Stanley . . . ? Where in the world have you been?"

"At the plant."

"I called a while ago. . . ."

"Must've just left. I didn't come straight home. . . ."

"Your supper's cold."

"Don't think I want any."

"I can warm it up. Or would you like some eggs scrambled?"

"No. . . . Thank you. . . ."

"I know! *How* about some nice cold watermelon!" He stopped short, then sat on the front steps in a sort of controlled slump. "Stanley, are you unwell?"

"Tired. So abysmally *tired*, Em. Tired inside, even."

She sat down next to him and linked her arm in his. "What'd you do with your day off?"

(What indeed.) "I lost my innocence." She laughed. "Don't you believe me?"

"Is that what made you so tired?"

"Yes. Beat. Beaten. I've been beaten, Em. Whipped. . . ."

"Who did such a terrible thing?"

"Wild Anthony Krumpit. And Old Beardsley. Did you know his first name is Anton, by the way?"

"Anton! But how lovely."

"*He's* not, though. He's a sonofabitch. Emily—a last-class bastard."

"What in the world did he *do* to you, darling?"

He told her all about the diary. (Now there were *three* people who knew.) And how finding out the truth about his "hero" had cut the fight and heart out of Stanley Stanhope. But he did not mention the rum-soaked watermelon and its unlovely aftermath; perhaps he would some day, but he could not do so now. "Needless to say, there will not be any Anthony Krumpit Guild, Em. It would be—grotesque."

"Oh dear."

"So I guess I should thank Old Bastard Beardsley, all in all. Besides saving me my home and business, he prevented me from making an unmitigated fool of myself. . . ."

She leaned closely against him. "You're not a fool, Stanley."

"What do you call a person who acts foolishly? A sage?"

She said nothing, just leaned against him. "I'm just like my father, you know. Just like old Jock. Jock the Joke, according to Anton with the lovely name. . . ."

"Why do you listen to him? He's just a crazy old man."

"But that's just *it*, Emily—he's *not*." He told her about the library, about the strange house with the windows up under the eaves, about the cellar filled with second-hand this and used that; and about how the old man had made a killing on old Tiffany lampshades and brass cuspidors and about how he awaited the renascence of chamber pots; about how he got along reading German and French and Spanish and Italian, as well as the mother tongue, of course; and about how Old Beardsley planned to market the rare books in his collection when he got too old to work. Emily marveled at it all. "God, I've got a splitting headache. . . ."

"Have you had anything to eat?" He had not. Not since morning, when he'd had a cup of instant coffee while Billy had slurped down his Wheaties. (There was the rum-soaked watermelon, of course, but he didn't mention that. For that was not strictly food—not the way he had partaken of it.) "Sounds to me like a hunger-headache, Stanley." She rose, pulling him up by the arm. "C'mon. We're going to get some food into you. No wonder you're tired, poor darling!"

Afterwards he wandered out to sit in his gazebo. Cissie's phonograph was still blaring away, but the myriads of crickets provided significant competition. Billy was in Osterville again. Which, Stanley wondered, attracted his son the more: the Perkins girl or her color television?

In the gazebo one had to create one's own world, one's own thoughts, one's own dreams. One raised the level of one's humanity there—which was why Stanley loved the place so. If he'd been a drinking man he would have repaired there with a snifter of cognac. In his heart he could not really believe that the gazebo had been built by Anton Beardsley, that shatterer of dreams and plans and thoughts of Patriotism.

Patriotism. The thought of it played in his brain like distant fife-music. It seemed to Stanley that he would have to define it anew, in the light of that day's discoveries. For Old Beardsley, inveterate cynic about so much in life, Patriotism was something distinctly *un*cynical: it was putting one's Country above one's own blood, guts, and rhetoric. For Anton Beardsley, Patriotism meant Peopledom. Hadn't he said that, hadn't he said that "We the People" should mean "We the Patriots"? Perhaps Old Beardsley was not quite the cynic he pretended to be—just as he was not quite the handyman town-clown people took him for. (*Might* he have built the gazebo after all, then?) Whatever Patriotism was, Stanley decided, it was somehow a coming to grips with *whatever* threatened the welfare of one's Country—a sort of wrestling with the Angel of Destiny. Wasn't it?

Anthony Krumpit had been intimately involved with the destiny of his Country yet had done nothing but exploit it, if his own testimony were to be believed. Stanley now regretted not having read Anthony's half-dozen letters from Paris. He could not have read them at the time, that was true; but now that he had fully recovered from his idolizing of Anthony, he felt he could safely read the letters. He *had* to read them. For a most tantalizing thought had sprung up in Stanley's exhausted brain: had Wild Anthony *changed* any, during those years of self-imposed exile? Might a European perspective of his Country have given him a different outlook entirely on the Revolution which had swept him to adventure and fame and wealth—however ill-gotten?

But there was the possibility (Stanley could not deny it) that the scoundrel Anthony had died rapaciously unrepentant. And yet, somewhere in those letters from Paris, mightn't there be—just perhaps—*something?* Some small yet cogent point, observation, summation, conclusion perhaps, which might well indicate that Wild Anthony *did indeed* have a change of heart? Perhaps the cynical Old Beardsley had not even been capable of seeing it. But the letters would tell. Stanley *had* to get his hands on them.

It would mean apologizing to Old Beardsley. Stanley would have to reestablish their never-too-steady rapport, and then he would ask to see the six Paris letters. Surely the old man would show them: he'd wanted to *will* Stanley the entire Krumpit Papers!

The moon was high now, sending its lackwarmth rays through the thousand little diamond-shaped chutes of the gazebo's latticework. Old fears of lunacy flitted through his imagination. He scurried back to the well-lighted sanity of his house. He slept, that night, in dreamless sleep.

He got up late. As he went to the bathroom a smell of roast beef awakened him fully.

He liked Sunday dinner to be a reassertion of familial ties, and both he and Emily were hard put to keep their kids from rushing through the meal, then off to the precincts of their own private worlds. It had not always been that way. Once, for instance, the rush had been to the Monopoly board, and that was but an extension of the familial spirit. But now, Billy worked weekends at the beach in summer and wasn't at table, and Cissie had taken to not being there in spirit, somehow, and her Sunday dinner usually got more played with than eaten. It was a hard and continuous battle, that attempt to weld a family anew around the Sunday roast, but Stanley steadfastly fought that worthwhile fight, every single weekend of the year. Yet that day it was Stanley himself who wanted to rush off.

"I thought I'd drive out to Old Beardsley's place today."

"Oh? Want some company?"

He looked up at his wife's bright face framed in raven hair, then he put his fork down on his plate. "Would you mind if I said no?" She seemed taken aback. "He's such a terrible, dirty old man. And I might have to apologize to him. . . ."

"What for, Daddy?" His daughter had an elbow poised on the table at a sophisticated angle, with her pretty, straight-lined chin just touching, but not weighing on, the curved fingers of her hand. She was a portrait someone should have painted. Perhaps someone would, some day.

"I told him to go to hell yesterday, Cissie. I shouldn't have done that—even if he deserved it—and I have to do the right thing now and apologize." One had to set examples for one's children, spell out the respons—

"May I be excused?"

"Cissie dear, we have ice cream for dessert."

"*I* don't want to get *fat.*"

(Jesus! Eleven years old and worried about . . . !) "You're excused." (Skinny little runt. Fat?)

Then they were alone, he and Emily. The ice cream was vanilla-fudge-royal-ripple-nut-supreme-delight and tasted nothing but cold. Someday—and not so very much later, thought Stanley—they would be alone for sure, he and Emily, alone in an empty house with Billy and Cissie rushed off, perhaps, to the far corners of the earth. Godonlyknew. It was a good thing that when he and Emily were alone, they were alone together. Yet here he was asking her to let him be alone by himself for the afternoon—and leaving *her* alone.

"Will you be gone long, Stanley?"

"Just long enough to apologize and to read those letters. The ones Wild Anthony sent from Paris."

"I thought you were through with Wild Anthony. Did I misunderstand you?"

"No. I am through with him. Dis . . . disabused. But all the same I want to read those letters, Em. I—I *have* to, actually." And he explained to her as best he could what it was he would be looking for in the Paris letters.

"Well, I've got some washing I can do. It'll have to be done tomorrow, anyway. . . ."

But the laundry room was in the basement. So was the vegetable cellar. The thought seared Stanley's consciousness:

would the pungent odor of rum be detected—and the melon remains discovered?

"Why—why don't you go over to your folks' instead? You ought to take the day off—it's Sunday, after all. The day of rest. . . ."

"But you're taking the car."

"I can use the van. I brought it home last night, remember?"

"You'll get a ticket driving that noisy thing."

"I'll use the back streets. If I get a ticket I'll give it to Harry; he was supposed to have had it fixed last week."

"Well . . . I *could* take them an apple pie. I baked two of them. It's Dad's favorite. And Cissie likes to go there."

"Fine, then. Maybe I'll join you there. . . ." (After I dispose of the melon.)

"If you haven't been arrested."

The delivery van's shot muffler bellowed horribly in the lower gears. The road past the town dump was a jarring experience as the van lurched and thudded through endless potholes. Along the empty racks in the rear of the truck, black metal coathangers with white cardboard foldovers chattered together like skeletal magpies. But Stanley Stanhope would have driven his red, white, and blue van down the road to hell in search of Patriotism.

When he pulled into Old Beardsley's front yard, the battered Plymouth was nowhere in sight. It hadn't even occurred to Stanley that A. BEARDSLEY might not be at home. He called out the old man's name but got no response. Had he come down that long rough road for nothing?

The door was unlocked. Stanley walked in and up the stairs, past the walls of restroom green, thinking how typical it was of the old man to have thousands in rare books and not even lock his door. But then, who would look for anything of value in the place beyond the town dump. . . .

The living room (the library) was unsettlingly quiet, the

floor-to-ceiling shelves of tomes emitting an almost oppressive silence. Stanley thought of turning back (for he did not at all like violating another's privacy) but his scruples were overcome by the belief that Old Beardsley really wouldn't mind and by the thought of Anthony Krumpit's last words in the secretary just across the room from him. He found himself retrieving the key from behind the end-volume of the shelf beside the secretary, and then he was unlocking the bottom drawer. . . .

The blue plastic-covered diary was easily identifiable, but he could not locate the six letters from Paris. Notebook after notebook he opened, but each contained personal scribbles of a more contemporary nature and Stanley was careful not to read any of them. There were several cardboard boxes in the drawer. The first one he opened contained old photographs. He was about to close the box when he spotted a large postcard-photo of his own mother!

She was young—perhaps not yet 20—and candidly lovely. She was sitting back onto her heels and looking up, smiling. Her hands were poised over a picnic basket like two lovely birds caught motionless in flight. The over-all impression was that the photographer had approached unexpectedly and cried, "Mary Louise!"—and she had looked up smiling and been captured that way on film before she was fully aware that her picture had even been taken. In a drawer of his own desk, back in his den at home, Stanley had many photographs of his mother; but he had never seen this one. He could not take his eyes off it. All her loveliness, all the gentleness he remembered yet from his own childhood days, all the ineffably sweet *tenderness* of his mother was caught in that incomparable photograph, and he could only drink it up with his eyes until he thought he would drown in the primitive memory of it. Were there other pictures? Only that thought enabled him to pry his eyes away in order to look.

There were. And photos of his father too. And of Anton Beardsley. And snapshots of the three of them together. Of the latter there was one in particular: three faces close together and laughing, his mother in an airy summer dress, his father to her right, sporting a straw boater, and Old Beardsley bare-headed on her left. Except that he was not then "old" Beardsley. He was just barely recognizable to Stanley—and may not have been were it not for the mustache, though it was not the Nietzschean affair of his later years. It was a full mustache trimmed neatly, not suavely but with a certain forthright elegance: he might have been a junior executive. He was dressed nattily enough to be mistaken for one. His mother—that sweet and tender memory of Stanley's own preverbal years—stood between these two men and laughed her beautiful laugh so that Stanley felt he might yet hear the echo of it, if only he strained his ears enough.

There were dozens of snapshots, some in the old Kodak postcard size and others smaller. There were photos taken on streetcars and bicycles, on the beach and before gigantic snowpiles, at picnics and at lawn parties. There were pictures of just his mother and father together, and there were others of his mother together with Anton Beardsley. And many, many pictures of his mother all by her shining self: holding a flower; sitting in a rowboat; laughing in a summer field; prettily posed with a baseball and glove; standing beside a sleek roadster of the Twenties.

There was also a pack of postcard-size pictures carefully wrapped in yellowed white tissue paper. No longer mindful of another man's privacy, Stanley unfolded the tissue, which broke apart in tiny dried-out flakes and split where the paper had been folded.

There were twelve photos, each solely of his mother. They had been taken, it was perfectly obvious, in a country setting amid the tall grasses of late summer. In every one of the photographs his mother was nude. In none of them had she made any attempt to conceal her sex. She did not smile in these photos: she was reserved yet not at all solemn, and, always, delicately but overwhelmingly beautiful. In the last picture she lay on her back deep in the grass, which had been matted down beside her, her eyes peaceful, a half-eaten apple in her hand. Stanley's own hand shook as he rewrapped the photographs, scattering the flaking tissue paper over the other pictures.

Distraught now, he pawed through the dozens of snapshots, inadvertently exposing an envelope at the bottom of the box. It was addressed, in a familiar script he had no difficulty identifying, to Mr. Anton Beardsley, 110 West Street, Krumpit. Still trembling, Stanley opened the envelope. There looked to be a dozen pages, in his mother's fine hand. A glance at the last-page signature "Mary Louise"—verified it, if he'd had even the slightest doubt, which he had not. Stanley Stanhope had no thoughts at all now about privacy or propriety. With a headful of anguish and a stunned heart, he began to read the letter.

January 31

My very dear Anton,

     I promised you an answer as soon as possible, and here it is. I will not keep you in suspense about it but tell you straight out: It is Jock Stanhope I've decided to marry. Forgive my telling you this via letter, Anton, instead of in person, but this is the only way I can tell you the reasons for my choice without being interrupted and without being half persuaded otherwise by your earnest arguments and dazzling talk.

Do I need to say it was the most difficult decision of my life? I suppose it is the complaint of most women that they are not loved well enough by one man. But I have been well loved by two, and, more's the pity for me, loved them both well in return. Sweet, fervent Jock and my witty, dashing Anton: no girl on earth should be blessed by the loves of two such; it is terribly unfair to the poorly loved and the unloved of this world. But life never is a matter of fairness, is it? I have been the most fortunate of mortals; I appreciate that and am grateful for it. But you must know, Anton, what anguish I had in making the choice I've made.

For I truly loved you both, and both seemingly as much as it is possible for a woman to love. I loved you both, exclusively and simultaneously—don't ask me how such a thing is possible because I couldn't begin to explain it, although I know it. Could it be, I wonder, because the two of you somehow coalesced for me into a single Perfect Lover? And yet I loved you *each*, as well as both, so perhaps that wasn't at all the way it was. That I slept routinely with each of you was not a wanton thing. (I know you wouldn't think of it that way.) The physical expression of that love was a deep-felt thing with me; I was fully as eager for each of you, dear Anton, as either of you were for me.

In all honesty I can tell you that the choice I've made would have been infinitely more difficult had I not this unborn child within me and was thus much freer to choose. I suppose this is scant consolation to you, but it *is* the truth, Anton, and I wanted you to know it. The life stirring within me limits my choice—and relieves me of the tyranny of choosing strictly on the basis of my own personal preference. For *what then* would I do, dear Anton? *How make* a choice? In a sense the decision has been made for me, by the life within me. I hope I can explain this. I can only try.

Our years together—the three of us together—were splendid and insane; not only will I never forget them, but I'll always be grateful for them. The times themselves were insane, I suppose, and we three but some of the inmates in that asylum-time. Perhaps the entire country went overboard, as we did. Certainly all the world we cared about appeared to. And perhaps this Great Depression is somehow deserved—necessary, perhaps: the logical consequence of our collective frivolity. Not just of the three of us, of course, but of everybody who in any way helped bring about these present hard times.

What lies ahead, certainly I don't know. Does anyone? In

New York people are jumping out of the windows of buildings they once owned. And I hear it said that the worst is yet to come. I don't know whether these "experts" and "prophets" are right or not (where were they, after all, while we were drifting into all this?) but I *do* know one thing and know it well, Anton: I want the best possible world for my child to grow up in. However hard the times do get, I want my child to have the *best chance possible*. My choice is based, then, in its most brutal simplicity, on the realization and conviction that Jock can provide my child with the best in this regard. He has neither your wit nor your great and varied abilities, Anton; but he believes in steady work and in not drinking excessively and in not gambling continuously at racetracks and all-night poker games. I do not bring this up to hold it against you, but to give you the explanation for my decision.

These are such perilous times—grown men beg in the streets! It's strange, Anton: in thinking about my baby-to-be I began for the first time to think—not about myself—but about how I've never before thought about anyone *except* myself. And now it's time to think about someone else, although I don't even know that someone, except in that very special way of knowing an organism that lives and feeds off one's own blood and tissue. And perilous as the times are, I simply will not expose my child to additional perils—not for love or money, Anton.

That the child may also be yours is not really a factor in my decision; for it might just as easily be Jock's (as you are both well aware) and the only fair position in the matter was to disregard the fact completely in making my decision. It's so clear and right and simple when I place the baby's welfare first and foremost! I don't know whether you will see it so clearly, however. I'm sure Jock doesn't, although he'd like me to think that he does. But does it really matter as long as you *accept* that priority, as Jock has? For one certainty in this sorry affair is, after all, that the child is definitely *mine*. And

Anton: I want its security—I demand it. I have an unwaver-
ing conviction that Jock can provide such security. I do not
really believe that you can. But please know that it isn't
mercenary: I love Jock Stanhope and will gladly be his wife.

I've loved you both—needed you both, I think. Wanted
you both, certainly. Sometimes when the three of us were so
very, very happy together, in New York or at the beach or
at countless outings or even here in Krumpit, I felt that I was
only truly complete as a person when both of you were with
me. Sometimes you and Jock even forgot that you were rivals,
and then there would be just *us*, musketeers three, laughing
at the world and riding on the wind. I remember wishing
that it would never end.

Anton, I could have been persuaded to live with you both,
if both of you had wanted that. Jock never could have lived
that way—and I do believe that you could not have, either,
for all the fervent bluster of your importunities. For why did
you ask me to marry you, otherwise? I do not feel that you
wanted marriage merely to spite Jock. I admit that I cannot
very well understand the male notion of exclusivity as re-
gards their women. I never felt that way toward either of
you. Quite the contrary: the two of you together provided
what I needed. I will be happy with Jock, I know, but I will
be less complete as a person somehow, without you.

Jock understands—and accepts—this situation. I explained
it to him this evening precisely as I have explained it here to
you. *His* position (aside from loving me, without which I
would never let him marry me) is that whatever the goings-
on of our threesome-courtship days, he cannot share me as
a wife. And if that is what marriage means to him, to behave
otherwise would be to court disaster. That I will not have,
not only for the baby's sake but for Jock's. Yet Jock is your
friend—I know he has been your friend for longer than either
of you have been *my* friend—and he does not want to end
that friendship. Well, I tell you now, Anton, exactly what I
told Jock earlier this evening: the friendship you two feel for

each other is entirely your own business—as long as it *excludes me,* from this moment on. I really don't think it can be any other way and still give me a chance for a successful marriage. I've no right to destroy your close friendship of so many years; but Anton, *you've* no right to destroy my marriage.

So here are the ground rules. Jock says you will abide by them, that he knows you will. I, for one, insist on it. This is a kind of farewell, Anton. I do not mean that we should not speak to each other on the street or not be civil to one another or not exchange Christmas cards and the like. I *do* mean that I do not want you in my home—and that I do not want anything *near* the easy comaraderie the three of us knew in past years. But I shall miss it, Anton. I deprive myself fully as much as I do you.

It was such an effervescent time!—perhaps the bubble had to burst. I suppose my own child will never believe that the Twenties could possibly have been as sparkling-crazy as they were for us. For my child's consciousness will have been formed by this terrible Depression and whatever horrible things may come of it or follow it. But we will remember, won't we, Anton: the three of us. Forever. It will be beautiful memory. *Must* be no more than that: resolutely and irrevocably, I hope you understand that. I depend on you—and on your love for me—to do the right thing. I know you will, so the memory might be kept untarnished. Goodbye, dear Anton. I wish for you only happy days.

Mary Louise

P.S. Jock and I will be married on Valentine's Day, for reasons symbolic of the love we share. You are invited, if you care to come. It will be the last invitation from the two of us.

"I'm sorry you had to find that, boy. . . ." Stanley raised his head in a series of little jerks and beheld Old Beardsley standing inside the doorway to the room. He was dressed in the kind of clothes one goes fishing in; he did in fact wear a battered hat with hooks and flies in the band. He stood there staring at Stanley, who could find neither words nor the ability to form them with his lips, which trembled uncontrollably. "I don't mind your coming here—you're welcome any time, day or night, whether I'm here or not—and I don't mind your going through my stuff: I expect it'll all be yours some day anyhow; that's the way it's been set up in my will for years." He took off his hat and tossed it onto the armchair near the window as he walked across the room. "That letter should've been destroyed years ago. The pictures, too—guess you found those, as well. I meant to, but I . . ." His hand went briskly through his mustache. "Goddammit Stanley, I tried to warn you. I *told* you the past is a kind of graveyard, that you ought to be careful where you dig in it."

"Y-*You* . . . !" (Jesus! JesusJesusJesusJesus*Jesus!*)

"I suppose I share in the blame, though. For showing you the Krumpit diary. I suppose you came here looking for the Paris letters, huh? Figures. I knew you'd want to see 'em sooner or later. I was reading 'em again myself last night—which is why they aren't there. I left 'em in my bedroom, on the night-table. . . ." He rubbed a sun-browned hand around the edges of his mouth, making a smacking noise that sounded indecently loud in the stillness. "Maybe it was a mistake showing you the diary. But I had no other way, boy—no other way to stop you from maybe ruining your life. Maybe you can understand why I felt that way, now that you've read that letter from your ma. But if I could have spared you the—"

"CHRIIIIST!" Stanley bellowed his anguish, brought it up from the depths of him. But it was lost—absorbed—among the voluminous bookshelves. He felt utterly alone, abandoned, very insignificant—a blubbering idiot amid a great universe of learning which he could never comprehend if he lived to be a thousand years old. For examine his first forty: what he thought he knew it turned out he did not know at all. He was like an ignorant primitive who thought the sun got snuffed out in the sea each evening. He was worse off than that, however: for even the ignorant primitive generally knew who his father was. "Christ, Christ, Christ Christ, Christ. . . !" Stanley felt his tear ducts turn to gushing springs as sobs arose from somewhere near the marrow of him. "Oh Christ! OhJesusChrist . . . !"

Old Beardsley went to the armchair by the window, picked up his hat, and sat down with it in his lap. He waited patiently until Stanley had regained a modicum of composure.

When he spoke the old man's voice sounded strangely metallic, like a bad recording. "It may or may not console you, boy, but I truly believe that you're Jock's son, not mine. Can't tell by the looks of you, 'cause you favor Mary Louise. But you got the same kind of mind and personality that Jock Stanhope had. I think I mentioned it before. . . ."

"I—can't tell you—the *contempt* I feel for you!"

"Maybe that'll pass. Or lessen, at least. I hope it will."

"Never. *Never!*" Old Beardsley retrieved a pipe from his shirt pocket and took a long time filling and lighting it. Stanley threw his invective at him with all the force he could muster: "NEV-ER!" And then it was dreadfully still in the room again.

"Waal . . ." (Puff, puff.) "That's a long time. I may not be around to see it, but maybe I will be. I've had a lot of nevers in my own time, Stan; but all of 'em arrived, I don't have any more."

Stanley could feel his eyes burning, with no tears left to put the fire out. But worse—far worse—was the fierce burning within him. And he was surprised by the words that came out of him: "I never thought I could kill a man, Mister Bastard Beardsley; but I think I could kill *you;* I think I *want* to." The old man merely took the pipe out of his mouth then put it back again. *"Didn't you hear me, you ancient creep? I said I want to* KILL YOU!"

(Puff, puff, puff.) "There's a loaded revolver in the top drawer of that desk." (Puff, puff, puff.) Was the old man *mocking* him? Even in Stanley's bottom-of-the-soul misery, was Anton Beardsley *mocking him*, and his anguish, and his desperate attempt to hold together what was left of his pitiful mental apparatus? Stanley jerked the top drawer open. There before him was an enormous pistol, something that looked as if it had come out of the Old West. He had to use both hands just to pick it up. "There's a safety-catch on the left side. You gotta release it, before you can fire it." (Puff, puff, puff.) *Was he mocking Stanley's immense hurt?*— mocking Mary Louise's boy—mocking the only incarnate memory of her whom he had defiled and probably deflowered, her whom he had undressed and laid amid the tall grasses of late summer and then had the effrontery to record the occasion on film? Was that *filthy* dirty old man defiling *yet* his mother, defiling the memory of her, Stanley's own beginning? His hands shook as he raised the weapon and aimed it at Anton Beardsley's face. Down, down the barrel Stanley sighted, trying to steady the revolver and line it up with the furrowed spot between the old eyes that gazed out at him from a nut-sweet cloud of tobacco smoke. Suddenly the revolver went off. Stanley was not aware that he had pulled the trigger. The roar of the weapon filled the room the way his cry of anguish had not, and the sound reverberated so that Stanley never even heard the tinkle of glass from the shattered window behind Old Beardsley. The old man finally lowered his pipe. Stanley Stanhope let fall the revolver. It fell with a heavy, deadweight KLUNK, abandoned forever by Stanley, who buried his face in both hands. "Waal . . . you shot your load, so to speak. Every man deserves the chance."

"I— Forgive me!"

"Lookit, son—Stan, where're you going? Don't rush off like that, boy!" Stanley stumbled out into the restroom-green hallway and down the stairs, nearly losing his balance altogether a half-dozen times. Behind him he could hear Old Beardsley: "Stanley, come back, for Chrissakes don't leave like this! Come back, goddammit! Come back!" But he climbed into his van, then backed it at full speed out of Old Beardsley's front yard. The old man had come out of the house and was standing amid the dust raised by the spinning rear wheels.

In another moment Stanley was crashing down the pot-holed road at breakneck speed, the magpie coat hangers in full alarm, the van itself protesting with wrenching grinding noises and shrill shrieks of metal on metal. The van shook as if it would be shaken apart, the pieces scattered along the road in front of the town dump, that place of broken and tarnished realities. Only its driver shook more. He was all the way into town before he could get the tremors under reasonable control. He drove down his own driveway and just barely stopped the van before it crashed into his garage door.

Stanley went at once to the vegetable cellar, to the deep-darkcool in search of the Mystic Fruit of Forgetfulness. The melon was aswarm with ants, who were having a tribal orgy with its pink flesh. Stanley fell on his knees before it, a gasping cry of anguish escaping him. He brushed away the ants then dug his fingers into the sticky watermelon, breaking off chunk after chunk of it and stuffing them into his mouth, and ants-be-damned if any of them clung to the pieces. Deeper and deeper into the melon remains he dug, seeking a coolness and release neither of which were there. It was a bitter fruit, bad to his taste this time. The only sensation he felt was nausea. Both halves of the split watermelon lay gutted before him, retaken by the besieging ants. He felt an explosive rise within him and vomited into the larger melon half. And decided that there had never been a greater fool alive than Stanley Stilmore Stanhope, son of Mary Louise and— *And whom?* He vomited into the other half of the melon.

AND WHOM? There was no other question in the world. It was bad enough that Stanley knew that his own mother— It was bad enough that she— (Mama! Nonononono!) The single, inadmissible notion violently sought entrance. When he closed his eyes he immediately saw Old Beardsley as he had seen him down the barrel of that enormous revolver. Stanley raised his empty hands as if to pull an imaginary trigger and rid himself of that vision. But there was no deafening roar; and the vision persisted, puff, puff, puff.

AND WHOM? Old Beardsley was a direct descendant of Jonathan Beardsley, who was of course Anthony Krumpit's cousin, which meant that *any son of Anton Beardsley would also be a relation of that same Wild Anthony*—at whatever remove—which meant— (No! Nonononono!) Then, like a fevered oracle who sees meaning in the random fall of sticks or spill of intestines, Stanley, horror-struck, saw new and supernatural significance in the very names Anton and Anthony. *Might Old Beardsley be*, actually, *Wild Anthony reincarnate?* And any son of his—

AND WHOM? (Mama—no!) He was his father's son— Jock Stanhope's boy. Even Old Beardsley had testified to their resemblance. Their *spiritual* resemblance, for physically he favored Mary Louise, who was, without a doubt, his mother. And he *was* a good deal like his father—like Jacob Stanhope—Stanley knew that. Surely those traits—the sound business sense, the dignified demeanor, the devotion to hard work, the generally liberal outlook—surely those traits told. Yet Mary Louise, his indisputably true mother, could not tell, was not certain. At least not at the time she'd decided to marry Jock Stanhope. But was she later, when Stanley had grown up and she had occasion to see for herself how very much *alike* Jock and Stanley Stanhope were? Weren't they? (Yes! Oh, yes!)

AND WHOM? Yet Anton Beardsley had made a will out to Stanley (hadn't the old man said that?) leaving him all the books and the Krumpit Papers and perhaps the chamber pots and the second-hand this and used that which filled his cellar. Willed it all to him, just as if Stanley were his— (No!) It was an old man's dream—a reaching-out for something to substitute for what he could not have: not getting Mary Louise—and not begetting a son off her—he wanted Mary Louise's son, Stanley. Yes, of course that was it! Maybe the old man planned it all, even: luring Stanley on with that diary, then making a great deal of the letters from Paris, then seeing to it that he wasn't at home when Stanley came, and— That box with all the photographs in it, and the letter, carefully yet obviously placed beneath the snapshots, and the key Old Beardsley had cleverly let him see hidden behind the end volume of a shelf beside the secretary: wasn't *that* also planned? Wasn't the whole sad show— (No. OhsweetJesus.)

Stanley's mind spun in his head with a ringing sound. He could think no more, and he was grateful for that. Slowly and with great care, he gathered the melon halves, puke-covered ants and all, into the burlap sack and stumbled out of his cellar with the mess.

The hole he dug behind his garage was three feet deep and nearly as wide. Into it went the burlap sack with its sorry contents, the melon halves—those chalices filled with vomitus and distress. He shoveled the dirt back quickly, trod it down firmly, then leaned against the garage and thought: "If only I could bury myself . . ."

Later he stood in the shower, letting hot water redden his nakedness. He thought he heard the phone ringing (unless it was his head again) but he did not budge, did not care. Might he turn the valve to hotter, and might he melt—run down the drain to some other, better existence? One with a certainty of parentage, even if that be but some humble bacterium?

If the phone *had* rung, it would probably have been Emily, wondering why he hadn't come over to his in-laws. As if he were fit for human company. As if he were fit for *anything*.

ELEVEN

*E*MILY FOUND him sitting in his gazebo, amid the darkgreenshade. He told her about his mother's letter to Anton Beardsley and about his worst fear —that he, Stanley, her very own husband, might conceivably be Old Beardsley's son. She sat beside him, close to him, holding his hand.

"I don't care *what* your parentage is, Stanley. You are who you are, and I love you for it." If she had more to say she hadn't time to say it, for Cissie was yelling out a window that there was a telephone call from grandma. "I guess she's wondering whether you got home all right. . . ."

Emily left him before he'd gotten around to telling her
about his near murder of Old Beardsley. But he would have
to tell her; it was not the sort of thing he could live with
alone.

He had no appetite at all and sat out supper in his den.
Afterwards, Emily was standing in the den doorway, sensing
that she was needed but not absolutely certain how.

"Come in, Em. And close the door." She sat on the edge
of his desk and folded her arms (what a picture of serenity
and strength she was!) then Stanley related the entire shabby
business of how he had actually fired a shot at Anton Beardsley: how he had tried to kill him; how he had *intended* to, at
least. Stanley neither spared himself nor sought to excuse
himself; he had to tell it straight or it would do him no good.

"Oh, Stanley . . . !" Her hands flew to her face, and she
seemed no longer the serene pillar of strength, the Corin-
thian column capable of supporting the temple of his sanity.
But gradually she regained an evenness of demeanor, if not
altogether a composure. "He wasn't injured, then? I mean,
you missed . . . ?"

"Yes. He wasn't hurt. Not that I could tell. He was talking pretty calmly afterwards, though I have no idea what
he said. Then I broke down. Completely. The next thing I
knew I was driving the van down that terrible road by the
town dump." He looked up at her with timid sheep's eyes. "I
had to tell you about it. I can't . . . carry it alone. . . ."

"Stanley, you're never alone; surely you know that. . . ."

"I'd like to be left alone for now, though; for a while, Em.
To try to put some pieces together. . . ."

She slid off the desk and onto his lap, and she kissed him
fiercely, holding his head in her hands. "I love you so much,
Stanley, it frightens me sometimes. I hurt when you do, so
please take care: you have both our lives in yours. . . ."
Then she slipped away and out of the den, closing the door
quietly behind her.

He was left with whatever thoughts he could muster—and
they were not many. Something in him (some safety valve?)

had shut off the more dangerous streams of his imaginings —the ones with the treacherous undertows. His mind was strangely at ease, as if the worst had already been done: what could happen now? His eyes wandered to the wedding portrait of his parents. He rose slowly and went over to it, forcing himself to look at it.

The serene beauty in the picture—she with the unafraid yet receptive eyes—had received perhaps more than she had bargained for. And the alert man beside her—he with the manly gaze leveled like a rifle—had it been he who had shot that tender beauty full of life? Full of . . . Stanley? Beneath that bridal gown, beneath that virginal whiteness, Stanley himself lay secretly and quietly growing—three months, perhaps? His mother knew, and so did his father—and so did his father's best friend (whichever way it worked out). But the photograph didn't show it. The photograph was a lie.

It did no good to dwell on it. Indeed, he found it difficult to do so: the safety valve in his head repeatedly shut off such thoughts. The organism protects itself, however it can. Wasn't that it? And what, he wondered, was the ultimate desperate act of self-protection? Insanity?

He sat at his desk and opened the top drawer. There was no revolver there, but there was a very potent watermelon stain. It stared at him like the Eye of God. Also in the drawer were Billy's peace pendant and the Yamaha motorcycle brochure. FEEL FREE. Peace and Freedom were there beside the Eye of God. . . .

What did Billy know of peace, he who knew nothing of war or of the battle that was life, he who knew of no other struggle than the anguish of adolescence, he who had practically a guaranteed security—even though he didn't have everything his Conspicuously Consuming little heart desired? Billy swam in the Sound and sunned on the sand, had a lovely girl in Osterville, and lived in a fine old house which he might someday inherit, along with a profitable and established business. *Who* was this upstart to wear a peace emblem, to imply that all his freedom to have such possessions and do

such things and be so blessed was not in itself a greater freedom than most men who have *ever lived* have known?

Stanley picked up the Yamaha brochure. The message on
its cover was succinct. For the first time Stanley thought he
saw a relationship between the motorcycle and the peace
pendant. The Indochina War was not involved; no war was
involved—not even the concept "war." Vietnam was mostly
a vehicle of convenience. What was at issue was, simply,
peace-and-freedom, freedom-and-peace, the freedom to be
peaceful, the peace to be free: and ask not whether the dog
wags the tail or the tail the dog. The freest people on earth
wanted to be impossibly free. Yet wasn't that *inhuman?*
Wasn't such perfect Freedompeace more correctly ascribable
to the Eye of God? Was that, then, what the peace-and-
freedomers *really* wanted—to *be God?* Whether they realized it or not? Stanley pushed the drawer closed and thought
no more about it. The safety valve had functioned again.

It was cool on the front porch when he joined Emily on
the glider. The honeysuckle flooded the night with its in-
toxicant and crickets chirped at a far less fractious volume.
All seemed right with the world, and he inhaled the sweet
night air as if it were sanity itself. His wife smiled broadly at
him. "How do you feel?"

"Hungry. Famished. Starved!"

"What can I fix you?"

"No, don't bother. Call the pizza place—the one on Sycamore, they deliver. Get the biggest one they have—sausages,
peppers, mushrooms, anchovies, the works! And if Cissie
doesn't want any, I'll eat her share!"

Cissie was crazy about pizza, though, and they divided the
huge pie at the kitchen table. Cissie drew out the melted
cheese in strings, then nibbled them in—reverting, for the
occasion at least, to eleven years old—and Stanley laughed as
his daughter got first cheese then tomato sauce then a tiny
piece of mushroom on her face—and laughed all the more
when she became incensed at his laughter. Billy came home—

early for a change—just in time to have the last two pieces
of the oversized pizza, and suddenly the four of them were
laughing together, a family again. Surely the world had
righted itself. Surely tomorrow a new sun would rise, and it
would shine on Krumpit-town. And on the Nation. . . .

Stanley Stanhope leveled the heavy revolver at the furrow
between Anton Beardsley's eyes and pulled the trigger:
slowly and deliberately, releasing an incredible roar that
echoed throughout the universe, even unto the Eye of God
—and presumably his Ear. Stanley's aim had been true: the
bullet from the enormous weapon hit Old Beardsley squarely
in the forehead, opening a gushing red orifice that size of a
half-dollar and spattering watermelon-pink brains out an immense hole blasted at the back of his head. So severe had been
the impact that the old man had bitten his pipe-stem in two,
and burning ashes spilled over his clothes and the armchair
and began to smoulder there.

Stanley went to the secretary and found the box of snapshots with the letter from his mother in it. Carefully, he
spread the dozen pages of her letter over the top of the desk
and upon them he placed the nude photographs of her, in
two neat rows of six. The revolver he laid atop the nude
photos. When he turned back toward Anton Beardsley, the
old man was swathed in flames, as was the stuffed chair he
sat in. Before the fiery wrap wound completely around Old
Beardsley, Stanley caught sight of the handyman's dead and
staring eyes full of fright and disbelief.

Then Stanley left the premises: out through the restroom-
green hallway, out the front door which was never locked,
out to his delivery van, which he slowly backed out into
the street. He waited, though he did not have to wait long.
Vindictive flames engulfed the house and sucked in the windows under the eaves. When the structure was a huge ball
of flame shooting loose ends up into the night consuming
Anton Beardsley, the Krumpit Papers, the nude photos of

his mother, her letter, the voluminous bookshelves in German French Spanish Italian and of course the mother tongue, the chamber pots and used this and second-hand that, then and only then did Stanley drive off.

He drove slowly down the pot-holed road past the town dump, being careful not to damage the van or disturb the slumbering magpie coat hangers. On the Krumpit-Osterville Road he pulled obediently to one side as a pair of fire trucks roared by in the opposite direction, their sirens churning the night. Before starting off again Stanley looked back toward the dump. Somewhere beyond it flames were leaping skyward as if some volcano had erupted. . . .

He was soaked with perspiration and awoke suddenly. Beside him, Emily slept peacefully, deeply, totally unaware of the crime. Stanley got up without disturbing her, found his bathrobe, and started for his gazebo.

It had done no good at all to murder Anton Beardsley. Stanley understood that completely as he set himself down on a gazebo bench. The act of murder—which had occurred the moment he willed it, whatever the actual outcome—was a purely selfish one of vindictiveness for a wrong which was wholly imagined. For did his *mother* hate Anton Beardsley? Her letter clearly demonstrated otherwise.

The murder of Anton Beardsley had been Stanley's own personal failure. He had failed in exactly the same way the power-brokers and the people who refused to be the People had failed: by placing his own interests and comforts above anything else; by not putting the good of the Country above his own blood guts and rhetoric—above his own good. In thinking his own predicament of paramount importance, in being concerned about how James Tarber might demolish him in print or how Anthony Krumpit was nothing but a scoundrel or how his mother posed nude for photographs and slept with her lovers or how not even she could tell for sure whom the father of her child Stanley was—in placing these strictly personal and (as world events go) insignificant occurrences on the center stage of his attention, Stanley had thereby *forfeited* any chance of becoming the Patriot he had dreamed of becoming. Stanley S. Stanhope was no better than the rest. Only more stupid, for he had gained nothing by his selfishness other than the unsavory taste of vengefulness. No wonder vengeance was said to be the Lord's: the human gullet couldn't handle it. On its surprisingly large proportions mere man choked to death. Or vengeance poisoned the system. As the very thought of his murder of Anton Beardsley poisoned him now.

In the moonlight he saw one thing with perfect clarity, and that was that the past did not matter. Old Beardsley had spoken well in calling it a graveyard. It was the present and the future which needed tending to.

Another corollary of the great Watermelon Correlative: "the future is in direct ratio to the seeds of the present." As in the famous parable, everything depends on what kind of soil the seeds end up in and how they are tended. It is precisely the task of the Patriot to tend those precious seeds of the present. By Wild Anthony's account, were not the first Patriots farmers? Countrymen for the Country—could anything be more appropriate? And with all the planting Stanley Stanhope had done behind his garage, *might he not* also qualify as a farmer?

Stanley Stanhope had no need of Anthony Krumpit or anyone else in the graveyard that was history. Now he could act; he could redeem himself. He inhaled the cool night air and was filled with the peace of knowing his own mind at last. He went back to bed without ever awakening his wife. As he fell asleep, he thought he heard a fife and drum a-playing. Or was it his own breath and heartbeat. . . .

Outside the Stanhope Cleaners a yellow modified Chevrolet with wide red stripes was parked in the morning sunshine. Stanley pulled the van up directly behind it, and Harry immediately popped out of the shop door. "Whaddya doing keeping the goddamn truck so late, for Chrissakes? Dontcha know I gotta take that-there goddamn thing inta the shop?"

"It's all yours, Harry."

"Ain't it bad enough I gotta use my kid's car for deliveries, that *you* gotta complicate my life basides?"

(Do you remember a summer evening? Do you remember watermelon slices under honeysuckle, and simple talk as sweet as life?) "Sorry. . . ."

Harry entered the truck, and in a minute more the red, white, and blue delivery van was tearing noisily down the street, its tailpipe finally breaking loose and scattering sparks.

"Hiya, Mister Stanhope." Irma stood by the legger and topper, waiting for the pressure to come up. She looked at him and smiled an enormous smile.

"Good morning"—and he went immediately into his little office. Last week's time-sheet lay atop his desk. It had already been approved and initialed: O.K.—H.P. Stanley added two hours to Irma Kasendorf's time, figuring it at double-time rather than the time-and-a-half she had demanded. Ah well, hard lessons were expensively learned. He signed the time-sheet and put it into an envelope to be mailed to the Krumpit National Bank, Att: Payroll Dept.

"Excuse me, Mister Stanhope." Irma stood in the office doorway, her voluptuous hips rolling as she settled her weight onto one leg. She wore the white Dacron dress with the short pleated skirt that danced when she walked. "I was wondering if you wanted me to come down any night this week. For the same kinda thing as Saturday night, I mean." She flashed an easy, conspiratorial grin. "I think I could work in a coupla hours a week, regular—for time-and-a-half, of course." One of her thighs twisted sideways a moment as she scratched herself there; it had not been done intentionally, Stanley felt certain, but quite unconsciously as she awaited his answer. "Or anytime, Mister Stanhope—anytime at all. If I'm free. . . ."

(Is this real? Is this happening?) "I—I'll have to let you know, Irma." (By the bleeding Jesus . . . !)

"Okay, Mister Stanhope, you let me know. Just about any time oughta be okay, I think." She beamed her dazzling white smile at him—and in a pirouetting turn a generous amount of bronzed thigh as well (now *that* was intentional) as she waltzed back into the workroom, her buttocks apparently doing a tarantella beneath those flying pleats. (OhsweetJesus.)

Stanley had it figured: Irma had related the strange (to say the least) business of Saturday evening to Freddie Winslow, and the conniving Freddie had suggested that since Old Stanhope (*old!*) only wanted to *look* and not touch, she'd be a fool not to make a regular thing out of it. Get the dirty old man hooked on the sight of her bouncing boobs and rolling thighs, then ask for double-time and then—who knows —days off, shorter hours at greater pay, a regular allowance on the side—anything she might work his mad lust for. That was definitely the way Winslow would think. Stanley knew his sort.

He felt an acute and profound embarrassment. To be the figure of discussion (and fun, no doubt) between Irma Kasendorf and Freddie Winslow (in bed, no doubt, after sex and during cigarettes), to be thought of as no more than a voyeur, an aging impotent suffering all sorts of sexual aberrations (Freddie would have read a book about them)—it was too much, simply too much. How could Stanley *ever* have his iced tea and tuna sandwich at Prescott's lunch counter again. . . .

But NO! that was just the failure he had discovered in himself last night in his gazebo: the preoccupation with his own sensibilities and self-interests, his own insignificant world and the unimportant problems in it. The past could bury the past. His foolishness with La Kasendorf was past. He was free of it and would not allow himself to be deterred by it, any more than by the rascality of Anthony Krumpit or the sardonic remarks of James Tarber or by the scarlet letter his mother had written or by his own attempt on Old Beardsley's life.

He got up and went into the workroom. Irma was laboring away. (Ssss-phtttt.) "Irma, when Harry gets back tell him I've gone for the day."

"On *Monday*, Mister Stanhope?" (SSss-ssss. . . .) She did not smile at him but only stared. She actually stopped working to stare at him.

"Yes. And if Harry says anything about it I want you to tell him something for me: I want you to remind him that *I'm* the boss here. Tell him I said that." Then he walked out of the shop. That goddamn Harry Putchek was getting out of hand—and it was beginning to rub off on Irma, who had *never once* questioned him. Even when he'd asked her to take off her clothes! It was time Stanley asserted himself around the plant.

Larry Putchek's car stood by the curb looking as if it were about to pounce. Harry would be only too happy to stick the sluggish delivery van into the repair shop for a day and grumble about the loss of it, but he goddamn enjoyed using his son's car, you could tell just by watching him behind the wheel. Would he give it back to Larry when the boy returned from Vietnam? Or was it Cambodia, or Laos. . . . It was no longer the Vietnamese War; it had become the Indochina War. It was a time for Patriots. It was a time for Stanley Stanhope to *act*.

When Stanley walked past Prescott's Pharmacy, Freddie Winslow waved good-naturedly at him. Stanley did not return the greeting; he knew the motivation behind it. That goddamn Freddie. . . .

Stanley hurried on. But as he approached Holgrove's Hardware, who was standing in front of it and looking directly at him but Old Beardsley, very much alive from the manner in which he turned abruptly and scuttled inside. Stanley stopped to look at the outdoor thermometer (which read a comfortable 75) and then forthrightly walked into the store. He found Old Beardsley alone, over by a counter of turnbuckles and braces. Anton Beardsley returned a brace to its bin, looked up, but said nothing.

"I want to apologize, Mister Beardsley." The handyman

appeared very old today, and very tired. Had the realization of how close a brush with death he'd had finally frightened the old man? Stanley thought he saw Old Beardsley's hands tremble. Maybe the geezer merely tied one on last night. The old eyes that gazed blinkingly at Stanley seemed bloodshotty. "Can you forgive me?"

But now Stanley felt acutely uneasy, as in his own mind he heard anew the roar of that revolver which may well have meant the destruction of Anton Beardsley. He had found it a terrible thing indeed nearly to have killed a man; but seeing the man directly before him, seeing the scraggle of his unkempt mustache and enlarged pores of his nose, it was infinitely worse.

Old Beardsley turned back to the bins. His voice was surprisingly calm. "Best thing to do is forget about it." He picked up a six-inch turnbuckle and began to work it. "Forget about *every*thing."

"I—I don't think I'll be able to. I don't think I *should*."

Anton Beardsley fished through a bin. "What's the matter with you, boy? Don't you ever learn anything? What's past is past. Forget it."

"I might have— I nearly killed you, Mister Beardsley."

"Maybe it was the other way around. . . ."

"Wh-What?"

"Maybe I nearly killed you."

"You're forgiven if I am."

The old man busied himself unscrewing a turnbuckle and measuring the extension against his hand. "I said it's forgotten. To forget *is* to forgive. Provided you *really* forget. Now, go on home, Stan—or wherever it is you're going. You only tend to remind me. . . ."

Stanley started to leave but stopped short and turned toward the handyman again. On the far side of the store Barney Holgrove was laughing and bidding a customer goodbye. "I'd like to ask a favor of you, Mister Beardsley. . . ."

"What the fuck is it?"

"Would you bequeath me the Krumpit Papers? I give you

my word I'll take proper care of them. And keep their secret." Anton Beardsley faced him again at last—stared at him steadily out of old bloodshot eyes as Barney Holgrove's easy laughter threaded its way toward them, counter by counter. *"Will you?"* Then Barney was between them, greeting them and starting immediately on the latest dirty joke and laughing to himself so irrepressibly that he had to pause and give full vent to his glee. Stanley repeated his question to Anton Beardsley, but only with his eyes: "WILL YOU?" As Barney Holgrove doubled with laughter, Old Beardsley nodded once, affirmatively, to Stanley, who turned and left the store before the proprietor even knew he'd gone.

It took him twenty minutes to walk to lower Sycamore, to the International Cycle Shop. He handed the salesman the Yamaha brochure. What should he say? "I want to Feel Free"?

"I'm interested in this model. Have you got it?" They did. It was a superb machine, a real— "Can you teach me to drive it, right now? The sale's contingent on whether I can handle it." There was no problem, no problem at all; would he come this way?

In the parking lot Stanley was shown how to start the bike, how to operate the brakes front and rear, how to disengage the clutch and shift, how to use the throttle and how to control the cycle easily by simultaneous use of throttle and rear brake. He was an avid student, paying the strictest of attention. The salesman took the bike around the lot a few times, then it was Stanley's turn. He was made to ride in wide circles and then, as his confidence became apparent, in sweeping figure-eights. It seemed ludicrously simple to drive, though the salesman kept coaching him to keep his feet in the proper positions and not to use the front-wheel brake in turns. Stanley was obviously getting the feel of the machine, and finally he was left alone to practice. It was nearly an hour later when he stopped the machine and went inside to the salesroom. "How much?"

"You can have that little baby for only seven forty-nine ninety-five, my friend."

(Not seven-fifty?) "I'll need a helmet too, won't I? And goggles? And put some dealer's plates on it; I'm taking it with me."

"Uh—you do need a license, you know. . . ."

"Yes. I'll write you a check, right now."

The cycle was his. He strapped the helmet on, feeling a bit absurd at first but rather like a fighter-pilot by the time he'd fastened it. The salesman had affixed the plates and fueled it up; he held it now, like some shining thoroughbred stallion ready for its master. Stanley mounted the machine and brought it to life—revving it expertly, he felt.

"Couple of things to remember!" The salesman had to shout over the throttled-up engine. "Use the rear brake first, downshift before you stop, and lean into fast curves." Stanley nodded his understanding and rolled off—a bit jerkily, but he controlled the bike immediately. "And don't forget the license . . . !" Stanley roared out of the lot and headed straight up Sycamore Street.

The bike was stable and responsive. "That little baby" felt like a living animal beneath him—a mount that roared like a wild beast yet did his bidding in perfect obedience. Stanley began to feel one with the machine, its vibrations becoming attuned with the vibrations in his blood vessels and with the beat of his heart—or was it the other way around? And he began to discover a strange kinship with the air around him: suddenly he was not so much moving *through* it as moving *with* it. He *did* "Feel Free"—there was no denying it; the brochure had not exaggerated. Stanley Stanhope felt, in fact, a delirium of sorts at his oneness with the same breeze that rippled the highest leaves of the tall old elms.

So complete was Stanley's leaping joy, that when he downshifted and stopped for the light at Sycamore and Main, he did not notice the yellow car with the broad red stripes waiting across the intersection from him. Nor was he aware that the car's driver took instant and open-mouthed notice of

Stanley. Perhaps that was because Stanley was busy pulling
his goggles down and putting his son's peace pendant around
his own neck. For hadn't *Stanley* the real right to wear such
a symbol? He who *really* knew what peace was all about?

When the light changed, Stanley revved his bike and shot
up Main, heading west. He turned off at Riker's Field
Road. . . .

Over the curb he rode—nearly unseating himself—and into
Riker's Field Park. There were a half-dozen young mothers
pushing baby carriages along the sunny brick walk which en-
circled Anthony Krumpit's shrine, but with shouts and shrieks
they shoved their precious bundles off the walk and into
flower beds as Stanley bore down on them on his machine
gone mad.

Round and round the upraised grave he rode, revving his
engine and shouting above the roar of it: "You failed! You
failed, Wild Anthony! Even if you have monuments that say
otherwise! But *you* know, and *I* know, and Anton Beardsley
knows, and his father, and his father's father, and on and on
and on, all the way to cousin Jonathan! And my *wife*, you
lustful bastard—she too knows you failed! Like you failed
with Nancy Primrose, who loved a Stanhope more! Like you
failed with the Patriot Cause, which you never even understood—which you hadn't the heart or mind to understand,
you selfish pimp and lecher! Like you failed with your entire
life, which got you just what you deserved—disease and dope
and death that not even your ill-gotten wealth, your filthy
lucre, could save you from! Do you hear me, Anthony?
YOU FAILED! But a Stanhope won't, you bloody bastard! A
Stanhope took your Nancy from you and another Stanhope
will take your goddamn *glory* from you! By out-performing
you! Do you hear me, Anthony? Do you hear me, with your
doped-up syphilitic soul rotting in hell?" Then, to the immense relief of the mothers standing terrified among the
marigolds, Stanley Stanhope spun off down a gravel path.

The woods muffled the roar of his bike, which swerved

sloppily, dangerously, on the gravel; but in another minute he had access to the broad meadow that was Riker's Field. He throttled open, hit a rise and rose clear off the ground— but his mount landed like a thoroughbred and he sped on across the meadow, aiming straight for the Krumpit Memorial Monument. He skidded around it once, remembering not to touch the front-wheel brake. How expertly he handled the steed; how exactly it responded to his guidance. "Do you hear me, you despicable bastard? A *Stanhope* will do the job for you!"

He charged westward across the expanse of meadow, ar- row-straight, having to swerve only once in order to avoid an elderly golfer who stood too petrified to move out of the way. Stanley shot the curb on the west side of Riker's Field and roared away down the boulevard there. He did not see the red-striped yellow car brake to a sudden halt, reverse, turn and start off after him. Stanley was too absorbed in the historic greatness of his task-at-hand to be aware of any- thing other than a sense of urgency.

He was on the highway north of Krumpit when he be- came aware of a roar other than the Yamaha's. Then, along- side him, a yellow and red blur appeared. He tried to ig- nore it, but the car pulled slightly ahead of him and sustained itself in that position. Stanley could see the driver motion- ing frantically at him. But Stanley could hear only the roaring and the wind: the totally free wind and the caged roar of engines. The yellow-red car whined as it revved up and pulled ahead of Stanley so that he could clearly see the car's driver.

"What the bleeding Jesus . . . !"—but he scarcely heard his own words, torn away as they were by the wind. Then the yellow-red car inched closer to him. "Get away! Get away . . . !" Stanley began to throttle down. But still he shouted at that goddamn Harry Putchek: "Get away—get away, I say!" But again the words were swept behind him. And still Harry inched closer, forcing Stanley onto the paved

breakdown lane. The maniac would kill him if he kept it up
—and he showed not the slightest sign of ceasing.

As Stanley slowed down Harry did also, staying alongside
him. Ahead of them the road rose to a crest of a hill. What,
thought Stanley, was beyond that? Would the breakdown
lane run out and would Stanley— He stomped hard on the
brake, fishtailing his bike. Harry pulled away to give him
room but stayed close enough to move back in if necessary.
The Yamaha had steadied itself, and finally Stanley thought it
safe enough to squeeze the front-wheel brake as well. The
cycle and the yellow-red car came to a halt together at the
top of the rise.

Stanley tried to still the quake in his arms and gain full
control of himself. He would fire Harry Putchek, that's
what he would do. Right there on the rise on the road in
open country. Regardless of the fact that Harry had been
with the Stanhope Cleaners since Jock Stanhope's time. Stanley would not stand for this. He removed his goggles and
helmet as Harry came rushing up to him. "Harry, you're—"

"*What the Christ are ya doing?*" His eyes looked crazed,
Stanley thought, and he was visibly trembling—more than
Stanley. Then Harry's powerful hands and arms picked him
right off the seat of the Yamaha. It toppled to the weeds at
the roadside while Stanley himself was thrown against the
yellow-red car.

"I said you're—" Harry began slapping him in the face,
right-left left-right right-left left-right, whack whack whack
whack whack.

"Ya goddamn fool ya coulda kilt yourself!" He shook
Stanley back and forth against the car, his vise-like grip
hurting Stanley's arms. "Are ya crazy, for Chrissakes? Have
ya flipped?"

"*I've got to save the Nation, don't you understand?*" Harry
released him suddenly, but Stanley found himself shaking
still: quaking from head to foot. And his voice, dry in his
throat now (from the wind, perhaps?) rasped out the ex-

planation. "There was nobody else, Harry . . . ! Nobody else. . . ."

"C'mon, get in." Harry opened the front passenger-side door and held it open until Stanley, spent somehow, entered the yellow-red car. Harry closed the door with a sad-sounding slam. In a moment, the trunk lid flew open. There were grunts and groans from the back of the car, and then the rear end sagged with a sudden weight. In another moment Harry was in the driver's seat. The engine exploded into its brutal metallic life, Harry paused to examine his rear-view mirrors, then he made a slow U-turn at the crest of the hill and drove toward Krumpit at no more than twenty-five miles per hour.

But he didn't stay on the highway. He went off down an unpaved road which led first into some trees and finally, after a mile or so, to a wide slow stream. The place seemed startlingly familiar to Stanley. Before them, the trees went clear to the stream, where mossy banks met the water's edge. On the other side, perhaps thirty feet across, was a splendid sunny meadow.

Was it—could it have been—the very spot where Anthony Krumpit had recuperated after his drunken caper at Riker's Field? Harry stilled the brutal engine, put the gearshift into reverse and set the parking brake with a daydream-shattering *crickkkk*. "Let's get out." Stanley obeyed meekly. He felt completely unwound, run down. It was hard for him to recall that just minutes before he was flying along the highway free as the wind, one with the machine that bore him, one with the air and the sky and even the road, which had seemed no more than an extension of himself, as if he had been riding up his own backside. . . .

Now they were sitting, with legs drawn up, on the mossy bank. The stream was brownish and bluish, in different places, and swept by them in a wide arc at this point, leaving deep quiet pools along the bank. The main stream flowed by in a gentle wash that made so little sound you didn't hear it at first, though after a while it became a clearly discernible and slightly hypnotic murmur. Across the stream, unseen birds twittered in the sunsplashed meadow grasses.

"Ever been here bafore?"

"No. . . ." (And yet . . . !)

"This-here's the Paquinock. It starts underground about nine miles north a here. It flows inta the Sound, a course. . . ." There was a sudden burst of twittering activity in the grasses across from them, then a rise of small brown birds, perhaps a dozen of them. "Me and Larry usedta come fishing here alla time. First day he gets back we gotta date ta come back here, even if it's ina middle a winter and we hafta fish through the ice—so I'm telling ya right now, Stan, I'm taking that-there day off."

"Yes, of course. . . ." (Did Anthony Krumpit sleep on this very mossy bank? Did he dry his clothes in the sun over there, precisely where those brown birds rose?)

"Where were ya heading, Stan?"

"To Hartford. . . ." (Anthony Krumpit, who was no hero at all, but rather quite the opposite. . . .)

"What for?"

(A scoundrel . . .) "I . . . had a crazy idea I could . . ." (He was a scoundrel when the Country sorely needed Patriots, as it does now. . . .)

"Could what?"

(A scoundrel who resorted to Patriotism in the Johnsonian sense—the SamuelJohnsonian, not the LyndonJohnsonian. . . .) "What?"

"What was ya gonna do in Hartford?"

"I don't really know, Harry. That's the truth." (Did Wild Anthony know what he did in fact accomplish when he charged down Riker's Field?)

"Ya musta had *some* kinda plan. For instance, why Hartford?"

"Because that's where the General Assembly is. . . ."

"Ya wanted ta talk ta them, is that it? Talk ta the legislators?"

Stanley laughed, slapped the mossy bank. Somewhere close by a frog jumped-plop into the stream. "I don't know . . . ! So help me. I thought I *would* know by the time I got to Hartford. I had some idea. . . . Maybe I *have* flipped, Harry. I had some crazy notion of myself driving the motorcycle right up the Statehouse stairs and into one of the Assembly chambers—of roaring right down the aisle of the House or the Senate and making them *listen* to me, Harry. *Making* the goddamn power-brokers hear me out. . . ."

Harry reached up and pulled a leaf from a low-hanging limb and began to chew pensively on the stem. "What wouldja have told 'em?"

"I don't know. I thought the words would come. They're all inside me, Harry—all bunched together, like a tumor."

"Well, just in general, sorta. What wouldja tell 'em, if ya could?"

(Christ!) "That I think there's a kind of sickness in the Country. Maybe one of epidemic proportions. I mean, *look* at us! Black Panthers and Wallacites; student hot-heads and bullying hard-hats; bomb-throwers and hate-mongers; left-wingers who would bring the whole Nation down and right-wingers who would stifle it to death; kids into drugs and parents into isolation; and always—always, Harry!—politicians who talk and talk and talk but who never *do* anything except the things they think will get them re-elected, so they can talk and talk some more!"

"Hell, that ain't nothing new. Is that all you'd tell 'em? 'Cause if it is, it wouldn't be worth the trip. Not ta Hartford, I mean. Maybe not even ta Osterville. . . ."

"No. I'd tell them the Country is so sick it needs a trans-fusion—a transfusion of the ideals of our own Revolution—if the Country's going to survive. That we can't any longer consider the Constitution merely a noble piece of paper but that we are going to have to put the principles contained in it into actual practice in American life, Harry. Things like Equality and Justice for all. They have to exist as something more than just words, or the Constitution won't *mean* anything anymore. I'd tell them that we're going to have to *stop,* while we still can, this mad pursuit we've developed for material things, for essentially needless things, for Conspicuous Consumption, for getting more and more while doing and caring less and less about anything and anybody else. That the Acquisitive Society is going to have to become the Sacrificial Society, at least to the point where the purpose of life becomes the quality of living, not the accumulation of material things.

"I'd tell them that we, the People, Harry, *as a Nation,* have got to become the truly Just Society. Not any 'New Frontier' or 'Great Society' or 'New Federalism' or any other catch-word nonsense designed only to gull the People into believing something will actually be done, but a truly Just Society: not one proclaimed in advance on the crest of political rhetoric, but one *achieved,* as a matter of workaday policy. Because that's what the Constitution's all about, I think. I really believe that its main purpose is Justice, Harry, and that we're having all the trouble we're having now because that purpose has been continuously thwarted. All the words, all the rhetoric, can no longer find any place to roost, because it can only roost in ignorance and there's less of that now. If the Constitution were *only implemented,* maybe we could *have* the Just Society. If it's attainable at all.

"But we've got to disenshrine it, Harry—get the Constitution out into the streets and into the Congress and the State-houses and the City Halls and the Town Halls. Because when the Just Society is finally achieved—not just talked about—won't we have everything else along with it? Law and order, true prosperity, the real brotherhood of man? If such things are humanly attainable. But if there is no Justice, isn't everything else a sham? Isn't law and order merely the haves keeping the have-nots in their place? Isn't prosperity based on some possessing things at the expense of others? Isn't brotherhood reduced to warring factions of ins versus outs? And if the politicians remain no more than power-brokers, isn't the Constitution rendered utterly and irredeemably impotent? And isn't it time that the *People*, Harry—you and me —rescued the Constitution from the hands of those who have betrayed it? While there's still *time?* Before we become the No Society and our enemies dine on our carcasses?

"I guess that's what I wanted to tell them. Tell *somebody* in a position to do something, to *act*. The General Assembly in Hartford was the nearest group, I guess. That's why I was going there. . . ."

Harry threw his leaf into the stream and it was borne away. "They wouldn'ta listened to ya, ya know that, dontcha. They wouldn'ta let ya speak, and if ya insisted they woulda had ya arrested and hauled your ass outa there for disturbing the peace and becoming a public nuisance. And they woulda clambed ya inta the jug. Later they woulda sent ya up for psychiatric observation and asked ya a lotta weirdo questions, like did ya ever wanna lay your old lady and did ya like little boys better'n little girls. And maybe, if ya kept your trap shut and said ya was sorry, maybe they'da let ya come home. If ya didn't, they'da locked ya up for keeps, Stan, and they woulda thrown the fucking key away. And that's the goddamn truth."

"Would I have deserved it? Being locked up, I mean. Being . . . put away. . . . Give me an honest answer, Harry. . . ."

"Naw. *Daserve* it! It's *them-there* bastards what oughta be locked up. There ain't a thing wrong with what ya just told me, Stan—not a goddamn thing. If ya run for President, I'll vote for ya."

"Then what *is* wrong with me? Why did I . . . mount that motorcycle and charge off to Hartford like that?"

"Ya know something? Ya remind me a lot a your old man. Sensitive, I mean. Very sensitive. Christ he usedta sit in the office and read the goddamn newspaper and get hopping mad—I mean *hopping*, right there, at something he was reading about, some dumb thing the government was gonna do or had done or was doing or wasn't gonna do. I mean he got *outraged*, Stan. Dontcha ramember? And it's a funny thing:

he wasn't so fanatic, neither. Sometimes we usedta talk about it—about whatever it was he was getting excited about—and nine times outa ten I'd agree with him completely. Just like I agreed with everything *you* been saying. But somehow, I dunno, things never got my blood up like it did his. And yours."

"Bad blood, do you think?"

"Nuts, ya mean? Naw. . . . It's just that ya got more amagination than the rest of us, Stan. That's your trouble. Ya got so damn much amagination ya get t' amagining ya can *do* something about things, that's all."

"And I can't—is that it?"

"How the hell should I know. Maybe ya can. Lemme tell ya: if there's one thing what's needed in Washington—and Hartford—it's amagination. Ya won't find *me* knocking it."

"But you said it was my 'trouble.' . . ."

"Keeping it on a leash is your trouble. Maybe that-there would be more accurate. Look, I aint no goddamn shrink, so don't ask *me*."

"You use the word 'shrink.' That suggests to me that you really, deep down, think of me as . . ."

"That's your amagination again. You ain't soft, Stan—I'm telling ya straight. I been around loonies in my time—lotsa them go ta sea, ya know—and I'm telling ya, you ain't one a them."

"How can you be so sure, if you're not a—a shrink?"

"I got news for ya, Stan: lotsa times the *shrinks* ain't sure."

"Harry . . . I've been behaving . . . strangely of late. Doing things I would've never *dreamed* of doing before. Crazy things. . . ."

"Happens ta everybody, one time or another."

"I think I might really be . . . somewhat deranged, Harry. Insane. . . ."

"Listen, Stan: What ya told me a minute ago was completely rational, see? It's what *everybody* should want. Anybody who *don't* want it is crazy. Now for the funny stuff, the strange bahavior and alla that-there, that ain't unnatural,

that's what ya gotta get through your skull. Stuff like that—
there happens ta people alla time. Balieve me."

"Not like it happens to me. Other people don't go flying
off to Hartford on a motorcycle because they don't like
the way the Country's being run."

"Naw. . . ." Harry plucked another leaf from the limb.
"They do other things. More private things, maybe. So's
other people don't notice. Or worse: maybe they just don't
give a damn. Most people don't, ya know. Others ain't got
the smarts. Others don't even know anough ta realize when
they're being screwed—by Uncle Sam or Lady Luck or
anybody else. But alla them, everybody on this-here earth,
Stan, does crazy things sometimes. Things they can't even
explain ta theirselves. It's the nature a the beast. . . ." He
was forming the leaf into a tiny vessel with the aid of green
twigs. His blunt fingers worked with a surprising agility.

"What shall I do, Harry?"

Harry launched the tiny leaf-boat gently into the stream
and watched it sail away. "Forget about it. It'll pass."

They were driving back into Krumpit. They hadn't said
a word since they'd left the secret stream, the one that began underground and flowed into the Sound, the one Anthony Krumpit may well have found solace by, the stream
called Paquinock. Whatever that name meant. The Indians
had a positive genius for place-names, perhaps because they
were far closer to the land and the water than the despoilers
who came after them. Stanley decided to give the stream a
meaning all his own—one he felt the Indians might have approved of. Paquinock: stream-that-renews-the-spirit.

"I don't want to forget about America, Harry. Or its problems. I want to *do* something about them. Even at my peril."
They were just turning into his driveway. Harry stilled the
bestial engine, then rested his big hands on the wheel.

"I didn't say ta forget about your country. I said ta forget
about the kookiness—about going overboard—because everybody does it, sometimes."

"I may again, then."

Harry took a deep breath, filling his barrel of a chest. "Ya know how ta handle that, Stan? I'll tell ya. Just try ta lead a full, normal life. Throw yourself inta your work—ya been taking too much time off lately; it ain't good. A man's gotta have something ta do, otherwise his head gets fulla funny ideas. I usedta see it aboard ship, alla time."

"Be a good dry-cleaner, you're telling me. Keep my nose to my spotting board. But I don't think that's enough. . . ."

"Be a good man, I'm saying. Lead a busy life. Ya'll still have time ta be concerned about what's happening—Christ, your old man was, and *he* was building up a goddamn business! Maybe that's what ya need. Didja ever think about opening up a branch somewhere? Osterville's big anough now. Ya could start a branch over there—that-there'd keep ya busy. Think about it."

Emily was coming towards them, her eyes widening. "Oh my goodness! A motorcycle! Oh Stanley, you've made Billy's summer . . . !"

Stanley helped Harry unload the bike from the trunk of the yellow-red car, which gratefully raised its tail six inches. He thanked Harry "for everything" and asked if he wouldn't come in for a cup of coffee.

"I ain't got no time for that—*some*body's gotta mind the store. That-there little girl's been holding the fort all by herself all morning long." He got into his son's car and stirred it to life. "Y'oughta give that-there kid a raise, Stanley. She works a helluva lot harder'n *you* do." Then he backed the beast out of Stanley's driveway.

On the front porch, under honeysuckle full of drowsing bees, Stanley and Emily Stanhope were having coffee and opening the morning mail. Emily was absorbed in a circular from Morgan's Department Store, while Stanley opened a letter from the American Dry-cleaners' Association. It was the announcement for the next National Convention, to be held in February.

Come Spend

WASHINGTON'S BIRTHDAY

in glamorous

☆ MIAMI BEACH! ☆

Sun and Fun Where Winter Never Comes!

Make your reservations NOW for:

THE 25TH ANNUAL CONVENTION

of the

AMERICAN DRYCLEANERS' ASSOCIATION

To be held at the
Glamorous NEW
Versailles-Schönbrunn Hotel

in Fabulous Miami Beach, Florida

The Last Word in Elegant Luxury!

Fill in the enclosed postage-paid reservation
card *at once!* Don't miss out on the F-U-N!
Make *your* reservations *early.* All reservations MUST be in by Sept. 15—

So HURRY! DO IT NOW!

See You In Swinging Miami Beach!

Stanley took the ball-point pen from his shirt pocket and
filled out the reservation card as instructed. "How'd you like
to go to Florida for a few days this winter, Em?"

"Fine. . . ." She was still engrossed in the Morgan's circular and he was not sure she had really understood him.

"I'm going to dust off the motorcycle—it got kinda dusty
getting here. Thanks for the coffee."

"Anytime. . . ."

Stanley washed down the bike with the garden hose, then

wiped it dry. The cycle shone in the sunlight as it stood in his driveway.

Was Harry right? Was the thing for him to do simply to *keep busy?* There was a certain logic to it, he had to admit. But he didn't care so much for the suggestion that he open a branch in Osterville. Maybe he would if he could get his son to work in it, even for a summer. But then, Bill would probably spend most of his time over at the Perkins girl's. It was not, he decided, such a good idea. Besides, the people of Osterville brought their clothes into Krumpit to be dry-cleaned—and the Stanhope Cleaners got its share. No, if he were to "keep busy" he needed something else. A project, perhaps—something that would really and truly absorb him and take his mind off . . . other things. What a pity he had no hobbies, as other men had. Might he start one?

Then it came to him: the perfect project, the perfect solution—for the summer and fall, at least. Dare he do it? Dare he try? It would certainly keep him busy (wasn't that Harry's prescription?) and it would definitely absorb his interest . . . !

He got an empty bucket from his garage, removed the cap from the motorcycle's gasoline tank, then tilted the bike until he drained most of the fuel into the bucket. From his kitchen he got a book of matches; and then, bucket in hand, he went over to the gazebo.

Carefully, strategically, he splashed the gasoline over the dark green latticework of the old, Beardsley-built structure. When he had finished, he twisted his handkerchief loosely and stuffed one end of it between the latticework. The other end he lighted—then he quickly retreated to the safety of his driveway. There was a tremendous WHUMP! and the latticework became an orange mesh of flame. Emily came running up the driveway.

"Stanley! What's *happened?*"

"I'm destroying it, Em. Doing away with the old. I'm going to build a new gazebo. I'm going to build it myself—

though I'm going to try to get Billy interested in working on it with me. I'm going to design it myself, too—from the ground up. I'm going to pull those old foundation stones and pour a concrete base, a single foundation, Em, all of one piece. I think I'll paint it white. I think I'd like a shining white gazebo. It's going to be an entirely new structure, Emily—one that'll last at least a hundred years. Maybe longer, who knows. . . ."

Stanley took his wife's hand, and together they watched the black smoke rise in an angry pall into the very blue sky of summer. The roof sagged of its own weight but did not fall right away. But finally the supports behind the latticework gave way, and the gazebo collapsed with a low rumble and flying sparks, only to burn away like kindling on the hearth of the foundation stones. Somewhere a siren pierced the July morning.